OPEN HEART

MARY BRINGLE

OPEN HEART

MARY BRINGLE

NAL BOOKS

NEW AMERICAN LIBRARY

TIMES MIRROR

NEW YORK AND SCARBOROUGH, ONTARIO

Copyright © 1982 by Mary Bringle

For information address The New American Library, Inc.
Published simultaneously in Canada by The New American Library of Canada Limited.

 NAL BOOKS TRADEMARK REG. U.S. PAT. OFF. AND FOREIGN COUNTRIES
REGISTERED TRADEMARK—MARCA REGISTRADA
HECHO EN HARRISONBURG, VA., U.S.A.

Acknowledgment
WHEELS AND BUTTERFLIES by William Butler Yeats
(Copyright 1934 by Macmillan Publishing Co., Inc.,
renewed 1962 by Bertha Georgie Yeats)

SIGNET, SIGNET CLASSICS, MENTOR, PLUME, MERIDIAN and
NAL BOOKS are published *in the United States* by The New American
Library, Inc., 1633 Broadway, New York, New York 10019, *in Canada* by
The New American Library of Canada Limited, 81 Mack Avenue,
Scarborough, Ontario M1L 1M8

Library of Congress Cataloging in Publication Data

Bringle, Mary
  Open heart.

  I. Title.
PS3552.R48506 1982   813'.54   82-12416
ISBN 0-453-00423-7

Designed by Alan Steele

First Printing, September, 1982

1 2 3 4 5 6 7 8 9

PRINTED IN THE UNITED STATES OF AMERICA

This book is dedicated to the Roundtablers, with all love and thanks.

The author wishes to thank Patricia Berens, Jane Edee, Fredrica S. Friedman, Jerry Friend, Hazel L. Haby, Joan Sanger, Tony Vercese, and Hans Vogel.

—Those who win the terrible friendship of
   the gods sometimes lie a long time as if dead.

—I have heard of such things;
   the very heart stops and yet they live after.

       —YEATS, *Fighting the Waves*

INTRODUCTION

They were all talking very loudly, raising their voices as if sheer volume would make her understand. Just now it was the man in the seat next to her, wanting to know if she felt ill. Before it had been the flight attendant, and before that the man at JFK Airport in New York who had directed her to her connecting flight to Houston.

It wasn't that she didn't understand English. She'd studied it as a schoolgirl in Genoa, and her knowledge of English was serviceable, if hardly fluent. She understood nearly perfectly the words being shouted at her; it was answering to them that was difficult. Fatigue, confusion, and a sense of terror had robbed her of her English; she felt it deserting her as palpably as she might feel, searching in her handbag, an empty space where traveler's checks were supposed to be.

"Are you all right? Are you feeling sick?"

She turned to her seatmate, who was now moving his lips in an exaggerated way, as if speaking to a deaf person. His innocent blue eyes, set in a clean, round face, gave him the look of a baby. He was perhaps fifty, a businessman probably, and she knew he meant to be kind.

"No, I am fine," she said, dragging the words out with a great effort. "Thank you."

She could not explain, even if she wanted to, the reasons for her odd behavior. She wasn't sure what she had done to alert him—quivered visibly? Grown pale, or cried out without noticing? She reacted to so many things now, things she might not even have noticed a few months ago. The slightest unexpected contact—people brushing against her in

3

the crush of the airport, the bump of a canvas carry-on against the back of her legs—seemed a dangerous assault. She was too fragile to sustain such surprises.

It had been a sudden jolt from the back of her seat this time. It was nothing more than someone's dinner tray being slammed back into the seatrest, but her reaction had been enough to alarm the man next to her. She looked at him now, her dark glasses protecting her from notice. He seemed satisfied with her few words of reassurance. He had returned to the newspaper he'd been reading and she felt relief. No further contact would be required.

Her journey had been a long one, begun at dawn in Genoa where she had said good-bye to her children. Anna-Laura had brought them to the airport where they had seen her off—a solemn party of three desperately trying to sustain the illusion of normalcy. She might have been going off on a holiday or a business trip. Somewhere over Zurich she had fallen into an exhausted sleep, but a sudden air pocket had brought her to a terrified, trembling wakefulness that had persisted all the way to New York. It had boarded the flight to Houston with her and now, as the plane prepared for its descent, it threatened to overpower her. She was too aware of the slightest change in pressure in the cabin; each small jolt seemed to be occurring inside her own body, as if she alone were responsible for the vast plane's descent through the air to the safe strip far below.

"Your first trip to Houston?" Her seatmate had folded his paper and was clasping his safety belt. She nodded yes. He felt inside his breast pocket and extracted a small blue and yellow object, handing it to her with a benign smile. "Enjoy your stay," he said.

She thanked him, grateful for the distraction. The object was a disposable cigarette lighter. On its clear yellow surface, printed in blue, was the single word GALVTEX. She supposed it had to do with an oil company and that her companion was a salesman. Although she didn't smoke, she found a very good use for the lighter. She held it tightly in her right hand, as if it were a talisman, folded her left hand around the right, and by clutching the little cylinder as hard as she could, forced herself to sit with rigid attention while the plane touched down in Houston.

She had arrived at the end of her journey and wished that she could have remained in the air forever.

"Enjoy your stay," repeated the GALVTEX man. Then he collected his belongings and rushed up the aisle, leaving her alone.

HOUSTON

BOOK ONE

Chapter 1

Rafaella and Aldo Leone had always planned to travel, and America was one of their targets. They had talked often of the places they would visit when the children were older, their income more stable. For the time being—they had said this every year of their marriage—they would be content with holidays in Italy and an occasional jaunt to Switzerland or France. But in the future! San Francisco had beckoned, as well as New Orleans. New York, of course, was a must. Somehow they had never considered Texas, but in poring over travel books Rafaella had picked up many scraps of useless information.

Houston, she knew, was on the same latitude as Cairo. This particular fact returned to her with new meaning as she waited for a taxi outside the airport. Dreaming over books with titles like *Let's Visit the United States* had not prepared her for the reality: herself, alone in America, struggling to draw a breath in air so tropically dense it seemed an alien element. The heat came as a physical blow after the air-conditioned interior of the airport; it pressed down on her and enveloped her with a menacing intensity, as if challenging her very right to exist.

As usual these days, she glanced around at her fellow humans to compare her discomfort with theirs. Everyone was sweating profusely, all around her they were removing jackets, mopping at brows, sprinting toward taxis. She was not alone in her discomfort; good, then. She had lost the ability to gauge her body and its feelings correctly, but as long as others were around she could use them as a sort of index.

The small inconveniences of travel seemed nearly insurmountable to her in her present state. How much should she give to the man who had reclaimed her baggage and waited, stoically, to load it into a taxi? How much to tip the driver when she arrived at her destination? She had no idea how far her hotel might be from the airport and even wondered if she could make the driver understand her English. She felt close to tears, and she detested herself for wanting to cry from simple exhaustion and helplessness. She knew from experience that tears would not be cleansing, not any more, and anyway, in this impossible climate how could you tell if you were crying? It would be like weeping underwater.

The interior of the taxi was so cold she had the unpleasant mental image of a meat locker. It seemed to have been designed so people wouldn't spoil on their way to the city. The driver nodded when she told him the name of her hotel as if he approved of her choice, and then they were leaving the long circular drive of the airport, spinning out into a bleak boulevard, part of a stream of moving cars hermetically sealed against the heat.

She saw Anna-Laura and the children again, waving determinedly back in Genoa. It would be the children's bedtime now; she saw every detail of the flat on the Via Vieri so clearly, so vividly, that it blotted out the landscape passing outside the taxi's windows. Since she didn't wish to think of her children now (later, when she was alone, was soon enough), she forced herself to pay attention.

Except for the size of the cars and the English words on the billboards, she might have been anywhere in the world. They were passing over a flat plain from which heat shimmered in small eddies without reflecting color. Far off, on the horizon, she saw the tall, cranelike shapes which she supposed were oil rigs, but all along the boulevard at this point were the shells of huge buildings under construction. One had been completed, but it looked more desolate than the bones of the others. The walls were constructed of a shiny, mirrored black material, as if the architect had planned a greenhouse in which only sinister things could be cultivated.

"Where do you come from?" said the voice from the driver's seat. She saw his face in the rearview mirror. He was a black man, but he had the same innocent, friendly face, the same kind eyes, as the GALVTEX man.

"From Italy," she said. Her voice emerged in a whisper and she repeated the words. The air-conditioned currents numbed her knees.

"I'm from———." The last word was unintelligible to her. Now the driver appeared to want to know what she was doing in Houston. She felt as if she were passing through customs. Her mind struggled to frame the correct tenses of a simple, untruthful reply. *To visit. I shall visit friends.*

"I am sorry," said Rafaella. "My English is not good."

The driver nodded, excusing her from further conversation. Outside the windows she could see a few scraggly palm trees and a red-brick building advertising "Barbecue— Topless Dancers." The cold seemed to have entered her bones now, but how could she ask him to turn the air-conditioner down? She had a brief view of herself, as if she stood outside her own body and judged the woman huddled miserably in the back seat: She saw a timid, easily frightened creature who would endure discomfort rather than engage in conversation with a stranger. She felt contempt for this spineless, shivering woman, but it was her old self who pronounced judgment. Her old self had been alive for thirty-four years, while the Rafaella she was now was only two months old. The old Rafaella had been cautious, but never, never, cowardly.

"Downtown Houston," came the voice from the front. The silhouettes of fantastic buildings appeared to her left like a mirage in the hazy, shimmering air, and then the taxi made a cloverleaf turn and the vision was gone. It had been like something from a dream, something glimpsed in the surface of a murky pond—Atlantis on the Gulf of Mexico.

She pulled her linen jacket more tightly around her. Anna-Laura would have been prepared. She would have produced a shawl from her totebag, or one of the gaudy cardigan sweaters she was forever knitting. Her sister-in-law packed for a simple day at the seaside as if she were relocating for good. She brought blankets and thermos bottles, folding chairs, umbrellas, radios, complete changes of costume. She believed in being prepared for all eventualities and was never caught off guard. Often she scolded Rafaella for being too austere. Why allow the children only one toy, one book, on a journey? What was the good, where the virtue, of traveling light? Life was too short to deny oneself. Rafaella thought that her sister-in-law, as usual, had been right.

By the time they were approaching the green-roofed monstrosity that was her hotel, she had achieved a kind of artificial calm. The disposable lighter, in the pocket of her jacket, soothed her. She clutched it as her mother, long dead, had often clutched her rosary beads, and thought that soon she would be able to lie down on a strange bed and rest. She held the vision of a warm bath and clean sheets before her with the desperation of one who knows she must progress one small step at a time.

Numb with cold, legs trembling with fatigue, she stepped out into the blast-furnace air of a Texas evening in June, trying to remember how much her guidebook had advised her to tip a taxi driver. As she produced the crumpled bills two things happened: her chest contracted with a sharp, brief pain; and a bird from the nearby shrubbery screeched out a long, double-noted call. The pain was familiar, the bird's call was not. Once she would have ignored, dismissed, the pain, and wondered what sort of bird could be welcoming her to this new place.

Now she heard the bird's call only as an alarming counterpoint to the pain. Part of what she despised in the new, foreign, Rafaella could be summed up in this one small incident. The world had receded and taken up residence in the small and unimportant area which was her body.

Cold. Unbelievably cold. The air-conditioning in the mammoth room the bellboy had shown her to was absolutely merciless. Rafaella thought she would see about turning it down, adjusting it somehow, but for the time being she had no energy. She sat at the edge of the huge bed, which seemed to have been designed with two giants in mind, and tried to calm herself. The pain had receded and was a dim memory, but she still had to press her hands to her knees to stop from trembling.

She forced herself to survey the room, take in the details. Beside the bed, the room contained three bureaus, a divan and two padded chairs, a large television on a pedestal, and a small refrigerator. Everything was on far too grand a scale. Even the closet, with its hangers which could not be removed, seemed big enough to live in.

At first she'd thought there had been some mistake, but this room on the twelfth floor of the Hibernian Hotel was precisely the one reserved for Signora Leone. The desk confirmed it when she asked the bellboy to call down. Signora Leone had reserved the room for five days, beginning today, the fifth day of June. Well, this was Texas. Things were supposed to be larger than life here.

She thought of the lobby, the crowds milling about as she'd entered. How fascinating she would have found such a scene, how much would have claimed her attention in the old days! Even now she was able to feel little shoots of curiosity, but she felt them as if through cotton wool, dully. The men in Stetsons and boots, the women in full evening dress heading for the Grand Ballroom—what glittering event were they going to attend? One couple especially had intrigued her. The man wore boots with his beautifully tailored evening clothes, and his companion, tall, tanned, and blonde, a chiffon dress of parrot-green. Like Rafaella's room, they were larger than life and seemed to dwarf her. She had always loved movies, had an especial fondness for American movies, and this couple made her think of the Texans in *Giant*, one of the favorite films of her youth. Rock Hudson and Elizabeth Taylor had grown old together gracefully, their hair a matching, muted blue; James Dean had struck oil, screaming maniacally while the black gold gushed over him like a benediction.

Get up. Keep moving. She went to inspect the bathroom. A paper band lay across the lid of the *gabinetto*; the drinking glasses were swathed in cellophane. What would Aldo have made of such a bathroom? The size and luxury of it. In most of their travels they had stayed at family-type hotels, the kind with a shared bathroom down the hall, European style. She avoided her image in the harsh, fluorescent light and returned to the main room. The tips of her fingers were icy. She could feel them tingling. *Unpack now. Draw comfort from the mechanical chore.* Then she would lie in a warm tub. The thing was to occupy her mind at all times; she would approach each task with a single-minded devotion, as if she were doing something very important.

Unfortunately, unpacking didn't take very long. She slid her few dresses and suits onto the immovable hangers and regarded them through Anna-Laura's eyes. "You dress like a nun," her sister-in-law was fond of saying. The garments in the closet weren't really nunnish, for Rafaella liked things to be fashionable and well-cut, but it was true they were far from colorful. Beige, white, pale sand, dove-grey—nowhere a hint of the bright colors Anna-Laura favored. *You don't want to be noticed. You're hiding.* Another accusation. Rafaella took her linen suit off, noticing how crumpled and forlorn it looked, and hung it up. She stood in a cream silk slip (she knew it was old-fashioned, but she always wore a slip) and felt the gooseflesh rise on her arms as the arctic air crept around her.

By the time she had laid her underthings and nightdresses neatly in the top two drawers of the dresser and aligned her shoes along the bottom of the closet, she felt sure she had used up a fair-sized chunk of time. The digital clock on the bedside table told her that precisely seven minutes had elapsed. She felt a wave of panic so acute it seemed to choke her. It had been a mistake to come alone to Houston; she would never be able to stand the solitude of the next five days. And yet what choice had she had? Anna-Laura, the only possible companion for her on this trip, was needed at home. Anna-Laura was looking after her children, and she was the only person in the world Rafaella trusted with that most precious labor.

"You'll like my sister. She's like Venice—always sinking, but never done for." That had been Aldo's description of Anna-Laura long ago, it seemed centuries ago, when he and

Rafaella were courting. It had been a marvelous way of describing Anna-Laura. She was a tempest of a woman—emotional, melodramatic, kind, passionate—at whose core lay a genius for surviving any difficulty, surmounting unhappiness as if it were of no importance. Although Anna-Laura had some of the grandeur of Venice—she was large, untidy, and colorful—she lacked its beauty, and she had never married. The loss, thought Rafaella as she ran a bath, was all on the side of the foolish men who had preferred prettier, more tractable women. Although Anna-Laura might conceivably still marry, it was unlikely that, at thirty-eight, she would have children, and that was another loss. The love and devotion she would have lavished on children of her own all flowed toward Rafaella's son and daughter, who absorbed it with casual gratitude, as if it were their due.

By the time she had bathed, wrapped herself in a kimono, and discovered how to turn the airconditioner down, another half-hour had passed. She stood at the window, looking down on the Hibernian's broad, sloping lawn. At the farthest edge a crew of men were working, erecting some sort of makeshift structure. She could see them pounding staves into the ground, stretching canvas; it looked as if they were preparing for a circus. Another mystery. She shook her head, clearing it for the next task.

She wasn't hungry, or was she? The empty feeling deep within was reminiscent of hunger, but the thought of food was sickening. What she really wanted was a glass of wine followed by a pot of strong espresso. She went to the telephone and informed the twanging, alien voice at the other end that she wanted a pot of tea. She was transferred to room service after an interminable period, and this time the voice was foreign in a different way. She hung up without knowing whether or not she'd been understood. Either a pot of tea would make its way to her, or it wouldn't. She was too tired to dress and descend to that cavernous lobby and find her way to the restaurant, jostled in the crowd of booted giants, too tired to lift an enormous menu and scan it for some familiar-looking item she could afford to order without guilt.

Only two objects remained in her traveling case. One was a flat, brown envelope, which she removed and placed on the dresser. The other was a large photograph, in a silver frame, of her children. She sat holding the photograph, not looking at the faces of Carlo and Stefania, drawing comfort from the smooth feel of the frame. She had designed it herself. Beyond her, the tropical sky was darkening in the square of window. It was nearly eight o'clock here in Houston. At home it was the small hours of the morning. Everyone she knew in the world was at this moment asleep. She had no existence in the consciousness of others; she had ceased to exist.

The picture wobbled, then came clear. Three men were discussing something that seemed very serious to judge by their expressions. One of them looked rather like the GALVTEX man, but he spoke so rapidly she could only catch every other word. She poured another cupful of tepid tea from the pot delivered by room service and strained to catch the English words. She had never cared much for television, but it had come to her that the TV in her room could serve two purposes: It could banish the awful silence and help her practice her English, both.

"Something—something—*foreign policy*," said the man in the middle, and then, "*The domestic issues are*—something —something—*clearly related to*—something."

She switched channels and encountered a dramatic situation. A man was threatening an attractive woman, stalking her with sinister tread in what looked like a darkened theater. He came close; a hand snaked out and twisted itself in her long, dark hair. She screamed in fright and pain and Rafaella, flinching, turned the dial again.

Now there was a young blonde girl in shorts smiling idiotically at two middle-aged men in a service station. "No problem," said the girl, and the room filled with the gleeful roar of an artificial laugh track.

Rafaella was about to change back to the three serious men when the program cut to a commercial. Two children ran through a field with a puppy. They ran in slow motion, their hair tossing in timeless, liquid arcs, lit by the sun so that they appeared to be golden idols. Surely they did not run in vain, these pretty children; surely some suitable reward lay waiting for them, and yes, there on the porch of the frame house stood an elderly woman in an apron holding a frosty pitcher of something good to drink. The children hurled themselves on her with cries of "Grandma!" and the old lady, miraculously spilling not a drop, poured them each a glass of what looked like rosé wine but was, the announcer said, Kool-Aid.

Rafaella thought cynically of additives and wondered what Anna-Laura had given the children for supper. Stefania, her daughter, would eat whatever was placed before her, but Carlo favored worthless treats, doted on Coca-Cola and chocolate-covered peppermints. While her mind made a hasty catalogue of the junk food Carlo found so appetizing, her body was betraying her again. From the moment the lovely children had appeared on the screen, running in their artificial paradise, a great stone had blossomed in her throat. It was made up of unshed tears, and it threatened to choke her unless it found some release.

On screen the children licked their lips with satisfaction as they gulped their Kool-Aid. The children in the silver frame, infinitely more beautiful to her, stared back at her, unsmiling, in the manner of European children in a formal photograph. The picture had been taken last year when Carlo was ten and Stefania seven. Her son looked very like Rafaella, everyone said so, even though he had inherited Aldo's more muscular frame. Beneath the fringe of black hair his blue eyes—northern Italian eyes, Aldo had called them—were her own, as was a certain look of determination. Stefania, younger, ethereal-looking, had been making a face at the photographer moments before the picture was taken. Consequently she had been smitten by guilt and wore an angelic expression in the finished product, her eyes as round and dark as olives. It was these Neapolitan eyes that caused well-meaning adults to tell Stefania she was the image of her father. The child was both pleased and perplexed at the thought, and Rafaella had often caught her daughter staring at photographs of Aldo with a calculating expression, as if searching for herself in her father's eyes.

If she allowed herself to think what would happen to her children if she died—and she had thought of little else these past two months—the wall of tears in her chest would explode. She would be alone with her terror, half a world away from the Via Vieri, where her children would waken without her for the first time.

"You are thirty-four, signora. A young woman, and healthy, apart from this condition. There is every reason for the surgery to be successful." Dr. Rinaldi, the cardiologist at the clinic in Genoa, had spoken these words of reassurance many times. He would not discuss risk, would not put odds on her life. "All surgery carries some risk, even a tonsillectomy, but you will be in good hands. The best."

Dr. Rinaldi's diagnosis, along with the X-rays of her faulty heart, lay in the brown envelope on top of the dresser. Two of Signora Leone's valves were badly occluded, perhaps as a result of an hereditary condition, and the doctor recommended coronary bypass surgery to correct the condition. He spoke enthusiastically of the marvelous changes this surgery would bring about—no more pain or shortness of breath. With her magically reconstructed pumping system, he said, she would be a new woman.

At times he reminded her of a subcontractor touting the virtues of a new system for laying plumbing; at others he reduced the whole affair to a simple, housewifely problem— her heart a cracked teacup in need of a bit of glue.

The poor teacup had served her well enough for most of her life. It had only been recently that the alarming symptoms had appeared. How could it be? The word "hereditary" had been the most terrifying of all, and the thought that she might have passed on some fatal flaw to her children, intolerable. Only the fact of Carlo's and Stefania's whole and healthy hearts, miraculously untouched by their mama's tainted heritage, had saved her from complete despair. When the reports came back, pronouncing them quite normal so far as medical science could tell, she had remembered the words of an old woman her mother had known. "It sometimes skips a generation," Signora Bianchi had said, nodding wisely. She had been discussing madness.

All of the day's fatigue and anxiety seemed to claim her at once, so that it was an effort to prepare for bed. When at last she lay beneath the blankets, the hum of the airconditioner the only sound in the cold, cavernous room, sleep eluded her.

"You'll be dead a long time," Anna-Laura used to say, in the days when these things could be said. "Time enough to sleep then." It was Aldo she'd so addressed, Aldo, who loved to sleep late on the few mornings such a luxury was granted him. Quite recently she had unthinkingly teased a sleepy Carlo with the old phrase and then, stricken, clapped a hand to her mouth as if to seal it forever.

Time enough to sleep then.

Chapter 2

St. Matthew's Hospital stood on land which had once been inhabited by mosquitoes and cottonmouths. A quarter of a century ago there had been only swamp; now the twenty-six-story tower rising above the quadruple wings represented Mecca to medical pilgrims from all over the world. They came with every conceivable disorder of the heart and—since heart disease is democratic—from every conceivable level of society.

For every famous heart made well at St. Matthew's, there were hundreds of humbler hearts delivered up to the magical hands of the chief surgeon, Dr. Martin Lassiter. For every sheikh who jetted in for pacemaker adjustments, there came a dozen people who had never been out of their native villages in Greece or Brazil. They arrived with aneurysms, occluded valves, pulmonary edema, malformations, transposed vessels. Some arrived almost in a state of cardiac failure and others with deceptively healthy looks, each bringing the time bomb in his chest to the one man whose reputation surpassed that of any other heart surgeon in the world.

From South America, Greece, and Italy came patients whose villages, aided by their churches, had taken up collections to save their lives. Between some countries and St. Matthew's existed complicated, bureaucratic arrangements for payment: the *regione* of Italy paid for its government workers but for no one else. From Holland came Dutch farmers, regularly airlifted to Houston because the death rate from heart disease in their country, coupled with a scarcity of hospital beds, had created a scandal. The Dutch government paid for their operations and hospitalization. It also paid for a family member to accompany them, because open-heart surgery should not be endured alone.

Still, there were patients who came alone. Desperately ill and speaking no English, they sometimes appeared in the lobby of the hospital hoping for a miracle. Someone back in Pakistan or Bolivia or Damascus had raised enough money to fly them to Houston and prayed for the best. Once such a person had died at the reception desk. Another had expired in the admissions office. The staff of St. Matthew's quite naturally did not like patients to die in full view of dozens of people, but everyone understood that St. Matthew's was not an ordinary hospital. It was a place of miracles, a temple consecrated to the almost supernatural powers of Dr. Lassiter.

The hospital was divided into three institutions—the hospital for adults, the children's hospital, and the heart research institute. On its site on the former marshland it was not alone—there were cancer research centers, diagnostic hospitals, neonatal and ophthalmological clinics in the medical complex—but it was the undisputed king of the group. Its tower soared far above any of the other buildings, its sand-colored, gleaming surface dominated the scene.

At noon, it presented a positively cheerful image to the visitor. The long circular drive was crowded with bright courtesy vans from various hotels, taxis, limousines, and flower trucks. The wheelchairs lined up in the outer lobby were made of lemon-yellow canvas and bright chrome. Even the woman behind the reception desk wore a jacket of bright purple. The elevators were color coded—cherry-red for the children's wing, grass-green for surgical floors. At first glance it looked like a very clean nursery school, except that the chairs scattered throughout the lobby were large and deep. There was no sense of urgency on the ground floor, only the usual cafeteria and gift shop where recuperating patients in bathrobes, some still attached to mobile IV's, mingled with visitors from the outside world.

At this hour of the day, Lassiter had performed his last bypass. His patients were all in Recovery Intensive Care, still unconscious. The surgical drama was over, barring emergencies, but the medical drama of recovery just beginning. On the following day, beginning at eight, the process would be repeated. The hospital functioned with a smooth, unerring efficiency; there was a proper time for each drama, and just now, at noon, one of the smaller ones was about to take place.

All of the non-English-speaking Latin Americans scheduled for surgery the following day had been shepherded down to the main floor for their preoperative conference. Generally these conferences took place in midafternoon when Lassiter's head cardiovascular nurse was freer, but there had been a shift of plans because one of the patients would be spending his afternoon in the cath lab.

Twelve people filed into the conference room, making an odd little procession as they straggled down the corridors. Lassiter's nurse and the head of patient relations walked with firm, determined steps, often turning to smile at their charges. They were both abundantly healthy-looking women, and the contrast between them and the little group behind was marked. There were five patients, and all but one was accompanied by a worried relative. A thin man of indeterminate age, his face gray and pinched, shuffled along listlessly beside his wife. It was obvious that his illness had taken its toll on her, for she was nearly as sickly looking as her husband. Only the fact that he wore a bathrobe and she did not marked him as the patient. A large, bossy woman was propelling her husband along by the arm, muttering to him in Spanish and casting baleful looks everywhere. Two elderly women, obviously sisters, followed timidily in her wake, and behind them a lady who appeared to be so ancient it seemed a miracle she could walk at all. She spoke no English, but she had waved the offered wheelchair away angrily. Her look was one of resignation, and it was she who had come alone.

The man bringing up the rear seemed designed to point out their pathos by contrast. He was a tall, tanned American, the sort of whom people said that he'd never been sick a day in his life. Unlike Lassiter's nurse or Mrs. Hewlett of patient relations, he neither smiled nor took bouncy, determined steps. He was trying to mask the look of anxiety that always came over his face before a preoperative conference, and at the same time he was cataloguing his patients. Julio Ramirez and wife, from Puerto Rico. Ramirez was thirty-eight and looked fifty. He was suffering from a ventricular septal defect, the commonest of congenital heart defects and generally the most easily remedied. He had probably been born with the hole in the septum between the lower chambers of his heart. Blood had been pumping into his lungs because the right ventrical was overworked. Lassiter would sew a Dacron patch into the damaged, flabby septum and hope for the best. Mr. Velasquez and wife, from Vera Cruz. A straightforward double bypass. Mrs. Reyes, of Quito, Ecuador, accompanied by her sister. Triple bypass. Ancient Señora Perez, Argentinean. Ought to have had a bypass years ago but had probably refused to consider it, as she had refused the wheelchair earlier. He had taken her medical history, along with the others, and been disturbed by the look of utter resignation in her unblinking, black eyes.

Except for the fact that they spoke no English, they had nothing in common aside from being very ill. They had no impulse, his patients, to talk to one another. They were sealed in, walled up, by the mystery going on inside their bodies. They had no room for commiserating; they were too frightened, and who could blame them?

He held the door for them and was the last to enter the room. In the next half-hour, every step of the ordeal they were about to undergo would be explained to them in the minutest detail. Nothing was omitted, nothing glossed over. It was his job to translate the information. It was in his careful Spanish that they first heard a full and unrelenting description of what it meant to have open-heart surgery.

Rafaella was shocked to find it nearly noon when she woke up. The shock came before she remembered where she was. All she saw was the clock; all she recorded at first was the hour. She was normally an early riser. She stirred beneath the heavy covers, felt the unfamiliar, artificial coolness of the air around her. Houston. She was in America. The fear was with her.

She had awakened with feelings of dread before, even before her knowledge of illness. Sometimes at home she imagined she had had a bad dream and waited for the suffocating terror to pass, only to have it increase. The nightmare had occurred in real life, and the dread was one of its manifestations. She would lie in her own bed, hers and Aldo's, with its ornate carved pineapples decorating the bedposts. They had selected it at a secondhand furniture store, laughing because it reminded them of a marriage bed they'd seen in a movie. The linens, the blankets, the pillow—all had known the touch of her husband. When she opened her eyes she would see his likeness in their wedding picture on the bureau. All was familiar, yet nothing was the same.

Now, on her first morning in Houston, she felt as she had in those days of morning dread, the first of them. The abrupt return was painful, frightening. Nothing to awaken to but a void. At least at home she had been forced to function for the sake of her children, but here no children required her, no telephone would ring. She might lie here undisturbed until night fell again and no one would know.

The pain in her stomach was only hunger, but the trouble with any pain these days was that she couldn't ignore it. How wonderful, she thought, when pain was a simple matter of needing something to eat, or having women's cramps, or feeling your back would break in the last weeks of pregnancy. How luxurious to take baths in water so hot you turned the color of a shrimp without worrying about the dizziness when you stepped out.

Everything in the physical world had an ominous meaning for her now. Ever since Dr. Rinaldi had showed her a large diagram of the human heart, tracing the areas where her heart had failed her, she had seen herself much differently. She no longer wanted to see her body in mirrors. Aldo had always teased her about her modesty, but now her reluctance to catch a glimpse of her naked flesh had nothing to do with modesty.

It had been home in Genoa that she'd realized what it was

she feared. Against all reason, she was afraid that if she looked into the mirror she would see her body stripped of flesh like the flayed man she had seen in a triptych in San Gimignano, all his organs visible, all the tiny conduits which pumped blood throughout his body pitifully displayed. Flayed alive. Saint Bartolomeo he had been; martyr and saint. The painting showed him, one foot held obediently up so that his torturers could complete their fiendish job, his face a mask of complacency to conceal the martyr's ecstasy at having arrived at his appointed end.

She was no saint and never would be. Beneath her own flesh, still young and supple and deceptively healthy-looking, was the hideous heart she had seen in Rinaldi's office, pumping feebly through its clogged valves. At the end of five days it would be displayed, like Saint Bartolomeo's, to the dispassionate eyes of strangers.

The silence was oppressive, the room sinister in its arctic peace. She wanted to be among people, to watch them going about their business in an ordinary way. Even if she couldn't speak to them, she could hear their voices, be reassured by their very normality. She dressed quickly, pulling her long hair back and securing it with the silver comb she always wore. Aldo had bought it for her in Ravenna on their honeymoon, and she would no more give it up than she would cut the hair he had loved.

Old-fashioned. The long hair, not quite so black as his, carefully coiled, and decorous. Her neat little suits; her preference for slips. Anna told her she belonged in another century. Rafaella looked at her face in the mirror and saw that it was so, but it was the way she preferred to look. Aside from a fondness for expensive shoes she couldn't afford and a penchant for fine fabrics next to her skin, she had very little feminine vanity. What she had possessed, she had laid aside, like a garment she wouldn't be needing anymore. It was preserved, intact, as a memento from another life.

"On the night before your surgery, someone from the OR will come to your room to shave your chest. If you are scheduled for a coronary bypass, your legs will also be shaved. This is to facilitate removal of the saphenous vein in your leg. Often several incisions are made which may extend from knee to groin."

Viola Phinney smiled encouragingly, as if she were discussing the hospital menu. "You will also be given an enema to prevent constipation after surgery. Prior to going to sleep you should take a bath or a shower. Then you'll be given a sleeping pill so you can have a restful night. You should not eat or drink anything after midnight."

Seven pairs of dark eyes hung on Lassiter's nurse with varying degrees of apprehension, waiting for the translation. She had not paused yet, so Stephen Morrissy allowed himself to look at Señora Perez. While Viola assured them they would be pleasantly sleepy when they entered the OR, Stephen searched for some sign of vulnerability in the old lady's face, but her expression never altered. She looked like a small idol carved in yellow stone.

"This medication may make your mouth feel dry. You may moisten your lips with a cloth, but do not drink any water. Your family may ride down with you to the surgical floor. Your family should remove all of your personal belongings from the room when you go to surgery because you will not be coming back to the same room."

Viola paused and indicated that Stephen was to translate what she had said thus far. He stood at the head of the long conference table, hands in his pockets, and repeated everything Viola had said, in Spanish. Since he had become a volunteer at St. Matthew's he had participated in over two dozen preops, and the words of the never varying message were so carefully memorized he didn't even have to listen to Viola any more.

What he was still working on was control over his own facial expressions. In the beginning, when he had come to the more distressing bits of information, he had not been able to prevent an earnest, sympathetic expression from creeping over his face. He was afraid this would alarm his patients, who were preternaturally acute about expressions and changes of tone when their conditions were being discussed.

"After placing pads on your arms and chest to monitor the activity of your heart," Viola continued, "your anesthesiologist will place a needle in the appropriate vein and artery, both to put you to sleep and to monitor your blood pressure. The induction of anesthesia is quite rapid and pleasant and you will—"

Hans Wolder, the Dutch-speaking volunteer, had assured Stephen that Dutch preops were almost jolly affairs. His patients, Hans said, sat about cracking jokes, ruddy and good-natured. Most of them were farmers accustomed to eating huge wheels of cheese with their breakfast bread; their hearts were so choked with fat it was a miracle they didn't all die on the plane coming over, yet they were optimistic and cheerful. Stephen's Latin American patients were frail, morose, although the lady from Ecuador had worn a gallant smile when he'd taken her medical history.

"—be unaware of further procedures until you start waking up in the recovery room." Viola paused. "As you wake up in the recovery room," she said briskly, "you will see many tubes and wires."

An understatement if ever there was one. When he had first heard the catalogue of tubes he'd been horrified at the graphic nature of Viola's description. "Why do they have to know so much?" he'd asked. "Isn't it bound to make them more apprehensive?" But apprehension before the event, he was told, was preferable to panic caused by ignorance afterward. "What if patients weren't warned about the breathing tube?" This from Hans. "They'd think they were choking and make matters worse." Most patients wanted to be enlightened; it was their right. Stephen had to admit that St. Matthew's policy was laudable, but it still made him uneasy. Only once had the process cheered him, and that time the patient had been a child of eight. Dolls with removable parts were used to explain the operation to children, and Stephen had explained to the little girl that *here* was where the doctor was going to make an incision and *there* was part of her heart that needed a new pump. The child had been delighted with the doll's versatility and obviously relieved to have matters explained. With the confidence of the very young, she'd told Stephen she'd be the first on her floor to be up walking.

"There will be a tube in your nose which leads to the stomach and keeps it empty," said Viola, beginning the inventory of lifelines. "There will also be one or two drainage tubes in your side to drain the fluid off your chest and help to reexpand your lungs. You will receive glucose through a small tube in your wrist, and another small tube will measure your blood pressure in the other hand. There will be four wires pasted on your chest, leading to the heart monitor. A catheter will have been inserted into your bladder to drain urine." Stephen translated, keeping his voice neutral.

Three of the group reached for cigarettes and lit them with haste. One of the smokers was the bossy woman from Vera Cruz, but the other two, Mrs. Reyes and Julio Ramirez, were patients. Smoking was not forbidden here; there were six ashtrays placed at strategic intervals around the table. If a cigarette helped to blur the image of that rain forest of tubes and wires, who was going to forbid it?

"When you first wake up, you will feel a breathing tube in your mouth. This tube goes to your lungs to make certain you receive enough oxygen. It may give you a slight choking sensation, but if you will relax and breathe through the tube it will make things easier. You will be asleep for most of the time the breathing tube is in place, but when you wake you will not be able to talk, since it passes through your vocal chords. You will be very sleepy, so we tie your hands to prevent you from removing any of the tubes. As soon as the breathing tube is removed, it will be important for you to take deep breaths and cough."

When Stephen translated, Mr. Velasquez raised his hand. He wanted to know when all the tubes would be removed.

"The breathing tube in a matter of hours, the others in two to three days." He thought of what it was like in the Recovery Intensive Care Unit while Viola explained they'd spend their first night there and an additional two to three days in one of the other ICU's. Time had no meaning there —it was always bright as some alien galaxy; vital signs were constantly monitored and there was so much movement and activity that it was about as restful and private as an airport. Two or three days might seem like two or three weeks, or a month, or any time at all. One of his patients had hallucinated there, but whether from drugs or the unrealness of the place, he didn't know.

Viola had now moved on to the importance of deep breathing and coughing after the patient had left the ICU and gone to one of the convalescent rooms. As she urged them to be "up and about" as much as possible, Stephen felt himself relaxing. They had passed from the arena of the OR and the ICU to pleasanter territory—in Viola's scenario they had all survived. She gave them a bright smile, consulted her watch, and thanked them for listening to her. While Stephen was translating her final remarks she was already out the door.

Now Janie Hewlett stepped forward and introduced herself. She was a small, vigorous woman who reminded children of their mothers, older people of their daughters. She had a magically flexible appearance, and all of her guises were pleasing. It helped that the information she had to give did not touch on incisions, tubes, or vital signs.

"I am the director of patient relations, and I want to welcome you to St. Matthew's." Pause. Janie paused often, possessing a different style than Viola and a cheerier line of patter. Occasionally during her talk Stephen felt they'd been caught in a vaudeville routine; at any moment he and Janie might link arms and sing a bilingual duet about visiting hours, waiting rooms, and reception areas. All this hopeful talk about laundry facilities and stamp machines assumed that even the most moribund patient would be as vibrant as Mrs. Hewlett herself in ten days' time. When she reminded family members to remove all personal belongings from the presurgery hospital room so they wouldn't be lost, she generally got a laugh when Stephen translated her final line: "And that includes dentures."

Señora Perez blinked, and the lady from Ecuador flashed her gallant smile.

By the time Stephen delivered his own brief speech the mood in the room had relaxed a little. "I am here to help you in any way I can," he told them. "If any of you— patient or relative—should need me, day or night, I'll be here. I am equipped with a beeper while I'm on duty, and when I'm not I can get to the hospital in ten minutes."

"How can you help us?" Suspicious Mrs. Velasquez with her hostile eyes. Worried about her husband, of course. Good question.

"I will translate for you when you meet with medical staff, just as I did when I took your histories. I can assist you in making calls to your country, perform errands, listen if you want to talk. I can even go out and get food for you if you're hungry and want something special. I can do all the things the medical staff is too busy to concern themselves with. I hope you won't hesitate to call on me. That's what I'm here for."

They murmured "*gracias,*" all except for Señora Perez, who refused his offer to see her to her room. She shook her head, rejecting him, and trailed off up the corridor with the others.

"Poor lady," said Janie Hewlett. "It always bothers me when they come alone."

On his way out to lunch, Stephen checked in at the admissions office. Near the desk Ernestine McGrath, one of the Greek-speaking volunteers, stood with a couple who looked as if they had just flown in from Athens. A few people sat in the chairs scattered through the room, but he wasn't needed. Just as he was about to leave he noticed a woman sitting quietly in the corner, an unread newspaper on her lap. She had a calm, detached air—although her dark glasses made it impossible to see her expression—and didn't seem to belong here. She sat very straight, like an alert schoolgirl, her hands at ease over the inky surface of the newspaper. She wore a ring on the third finger of her right hand. Something about her interested him. She had neither the anxious air of a patient nor the exhausted, resigned demeanor of a relative. You could tell a lot about people by the way they sat, and this woman's position was one of an observer.

But what could she be observing? She was too tranquil to be a television reporter, and he knew all the local newspaperwomen. A foreign journalist? Possibly. Her clothing was elegant, if simple. The suit was real linen, wrinkled slightly. Someone new to Houston couldn't know that a five-minute contact with the heat would ruin the effect of clothing that would stay immaculate in London, say, or Copenhagen.

His trained eye took in the fine lines of her jaw, the delicate wings of dark hair drawn back with an old-fashioned silver comb. She would photograph well, he thought. It had been weeks now since he'd been behind a camera, but you never forgot, never lost the sensation of pleasure when you saw an object you wanted to photograph. He had seen many more beautiful women, but this one fascinated him with her aloof, unapproachable demeanor.

The wife of a doctor? Wives of cardiovascular surgeons didn't sit in Admissions; nobody sat in Admissions without a good reason. She shifted slightly. It almost seemed she might be looking in his direction. His earlier impression of aloofness vanished, and now he sensed something vulnerable and lost about her.

Years ago, when he had been a boy, he had seen a doe standing motionless at the edge of a busy highway in northern Wisconsin. She must have picked her way from the heart of the forest to the edge of the perilous road in search of something, but whatever it was she had tracked was forgotten in her distress at the roaring traffic. The woman seemed somehow like the deer, alert and guarding herself against danger. Caught in a stream of moving traffic, he had been unable to help the doe. He wanted to help the woman, but realized it would be presumptuous to do so. Someone else would come along to help her, if it was help she needed.

Probably it was his own overworked imagination that prompted such images. A few moments ago he had been desperate to leave the hospital—to head for lunch, freedom, a world where people weren't sick. Now he idled in Admissions, wondering why the sight of a rather pale, slender, dark-haired woman should detain him so powerfully. She made him feel tranquil and peaceful. He imagined the sound of her voice. It would be low and sweet. It would be the voice of the doe when she had leaped across the road to safety and was once more in the familiar forest—her domain —or the voice of a woman captured in a painting hundreds of years ago.

He really did not want to be caught staring. Admissions was not a place for indulging fantasies, and the woman was now settled in her old, unapproachable pose. He pretended to consult his watch, and left, abruptly, for his freedom.

Chapter 3

Rafaella sat in the admissions office watching the life of the hospital eddying all around her. Two nurses in surgical scrub gear were entering the cafeteria across the way. They stopped to talk to a man in a bathrobe; they smiled, made jokes. The man was attached to an IV pole, the needle concealed by the sleeve of his plaid bathrobe. Nothing too alarming about IV's—she herself had been nourished by an IV after the birth of Stefania. A child slept upright a few chairs away from her. His mother, she knew, had gone off to the gift shop to select something for the boy's uncle. Rafaella had understood the conversation because it was in Spanish, close enough to Italian to be intelligible. At the desk someone was filling out forms of admission for an old couple dressed entirely in black. She thought they spoke Greek. So far, so good.

What had she expected? A grim atmosphere, a lobby crowded with suffering multitudes? Voices on the public address system paging doctors with frantic urgency? She hardly knew what she had expected, but the calm, cheerful efficiency surrounding her was exactly what she needed. Inwardly, she began to compose a letter to Anna-Laura. *You see, cara, I was right to insist on some time on my own. You thought I was being temperamental—so unlike me, you said! —and unreasonable. Wouldn't I rather get it over with immediately, you said, and how could I bear to be all alone for five days in a city where I didn't know a soul? Perhaps it crossed your mind I was being selfish, demanding this time, but when was the last time I was selfish? Haven't I earned the right?*

Mentally, she crumpled this letter. It had too great a tone of self-pity, which she despised, and it wasn't her intention to lecture her beloved sister-in-law. *You know,* she began again, *how I am when we go to the seaside? I am always the last in the water, first one toe, then up to the ankle—slowly, gingerly. I need to take a good look around me, always. To get my bearings. I will have more courage this way. That is the way I am.*

She had ridden over in one of the Hibernian's small courtesy vans. They plied back and forth between hotel and hospital hourly, ferrying their frightened, anxious cargo free of charge. Medicine was big business here; it brought as many people to Houston as did oil. The heavy air had stunned her once more, sucking away her vitality simply by pressing in. Waiting for the van, she had felt a return of yesterday's disorientation and helplessness. She stared at the thin shoulder blades of the man ahead of her, jutting through the material of his shirt, and wondered if he too was destined for surgery. The shirt was a gaudy affair, printed with bright jungle parrots. A gesture of defiance? She decided they were a pathetic little band—two Spanish-speaking sisters who fanned themselves futilely against the heat, the parrot man, a boy who looked Lebanese or Syrian, his color poor beneath his naturally dark skin, and herself. Invalids all. This was where she belonged.

Small puffs of wind had set the tall palm trees to rattling far above her head, and the effect was that of an electric fire. It banished the humidity for a moment but brought a scorching, fiery blast which was almost worse. She'd been grateful when the van opened its doors to the waiting group, but then there was a new humiliation. The driver, a small, round woman, had helped her in, grasping her arm. Did she look sick? Even Dr. Rinaldi had said that her color was remarkably good, under the circumstances. She had always been pale, but there was none of the faint bluish cast observable in some heart patients.

On the short drive over down the humming boulevard and past the Hibernian's lawn, where the odd structures had been erected in the night, she told herself she would dread the hospital less if she became thoroughly familiar with it. By the time she checked in, when they would be expecting her, it would be a known quantity.

She had bought the newspaper to have something to carry, but she wouldn't have read it, not even if it had been Italian. She knew what it would tell her, it was the same all over the world. Terrorists Hijack Plane to Cuba . . . Red Brigades Abduct Industrialists . . . Missing Boy Believed Dead . . . Student Goes Berserk, Murders Seven . . .

Since she'd become ill, reading had been banned from her list of pleasures. Horror lurked everywhere in the printed word—accounts of violence, mayhem, political torture, now seemed so significant she couldn't think of them without trembling, weeping. She felt the bullet, the rubber truncheon, the electric shock, as if she herself had become the victim of every horrible crime she read about. The pity and revulsion she felt were beside the point because they were felt for herself.

Even the harmless mystery novel Anna-Laura had slipped into her bag for plane reading was dangerous. It was an English country mystery (the sort she'd always enjoyed) translated into Italian. She knew it would be full of cozy vicarages and leafy lanes, but it would also contain an act of violence. When would it come? She would be waiting for it, dreading it, the way a soldier anticipated a land mine. So she sat, the unread paper smudging her linen skirt, watching.

A man came into the admissions office, looking around as if he'd forgotten something. Here was a man who definitely wasn't ill, who had probably never been sick. A doctor? He was dressed casually in light-colored trousers and a pale-blue shirt open at the neck. He had removed his jacket and carried it over one arm. She thought he must spend much of his time outdoors. He was tanned and athletic-looking. He moved quickly, as if he were anxious to be away from the hospital.

She judged him to be a little older than she was. Instinctively she knew he was American. He might not be wearing cowboy boots and a Stetson hat, but he was as American as the *Giant* people in the lobby of the Hibernian. His hair was light and shaggy. Even as she watched, safe behind her dark glasses, he ran one hand over his hair in an impatient gesture.

"All American men are boys, really." This was Anna-Laura's opinion, pronounced without scorn as a simple fact.

A memory was crowding in; suddenly she was back in a darkened movie theater with her best friend Gina. They were thirteen, and giggling. They'd come to see the latest American surfer movie, dubbed in Italian and rechristened *Sci Acquatico*. Rafaella and Gina formed their opinions of American character from movies such as this, but even they could see the dubbing was all wrong. The large, blond boys lived almost entirely in their bodies. Their verbal flirtations were laconic; they didn't snap and flick their wrists, gesticulating as an Italian male would do. They spoke slowly, choosing words with deliberation. Yet on the screen torrents of Italian poured from their lips. Passionate declarations hung in the air long after the lips had actually closed. Rafaella and Gina admired the boys physically, but the silly dubbing forced their admiration to the background. Clinging to each other, weak with laughter, they tried to stifle their giggles before someone complained.

That was what the man reminded her of—a California surfer who had grown up. When he turned and left she was sorry because while he'd dominated the room something surprising had happened.

She had stopped thinking about herself.

In the volunteers' office at St. Matthew's a color coordinated chart advised bilingual volunteers of new arrivals requiring assistance. Green tabs denoted Dutch patients; blue, Italian; red, Latin American; yellow, Greek; and so on through Japanese, Arabic, Turkish, Greek, Persian, and almost every language known to the modern world. A notable exception was French.

Jacqueline Talbot smiled, remembering the explanation for this omission. "The French, Miss Talbot, are a chauvinistic people. They prefer to have their surgery in French hospitals with French doctors attending." She had been working as a volunteer for nearly a year now, living with her family in River Oaks and spending as much time at the hospital as possible. She liked to think she was doing some good for once in her life, although she'd bite her tongue out before she'd express such a sentimental thought to any of her friends. She knew what they thought, and said, behind her back. Dear Jackie was trying to distract herself after that unfortunate marriage to the Roman photographer. Acting as a volunteer was her *therapy;* instead of crawling home to River Oaks, tail between her legs, she pretended to find fulfillment working with those unfortunate Italians at St. Matthew's. It never occurred to any of her friends that Jackie might honestly enjoy the work.

She scanned the chart for blue tabs, but there would be no new arrivals in the next day. Three tabs indicated patients on the recovery floors, one a three-year-old in the children's hospital. They were all doing well, thank god. What would she do if one of her patients, particularly one of the babies, should die? It was a problem she'd never confronted. It pleased her to be able to comfort Mrs. Donitello, a child's frantic mother, to make Graziella giggle or to have old Signora Della Croce confide in her. What would they do without someone who could speak to them in their language? How much greater the terror would be if they didn't understand what was happening to them.

Another thing that pleased her was that she'd carried something useful away from the shambles of her marriage: Italian.

"I'm so impressed," Mary Jo or Eugenia would coo at her. "However did you learn to speak such good Italian?"

"We had marathon quarrels," she'd replied with the brittle, jokey tone she always used when discussing her marriage. "They were better than Berlitz. I learned fast."

The truth was that she'd always been quick with languages, but until recently there had seemed no point in developing her skill. There'd been no particular point in anything except enjoying your good luck if you were Jackie Talbot. She'd enjoyed being the daughter of a millionaire neurosurgeon, enjoyed being tall, blonde, and beautiful, without even knowing there was anything else to be. All her friends were rich and beautiful too, enabling her to feel lucky without thinking she was special. She'd gone right on enjoying her life until, at twenty-one, an Italian photographer had noticed her in a fashion layout in the local papers (it had been for charity, the sort of thing all Jackie's friends modeled for) and called her all the way from New York.

Only a fool would have married Eduardo, and Jackie had not only married him, she'd gone to live with him in Rome. He was ridiculously handsome and had a voice like dark velvet. He also had dark eyes of such an endearing sincerity it had taken her over a year to discover that he was an accomplished, a *virtuoso*, liar. Lying, making love, and photographing women were what he did best, in that order. She minded the infidelities bitterly, but what she minded even more was Eduardo's assumption that she didn't. He was capable of wooing her, swearing on his mother's head that he would never again so much as touch another woman, and then going off to keep a date with a starlet on the Via Margutta.

The marriage had lasted five years and now, at twenty-six, Jackie marveled that it hadn't ended after five months. She still felt spiritually bruised, bewildered. She didn't want to trust herself to a man again, although she knew the feeling would pass. She wasn't a bitter woman. Her natural resiliency would buoy her up and gradually return her to a sunnier outlook, but for the time being she thought of herself as in a kind of limbo. What better way to pass through limbo than to help people who were genuinely suffering?

Jackie went into the volunteers' lounge, where Ernestine McGrath was making notations on a yellow pad. Ernestine was a sallow, frowning woman, a noted cookbook writer who devoted at least twelve hours a week to her work as a volunteer. She and Jackie had two things in common—they had both learned a language from the man they had married, and both had lost the husband who had taught them. Ernestine's husband, a Greek, had died on the operating table in the middle of open-heart surgery. Ernestine had stayed on in Houston, reverted to her maiden name, and been certified by Berlitz as competent to work as a bilingual volunteer.

Most of the volunteers had full-time jobs on the outside. Hans Wolder (Vol. bi-lin: Dutch) was an air traffic controller at Houston Airport. Joe Gonzalez (Vol. bi-lin: Spanish) was an insurance adjuster. Leila Coury (Vol. bi-lin: Arabic) owned a restaurant in downtown Houston. Only Jackie seemed to fit the classic mold associated with hospital volunteer work; only Jackie was described as a socialite in the gossip columns; only Jackie went home to River Oaks.

"Hello, Ernestine." Jackie waited for the look of barely concealed annoyance which always crept over Ernestine's face at sight of her. Ernestine no doubt thought of Jackie as a dilettante. Frivolous. The only person who annoyed her more was Stephen Morrissy.

"I was wondering if you'd seen Morrissy?" Jackie's voice was politely neutral.

Ernestine removed her glasses and frowned more deeply. "Mr. Morrissy left Admissions five minutes ago," she said. "I suppose he was going to *lunch*." She pronounced the word with delicate disapproval, conveying a sense of Morrissy's ethical inferiority. She herself always lunched in the cafeteria or from the contents of a brown paper bag in the volunteers' lounge.

"Why do you dislike him so much?"

"My dear Jacqueline, I don't *dislike* Mr. Morrissy. No doubt in his proper sphere he is most competent. I just don't think he belongs here. A hospital devoted to cardiovascular surgery shouldn't have to concern itself with show business."

"Ernestine, honey, the man's a documentary filmmaker. It's not as if he's come to shoot an X-rated movie or something." She was afraid she would laugh and offend Ernestine even more. She pitied the woman for her rigidity, her loss. "Some of his work has been very good, you know. He's won awards. He's a serious person."

"As I said, I'm sure Mr. Morrissy excels at his chosen field. I wouldn't object to his quietly gathering research for the project, but I draw the line at his being certified. I don't think he should be allowed to work with patients."

"Why ever not? He speaks good Spanish. He knocks himself out for them. What better way to research?"

Ernestine replaced her glasses, signifying that she wanted

to return to her notes. "I have reason to believe that Mr. Morrissy is uncomfortable around sick people. I'm not even sure he likes them."

What to say? That you didn't *like* sick people as a particular class, that they were people who happened to be ill whom you could help? That to like sick people, in particular, would be weird, like having a fetish for cripples? Nothing would make an impression on Ernestine. Jackie left the lounge and went out into the main reception area. She thought Stephen would have headed for the little French cafeteria on the boulevard. The food was reasonable, and you could get wine. She'd go join him and have a few laughs. They frequently lunched together; in a limited way they were friends.

Friends, thought Jackie with amusement. *Morrissy and I are friends.* There'd been a time when she hadn't believed a man and woman could be friends, not unless the man was gay or the woman over sixty. She and Morrissy enjoyed each other's company, he wanted nothing from her. He admired her beauty quite impersonally, but she knew she didn't move him to any direct or personal desire. He'd been married, and divorced, but he never had to be lonely. There would always be plenty of women for a man like Morrissy. Most important, he sensed the limbo quality of Jackie's life at present and respected it.

There was a small commotion in the lobby, caused by the gregarious sheikh with pacemaker problems. He liked to walk about the hospital in his billowing robes, entourage close by, as if he were reviewing the troops. Today he was wearing natty, mirrored sunglasses and carrying a copy of the *Wall Street Journal.* The whole scene looked like an OPEC conference and Jackie thought of Ernestine's remarks about "show business." Morrissy wasn't in the least concerned with the sheikhs and movie stars. He wanted to document the everyday life of the most celebrated heart hospital in the world, and Jackie was willing to bet he would do it superbly.

Lassiter had looked down from the heights and pronounced approval. Now *there* was a man, thought Jackie (aware of the many dark eyes glued to her departing back), who understood the value of show business. Lassiter was a genius of a medical man, but he was also a star.

The King of Hearts, as he had been dubbed by the press, didn't look the way he was supposed to. Great Doctors, at least in TV dramas, came in two recognizable models. The first was the gentle, harried savior who was too busy saving lives to notice whether or not he had put on matching socks that morning. The second was a brusque autocrat, capable of towering rages, whose eyes, on closer examination, revealed a kindly twinkle.

Lassiter resembled neither. His face was smooth, unlined, and untroubled, and he looked much younger than his fifty years. His brown hair was still abundant, and nowhere in his pale, rather large eyes was there so much as a hint of a twinkle. He carried himself well and was always beautifully tailored. Even his surgical suits looked as if they'd been turned out for him on Saville Row. He looked as if he would be more at home on a polo pony or lounging beside a pool than standing in an OR and grubbing about inside somebody's heart.

It was difficult to imagine those fastidious hands *wanting* to enter the cavities of the human body. It was even more difficult to look into the opaque blue eyes and believe that Martin Lassiter could care about the outcome. He was courteous, of course, and particularly gentle with children, but there remained a shield of reserve which was never lowered. He was aloof.

"Which would you rather?" his defenders often asked. "A good bedside manner or the best doctor in the world?"

"But why," a detractor would reply, "should one preclude the other?"

At St. Matthew's he was usually referred to simply as *he*. *He* had done six bypasses before lunch. *He* had terrorized a cardiologist, offended a journalist, shown a shocking lack of sympathy to an hysterical woman whose baby had been born with the Great Vessels of her heart transposed. *He* had sewn a Dacron patch into tissue so deteriorated it was like patching pasta.

He occupied a rarefied position available to only a handful of human beings in every profession; on the Olympus of success and power, he dwelt at the very top. Other doctors might be famous in medical circles, but outside their own professions they were anonymous; Lassiter's fame was of the international variety, and he moved in an aura of celebrity almost as palpable as that of a film star.

Nobody disputed his brilliance or skill, but in a world teeming with skilled surgeons it sometimes seemed puzzling that Lassiter had shot so far beyond them. Hundreds of doctors might be able to mend hearts as efficiently, but that was beside the point. Lassiter's skill went beyond mere brilliance into a shadowy area customarily described with mystical words. Magical. Miraculous. Superhuman. Hands of a wizard. In an earlier age he might have been burned at the stake.

A part of his mystique was his supreme, unassailable confidence in the operating room. He seemed to know instinctively what to do; almost at first sight of the heart laid open for him his course was clear. Other doctors hesitated, pondered, made decisions, but Lassiter literally plunged in. It was as if the circuits between his hands and brain were swifter, more sure, than those of other surgeons. He could operate on any given day on more patients than any other cardiovascular surgeon, and he had done it day after day, year after year, until the number of human beings he had repaired and sent back into the world could populate a city.

His private life was unexceptional. He lived in River Oaks with his wife of twenty years. There were no rumors of other women; indeed, when would he find the time? He was a natural athlete and liked to sail on those few occasions when he took a holiday. He appeared, briefly, at all suitable social functions and as a guest on television talk-shows.

If he suspected that people called him a cold fish behind his back, it did not disturb him. All of his energy and emotion were carefully conserved to spend in the arena of the operating room. He rarely raised his voice in anger if a colleague did something inept, but the chill air of his disapproval was more frightening than a tantrum would have been. It was his very lack of drama that made him such a dramatic figure.

His anger only surfaced when he failed, and a patient died. Martin Lassiter, it was said, took death as a personal affront.

Rafaella had reached the edge of the crescent drive outside the hospital when it occurred to her that her doctor's orders—to walk a little each day—were the advice of a man who had never been in Texas. The sun bleached everything; except for the cars speeding by the pedestrian walkway she might have been forging through a desert. The long white boulevard was merciless. There was no turning back, no place to rest.

Every discomfort was magnified by the heat. The pavement beneath the thin soles of her shoes shimmered dizzyingly; her silver comb dragged downward through her hair, making her temples ache. The malevolent cars roared past the narrow walkway as if determined to leap the low embankment and mangle her beneath their wheels.

She could see the long lawn of the Hibernian from where she was. It really wasn't much farther, she was almost halfway, but it seemed an impossibility that she would ever again enter that cavernous lobby. Slowly. She would continue, one foot in front of the other, slowly. A walk only had value for the heart if it was brisk, but in this merciless climate a brisk walk might kill her.

What would she seem to be if she could look down on herself at this moment? A lizard. One of the small lizards so numerous along the Adriatic coast. She had opened her eyes once, lying on the beach at Cesenatico, and seen one clinging to a rock near her head. Beneath the taut skin the creature trembled violently, as if gathering strength for some daring action. It pulsated against the rock for a while, nearly transparent, and then skittered off. She was like a weightless lizard, stunned by the heat, scrabbling toward a rock where she might hide. She thought of the cool, dim admissions office with longing and wished she'd never left. For the first time she doubted the wisdom of staying in Houston for five days, alone.

Fifteen minutes. The Hibernian's clock told her that the grueling walk had lasted only fifteen minutes. She went straight to her room. The chambermaid had tidied it and set both airconditioners on high. On the low table a bouquet of flowers had been placed—freesias and carnations ringed with soft fern. She stared at them dumbly, sure there had been a mistake, but the card, when she thought to look at it, proved her wrong.

"My thoughts are with you. All my love, Maurizio."

Chapter 4

Maurizio had been Aldo's lawyer. It was Maurizio who had read Aldo's will to her, Maurizio who had explained that —aside from the life insurance she intended to reserve for the children's education—there was barely enough money to see her through a year. He was delicate, Maurizio. He offered his condolences without dwelling on the tragedy of Aldo's death; at the same time he had allowed her to understand that he would be available to help her. He did not try to penetrate the opaque wall of her grief, knowing from experience how unwelcome such gestures are to the recently bereaved. He had lost his own wife a decade earlier.

Even now, three years later, the day of Aldo's death was clearer in her memory than any other day in her life. She had lost many of the details surrounding other important events. The deaths of her own parents, her first meeting with the man she would marry, her wedding day—these were slightly blurred around the edges, like old photographs, but her last day with Aldo might have happened a week ago. She often wondered why this should be, since she'd had no way of knowing how that day would end. No premonition had warned her, nothing to make her mark so carefully the trivia of a day that should have been like any other, only happier, because they were on holiday.

She had wakened, as always, before him. He was sleeping with his back turned to her so that her cheek rested against the green-and-white-striped pajama tops she'd bought for him in Genoa. Their room was in a chalet-style hotel in the

Dolomites, outside Cortina below the Tre Croci Pass. Its chief beauty lay in the panoramic view of the mountains beyond the shuttered windows. Aldo stirred and Rafaella stroked his back gently, wanting him to sleep for a time as all hard-working men deserved to do when on holiday. The light from between the wooden slats of the shutters was pale and tentative, a lettuce-green light. Aldo's black hair was rumpled and longer than usual. Soon he would cut it, but Rafaella secretly liked it a bit shaggy. Her husband, so gentle and kind he disliked raising his voice when the children misbehaved, assumed a brigandish, dangerous look with longer hair. She never prompted him to go to the barber.

She smiled at the sight of the green-and-white pajama tops. They were the badge of a holiday, since Aldo never wore pajamas at home. When they traveled he packed several pair for the journey down the hall to the bathroom. Rafaella always wore a nightdress. This morning her white batiste nightgown had rolled up around her waist in sleep. Modestly, she pulled it down and then nudged Aldo's knees, her bare legs against his pajamaed ones. *Sleep a while longer, darling.*

Quietly, she slid from the bed and went to the door that led to the children's room. Stefania lay on her back, her face at five still that of a baby when she slept. Carlo (eight, then) had kicked the covers away as usual and lay with one leg half off the bed, as if he had been performing calisthenics in his sleep. He frowned, deep in some dream. Even unconscious, Carlo was fiercely single-minded, and Rafaella smiled in sympathy. She had been called stubborn more than once, and she supposed her son had inherited this trait from her, but where her stubbornness was tempered with a woman's practicality, Carlo was moodily male. They had visited the church in Cortina the day before to admire the pale-green marble walls, the Grecian font, and St. Peter, crucified head down. Carlo had marveled most at the skeleton, whose bony fingers were decorated with heavy rings, and before going to bed he had attempted to make a drawing of the skeleton. Three sheets of paper lay crumpled in the wastepaper basket; three times he had hurled his bejeweled skeleton drawing to the floor, angry because he couldn't capture the complicated articulation of the bones.

"I can't get the fingers right," he had muttered. A perfectionist.

Aldo, with his architect's draftsman skill had tried to help, and then Rafaella, who had studied art, pointed out how difficult it was to draw a skeleton without a knowledge of anatomy.

"The skull looks like a dog," Stefania said, giggling. Carlo had ripped the drawing and turned on them in indignation.

"*Basta,*" Aldo had said sternly, knowing when to call a halt to such temperamental outbursts. "To bed, Carlo."

Rafaella thought she would buy her son an anatomy book when they returned home. It was the fifth day of their holiday—nine days remained to them before they would go home and paste their photographs in the family album. Today they would drive to Misurina, the mountain lake, and picnic there. Aldo wished to climb a spur of rock near Monte Piano and had arranged to meet a guide after their picnic. Aldo was athletic, surefooted; he had always enjoyed climbing and had purchased new boots before leaving Genoa. Rafaella, who was afraid of heights, would remain by the lake with the children. Perhaps, she thought, going back into the room where her husband slept, she would sketch a bit. She never thought of herself as an artist and did her modest sketching and sculpting with an almost apologetic air, as if she were being a trifle self-indulgent.

Aldo's eyes were open now. The covers had slipped down and he plucked sleepily at the sleeves of his new pajamas. "I feel overdressed," he said, and smiled, and when she burrowed back into the bed, beside him, he adroitly imprisoned her by throwing one leg over her legs. His hands stroked her hair; she felt his hand cupping her skull, then the fingers sifting gently through her hair, lifting and weighing it as if he had discovered treasure. They often lay like this, quietly, without words. Sometimes it led to lovemaking, but this morning they were lazy, peaceful. She sometimes thought of Aldo as the source of her physical strength. When she lay close to his body she could almost feel herself being charged by his superior energy and strength. "I have a peasant's body," he had said once, referring to his sturdiness, the compact musculature of a man born to do physical labor. By contrast, her slender limbs, the small ankles and wrists, the delicate bones of her fingers, seemed patrician and elegant. She had never considered herself frail, but the image of drawing strength from his body was one which had persisted through all the years of their marriage.

Basta, said Rafaella to herself, echoing Aldo's caution to Carlo that night outside of Cortina. The word was alien in the room in Houston. *Enough remembering*, she said, but the mechanism, once set in motion, did not stop so easily. She saw them at Lake Misurina, 1,800 feet higher than Cortina, where the air was cool and almost wintry. The lake was beautiful, of course, like all lakes in the north of Italy, and Stefania said it was the exact color of her parka. Aldo wore a red parka, and so did Carlo. Rafaella herself had on a turtleneck sweater the color of the dark spruce trees ringing the lake.

Directly in front of them lay the remains of their picnic lunch, in the image Rafaella so persistently chose to see. There was an inch of red wine in the little half-liter bottle of Bardolino, and on Carlo's plate a half-moon of pale, uneaten cheese. *Now!* Aldo was walking away from them, his feet looking unnaturally large in the new climbing boots, to meet the guide as he had arranged.

"Ciao, Papa," called Carlo. "Take a picture at the top."

At that precise moment Aldo had only another hour to live. He turned and called to her that if she tired of Lake Misurina she should take the car and return to the hotel. He would find his way back.

And had she, at that moment, thought of how kind, how considerate, her husband was? Had she felt gratitude at being so happily married? She had not, because when one is happy one does not think about it. Weighing the moment, examining the event, is an occupation for the dissatisfied. She did not think of how she loved Aldo, because for seven years she had lived in the secure climate of that love. She smiled and sent him on his way without the slightest premonition of disaster. Just as he disappeared into a grove of trees she was reproving Carlo, who was making a hideous face at Stefania, and so she never saw him pass from her sight. In her memory he would remain forever walking away.

The guide who told her was Austrian. In heavily accented, formal Italian, he tried to explain to her that it had been a freakish sort of accident. Nobody was to blame, he said, and then blushed at his words, afraid she would think he was exonerating himself. Signor Leone was not to blame. He had not been foolhardy or taken unnecessary risks. "But," the guide concluded sorrowfully, "there is always some risk, even in the simplest climb."

Aldo had fallen from a spur of rock and plunged fifty feet into a small crevasse still covered over with snow. A fall of fifty feet, cushioned by snow, was not usually fatal, but Signora Leone had to understand that her husband had fallen in such a way that the neck had been broken. There had been no pain for Aldo; he had not suffered. They brought him down in a canvas stretcher which was bright orange, as if it had been designed for festive occasions.

Her memory of the day stopped short at the guide's explanation, as if the clock had literally been smashed at three twenty-five in the afternoon. Somebody—the chambermaid? —packed all her belongings. The police took care of the return of the rented car and called Anna-Laura, asking her to meet the train at Genoa. Rafaella never knew if Aldo's body traveled with them on that trip or on a separate train. She brought all Aldo's things back with her to Genoa. She was not a superstitious woman. She did not believe that her husband's spirit lingered somewhere amongst his possessions —she knew he was dead and would never return to her in any form. She brought them because she could not bear the idea of anyone else touching the garments which had so recently lain close to his warm and living flesh.

The day that had begun so happily hadn't really ended, for her, until a week later. Then, in the office of Maurizio Guidi, she learned that she would have to work to support her family. Maurizio discreetly acknowledged that she might expect a struggle if she refused to use the life-insurance money. It was all very well, he told her, to set that money aside for her children's education, but the savings of a thirty-four-year-old architect were not large, and Aldo had not expected to die. She felt only a sense of gratitude at this news, since the struggle he alluded to would be a reason to go on living.

Now, with the same discretion, Maurizio led her to understand that he would like to marry her. He had courted her calmly, patiently, for the past year. Looking at the bouquet of freesia and carnation he had sent her, she conjured up his face. It was the face of a man in vigorous, early middle age. He wore spectacles and a responsible, kindly look. Occasionally, when Maurizio smiled, he could be quite attractive. His expression in regarding Rafaella was always the same. It seemed to say *I have patience. I can wait. You may think you are done with love, but I know better.*

As grateful as she was to Maurizio Guidi, she could not conceive of marrying him, but ever since the diagnosis of her doctor she had had an ugly thought—Maurizio was secretly glad that she was ill. A healthy Rafaella might continue to gently reject him forever, but an invalid whose body had been mutilated by the surgeon's knife might be very glad, indeed, to have him.

Like all healthy men, Stephen Morrissy had never considered the varieties of ways in which the human heart could fail to function. Men—and occasionally women—had coronaries. Older people had strokes. He had never considered exactly what it was a surgeon did in open-heart procedures. In his career he had examined many phenomena, but the project at St. Matthew's was the first in which the inner workings of the body played a part.

When he'd first thought of the film he'd imagined it as a documentary on the daily life of a great American hospital. There had been a certain cynicism in his approach—he had fully expected to find the great Lassiter intolerably arrogant, a man elevated to the position of a god by the American public's reverence for physicians. He had also expected to find St. Matthew's country clubbish and extravagant in the way only Texas institutions could be. Sheikhs, shahs, film stars, and millionaire oilmen would comprise the vast majority of Lassiter's patients—people who could afford to come to Houston for some retooling of their hearts as casually as they might travel up to Scotland to shoot grouse in season.

He'd quickly learned how wrong he had been and felt rather humble as a result. In the month he'd spent as a volunteer he had learned more about people, inside and out, than he would have thought possible. They were tougher and more courageous than they seemed. He had done films on every sociological problem from the tormented psyches of Vietnam vets to the fears of harassed old people living in crime-ridden urban areas, but he had never studied so closely the behavior of people risking their lives. That was exactly what the heart patients were doing, although the odds were in their favor. Without the operation most of them would die before their time, some immediately, but the fact that they chose to trust their very hearts to Lassiter fascinated him.

Waiting on the sixth floor to confer with the cardiologist Blanchard, he compared the heart patients to other subjects he had studied in high risk situations. Marines in combat, kids living in Belfast's Murder Triangle, Navy test pilots—all of them knew they were at risk. The bullet, the fire bomb, the crash could come at any time, and they knew it. Except for a few crazies who believed they were immortal, none of them doubted the power of the danger all around them. Some even gave themselves odds. But none of them could say for certain that the dreaded event would definitely occur, much less when.

The heart patients knew that at precisely such and such an hour their chests would be sawed open and their hearts laid bare; they knew it was *conceivable* they might never come out of it, and yet they talked and ate meals and sometimes even managed to smile, precisely like other human beings. Most of them had resolved their crisis of fear and were resigned when it came to the actual event. It was afterwards, when they were on the mend, that the strange feelings surfaced. One man had told Stephen that he felt a part of his soul had escaped when his heart was invaded; he was sure he was not the same man.

"Okay, Morrissy, make it quick. You know I'm not supposed to feed you information." Blanchard had come from the catheterization lab, where further X-rays had been taken of Señora Perez's heart. His words were harsh, but he was smiling. He liked Stephen and—more importantly—enjoyed educating him. As a cardiologist in a hospital dedicated to surgery, Blanchard was very much a second fiddle.

"How do they look?"

"We got a good picture, got it quickly too. The whole business only took an hour. The old lady's in better shape for surgery than you'd think. She shows narrowing in the beginning portion of the left main coronary artery. Medical therapy is less effective in these cases than surgery." Blanchard lowered his voice. "If you want to worry about someone, I'd pick Ramirez. So much deterioration there—he might as well have the heart of an eighty-year-old man."

Blanchard often spoke of his patients to Stephen as "the ventricular" or "the Fallot," as if they could only be identified by their particular defect, but this detached tone never emerged when he was in their presence. He was as leisurely and concerned in his handling of them as Lassiter was abrupt, aloof. He might refer to a candidate for double bypass surgery as "the times two," but he would know the patient's name and use it often, and reassuringly, in his presence. "Got to go," he said and wheeled off, a portfolio of X-rays as thick as a phone book under his arm.

Stephen was no longer needed. Tomorrow, when his patients went to the OR, he would put in a full day. He would wait the endless hours with the relatives, escort them to the ICU when the ordeal was over. This was the hardest part of his job. It tired him more than any physical activity would have done. He thought ironically of the sort of activity customary in his line of work. Cutting through the jungle with a machete, struggling down the powdery side of an extinct volcano—these were perfectly natural exercises. His body was happy when it was exhausted and he then slept as deeply and satisfyingly as a child. After a surgery day he was jumpy from inactivity, his mind dull from emotional strain. Tonight he would go to the party Jackie Talbot had invited him to in River Oaks; the opulent banality of the hostess, whom Stephen had read about in the columns, was just what he needed after a day at the hospital.

Nobody at Eugenia Fowler's party would be a times-two, a Fallot, or a ventricular; nobody would be in pain, or frightened out of their wits, or unable to speak English. He thought guiltily of what Jackie had told him at lunch. Ernestine McGrath was convinced that he was uncomfortable around sick people. Ernestine, he remembered with a swift, unpleasant jog of memory, was not alone in this conviction. His ex-wife, Natalie, had accused him similarly in a hotel room near Mesa Verde, Colorado. He had taken her along on that assignment because she'd complained they weren't together enough. Natalie had spent the whole time bitterly lamenting the heat and discomfort on the mesa, constantly looking out for scorpions, ticks, and snakes. She had refused to wear a hat while riding through the ruins of the cliff-dwellings, and she'd come down with sunstroke.

"You don't really care how I feel," she'd wailed. "You're only annoyed because I'm slowing things up." This had been unfair. Stephen had cared very much, been stricken with remorse when poor Natalie whimpered that her head was splitting apart, but the more she accused him of a lack of feeling, the more it became true.

Riding down on the elevator, he had an extraordinarily clear memory of her face as it had been in the darkened room in Colorado. The long, clear brown eyes were muddied with fever and her lips were dry, a little cracked. This dimming of her beauty had touched him, even as he braced himself for one of her diatribes. What exactly had she said?

"Do you know why you can't stand to be in this room with me? You *hate* sick people. If I were some old Indian woman dying in a hut, you'd be right at home. As long as you can trap suffering and slap it in a can you're happy. You think all of life is a documentary film. You think our marriage is a documentary film! Well, I have news for you, Stephen. This is me. Your wife. I feel like hell and I want to go home." Something like that.

The elevator stopped at the main floor and he headed for the volunteers' lounge to turn his beeper in. Ernestine was sitting in a leather chair, working on one of her cookbooks.

It would have to be Ernestine, of course. Perfect. He gave her the number where he would be in River Oaks in case of an emergency.

"River Oaks, eh? Party, party."

Several clever replies came to mind, but he swallowed them and said good-bye politely. A duel of wits with Ernestine McGrath was not high on his list of priorities, and he felt sorry for her. He knew that every time she looked at him she wondered why he should be alive and healthy while her husband was dead.

He left the hospital and loped down the long drive toward his motel on the boulevard. There in his rented unit, he would shower and have a drink. Then he would get into his rented car and drive to River Oaks. Nothing in his life was permanent; everything was rented, borrowed, temporary, and that was exactly to his liking. Forty-four-year-old men were supposed to crave permanency, but Stephen liked the ugly, impersonal interior of his room at the Tropicana Motel. It suggested a short-term stay, just as the floor of a rain forest or a lean-to in Alaska did. He had a fifth of Polish vodka in the fridge and also a packet of Marlboros. He had been trying to give up smoking—nothing like a heart hospital to convince you to give up that particular vice—but he badly wanted a cigarette now.

He entered the air-cooled dimness of his room, all vinyl and polyester, and began to remove his clothes immediately, letting them fall where they would, then kicking them in a neat pile in the corner. This was a habit which had infuriated Natalie. No matter how many times he had told her that her fury was unwarranted—after all, he always got around to collecting them and putting them in the laundry hamper—she placed it high on the list of his faults. Not, she assured him, that it was the gesture that mattered. It was the underlying attitude, the absolute male arrogance the gesture reflected, that drove her crazy. Standing in the shower he amused himself by recalling the long list of sins against women Natalie had laid at his feet.

He was selfish in a way fundamental to men, a way bred into him. Stephen, she said, didn't even understand why he was selfish. He was also reckless, and his disregard for his own safety reflected his basic disregard for her. He would never settle down because he was terrified of living a life of routine like other men. He thought he was above it all; he would never realize it took more courage to lead an ordinary life than it did to court malaria in the tropics or frostbite on Baffin Island.

It wasn't until he was lying on the bed, a towel wrapped around his waist, two inches of Polish vodka in the motel glass beside him and a cigarette (unlit, after all) between his lips, that he remembered what else she had said that day in Mesa Verde.

"You're Mr. Objective, aren't you? Mr. Detachment."

He raised his glass in a silent toast to her, realizing the basic justice of the words. *Mr. Detachment. Mr. Objective.*

She kept her face carefully composed so that no one could realize how shocking the prices were to her. She had become used to economizing, but during her most carefree days she had never paid hundreds of thousands of *lire* for a belt or scarf. Even the rich women who'd patronized the store on the Via Marconi, where Rafaella had worked for a time, might hesitate before the staggering price-tags at Neiman-Marcus. The very air here smelled expensive.

She had already spent more for Stefania's cowboy hat than she had planned on using for all her gifts, and it was plain and unadorned. For fifty dollars more, the glamorous salesgirl had explained, she might have one with two feathers in the band.

She watched while a woman ordered one dozen pigskin driving gloves, converting the dollars to *lire* and multiplying by twelve. Over seven hundred dollars! *Basta. You are acting like a peasant!* She smiled pleasantly at the woman, as if to say that she approved of her taste in driving gloves, and went to examine an object that seemed to belong more in a museum than a department store.

It was a vest fashioned of stiff, quill-like darts and bound together in leather so soft it felt like crushed velvet; it dripped with beads and dangling feathers and small, strange objects which chimed together musically when she touched them. Entranced, she examined the vest more closely. It seemed something to be worn in an Indian ceremony. She pictured it as a joyful ceremony—a wedding or christening —and thought how Anna-Laura would adore it.

The price tag bore a sum well up in the four-figure range, and ruefully she turned and went in search of something less flamboyant. Eventually she settled on a rather plain blouse, redeemed by its awesomely bright color—a screaming cerise, Anna-Laura's favorite.

She had begun to despair of finding anything for Carlo, whose tastes were eccentric and who would have struggled to conceal chagrin at a gift of clothing, when she saw the candle in the alcove. It was shaped like a cowboy boot, and life-sized. There was an even larger one—a giant's boot—but the thought of transporting it back was staggering. The smaller boot was two feet high, and the candle wax was carefully carved to resemble snakeskin. Carlo would love it. No other boy in Genoa would have such a peculiar thing to call his own.

When she was leaving the store with her purchases, the boot awkward in a shopping bag, she did some mental calculations. She had already dipped into her "emergency fund" (at home she and Anna-Laura had agreed on the necessity of such a fund without ever wanting to say what it could mean), and instead of feeling alarm she was exhilarated. One had to be generous, and she was pleased with her choices.

As she got into a taxi she tried to see herself as the driver might: an ordinary, happy woman, returning from an impulsive shopping spree.

Chapter 5

Rafaella waited for the call to Genoa to be put through. It was the second day of her five-day grace period; she had agreed with Anna-Laura to call twice, the last time just before she entered the hospital. She could wait no longer. It seemed vital to her to hear the voices of her family, even if she couldn't afford the transatlantic call.

She breathed deeply, trying to calm herself. It was important to sound normal, cheerful even, for her children. When the operator rang back to connect her, the phone felt slick in her hand. She had to grasp it until her wrist ached to hold it firm.

"Rafaella!" Anna-Laura's greeting was a shout. In the single word her sister-in-law managed to convey concern, love, fear, and joy all at the same time. This was very much Anna-Laura's style. In the background, she could hear a sort of low-key pandemonium made up of the drone of television and the raised voices of Carlo and Stefania. It was the familiar chaos, and it made her so homesick she felt a wave of longing sweep over her.

Anna-Laura's voice was like a cello, capable of sustaining long sweet notes and then descending to a thrilling deepness. She let the voice comfort her, mechanically answering the questions. Yes, she felt well enough. Yes, it was barbarically hot in Houston.

"Maurizio is here," said Anna-Laura. "He had supper with us. The children are fighting over who will speak to you first, and Maurizio has just told them to go in alphabetical order."

Now Maurizio's voice—calm, courteous, soft. "Rafaella— how are you?"

"Your flowers are lovely. Thank you."

He dismissed the flowers and his voice became more urgent. "I could fly to Houston," he said. "I could be with you. You shouldn't be alone."

"It's better for me to be alone," said Rafaella. It was a meaningless statement, but she could not accept his presence and what it would imply. A silence stretched between them, minute, but enough to remind him of her longing to speak to the children. "God bless you," he said.

"Mama!" It was Carlo's turn. His voice, which was faintly tinged with the huskiness which would one day turn his treble into a man's voice, made tears rise in her throat. "A boy in school, Marcello, you remember him, he showed me a picture of the Houston Astrodome. Isn't that a coincidence?"

"*Stupefacente!*" She felt tears sliding down her cheeks even as she smiled at his intensity. "I bought you a wonderful present today. I bought presents for you and Stefania and Anna-Laura. You'll just have to wait until I get back, because I won't tell you what they are."

"I don't need a present," said Carlo. "I just want you to come back well." He spoke self-consciously, aping the words of adults but meaning them so urgently his voice shook. She knew she must not allow him to cry; crying would shame him.

"What did you have for supper?" she asked. Carlo informed her that Anna-Laura had made *pesto* and Signor Guidi had brought *focaccia* from Brandini's. She could taste the *pesto*, see the red and white striped awning over the pastry shop. It occurred to her that ordinary life was bliss. "It's Stefania's turn now. I love you, Mama."

"What did you buy for me, Mama?" Stefania's voice emerged in amplified form; she was, as usual, holding the phone too close to her mouth. "Did you buy me a cowboy hat?"

"I can't tell. It wouldn't be fair. How are you, darling?"

"I had a fight with Maria Panero, in school. She said Texas was on the other side of the equator."

"Ah, you win, Stefania, but you mustn't fight, my love. The geography teacher can show Maria, on the map. Are you helping Anna-Laura?"

"Oh, yes," said Stefania piously. "I'm being very good. I miss you, Mama. Here are ten kisses." She smacked them off quickly. It was going by too fast; Rafaella wanted to hold onto the illusion of being with them, the comfort of speaking Italian.

They all seemed to say good-bye at once, although it was Anna-Laura who had the final word. "We love you," said Anna-Laura's voice. "We pray for you." Anna-Laura was not at all religious. "The prayers of unbelievers are more powerful," she'd said once, "because they are more rare."

Before the line went dead, Rafaella could hear the children calling a final good-bye. "*Ciao, Mama. Ciao!*"

Ciao, Papa.

By midafternoon, all of Stephen's patients were in the recovery ICU. The prognosis for three was very good. Julio Ramirez, the man with the ventricular septal defect, had waited too long to come for help; it would be some time before his surgery could be pronounced successful.

As soon as his heart had been opened, it was apparent to everyone in the OR that Ramirez was fortunate to be alive at all. The heart was ancient, the tissue around the hole so tired and flimsy it seemed impossible that any sutures could secure the necessary patch. There had been no hesitation in Lassiter's movements. He had sewed the Dacron patch as deftly as if he had been mending a young, resilient septum rather than the flabby, deteriorated organ that was Ramirez's heart. Twice the patient's heart fibrillated when he was removed from the pump; twice Lassiter had shocked it back with a jolt of electricity. Now Ramirez lay with the others, still mercifully unconscious, in intensive care.

Stephen sat with the relatives in the Recovery waiting room. Mrs. Ramirez had been doing needlepoint for three hours, resisting all offers of coffee or tea. This was her method of controlling her anxiety. In Stephen's time as a volunteer he had learned to recognize which personality types withdrew during the long vigil and which needed constant contact. The Ecuadorian lady was of the latter variety.

She was gracious, talkative. She questioned Stephen about every facet of hospital life, complimented him on his Spanish, and showed him photographs of her children, now grown. Mrs. Velasquez, the bullying woman from Vera Cruz, was yet another type. She couldn't bear to remain quiet and came and went like a tropical storm.

"Where is the doctor?" she demanded suddenly. The skin beneath her eyes was black with fatigue. She had smoked so many cigarettes during the long vigil the odor of nicotine had seeped into her pores. She smelled like a heaping ashtray. "There have been complications," she announced bitterly. "That is what is taking so long."

"Dr. Lassiter never appears before four," Stephen explained. "That is the earliest he can report to you—it would be useless before." He went on to describe Lassiter's busy routine—surgery in the morning, rounds with recuperative patients in the afternoon shuttling from the ICU's to the convalescent rooms, rounds in the evening to visit the next day's patients—but Lassiter's whirlwind schedule meant next to nothing to a woman wondering if her husband were still alive. Mrs. Velasquez lit another cigarette. Across the room an American woman had begun to weep softly.

At five minutes past the hour of four there was a commotion at the door and Lassiter entered, nearly at a run, trailed by Blanchard the cardiologist and another surgeon. The room became charged with galvanic energy, and Stephen wondered what it must be like to be Lassiter at this particular moment. No audience in a theater could wait for a star's entrance with such intensity; no head of state could command the utter, electrified attention accorded this figure. It was absolute power, undiluted and frightening.

Lassiter's words were always an anticlimax. His delivery was terse, almost casual; as he went to each relative with his news bulletin he might have been describing the outcome of a tonsillectomy. "Your husband is fine." "Your wife is doing well." "Your daughter responded well." "Fine, fine, fine." "You can see him at seven o'clock." "Things are looking good. . . ."

The flat words didn't seem equal to the drama of the situation, but how could they? It had been said that Lassiter escaped the relatives quickly to avoid embarrassing demonstrations of gratitude. People had been known to try to kiss his hands or thrust statues of saints on him. Now he was in front of Mrs. Ramirez.

"I've put in a Dacron patch," he said. "Your husband should be just fine, but we'll keep him in intensive care an extra day, to make sure."

While Stephen translated for Estella Ramirez, he remembered another witticism about Lassiter. Blanchard had warned him during his first week, "Martin is a very articulate man, but when he meets the relatives his vocabulary is confined to twenty words or less."

"Your sister's responding well," he said to Mrs. Reyes. "Things are looking good."

He had sped on to the next group before Mrs. Reyes could thank him. She turned her gracious smile on Stephen; he could see tears beginning to form in the corners of her eyes. She had been very brave, concealing her anxiety with an heroic effort.

He thought ahead to the time when he would take his charges to the recovery ICU for their five-minute visit. He imagined Estella Ramirez would weep at sight of her husband, his orange-painted chest making a dramatic contrast with the colorless rest of him. Mrs. Velasquez might be struck dumb, perhaps for the first time in her life.

It would probably be his gallant lady from Ecuador, she of the imperturbable, smiling demeanor, who would faint.

Nearly five o'clock. The worst heat of the day was over. Rather than stay in her room, where the voices of her children still seemed to echo in the walls, Rafaella descended again to the Hibernian's lobby. If anything, the *Giant* people were more numerous than on the evening she'd arrived. They were streaming in and out of the front doors, involved in some mysterious activity on the hotel's long front lawn. She decided to join them.

The structures erected during the night seemed to be pens,

the sort in which animals were housed. Brightly striped tents enclosed the pens, and people milled about as if at a fair. She made her way down the walk, drawn toward the tents and people by curiosity and a desperate need to distract herself.

A rich mixture of smells hung in the air—straw and beer and the warm, comforting odor of healthy animals. The beer was being dispensed from a wagon nearby; everywhere she looked cans emblazoned with the word *Pearl's* were lifted to parched lips. The heat lay over the land, even at this hour, like a fiery cloak.

It was cooler under the shade of the tents, but close and humid still. The livestock had been arranged in two lots on either side of the walk, and Rafaella joined the crowds who wandered from pen to pen appraising the horses. The first was a stallion belonging, so the sign said, to the Jamison Ranch in Medina. He was a magnificent beast, seventeen hands high at least, with chestnut flanks that seemed to shoot forth rays of light. His high, round rump shone as if polished like fine old wood. A roan was next, and Rafaella recognized the owner's name. He had once been a governor of Texas, but everyone in Italy knew him as the man who had been riding with President Kennedy that day in Dallas. Each horse was more beautiful than the last, and she walked on, heels sinking into the damp straw, admiring them impartially. Here was a black stallion from the King Ranch, there a white filly so delicate and pretty it might have been a palfrey in a medieval tapestry. A man in a Stetson jostled against her, lifted his hand to his hat in apology, and broke her mood of temporary enchantment.

She crossed over to the other enclosure and felt an instant, unreasonable alarm at what she saw there. The creatures seemed like something from a child's nightmare, massive and long, gleaming with health, but unrecognizable as what they were: bulls. Santa Gertrudis bulls, she read, and then looked again to see if they were really as large as Rolls-Royce automobiles. They looked back at her, indifferent, unlike the horses whose arrogant, fierce expressions were all of a piece with their beauty. These creatures were all menace, she thought, and she was glad for the bars which separated her from them. The old Rafaella would have been fascinated without feeling fear; the new Rafaella, who saw everything as a potential threat, was fascinated *by* her fear.

In the aisles between the pens were large, standing bales of hay where people sat drinking their Pearl's beer. A group of four seemed to be having a private party. The men drank from silver flasks while the women, blonde heads close together, scrutinized the crowd and laughed. Rafaella selected an empty bale and sat, tucking her skirt beneath her modestly. The hay was rough and prickly; no matter how she shifted her position it poked at her thighs through the material of her dress. She watched the women from behind her dark glasses.

They were definitely members of the *Giant* breed—deeply tanned, sporting identical hair styles (long, streaked manes of blonde hair), and identical tight blue jeans. Rafaella's practiced eye told her that the women's boots cost more than any item in her entire wardrobe. One pair seemed to be made of black and white snakeskin, patterned like a fresco or a mosaic; the other was handpainted on rough hide that looked like elephant skin. Diamonds flashed from their fingers, gold chains glimmered at the open necks of their shirts. Rich women they were, possibly the wives of the ranchers who were displaying their animals. They advertised their wealth by wearing their jewels with their jeans, donning— she quickly made a conversion from lire—eight-hundred-dollar cowboy boots to muck about in the mire! This satisfied Rafaella's sense of the dramatic. It was very much what she might have expected of Texans. She turned to look in the other direction and saw, sauntering up the path toward the tents, the man she had noticed in the admissions office yesterday. He was coming from the direction of the hospital.

Today his shirt was white and turned back casually at the cuffs. His hair was much blonder in the sunlight, but otherwise he looked the same. He didn't wear a Stetson or boots, but he was still one of them. His tanned skin and light hair, his height and health, even the way he walked were his badges of membership. She watched as he stopped in front of the governor's stallion, head cocked to one side as if he knew how to evaluate horseflesh. A loud country and western band came blaring over the loudspeaker system. Had the music just begun, or hadn't she noticed it before?

The man moved on, heading for the wagon where the Pearl's beer was being sold. She watched while he purchased a can, noted his fingers as they wrapped around the shiny aluminum. Were they the hands of a doctor? She thought not. The hands were too large and square. She couldn't imagine them performing delicate tasks. Now he was heading back in her direction and she looked away, but before she did she saw a look of surprise and recognition cross his face. He nodded at her, as if they were acquainted. He was coming closer, even smiling slightly. He was standing directly in front of her bale of hay. "Americans slide into conversations with strangers all the time," Anna-Laura had told her. "It's second nature to them, doesn't mean anything."

"Excuse me," he said. "Is this bale of hay taken?"

His voice was deep and rather soft. It lacked the twanging resonance of Texas voices. Except for the "excuse me" she didn't understand a word of what he had said. She nodded politely, and he sat on the bale next to hers.

"I saw you in Admissions yesterday. What do you think of all this horseflesh?"

This time she understood but couldn't frame a reply. She was more than ever aware of the prickly hay against the backs of her legs, of the noise and the odor of animals. Her confusion must have been evident because he spread his hands and gestured around him, taking in the horses and bulls, the women in their boots and diamonds. "All this," he said. "Do you find it interesting?"

"It is very interesting. So colorful." She saw the familiar look, the one indicating he was trying to place her accent.

"My name is Morrissy, Stephen Morrissy. When I first saw you yesterday I had the feeling you'd just arrived in Houston. Arrived from somewhere, but I couldn't tell where."

As if it was any of his business! She disapproved of his casual manners; he made things seem too easy. Still, she had always been polite; she didn't want to be rude to someone who was just obeying, as Anna-Laura would have it, his second nature. "I come from Italy," she said. "Genoa."

64

He cleared his throat. "Ah, Genoa," he said. "I've been in Rome, and Milan, and Venice, but I never got to Genoa." He said this gravely, as if in apology. Abruptly, she felt sorry for him. He must be wishing he'd never started such a conversation.

"Perhaps you will someday," she said more kindly.

He smiled at her, and she saw that his eyes were *nocciuola*—the color of hazelnuts. Fine lines radiated from his eyes; he was older than she'd thought, maybe forty. His physical presence seemed to demand more space than was possible in the confines of the tent. She could see traces of the boyish surfer quality she'd noticed earlier, but there was something she hadn't seen, something male and commanding, which made her uneasy.

"Do you have a friend, a relative, in the hospital?"

She shook her head. Of course he had to ask it; why else would she be sitting in Admissions?

"Then you're visiting. A tourist."

"Yes, visiting." This was a lie only in the strictest sense. How could she tell this inquisitive stranger the truth? It seemed ludicrous, like something from a foolish dream, to be sitting on a bale of hay, submitting to relentless questioning. If the man had been vulgar, or stupid-seeming, it would have angered her, but his soft voice and polite expression made it difficult to be angry. In fact, if she were truthful, she wasn't angry at all. It was as much a part of her training and background to behave coolly toward inquisitive males as it was, apparently, a part of his to ask questions. She was bewildered by his attentions to her. Why should this vigorous man, so pleasing to the eye that she wished she could study him more frankly, seek her out? She inclined her head downward, toward the straw, and waited to hear what he would say next.

"People come here, to the hospital, from all over the world. I thought you might be the wife of a patient when I saw you."

"My husband is dead," she said. Instantly, she heard the bluntness, the crudity of it, saw him lower his eyes in a conventional gesture of sympathy, and felt she had flailed him with her widowhood. It was not the first time she had announced it to a stranger, but never before had she done it with such a lack of grace. In her own language it would have come out much differently.

"Are you a doctor?" Her voice emerged with just the right degree of casual curiosity, which surprised her. The green eyes looked up again, grateful.

"I'm a volunteer. I work with Spanish-speaking patients. I don't speak Italian, but I can understand it." Again he smiled, and suddenly she knew it was important to put space between herself and this man who charmed her even as he pried. She had already told him a lie; he was dangerous to her.

"Excuse me," she said. "I must go now."

"Do you have an appointment?"

Now she was sure he was mocking her. Why couldn't he behave properly, refrain from interrogating her? "I am only tired," she said. "It is so hot."

Instantly he was on his feet, looming above her. "I forgot how the heat affects people who aren't used to it. It's very tiring. *Fatigozzo?*"

"*Faticoso,*" she said, automatically correcting him. She was instantly appalled at her bad manners; so few Americans even attempted to speak Italian, and this man apparently knew Spanish.

"The two languages are very close." His voice was earnest, and for the first time she understood something: he was as uncomfortable as she. The stilted little conversation, his endless questions, embarrassed him. Then why did he seem to be walking along beside her back toward the Hibernian?

"There's a nice, cool bar in that hotel," he was saying. "If you'd allow me to buy you a drink I'll apologize for imprisoning you with the livestock."

"I live there." This was no answer, but she had begun to despair of escaping from him. Now he was telling her about the builder of the Hibernian, a famous wildcatter he said, a driller of oil. He'd struck it rich and built the hotel to commemorate his good fortune. He made her understand by pantomiming a gusher springing up and raining its riches down on the astonished man.

66

"Like James Dean in *Giant*," she said, triumphantly displaying her knowledge of Americana.

"*Exactly* like James Dean. The man James Dean played in *Giant* was based on him." The *nocciuolo* eyes looked at her with amusement and approval. "You like movies?"

"Very much."

How could she not have a drink with him after that? Feeling inexplicably happier than she had for a long time, she followed him into the dim recesses of the Hibernian's bar. He had said he had to be back at the hospital soon; what harm could it do? She wouldn't ever see him again, but for half an hour she could pretend she was a normal woman, a tourist, having a pleasant conversation with a strange man in a strange town.

I never thought I could feel this way. Don't you see? It's all so new to me!

Darling . . . darling . . . don't waste precious time with words! Oh, my love!

Don't speak . . . hold me. Hold me close . . .

Rafaella sneezed. She drew one of the hotel blankets up around her shoulders and continued to watch the flickering figures on the TV screen. The man was now kissing the woman who had said it was all so new to her. They kissed carefully, in full profile, so the camera could highlight their fine cheekbones and the woman's long, arched-back neck. From what Rafaella could glean from the dialogue, the course of their love would be rocky because the man was married to a selfish and domineering woman who would never agree to a divorce. The woman was weeping now. Rafaella sneezed again and crossed the room to turn the air conditioning off. On her way she addressed the woman on the screen, "Signora, what would you do if you had real problems?"

The movie had been made in the fifties, judging by the skirt lengths. She was watching it to pass the time and to strengthen her English. Soon, she told herself, she would turn it off and go to sleep. What did she care about the fate

67

of the heroine—a sulkily pretty woman with no visible means of support who fluttered about New York in a series of chic cocktail dresses? Her clandestine meetings with her lover especially irritated Rafaella, and gradually, with shame, she realized that she was envious, actually envious, of a cardboard figure in a harmless, melodramatic movie. It was not the heroine's wardrobe or wealth or glamorous life she envied, but her simple delusions. She believed that she deserved to be happy because she was in love and her lover returned that emotion. It was a situation Rafaella would never again experience, and until now it had not occurred to her that she could miss it.

She turned the television off and went to prepare for bed. The long day had exhausted her. It seemed ages ago that she had bought the presents for Carlo and Stefania, an aeon since she had heard their voices. She saw herself seated in the Hibernian bar, sipping her Campari and soda, listening to the stranger while he told her about his real profession. No doubt he had found her standoffish and cold. Also boring. The truth was that she felt safe when he talked about himself because it steered the conversation away from herself.

It made her smile to remember the strange Italianized Spanish he used on her if there was something she couldn't understand. *Documentario*, he'd said, explaining about the kinds of films he made, and she had understood immediately. From what he'd told her, his work seemed to embrace every possible sort of dangerous climate, country, situation, and activity. He had been in the Amazon, the Yucatan, Belfast, and Vietnam. He had made films in prisons and slums. He seemed to thrive on danger.

The time had passed for her to tell him the truth about her reasons for being in Houston, and so she sat on, an imposter. What would she have seen on his face if she had been truthful? Discomfort, sympathy, quickly masked by the falsely cheerful look people assumed when confronted with illness. She'd seen that look too often; in some ways being pitied was the worst trial of all.

Performing the simple, repetitive bedtime rituals, she felt self-conscious, like an actor in a play. She was too aware of the light pressure of her fingers as she applied a moisturizing cream to her skin, the sibilant sound of the brush as it moved through her hair.

Without any warning, her fingers grasped the hem of her nightgown and pulled it up over her head so that she stood naked in front of the mirror. She forced herself to look at her body, the betrayer, as she had not done for a long time. She saw, not the flayed man she had imagined, nor any other sign of her imperfection, but the slender, graceful body of an unknown woman. It was a pleasing body; it had been capable of pleasure in its day. It had received and given pleasure. The breasts had suckled children, yet remained firm and youthful. Only if she moved slightly could she detect, in the dim lamp light, the faint silvery marks, like laurel wreaths, on her belly. Otherwise the woman in the mirror might have been a virgin.

She placed one finger lightly over her breastbone and moved it downward, tracing the path the surgeon's knife would take. It was some time before she put the lights out and got into the bed designed for two.

Chapter 6

The little girl was five years old, and she had been born with the Great Vessels of her heart transposed. She had the unhealthy coloring and sad eyes of a child who has always been sick, and she spoke no English. She and her mother had come from Naples that day.

Jackie didn't know whom she pitied more, the little girl or her frantic, exhausted mother. Signora Camaratta gave her the child's medical history in her soft Neapolitan accent. Lucia had turned a peculiar color six weeks after she'd been born, but the local doctor had attributed her lack of vitality, her unusually thin arms and legs, to some vitamin deficiency.

"Sometimes she will be playing, like a normal child, and suddenly, in moments, she is pale and drained. There is nothing I can do, you understand."

That, Jackie thought, was the greatest anguish for the parents of such children. They were powerless to protect or help, and some of them even felt guilty, as if they had transmitted the terrible defect knowingly. Lucia lay in her bed in the children's wing, an emaciated child with knowing dark eyes, surrounded by a bright motif of capering chipmunks on the walls.

Her defect was one of the most common congenital defects of the heart, and it could be cured in two steps. Using a technique called Mustard, after the Canadian surgeon who had invented it, Lassiter would perform surgery to improve oxygenation. In effect, another defect would be created to replace the original one. By the time Lucia was a few years older and able to tolerate major surgery again, there was every chance that her heart could be totally corrected. Lassiter had probably performed more Mustards than any other surgeon on earth, but his skill and the fact that Lucia's condition was common—as congenital heart defects went—were not likely to comfort Signora Camaratta. Jackie had no children, but she knew no mother thought of her child as a statistic.

"Is there anything I can do for you now?" she asked. It would be several hours before Vi Phinney would appear to help her explain the surgery to Lucia. "Would you like me to bring you something from the cafeteria?" Signora Camaratta shook her head, but when Jackie left she pursued her to the corridor, out of the child's hearing.

"Please," she whispered, "tell me what is the risk? I know she must have the operation, but what is the risk?"

Volunteers were not allowed to discuss medical procedure, except when translating, but Jackie had heard the question dozens of times. It meant *Will my child die? What are the odds on my husband's life? Does my wife have a fifty-fifty chance, or is it more like seventy-thirty?* Lassiter was known to say "I don't give odds."

Jackie gave the woman her most reassuring smile, cheating a little, because the smile seemed to gently mock at the concept of risk. Then she gave the standard answer. "Dr. Lassiter has done more operations of this sort than any surgeon in the world. Lucia is in good hands. The best."

It was all she could say, but it seemed to work. All the way down in the elevator she saw Signora Camaratta's eyes, begging for the right answer, and her nails, which had been bitten to the quick, and the small, wise face of Lucia, which might have been a hundred years old.

"I can't say how much I admire you, Jackie. Hiding yourself away in that dreary hospital, being a ministering angel to all those unfortunate people. I think it's marvelous, really I do, but it must be awfully depressing." The words of Eugenia Fowler, one of her oldest friends. No Florence Nightingale, she. Genia was a shark, had been at ten. What had prompted her to invite Morrissy to Genia's party? Intrigue really wasn't her style, but she'd done it because she wanted to see if anything short of an erupting volcano or a Stone Age savage viewed through a camera lens could turn Morrissy on.

In the sixth grade, Genia had prompted a boy named Raymond Beale to swallow a fly. He'd done it because Genia had promised him a kiss. When Raymond presented himself for his reward, she had shrieked, "How could I possibly kiss lips that have touched a *fly?*" There had been this nagging curiosity to see how Morrissy would behave in a social situation, how he would cope with a woman like Eugenia. That's why she'd invited him to the River Oaks party.

Genia's house had been redecorated in shades of watermelon-pink and tangerine. Her husband, a plastic surgeon, had paid for every scrap of it, and Genia waited for the redecoration to be completed before she filed for divorce. The cosmetic surgeon had also paid for the jewels Genia wore, the pre-Columbian sculptures she favored, and the life-sized statue of her, in marble, which presided over the pool. He had personally supervised the enlarging of her already quite adequate breasts, and she stood—a living tribute to his skills—welcoming her guests, dressed in a Balinese drapery fastened at strategic places.

She'd zeroed right in on Stephen, fluttering lashes and dazzling smile working overtime. "I think I'd die if I had to go into those intensive care units every day," she'd said, continuing her praise of Jackie's volunteer work. "When my grandpa had a coronary, I saw him, you know? Right there in the ICU? Martin Lassiter was a perfect *charm,* he did all he could, but honestly, my grandpa looked just like *blue meat.*" She shuddered dramatically. "I never got over it. To this day I have nightmares about it."

Jackie had sought Morrissy's eyes and seen there a glimmer of wicked amusement. Behind the amusement she also saw a certain weariness. He was bored. "Sorry," she mouthed at him as Eugenia turned away to grab a drink from a passing tray.

He winked at her. Say what you like about Stephen Morrissy, he was no Raymond Beale.

"Jehovah's Witnesses are forbidden to accept blood transfusions. They interpret the words 'Ye shall not eat blood' as a ban on the *use* of blood. Lassiter is one of the few surgeons who will operate under these circumstances. He uses saline solutions to replenish body fluids. Results are surprisingly successful. Low death-rate. . . . Note for myself: Ask Blanchard if Lassiter ever cheats in an emergency situation?"

Stephen switched off the tape recorder. It would be an interesting aside to the film if he could show that Lassiter—a man of science—scrupulously respected the Jehovah's Witnesses' religious wishes. Would it be more ethical to disobey and save a life or play it straight and let the patient die?

He walked to the window, parted the hideous fiber-glass curtains, and looked out across the boulevard toward the Hibernian. The livestock enclosures had been dismantled; the auction in the hotel's huge annex had been a great success. The finest of the Santa Gertrudis bulls had gone to an Oklahoma rancher for $500,000. The site of his meeting with the Italian Widow, as he thought of her, had vanished. So had she. After their drink she had thanked him and simply vanished. He had learned almost nothing about her, and this was not because of the language barrier but because she offered nothing.

She reminded him of the women one occasionally saw in Italian films, chosen by the director to symbolize some virtue or call up a specific emotion. They rarely had lines; they existed as symbols, icons, physical reminders of what they were supposed to evoke. Yet those women were only actresses; in real life they squabbled with their agents, took lovers, got themselves photographed by papparazzi in yachts off Sardinia. The Italian Widow seemed to have no other life. She simply existed, mysteriously, as a visitor to Houston whose purpose in visiting he could not imagine.

Yesterday, surrounded by all those Neiman-Marcus cowgirls, she had seemed as out of place as a painting by Caravaggio would be on the walls of his motel room. Pure curiosity had forced him to speak to her, and the strength of that curiosity still amazed him. He'd been deeply embarrassed, battering away at her reserve when she so clearly wanted to be alone, but he hadn't been able to help himself.

The few times he had made her smile seemed like such triumphs that he wanted to make it happen again and again.

"Thank you for such hospitality," she'd said quaintly, and then done her vanishing act. He shook himself irritably. It was foolish to think in terms of icons and mystery. She was just a shy, reserved woman who thought he was trying to pick her up. Probably she was the rich widow of someone who had relatives in Houston. She would shop at Neiman-Marcus, go to a few parties, and fly back to Genoa. He would never know why she had been sitting in Admissions, and it didn't matter.

Except it didn't ring true. He couldn't imagine her at a party like Eugenia Fowler's. He couldn't imagine her anywhere; Signora Leone seemed to have no existence beyond his brief glimpses of her. He switched the tape recorder on again.

"Ask Blanchard 1. Are certain ethnic groups more prone to heart disease? 2. What percentage of heart disease can be considered congenital?"

What would Natalie think if she could see him now, bent over a tape recorder in a tacky motel unit, dealing with the *real* problems of the human heart? She had considered herself an expert on the theoretical ones. *You have no heart. How can you be so heartless?*

It was true he rarely thought of her. He had thought more about her in the last two days than in the entire year before. She had been a long-limbed, tawny girl, supple and resilient with the dancer's secret, wiry strength. Part of his initial attraction to Natalie had been for that strength; he loved to see her walking toward him, moving with proud precision and a wholly instinctive grace. It seemed to him later that he had mistaken her physical dignity for a radiant inner life which Natalie did not possess, just as he had confused her fascination with filmmaking for approval.

Even when her flaws became apparent, it didn't seem to matter. He was twenty-nine, Natalie twenty-four. It was time he married, and if his marriage proved less than idyllic he would have ample opportunities to escape it for long periods of time. He had still liked Natalie better than any other woman at that time, and her physical self enchanted him.

Whenever he saw her dance on stage he experienced a thrill of sensual delight that the splendid creature up there was his. She was less gifted as an actress. On the rare occasions when she was cast in off-Broadway plays his feeling had been one of embarrassment for her. She was unnatural, stiff, mechanical. The sure, sweet movements of her knowing body were somehow trapped in artifice, and her voice grated painfully. It wasn't until she'd played her deathbed scene in Mesa Verde that he understood why she failed so as an actress—Natalie on stage simply magnified the real-life Natalie, no matter what part she was playing, and thought that was enough.

Mr. Detachment. Mr. Objective. He recognized the justice of it. Hadn't there always been something indifferent at the core of his feelings for her? Even at the height of his physical passion for her, there were great, unexplored areas within him he had never allowed her to enter. She would have been a poacher there, an interloper crossing the "Do Not Trespass" sign at her own peril. Whether it was something lacking in him or Natalie's fault for being less than her radiant outer shell suggested didn't matter. She'd been right that time.

In the later years of their marriage they'd had a pact: Stephen would work on projects in the Eastern seaboard area only, and Natalie would attend her daily ballet class and pursue her acting career. Gradually, the pact dissolved. Stephen urged Natalie to accept a part with a touring company and then went to Mexico to collaborate on a project in the Yucatan. When they met, back in New York in their Greenwich Village apartment, they met as good friends who enjoyed themselves in bed. At the beginning both had claimed to want children, but the subject was abandoned by tacit consent. When Stephen was alone, women dropped in and out of his life as pleasantly and briefly as fragrant summer showers, but he never went looking for them and Natalie never asked.

The end of their marriage was surprisingly painless. It was she who had asked for a divorce. After a brief stint with the Stuttgart Ballet, Natalie had married a California real estate developer she'd met in Europe. She lived now in Mill Valley, had two children, and always sent Stephen a Christmas card. He thought of her with affection and wished her well. She was quite a nice woman, really; it had taken them a long time to perceive that they were badly matched.

He thought briefly of the few women he'd considered marrying in the last ten years, but he was happy as he was. He liked his permanently temporary life. If he needed a woman's company, there were scores of ready partners. Eugenia Fowler, she of the plumped-up breasts and pre-Columbian art, would be only too happy to entertain a lonely filmmaker, but she presented a problem. He really preferred to make love to women he liked.

Guiltily, he lit one of the Marlboros from the secret cache in the fridge. The first drag was good, the second indifferent, the third foul. He crushed it out and prepared to go to the hospital. It was time to see how the relatives were bearing up.

Just as he was leaving, it occurred to him to wonder if the woman existed whom he might love as Natalie had wanted him to love her.

Jackie watched while Vi Phinney produced a big rag doll and held it up for Lucia Camaratta to see. Lassiter had already conferred with the child's mother, and Lucia's surgery was scheduled for the next day.

"Hello, Lucia. I thought maybe you were curious about some things, so I've come to answer any questions you might like to ask me."

Jackie translated, watching for a flicker of emotion in the little girl's eyes. Lucia regarded them somberly. The only sound in the room was the accelerated breathing of her mother.

"We're going to fix your heart tomorrow," said Vi. "You'll be asleep. You won't feel anything at all. But when you wake up, this is how you'll look. We don't want you to be scared. This is how everyone looks after they get their hearts fixed, and it's only for a little while."

Vi's dextrous fingers rigged the rag doll with miniature tubes and catheters, as if she were decorating a grotesque

Christmas tree. Lucia watched intently, but the dark eyes remained expressionless. Some children asked many questions; some were confident, others terrified. A few screamed at the very sight of a doctor or nurse. Most asked if there would be any needles, which they feared more than surgery. Lucia was silent, accepting the presence of these strangers in her room as she had accepted everything in her short, bleak life. She had been sick for as long as she could remember and expected nothing good.

Jackie had never yet had one of her patients die. Some volunteers quit when it happened; they couldn't accept it. For the first time she had a premonition about a patient, and it shocked and frightened her.

She felt almost sure that Lucia would die on the table.

Chapter 7

On her third day in Houston, Rafaella felt she had become a prisoner. She could not afford to take taxis across the endless expanses of the city, even if she'd had a destination in mind. It was too hot to stroll aimlessly, and there was only the humming, perilous boulevard in any case. Since she had met the Morrissy man she couldn't even go to the hospital for fear of seeing him there. Her own room had the feel of solitary confinement.

Sitting in the Hibernian's coffee shop and contemplating her lunch without enthusiasm, she felt her loneliness as something tangible which pressed against her. Lately there had been none of the terrible shortness of breath—the fight for air—that had sent her to Dr. Rinaldi; she had not felt the crushing chest pain either, but this feeling was nearly as bad.

The salad she had ordered was overabundant. Beneath the strips of ham and turkey, the halved, hard-cooked eggs, and tasteless tomatoes was an enormous bed of greenery too dense to penetrate. More mystifying were the peach halves which had arrived with the salad. They were filled with something ominous—a pale brown glistening substance she tasted timidly and found to be peanut butter. *Santa Maria*—peanut butter in peaches! Carlo would approve of it.

She knew a sudden and acute longing for the dishes of her native province. If the unwieldy salad would only vanish and be replaced by *trenette* with *pesto* or a small plate of the shellfish—*cannolicchio*—the Genovese called spaghetti of the sea, she thought the awful feeling might recede.

If Anna-Laura were in her position, she would know how to conquer such loneliness. All sorts of exciting things would occur. Anna-Laura would make friends with strangers, strike up an acquaintance with one of the limo drivers and get free rides into the interior of the city. She would have sneaked into the invitation-only auction and watched while a rancher paid half a million American dollars for one of the fearsome bulls. She might even know how to conjure up *pesto* in Houston.

Right up until the moment they wheeled her into the operating room, she would be holding animated conversations with everyone in sight. Most especially, Anna-Laura would have befriended the filmmaker. She would have him for a friend without any hint of impropriety unless, of course, impropriety was in the cards. Here Rafaella smiled wryly. Anna-Laura often desired intimacy with men who saw her only as a friend, whereas Rafaella had the opposite problem. She ran from any hint of offered intimacy.

Anna-Laura's face floated over the huge salad and gave her a mocking look. It seemed to say that Rafaella was afraid of the filmmaker because he was such a masculine presence. Dangerous. Not at all like the men she permitted herself to know back home. He wasn't calm and paternal, like Maurizio, or friendly and sexless like the fortyish poet from Trieste she'd met at Anna-Laura's flat.

Rafaella knew if her sister-in-law was here in the flesh, she would draw a vulgar analogy. She would say Rafaella was uncomfortable in the presence of the filmmaker just as—the day before—she had been uneasy looking at the bull.

She couldn't make lunch last forever. When she paid her check, passing the bills over to the cashier whose long, lacquered nails looked like the claws of a Mandarin, it was only one-thirty. She would take the daily walk her doctor recommended in the halls of the Hibernian, briskly striding past the gift shops and pharmacy, the ballroom and bar, and if anyone thought she was crazy, too bad.

Things had calmed down some; the cattlemen had all decamped and the lobby was full of ladies in peach-colored coats who were attending a medical supply convention. Occasionally she passed people she felt sure were patients at the medical center. They moved as she had done on her first day in Houston—hesitantly, as if they were afraid someone might brush against them. One man wore carpet slippers. Her own fear had taken a new form, and she wasn't sure she understood it.

On her third lap past the gift shop she saw a woman inside who drew her attention. She was perhaps sixty-five, handsome and well-groomed, and definitely a Latin of some sort. She looked up from the counter where she was browsing and—for no reason—smiled at Rafaella. She wanted to smile back, if only to be polite, but she was moving swiftly and the moment was lost.

Passing the lobby a few minutes later she saw the woman again. She was holding a gift-wrapped package and scanning the door anxiously, as if waiting for someone. Just on cue, a group of medical conventioneers parted and revealed Stephen Morrissy entering the Hibernian. The woman waved and moved forward to greet him. Rafaella felt a superstitious dread, as if she had called him here by thinking about him. She watched as he took the woman's arm and settled her in one of the deep sofas near the desk. They were conferring earnestly, heads close together.

The woman took a cigarette from a gold case, then offered one to the filmmaker. He hesitated, then accepted. He felt in his pockets for matches or a lighter, came up with nothing, and allowed the woman to light both cigarettes. *I didn't know he smoked*, thought Rafaella. And then, *But why should I?* Later, she would see herself in the light of a schoolgirl, lurking in a hallway, spying on a boy who had seized her interest, but for now she had no thought except pleasure in seeing him. Perfectly natural, of course—he was the only living soul she had spoken to in Houston except for the waitresses in the coffee shop, the bellhop, and desk clerk.

They were rising now, preparing to leave together. *Goodbye, filmmaker.* But no. The woman searched in her handbag, then lightly hit her forehead—the gesture of one who has forgotten something. She headed for the bank of elevators, and Stephen stood politely, watching her go. Then an expression of surprise crossed his face, and Rafaella knew he had seen her. He was heading in her direction.

"Hello, signora. It's nice to see you again."

She was determined to appear more casual. More *normal.* "Is the lady the wife of one of your patients?"

"The sister. They're very devoted. Mrs. Reyes's sister is still in intensive care." He paused, shifted from one foot to another. "Are you enjoying your stay?"

"Yes. The salad for lunch was much too large, though. I believe it is true that everything in Texas is more large than life."

"How long will you be here?"

"Two more days."

"And then you'll go back to Italy?"

"Eventually."

"I like your earrings very much. They're unusual. Are they Italian?"

She touched the lobe of one ear involuntarily. The familiar earrings felt fragile beneath her fingertips. They were fashioned in the shape of a spiky flower, an anemone perhaps, and they lay flat against the lobe rather than dangling. Anna-Laura said they called attention to the line of her jaw.

"They are my own. I designed them."

"You're a designer."

"Yes. Also a silversmith. A goldsmith. Whatever. That is my profession." The words emerged awkwardly, but it had taken her a long time to think of herself as someone with a *profession.* Her mother-in-law still thought there was something unseemly in it. The filmmaker seemed to be making a decision. He was still holding the cigarette in his hand, but he had barely smoked it. He bent quickly and extinguished it in a standing ashtray.

"*This,*" he said significantly, "is an Ecuadorian cigarette. Very strong." And then, as if he were continuing an analysis of South American cigarettes, "Would you have dinner with me tonight? If you're not busy, of course. You have so little time left in Houston, and there's a funny place you might enjoy. It's down on the Ship Channel."

"It is kind of you to ask me," said Rafaella, feeling that her conversational skills had lapsed back to guidebook phrases. "I think I will be engaged."

He cleared his throat. "If you find yourself free, you can reach me at the Tropicana Motel after five-thirty. I have a night off tonight."

The lady from Ecuador reappeared, and Stephen introduced them.

"Señora Reyes, this is Signora, ah, Leone."

Mrs. Reyes unleashed a torrent of Spanish in Rafaella's direction before Stephen could explain that she was Italian. "Please tell Señora Reyes I hope her sister will be well," said Rafaella. When Stephen imparted this information the lady from Ecuador wanted to know if Rafaella had a relative at St. Matthew's. Rafaella could understand his reply. He told Mrs. Reyes that she was a visiting artist. They left after a complicated series of good-byes.

Rafaella took the elevator to the twelfth floor, feeling that something momentous had happened. *Dear Anna-Laura,* she composed on the ride up, *When you are very sick, and afraid all the time, the world shrinks to very small proportions. The tiniest things assume an importance which would seem silly to a person who is not afraid. It seems glorious if someone from the real world accepts you, not knowing you are flawed. You are willing to do anything to preserve this illusion. Certainly you will lie—*

When she entered her room the first thing she noticed was Maurizio's flowers. The chambermaid had, for some reason, placed them in a new position. They were blooming ferociously, and to Rafaella's eye they seemed almost reproachful.

"Mama! I want to know how hot it is in Houston!" Stefania spoke first this time, because Carlo had had the privilege last time.

"It is one hundred degrees," said Rafaella.

"No, but really, Mama. What is it *really?*"

Her literal-minded daughter. She knew the questions boiling in Stefania's head. *If you don't come back, will we live with Anna-Laura? May I bring my goldfish?*

"That's Fahrenheit, darling. Ask Anna-Laura to show you what it is centigrade. It is very, very hot."

"Do you miss us?"

"So much." God, yes.

"Mama?" Carlo. "Are you feeling well? You must be lonesome there." His voice was level, serious. He was trying to be very adult. "I wish I could be with you, to keep you company."

"I do too. You're very good company, Carlo, but you mustn't worry. There are many friendly people here. I've had lots of interesting conversations."

"Really?" He sounded dubious. "What are they like, the Americans?"

Rafaella considered the only American she had met. "Very gracious and cheerful. A bit curious. They ask lots of questions, but they mean well. And big—they're quite large."

"Also quite rich."

"Well, some are, of course." She told him about the livestock show, right on the lawn of her hotel, and about the bull who sold for half a million dollars. She converted the dollars into lire for Carlo's benefit. He was suitably impressed. They might have been conversing in the parlor at home. This was the way she had to talk to her son because Carlo, unlike Stefania, was able to appreciate the seriousness of her illness. Everything she said was meant to soothe him, to give him the impression that all would be well. They played the game very nicely together, each holding in emotion for the other's sake.

After she had hung up she sat on the edge of the bed, quite still. Everything in the room, including herself, seemed unreal. She thought if she looked into the mirror now there would be no reflection at all. People thought she was courageous, they always had. After Aldo's death, when she had sold their house and gone to work in a shop, everyone remarked on her strength and bravery. Such praise angered her because it seemed naive. What did they expect her to do? She had children, and a woman with children had no choice but to go on, day after day. She couldn't abandon herself to the luxury of grief, become a hermit or a drinker. She couldn't even show her feelings much, because no one would hire a woman who wept at the smallest things or came to work with her eyes red and swollen, looking a mess. At the smart shop on the Via Marconi she was always neatly dressed, always courteous. She rarely smiled, but she was never seen to weep either.

Did this mean she was a courageous woman? Of course not! It meant that she was working hard to survive, and her survival was important because the survival of her children depended on it. Now, alone in her hotel room, she could certainly afford to let go. Carlo and Stefania wouldn't know their mother lay writhing on a bed, crying and pulling at her hair so that temporary pain might minimize permanent fear; all they would know was that Mama had called, sounding cheerful and unafraid. She was absolutely free.

"I am afraid," she said out loud. "I am afraid of pain and afraid of dying on the table. I am afraid of being mutilated." No tears came, only a heightened sense of unreality. Her voice wasn't her own, because there was no one to hear. She lay down on the big bed, pulling the covers over her. She had read somewhere that the ability to sleep for long periods of time during the day was an indication of depression. Whatever it was, she was grateful for it.

She slept dreamlessly, so when the phone rang she was disoriented. She believed she had been lying on the bed for only a few moments and expected the voice of the overseas operator confirming the cost of her call to Genoa.

"It's Morrissy here," said the voice at the other end. "I just thought I'd check to see if you were free tonight."

"Free?" she said thickly. The clock stood at five-thirty. He was asking if she would have dinner with him, of course; she remembered now. If she agreed she would be spared the bleak hours stretching ahead, yet how could she agree?

"It's very kind of you—"

"No, signora. It has nothing to do with kindness. I would enjoy your company. If you're busy, or if you feel you would *not* enjoy *my* company, only say so. I'll be sorry, but it won't break my heart." He spoke distinctly, in formal sentences. Whether this meant that he wanted her to understand him, or that he was impatient with her, she didn't know. She hadn't dealt with a man in this way for so long she felt awkward. A novice. It was almost as if she were back with Aldo in the days of her marriage. Was she having a quarrel with a stranger?

"I am not busy, Mr. Morrissy."

"Does that mean you'll have dinner with me?"

"Yes," she said. "I believe it does mean I will have dinner with you."

For almost the first time in her life, she had surprised herself.

The road leading to the Ship Channel branched sharply from the main highway. In the last light of a gaudy sunset, the man's hands on the steering wheel were stained copper. Rafaella turned and dutifully looked out the window, but there was nothing to see except a long expanse of scrubby grass and weeds stretching away on either side of the road.

She was acutely aware of his presence in the confines of the car. Except for Maurizio, she hadn't ridden in a car with a man for a long time. Aldo had been a careful, competent driver, sure and precise. Maurizio, as if to make up for his essentially conservative life, drove like a man possessed. He became enraged when his car was delayed in traffic, cursing and wishing picturesque torments on the other drivers.

Stephen Morrissy seemed not to drive at all. His hand lay lightly on the wheel, as if in benediction. He appeared to steer with his thumb. His physical nearness, the fact of him so close to her, seemed menacing. She turned to look at the road ahead and found herself studying his hand again. The nails were pale, well-shaped, and he wore no rings. The hairs on his wrists had been bleached by the sun so they seemed white.

"What did you buy for Carlo?"

His voice uttering the name "Carlo" seemed oddly intimate. They had been talking about the cowboy hat she'd bought for Stefania, and about her children in general, so the question was a perfectly normal one.

"A tremendous cowboy boot made of wax." She showed how large with her hands. "It is also a candle. He likes such odd things, it will please him."

85

Stephen laughed. "I hope you have a big suitcase," he said.

"It will be a problem. I'll have to take the candle in the Neiman-Marcus marketing bag. Is that what you call it?"

"Shopping bag. They'll arrest you at customs. They'll think you're carrying concealed drugs."

"You are joking."

"Yes."

They turned again, bumped down along a rutted road, and came to rest in a crowded parking lot. The restaurant was a long, ramshackle building constructed of wood and shingle; the boards had weathered to an ancient-looking silver-gray. Additions had been slapped on to the central building, and they leaned at odd angles as if the whole structure might collapse and send the new wings tumbling into the water. The bayou, still and thick as oil, barely lapped at the hoardings.

He helped her from the coolness of the car into the swampy heat, giving her his arm as they walked over a narrow path strewn with pebbles. Her fingers rested on the cloth of his jacket; she felt the shape of his arm beneath and wanted to withdraw, but the path was uneven and her heels were high.

Inside, the restaurant was a maze of passages and ramps and stairways leading to mysterious alcoves. Country music wafted out in one direction, a babble of voices from another. He led her up a stairway to an open gallery, entirely glassed in, looking over the bayou. Deep sofas were scattered everywhere and people sat drinking, sprawled casually as if in their own living rooms.

"It's like being on a boat," she said. They sat together on one of the sofas and Stephen ordered Campari for her and a vodka martini for himself. He began to tell her about the turning basin, about how Houston was once merely a prosperous timber and cotton port, how with the discovery of oil everything changed overnight. They dredged the Buffalo Bayou and widened it so ships could steam in, turn around, and head back into the Gulf of Mexico and to any port in the world.

"Houston is all about change, constant change," he said.

"I was born here. When I was ten my parents moved to the Midwest, but I remember what it was like. The hospitals at the medical center hadn't been dreamed of. That whole area was useless marsh."

"How is Mrs. Reyes's sister?" Dangerous territory, but she had to ask.

"Doing pretty well. She'll be in intensive care for at least another day."

Rafaella sipped her drink slowly, beginning to feel more at ease. The soft cushions were relaxing, the lights dancing on the water hypnotic. She concentrated on playing the role she had chosen, only occasionally feeling a pang of envy for the woman she was pretending to be. When their table was ready and she walked ahead of him to the secluded alcove, she was glad she'd taken pains with her appearance. She felt the scalloped hem of her light dress cling to her legs and then move away to float freely. It was a cream-colored dress; small flowers, terra-cotta and mauve, dotted its surface. She had arranged her hair less severely than usual, and because she was out of practice, it had taken half an hour to fashion the loose coil at the nape of her neck. She wore the earrings he had admired and a light perfume. She could never be a glamorous Texas blonde, but she could do her best to show that Italian women knew what to make of their assets.

Morrissy drank most of the bottle of wine he ordered with their dinner, which was just as well. Her doctor had forbidden her more than one glass, and the Campari she'd had before had made her feel light-headed. The portions of food were enormous and she was unable to finish her scallops, but she enjoyed what she ate and was beginning to feel *benessere* —"well-being." This was a dangerous state, she thought. She must not mix illusion with reality.

They talked easily, sometimes in English and sometimes in Italian, Morrissy switching into the peculiar Italianized Spanish she could understand. Often she was unaware of which language was being spoken, and then he would say something so foreign to her it made her laugh.

It was when the coffee arrived that he searched in his pockets for a cigarette. "I'm giving it up," he explained. "I rarely smoke now." He withdrew a rather elderly pack of

Marlboros and then searched for a light, as he had done with the lady from Ecuador.

"I have a present for you," said Rafaella. She reached into her bag—the same she'd carried when she arrived in Houston —and located the GALVTEX disposable lighter. She offered it to him gravely.

He held the lighter up, looked from its blue and yellow surface to her eyes, and then hastily lit the cigarette. "Thank you," he said. "It's very nice."

He looked so solemn she wanted to laugh. She knew exactly what he was thinking and could have told him, in Italian, but she controlled her laughter and said:

"It is *not* very nice. It is a perfectly ordinary thing. A cheap lighter. A salesman gave it to me on the plane. Don't you think I know the difference?"

"I thought—" Stephen considered. "It's not easy to know what you're thinking."

"Stephen. I am from Italy, not Mars. I am not so very strange, am I?"

"Not strange. Mysterious, maybe." He shrugged, embarrassed, and smiled at her. "I was going to say 'special' but that would be trite. *Trito?*"

At that moment a tanker slid into view, huge and ghostly in the dim light, maneuvering up the channel like some emissary from the spirit world. They studied it in silence, as if it were an omen of some kind, and left shortly after.

It was midnight when he delivered her back to the Hibernian. On the ride back he'd proposed an excursion to the Rothko Chapel the next day, but everything was vague, indefinite. He wasn't sure of his schedule at the hospital, and Rafaella had lapsed back into difficulty with the language. He escorted her through the lobby, past the ladies in peach-colored convention coats who still sat talking amid the potted palms.

At the bank of elevators he took her hand, thanked her for dining with him, and brought her fingers briefly to his lips. It was a cavalier little gesture, but his face was impassive.

"Good night, signora," he said. Then he turned and went back to the real world, while she boarded the elevator which would return her to her cell.

Chapter 8

Two of Stephen's patients were being troublesome. On the morning after he had dined with the Italian Widow—he couldn't think of her as "Signora Leone" and he had never yet called her Rafaella—he found himself in Intensive Care trying to persuade Señora Perez to squeeze Blanchard's hand once for yes and twice for no.

The breathing tube had long since been removed, but the old woman appeared unable to speak. She seemed no larger than a doll; pierced by tubes and wires, hooked up to machines which beeped and hummed, Señora Perez seemed little more than a fragile sack of bones which had been thrown from a great distance and miraculously landed among the life-sustaining equipment. Her hands were still tied down. Blanchard had explained. She had several times tried to forcibly remove the tube in her nose; restraint was necessary for her own good.

Stephen looked down at the wizened face, the tiny hands scrabbling feebly against the restraints. The ICU always made him think of a torture chamber—an unfortunate comparison but one which Blanchard assured him was almost universal. Señora Perez was a pale yellow color. Since her natural hue was something like teakwood, this was not alarming. He thought she must have a good deal of Indian blood. *Blue meat.* Eugenia Fowler's phrase. One of the dozens of scraps of information he had culled since becoming a volunteer was writing itself across his consciousness. If the patient dies from a failure of the lungs, the color is blue. If from heart failure, it is gray.

"Señora." He bent close to her, speaking slowly, intimately. The Spanish words arranged themselves in his mind. "It is very important for you to tell Dr. Blanchard certain things. If you don't wish to speak, then answer him by pressing his hand. Once for yes, twice for no. Will you do that? He wants to help you."

The black eyes, nearly obscured in the hooded ridges, regarded him without comprehension.

"You're doing very well, you know. Did you know that? Your vital signs are very strong. I imagine you would like to have your hands untied, wouldn't you?"

A flicker of interest stirred in those impassive eyes. He repeated what he had said. Her lips wriggled impotently, trying to find their way back to speech, and then she whispered a single word. "You."

Stephen thought, *Me. What does she mean?* The bony fingers clawed about, as if seeking contact. Tentatively, he touched his fingers to hers and found his hand enclosed by fingers as weightless and dry as the claws of an iguana. It was *his* hand she wished to press; his hand through which she would communicate. Blanchard nodded, asked Stephen to ask her if she understood that she must not rip the life-sustaining tubes from her body.

The fingers squeezed back once.

"They will all be removed soon, Señora. You will go to the regular intensive care unit, and then to your room. But you must promise me not to try to remove anything. Promise?" Another single pressure. "Is there anything you want to ask?"

Again the lips moved against each other, as if summoning up enough friction to produce a sound.

"What day?" she asked. "How long?"

"You have been here for two days. It's ten in the morning now."

She nodded, and Blanchard removed the restraints. "You guys in the glamor professions," he said. "She'd rather hold your hand than mine." He laid his hand briefly on her forehead, fingers touching her wispy hair with the gentleness which was his hallmark. "Tell her she has the body of a seventeen-year-old girl," he said. "Tell her something nice."

The other problem was Julio Ramirez. He wasn't responsible for the trouble he was causing. Unlike Señora Perez, the atmosphere of the recovery ICU didn't disorient him, because he had suffered three separate heart attacks during the night. Each time he had been shocked back with the paddles, but he seemed unaware of anything. He looked nearly dead to Stephen. Blanchard good-humoredly assured him that he had seen patients suffer up to ten heart attacks in ICU and leave two weeks later in great shape, but this seemed unlikely to Stephen.

He thought of Ramirez's body as one of the satellite weather pictures seen on television. Squalls, hurricanes, deadly pressure centers, were brewing there. At any moment some elemental disaster might sweep through and wreak havoc. He pictured the Dacron patch shoring up the hole in Julio's heart, saw the flabby heart muscle as Blanchard had described it. He imagined the blood pumping into that prematurely ancient heart and ripping away the patch the way a flash flood could tear a tree from the side of an arroyo.

The man from Vera Cruz and the lady from Ecuador had already been removed from recovery ICU to a regular intensive care unit. That, at least, was good news. Two out of four were doing well. With any luck Señora Perez would join them.

In the waiting room he encountered Estella Ramirez. She had aged another ten years in the last forty-eight hours and was trembling with fatigue.

"Let me take you to your hotel, Mrs. Ramirez. You need to sleep."

"I would rather wait here. I will wait until seven when I can see him. Then I'll go back."

"How long has it been since you've had some sleep?"

She considered, as if he had asked her an enormously complicated question. The whites of her eyes were shot through with red threads, like blood in a broken egg-white. At last she shrugged. "I sleep here, on and off," she said.

"Would you like something from the cafeteria?" But she had closed her eyes and seemed to be asleep. He took the elevator down to the main floor and entered the volunteers' lounge just as Hans Wolder was checking in. A party of

Dutch patients were due to arrive. Jackie Talbot was over in the children's hospital; outside on the circular drive, a Daimler waited for the departing sheikh. The teenaged girls who worked as volunteers in the gift shop had lined up in the lobby to see him go. Business as usual.

Stephen thought of all the questions he wanted to ask the Italian Widow and probably never would. She seemed a study in contradictions to him. Just when he was beginning to see her as a waiflike creature, too shy and timid to make much of her time in a foreign country, she appeared for their dinner date elegantly dressed, transformed into a chic European woman of the world. What he had seen as shyness, conventional reserve, might have been the coolness of the Old World dealing with the New.

For the first time in years he had felt unsure of his ability to entertain a woman. He was plunged back in time to the awkwardness of boyhood, to adolescence itself. Would the girl approve of the Morrissy family car (a Buick, it had been), or find it lacking in glamor? Would she think he talked too much or not enough; was the silence a comfortable one, or strained and anxious? It was ludicrous for a man of forty-four to harbor such insecurity, but that was the effect she had on him.

He wanted to know how long she had been a widow, what sort of man her husband had been, the manner of his death; but these were questions he didn't dare to ask. Her manner forbade it. He thought perhaps the husband had been much older. It would explain much about the helplessness he'd detected in her on the day of the livestock exhibition. He pictured her married to an adoring older man, a banker or a university professor, who had shielded her from unpleasant realities, pampered and spoiled her.

He discarded the image. She had a career, she designed jewelry. This still seemed the only possible solution to the most pressing question of all—why was she here? If she was a tourist, she was the most inept tourist he had ever run across. A new thought came. For all he knew, she was a famous designer. He knew nothing about such things. She might be selling a line to Neiman-Marcus: Rafaella earrings.

92

It would explain her gentle mockery when she gave him the disposable lighter.

She was a chameleon. If she could only remain one thing or the other, he would know how to talk to her. He could touch her. He took the lighter from his pocket and pressed the catch. Three times the flame sprang up without wavering. She was leaving tomorrow; what was the point? *I am from Italy, not Mars.*

He went to the pay phones in the lobby and called the Hibernian. The phone in her room rang seven times. He hung up but had a sudden vision of her the day he'd been with Mrs. Reyes. The Italian Widow hung out a lot in the lobby, it seemed. He called back.

"Will you page Mrs. Leone, please?"

Three minutes later she was on the other end, agreeing reluctantly to see the Rothko Chapel with him. She sounded very stern.

"I don't suppose Rothko is your kind of artist," he said, "but I thought you should see it."

"Who do you think is my kind of artist?"

"Botticelli, Tintoretto, Duccio, Caravaggio . . ."

"Oh, of course. Everybody likes them, it's only natural. But this is different. I could work here."

The remark puzzled him. She could see it in the slight contraction of his eyebrows. He was wondering if he had heard her correctly. She wished she could explain how this austere room, its white stucco walls relieved only by the Rothko panels, reminded her of her studio at home. The panels sometimes seemed to be the color of dark plums and then again they were richly and profoundly brown as the coats of seals or otters. They made her feel a tranquil emptiness.

"I work in a small studio near my flat," she said. "It is white and bare, like this."

"Are you very well known in Italy?"

She looked up to see if he was mocking her. They were alone in the room and he stood a few paces away, hands in his pockets, head bowed. He had asked the question shyly, she decided, and she smiled.

"No. Not even in Genoa. But I am beginning to get—commissions, they're called?—from Milan and Rome."

It seemed unlikely that he would be . interested in her career, but he asked many questions and she answered. It was a safe topic, perhaps the *only* safe topic. They got back in his car and he headed onto one of the innumerable boulevards; she didn't ask where they were going.

"I went to art school for two years—a special diploma. When I got married I sketched and painted as a hobby. I never thought of myself as an artist; I don't now. I am an artisan."

"What made you start to take yourself seriously?"

"*Necessità.* I had to support my children. But first I worked in a shop. I sold handbags, leather goods. I never thought to design at first." She wondered whether to tell him of her mother-in-law's reaction to this job.

"A shopgirl. You have become a shopgirl!" Gemma Leone had moaned her disapproval all the way from Naples. Better, she had said, for Rafaella to bring the children there and live with her. She had bullied and pleaded to no avail until at last she could only make a bitter pronouncement: "*senza dignità.*" Rafaella was undignified.

She decided against telling Stephen. It was too intimate. Also disloyal. Whatever she thought of her mother-in-law, she could not hold Gemma, mother of Aldo, up to ridicule.

Instead she told him how she had stumbled on her career. There had been a new line of handbags—supple, creamy leather, as expensive as they looked. They weren't selling well, and Rafaella thought she knew why. Either from a lack of vision or in an effort to save money, the manufacturer had given the bags ugly, pedestrian clasps. This was difficult to convey to Stephen. She pointed to the clasp of her own bag so he would understand and searched for the right phrase.

"These ones lacked beauty," she said, proud of her choice of words. Even now, it made her angry to remember the clasps. Shoddy workmanship had defiled the lovely handbags. She had never been able to tolerate the ruin of beauty

—graffiti on marble statues, soft-drink bottles cast into the sea, paintings mounted in garish frames, all had the power to make her tremble with outrage. Stephen was smiling again. She wondered if she had said something ridiculous.

"Lack of beauty makes you very fierce," he said.

When the woman who managed her department asked her why the bags weren't more popular, Rafaella told her. On her salespad, she sketched a vastly superior clasp—simple, elegant, and pleasing to the eye. The manager was impressed.

"This lady wished to give her husband a gift for his *compleanno*—day of birth. A thing for lighting his pipe, like the GALVTEX, only gold. It would have his *iniziale*." She wondered if he understood about the initials, not knowing if the word was similar in English, but he nodded and she went on. The more she talked, the easier it became.

The manager had wanted to make the gift more personal, more expressly designed for the tastes of her husband, and she asked Rafaella's advice. It seemed that the man, a prosperous dentist, had a passion for Oriental art.

"On my hour at midday I drew small Chinese dragons. One has a tail, like this"—she showed him, sketching in the air above the dashboard—"with space for his *iniziale*." She wished she had the English, or he the Italian, for her to describe the intricacy of the scrolls in the dragon's tail, the clever way with which she had concealed the man's monogram inside.

"I am sure," said Stephen, "your dragons did not lack beauty."

"They were pleasing," she said. She could not bring herself to use a more complimentary word to describe her own work. It would seem *indecoroso*. The manager had exclaimed over the dragons and promptly hired a goldsmith to reproduce them and mount them on the surface of the lighter. "I was surprised, because she paid to me a commission. Then she put, transferred, me to the jewelry department."

Stephen lit a cigarette, using the GALVTEX lighter with a small nod in her direction. "There," he said, "you redesigned every earring and belt buckle—whatever they sell—until the salesmen had to admit you were better than their clients."

"Not at first. I did not wish to push my way. But finally, yes." She had made many sketches but couldn't afford to buy silver or gold. She had sculpted in wax. How did you say wax? It had been a year before she could afford to cast a brooch in silver. "I went to—you call them flea markets. I bought odd bits of jewelry so I could have the tiny gems and the metal."

The shop on the Via Marconi began to take notice of her. She had already been made a consultant to the buyer, and when she showed her brooch it was agreed that the shop would carry a small line of Rafaella's imaginative designs. In another year there was a modest but steady demand for her work. When she received a private commission from Rome, she knew it was time to set up on her own. Her shop on the Via Acquatania represented a triumph she wouldn't have dreamed possible a short time ago. When she deducted the rent, her assistant Nina's salary, and the price of her materials from the money she now earned, it was only slightly more than what she'd made at the shop.

"But I am independent now, and I can spend more time with my children." *My mother-in-law now refers to me as artistico.*

Stephen stubbed his cigarette out. She noticed that he never smoked more than half a cigarette; this was his way of quitting. "I admire you," he said. "An independent woman. A resourceful artisan. Do your designs have a name?"

"*Bagatelle.* I can't translate."

"Baubles. You're too modest, signora."

They were passing into a realm of lush greenery, as if by magic. Where before there were only tall, forlorn-looking palms lining the boulevard, now jungles of cypress, groves of oak and pine appeared. The vast lawns, immaculately trimmed, were parrot green. Great houses, some as magnificent as the *palazzi* along the Via Garibaldi in Genoa, stood in splendor set well back from the road. "This is River Oaks," said Stephen. "This is where all those people you saw at the Hibernian live. It's Houston's showplace neighborhood."

Rafaella thought of the legions of gardeners it would take to manicure River Oaks. This beautiful jungle, made neat and civilized, was a remnant of what Houston had been before the bulldozers came to level the ground and make way for the skyscrapers. The people who lived in the ice-cream-colored, pillared houses were safe from nature because they hired others to keep it at bay.

"That's a magnolia tree," he said instructively, or, "that's Spanish moss." Once he said, "That house belongs to Martin Lassiter, the head surgeon at the hospital."

Rafaella turned to admire the house, but the fragile texture of the afternoon was ruined. Any reminder would have done it. For the first time in her life Rafaella wondered if she might be mentally unbalanced. She had actually succeeded in convincing herself, for a little while, that she *was* the woman she pretended to be. The fact that had dominated her life since that day in the doctor's office back home had—incredibly—receded to a tiny, unpleasant point in her consciousness. A sane woman could never achieve such a feat.

The salmon and vanilla mansions, the jungly green of the foliage, all slid past now in a blur. She knotted her hands together in her lap to keep them from shaking. The air-conditioned interior of the car seemed menacing, and she felt her heart inside her like a block of ice.

When Stephen Morrissy dropped her off at the hotel on his way back to the hospital, he asked if she felt well. She told him she thought perhaps she'd caught a virus, something going round. Before he had a chance to answer she thanked him for the afternoon and got out of the car.

He was in a stream of traffic and couldn't follow her. She saw him looking perplexed and anxious, and then the car ahead of him moved on, and he had to follow.

Dear Mr. Morrissy, I have deceived you, but I didn't mean any harm, and

Dear Mr. Morrissy, It is quite impossible for me to see you because I am going to be a patient at

Dear Stefan, Thank you for your kindness, but

In the end they all landed at the bottom of the wastepaper basket. She had been sitting for what seemed hours, her "Traveler's English" nearby to help her spell words correctly, trying to compose the proper letter. She had looked through the Houston phone book to get some idea of the spelling of his last name. There were several ways, but she chose the one she thought looked best. In the last letter, which had gone on for half a page, she had discovered she was crying only when small water marks appeared on the Hibernian stationery.

You will not cry, she told herself. *Basta*. She fixed her gaze on Maurizio's flowers. It wasn't as if she were so starved for a kind word, like a mistreated dog. Her children, Anna-Laura, loved her. Neighbors, acquaintances, Nina, her mother-in-law, all cared for her in their separate ways. Even if she could not return Maurizio's affections, the fact of their existence warmed her. But it was a fragile warmth, like that of a wintry sun in March.

If Morrissy's words fell upon her like rain into a parched tract of earth, it had nothing to do with the words themselves. It had to do with the man.

She went down, eventually, to the Hibernian's formal dining room to eat her solitary dinner. There weren't many customers and she had three waiters all to herself, a distinction she didn't appreciate. No sooner had the chilled soup arrived than one of them dashed up to ask if everything was to her liking. She could see them coming, running along under the light of the crystal chandeliers, faces solicitous. Dishing up her veal, they collided in their efforts to be helpful.

She wasn't hungry, but she forced herself to eat, chewing mechanically, sipping her one glass of wine with deliberation. Like an officer in some remote outpost, she tried to preserve the illusion of normalcy by dressing for dinner, eating with civilized delicacy. What difference would it make if she plunged her hands into her salad and tore at the veal like an animal? None.

After her dinner she sat in the lobby, a newspaper on her lap. When she thought it was late enough, she went up to her room. As she was preparing for bed the phone began to ring. From habit she stretched out a hand to answer it, then stopped herself. It was five in the morning in Italy; the call was not from home. There was only one person who could be calling her, and she didn't trust herself to speak to him.

It rang again and again. On the fourth ring she began to tremble violently. What if something had happened to one of the children? Accidents, calamities, could occur at any hour. She lifted the receiver, full of contempt for herself. How could she have thought, even for an instant, that she was free to ignore the ringing of a phone?

"*Prego.*" Her voice shook alarmingly. She had been so sure she would be greeted by Anna-Laura that Stephen's voice at the other end filled her with relief. Nothing had happened to Carlo or Stefania after all.

Stephen mistook her whisper of terror for sleepiness. He apologized for wakening her, sounding wretchedly embarrassed. He had given her the perfect excuse.

"Good night," she said, and dropped the phone back into its cradle with finality. He would believe in her virus now and leave her alone. There was no other way. "Good-bye," she said to the empty room.

That night she had a dream. She and Aldo and Stephen Morrissy were having a picnic in River Oaks. They sat crosslegged on a bright green lawn. The air was full of the light of innocent dream-ecstasy. Rafaella sat between the two men, handing them sandwiches and hard-boiled eggs, pouring out wine, attending to their needs with impartial tenderness. She smiled at each in turn, and they exchanged glances, then bent toward her. *We like it when you're happy*, they said. *We want you to be happy.* They all held hands, like children, and felt very happy and virtuous.

Chapter 9

"How's the little girl in Children's?" Joe Gonzalez put his paper cup of coffee down and gave Jackie an expectant, sympathetic look.

"She's fine so far." Jackie couldn't restrain the wide, relieved smile spreading over her face. It was partly caused by nervous guilt at her own morbid imaginings. She'd thought Lucia would die on the table, and why? Because she couldn't bear the thought of a child dying, she was sure it would happen. The unbearable always seemed to happen, but not this time. Lucia was doing well in Recovery.

"I'm glad. I've got a three-year-old coming in from Venezuela. A Fallot."

Fallots were classic blue babies. Joe Gonzalez, like Blanchard, always spoke in medical shorthand. He had had two years of medical school before he dropped out and became a businessman. He was one of the most conscientious volunteers, one of the five Spanish bilinguals. Unlike Ernestine McGrath, he liked Stephen Morrissy.

"Who's Morrissy got up in ICU?"

"Three bypasses and a VSD. They've wired the VSD up with a pacemaker now because his heart was beating arhythmically."

Joe scanned the schedule board. "I see half of Holland is here again," he said. "No Arabs?"

"There's a man from Morrocco named Beauvais. He didn't speak any Arabic so Ernestine McGrath flew at him with her fluent French. God knows she doesn't get a chance to use it; nobody does. It turned out he was an American who'd been living in Rabat for twenty years. His wife is English."

"Who do you have coming in?"

"Nobody until tomorrow. It's"—she consulted the card she'd plucked from the board—"a Mrs. Leone, from Genoa. She's only thirty-four, and she's coming alone. That seems sad, doesn't it?"

"Don't start thinking like that. *Sad.* Shit, it's all sad."

His beeper went off then, and he stood up immediately. "That'll be my Fallot from Venezuela," he said. "You can finish my coffee if you want."

He went off to Admissions, leaving Jackie to wonder for the hundredth time why he had left medical school and why, under the circumstances, he chose to hang around a hospital.

Her last day. She became ferociously efficient. She packed everything she would not be needing and left the suitcases open near the door. She counted her money and allotted so much for the bill, so much to leave for the chambermaid. Meticulously, she manicured her nails, plucked the few stray hairs from her slender brows. She shampooed her hair and rubbed creams and unguents into her flesh as if she were preparing for her bridal night. At home in Genoa, she had left letters in the care of Anna-Laura. They were for Carlo and Stefania to read in the event of her death. Her will was also back in Genoa in Maurizio's office.

Now she wrote to Anna-Laura. The words flowed easily because she was merely telling her sister-in-law what she had mutely acknowledged for so many years—that she loved, admired, and respected her, that she had drawn courage from her, that the only comfort she had known in the years following Aldo's death—aside from the love of her children —stemmed from Anna-Laura's vastly generous and loving spirit. Anna-Laura had agreed to be the children's guardian if the unspeakable happened; nothing more needed to be said on that point.

On impulse, she purchased a postcard and addressed it to her old schoolfriend, Gina, who now lived in Switzerland. "Here I am in Texas," she wrote gaily. "Do you remember when we saw *Sci Aquatico* and laughed so much? I hope you are well and happy. God bless you. Rafaella."

Then she left the letter and postcard at the desk and asked a taxi driver to take her to the nearest movie theater. She watched a film about teen-aged gangs in New York City, not minding the violence because it was so obviously false. Because the actors spoke in peculiar accents and fragmented sentences, she had difficulty understanding their English.

When she returned to the hotel, there was a message for her. It read:

Dear Signora, I hope your virus is better. If you are really ill, it would be unwise to fly tomorrow. If not, I would like to say good-bye to you. I will be at this number all evening. Please call, if only to cement Italian-American goodwill. Ciao. S. Morrissy.

The number followed.

She studied his handwriting avidly, as if some miraculous message could be transmitted there. It was large, bold, arrogant. It touched her because it seemed the hand of someone not accustomed to penning humble, friendly messages. It touched her because she could picture the hand holding the pen, the same hand she had studied on the steering wheel.

In her room, she dialed the number. He answered on the second ring.

"*Prego*," he said.

"How did you know it would be me?"

"No one calls me here. Hardly anyone."

"I telephoned to say good-bye. I leave tomorrow."

"Your virus has disappeared?"

"Yes. I think I was only tired."

"So. It's back to Italy, is it? Back to Bagatelle. I hope your son appreciates the candle."

"Thank you for being so kind," she said. "Thank you for taking me to dinner at the Ship Channel."

"Signora. Rafaella. I wish you would stop calling me *kind*. In English it's a very bland, *blando*, word. I am not particularly kind. Do you have time to see me tonight? Will you dine with me?"

"No, not dine. But I would like to see you. To say good-bye."

"I'll pick you up at the hotel then, shall I? About nine?"

"Yes."

When she replaced the phone she sat perfectly still for a moment, then picked it up again to place a call to Genoa. It was past the children's bedtime, but Anna-Laura had kept them up on the last night.

She hardly remembered what they said, only the sound of their voices. She wanted to bless them formally and say a real good-bye (in case, in case), but this was impossible because it would alarm them. That was why she had written the letters, to say good-bye and to help them understand later, when they were grown.

Only to Anna-Laura did she say *addio*. To her son and daughter she said *ciao*.

She was waiting in front of the hotel when he drove up. She got in quickly, as if it were a getaway and she a thief. A long, flat package lay on the dashboard.

"Where would you like to go?"

"A place where it is quiet. I would like to talk to you."

The car moved off up the dark boulevard. He was quietly presenting choices. There was a club at the top of a sky-scraper. He wasn't a member, but he had a friend's card. The bar at the Warwick was reasonably quiet, or she might like—

"Not a bar, please."

"We could just drive around Houston without ever stop-ping. Like the Flying Dutchman."

She heard the amusement in his voice, but she was also aware of a darker, subtler meaning in his tone. It wasn't his fault; he was a man. He had every reason to believe she was being coy. Perhaps the car would be best. It would be dark and close, like a confessional. She would tell him about her fraudulence while they sped through the night, and then he could leave her at the Hibernian. She wouldn't have to look at him once.

"What is it?" he asked. "Is something wrong?"

What is wrong is that you work at the hospital, she thought. *If you didn't, none of this would be necessary. How shocked, disgusted, you would be to see me unconscious in the intensive care place. And what if you overheard one of the nurses saying, "The Leone woman? From Italy? She died on the table that one. Too bad." In the end it wouldn't matter to you greatly. You wouldn't grieve. But you would be sorry, and you would feel bewildered. It isn't right. I cannot let that happen.*

"Yes," she said. "Something is wrong."

"Is one of your children sick?"

She heard herself laugh strangely. A vulgar sound, unlike her. "No." A peculiar thing was beginning to happen. She felt, actually *felt*, her English deserting her. She could see it fly about in the interior of the rented car, seeking a way out. It was much more severe than on her first day in Houston. She thought it might be permanent. She tried to describe this phenomenon to him, speaking rapidly in Italian. The words emerged in a torrent; her tongue tripped again and again.

She felt him turn the car and head back in the direction of the hotel. His hand imprisoned her hands, which were tightly clasped, and the thumb soothed her as if she were a child. He was speaking, but she couldn't understand him.

They were passing the hospital now, circling the huge block of medical buildings, decelerating in speed until the car crept to a halt in the parking lot of something called the Tropicana Motel. This was where he lived. A neon sign showed a tall, lime-green palm tree; cars bulked darkly in front of the units, which were painted in orange and aqua hues. He helped her from the car. She clung to his arm and meekly accompanied him to a room in the far corner. He thrust the key into the lock with one hand while the other protectively hovered at her shoulders. The door swung open and then they were inside.

Gently he propelled her toward a hideous chair and forced her to sit in it. Then he turned on a lamp and went to a small refrigerator, returning with a glass of pale, icy liquid in which fat ice cubes floated and tinkled. He handed the glass to her and then sat on the edge of the bed, elbows on his knees, hands cupping his head.

She cradled the glass in her hand without sampling its contents. This was better. She felt calmer. Some English returned. "I am sorry," she said.

He waited for a while in silence, but when she said nothing else he raised his head and laughed softly. "Signora, you really do beat all. That was an expression my father was fond of, by the way. It means you take the cake, defy understanding, make your own rules. What is it, sweetheart? Are you in trouble?" He repeated the last phrase in Spanish and—getting no answer—went to the fridge and poured himself a hefty glass of the pale liquid. He also lit a Marlboro cigarette, ironically bowing in her direction when he used his GALVTEX lighter.

"I mean," he continued, resuming his place on the edge of the bed, "you are one big mystery. *Enigmatico*, right?"

"I lied to you. I am sorry."

"Oh, terrific, you lied to me. What did you lie about? Age? Personally, you look about twenty-eight to me. Marital status? Is that it? I've got it. You're a swinging Italian housewife who flew all the way to Houston to have a hot affair and then chickened out. You have a husband and ten kids back in Genoa, but you pass yourself off as this Madonnalike, indomitable little widow who happens, just *happens*, to be passing through Houston for no known purpose."

It wasn't necessary to understand every word he said. It was clear enough.

"No," she said, "you are wrong. I am a widow."

"How did your husband die?"

"In an accident, at Misurina, climbing rocks. Three years ago. He was thirty-four years old. I did not lie about that." She watched him, speaking into his eyes. It was very important not to be cowardly. The expression on his face was unreadable. In the dim light, anchored firmly to his position at the end of the bed, he seemed vulnerable. She spoke to him as if he were Carlo. "I dreamed we all had a picnic at the River Oaks. You, me, and Aldo. It was so nice. You said you wanted me to be happy. Both of you."

He rose from the bed and came toward her. He was kneeling in front of the chair. He took her hands and held them tightly in his own. When she didn't protest, he touched her face, his fingers light and searching, tracing the line of her cheekbones, smoothing her forehead. She felt his fingers on her hair unclasping the silver comb, drawing it away until the hair tumbled loose and came in a warm rush around her neck and shoulders.

He spoke her name. "Rafaella." He spoke it again and she felt a love for her name, the separate syllables as spoken in his foreign accent. She wanted to hear it again and again.

He drew her to her feet and kissed her. So this was what she had forgotten: the sweetness of a man's lips searching— a sort of hello, a breaking down of doors and barriers by heat, not battering. I have power, too, she thought. I am white-hot with power and tenderness. Her hands moved to touch him. The cloth of his shirt where it lay over his back, the back beneath, the soft, shaggy hair at his nape. The infallible nerve endings at the tips of her fingers tingled with creation, as if she were sculpting him.

It was only five feet to the bed. Without seeming to have moved in that direction, they landed there together—travelers washed up on a friendly beach, panting softly. She lay back and looked up at him. Her hands were at her sides, palms up, fingers curling as if to catch rain. He took one of her hands and held it to his lips. Again her name, murmured against her palm. She reached up and drew him down to her.

She had never felt so strong and whole; his hands, at her breast, her thighs, seemed to contain miraculous healing powers. She smiled into his shoulder, against his chest, up at the ceiling. *We want you to be happy.* She helped him to undress her, their hands meeting on her flesh. She could read it in his eyes, that she had come into her own, was beautiful. It was a good thing, because he was beautiful, too. She remembered the laconic surfers; she would tell him one day and they would laugh. The surfers were boys, glistening and stupid, their beauty inconsequential. This man who stroked her so gently had lived in his body for forty-four years. It was as hard and well-made as the surfers' bodies, but it had suffered some damage. The soles of her feet discovered an uneven bone in the shin of his left leg—it had been broken at some time. He had a small scar on his back, long since healed in a half-moon shape, and another on his chest.

She felt she could go on like this forever, memorizing him and discovering him at the same time. Last time, and first. But her body was responding to his lover's tricks, quite independently. Her heart now beat so audibly she couldn't ignore it. Her veins hummed like tight wires in a high wind and she thought she could feel the chambers of her heart contract and expand in every part of her body. *No, stop. Please stop. You will kill me.*

When she felt him invade her, inside now, she imagined the blood blasting through the damaged valves. He would drive it through and miraculously heal her, because he was not killing her but making her well again. She clung to him, accepting the pleasure with terror. There was nothing she could do in any case, no turning back now. At the very height of her pleasure she was free from fear for the first time; in the extremity of pleasure she was blessedly mindless, but as it receded dread returned. Her heart couldn't beat like this without exploding. At any moment the fatal blow would come. She shut her eyes, wondering when she had shed the tears that covered her face, and waited to die.

"Rafaella." His voice was close to her ear. How much time had gone by? There was no pain, only the echoes of pleasure. She could breathe. She wasn't dead. She opened her eyes and found herself looking at his back. He was in the act of drawing a blanket up over their naked bodies to protect her from the ferocious air-conditioning. Already she shivered, deprived of his warmth.

Now he was back, beside her, propped up on one elbow. He looked so happy, hazelnut eyes softer than she had ever seen them. He smiled, bent, kissed her forehead. "I wish you weren't going away," he said.

She placed her hand over his lips, then tried her voice. She spoke his name. Now she was thinking clearly again. She had to tell him, but she could allow herself one last moment before she stopped being his lover and introduced him to a sick woman. She drew his head down to the pillow and kissed him. She felt each separate point of contact, warm lips, soft hair beneath her fingertips, cheekbone beneath her thumb. *Good-bye.*

"Do you remember I said I lied to you?"

He smiled. "How could it matter?" When she was silent a shadow passed over his face fleetingly before he smiled again. "Are you a spy?" he asked teasingly. He reached out and toyed with a strand of her hair. "If you are, you're the worst spy I've ever run across. You don't even have a cover."

"I came to Houston because I need surgery. I will be a patient tomorrow."

Several things happened. At first he seemed to freeze. Hand still holding a loop of her hair, smile on his lips, he became a statue. Rafaella remembered playing statue maker in her childhood and thought Stephen Morrissy would have been good at it. Next he shook his head abruptly, as if chasing off a pesky insect. "No," he said finally. "That can't be true."

"But it is. I'm sorry."

"What kind of surgery? What's wrong with you?" The questions were sharp, angry.

"My heart."

"*Brava,* signora, I'd figured that out. What exactly is wrong with your heart, or didn't you care enough to ask?"

"Two valves. I need a bypass for two valves."

"Lassiter?"

She nodded. He left the bed so quickly it seemed to vibrate beneath her. Naked, he went to pour himself more vodka. She watched him fearfully. It was natural that he was angry. She had already said good-bye to him. His hand shook as he poured the vodka neat into the glass. Some of the liquid sloshed over. He cursed softly, then slammed the bottle down with such force it nearly shattered.

"What the hell did you think you were doing back there?" He gestured at the bed with a kind of hatred, as if it had suddenly revealed a nest of rattlesnakes. "Christ, lady, that little romp could have killed you. Were you trying to get yourself killed? Is that it? Are you sorry it didn't work?"

"I never thought about it," she said. "Not until it was too late."

"Balls. Everybody thinks about it. There's not a heart

patient in the world who doesn't wonder if sex will knock him off."

"But you see," said Rafaella, "sex wasn't a part of my life. I never asked my doctor because I never expected to make love."

And then she tried to explain to him, speaking very rationally, why it was she'd never told him. At first it hadn't seemed necessary, because she thought she'd never see him again. "Later, when we went to the Ship Channel, I couldn't do it. I couldn't bear for you to pity me. Also I was selfish."

"Selfish?"

"It made me happy to be with you. It mattered more to me than you. So. Thank you for making me happy, and I am sorry I lied."

"Tell me something. Would you have told me if I didn't work at the hospital?"

"No. Never."

"Do you feel all right now? Or are you going to die in my bed?"

She understood the reason for his cruelty and forgave him, but the harshness of his words made her flinch. He disappeared, without waiting for her reply and returned with a glass of water. He was wearing a terry-cloth robe. "Here," he said, handing her the water. "Do you have any medication?"

"I've taken it, thank you."

She pulled the sheets around her and sat up, drinking obediently. They were being very polite now. At any moment he would ask her if he could drive her back to the hotel. She watched while he gathered his clothes, strewn about on the floor. Instead of dressing he threw them all into the corner. He picked her dress up, shook it out, and hung it in his closet. He aligned her shoes neatly on the bureau, discreetly gathered her underclothing and put it in a drawer. When he had finished all these tasks he sank into the chair, looking forlorn. "Oh, Jesus," he said. "Oh, Christ." He sounded like a boy who had been kicked off the football team.

"I am sorry," she said again. The stupid tears were coming again, prompted by his distress. She had wept more in the presence of this man than in the entire time of her illness. "I think I must go now."

But Stephen Morrissy crossed the room, shaking his head. He lay beside her on the bed on top of the covers. He took her in his arms and told her that everything was going to be all right, that Lassiter was the finest surgeon in the world. Rafaella would be safe, he said; she would recover and be twice as good, he said, as new.

He repeated this litany over and over throughout the night. Neither of them slept. All night long they lay in each other's arms, waiting for the dreadful day to dawn.

THE HOSPITAL

BOOK TWO

Chapter 1

Jackie was in Admissions at nine o'clock, waiting for the woman from Genoa. She glanced out into the corridor and saw Stephen rounding the corner, carrying two suitcases and a large Neiman-Marcus shopping bag. Next to him was a small, delicate-looking woman wearing dark glasses. Her face, what Jackie could see of it, was impassive.

They came into the admissions office together. Stephen put the luggage down near a chair, then came toward her. He held the woman's arm tightly.

"This is Signora Leone," he said. Then he told the woman, whom he called by her first name, who Jackie was. The woman extended a hand and said hello. Her voice was steady, but the hand was icy cold. Jackie was wild with curiosity—how had Stephen become acquainted with a woman who had presumably flown to Houston that morning? Perhaps they were old acquaintances, but in that case why wouldn't he have mentioned it?

"I have to go up to Recovery," he said. "Will you please leave a note for me so I know what Mrs. Leone's room number is?" Jackie nodded. He touched the Italian woman's shoulder gently, and then he was gone.

Jackie brought Mrs. Leone the Italian-language admissions papers and sat with her while she filled out the document. She wrote in a fine, beautiful hand, meticulously setting forward the bare bones of what had been her life. Maiden Name: Francini. Age: 34. Spouse: Deceased. Address: 50 Via Vieri, Genoa, Italy. Nearest Relative: Sister-in-law. The *regione* was not paying for her; Signora Leone was paying for herself and had brought a check in the sum of $12,000. In case of an emergency, it was the sister-in-law who was to be called.

It was a melancholy document. This woman, who seemed so young to Jackie, had neither parents nor brothers nor sisters. Her husband was dead, and nobody apparently cared enough to accompany her on such a momentous journey.

"Do you have children?" Jackie smiled to show the question had nothing to do with admissions and was designed to be friendly.

"A son and a daughter." Her voice was very low. She was frightened, of course. "My sister-in-law is caring for them."

Then Jackie saw, protruding from the lip of the Neiman-Marcus bag, the toe of a huge wax candle, fashioned in the shape of a cowboy boot. "I have one of those," said Jackie. "The minute I saw it, I had to have it."

The Italian woman smiled wanly. "It is for my son," she said.

"I'll just go and make sure your room is ready," said Jackie. "Do you speak any English, Signora Leone?"

"Yes. Quite a bit. Not as well as you speak Italian though."

Jackie was pleased. Her new patient's instincts were as nice as her calligraphy. Who but a very nice woman would think, upon entering a hospital, to compliment a volunteer on her command of Italian?

"*Grazie, signora.*"

"*Prego.*"

The room was small and white. Everything was glaringly modern, from the complicated touch-lighting to the gleaming fixtures in the bathroom. One wall had been painted blue in an effort to minimize the austerity. It was, as Jackie had explained, temporary. She would only spend one night in this room, and there was no need to unpack even.

Rafaella took her toilet articles out and ranged them on a steel shelf in the bathroom. Then she changed into a plain white batiste nightdress and her Japanese kimono. She left her hair up with its silver comb in place and went to sit in the chair by the window. The view showed her the east wall of the Hibernian; by counting up from the ground floor she could almost figure out which room had been hers. She avoided the bed. She would be having enough of beds soon.

Her eyes burned from the long, sleepless night. At times she had lain very still, pretending to sleep, so that Stephen could drop off, but he never did. All night he had stroked her, murmured to her, and held her in his arms. When it grew light he had risen and showered. He had gone over to the Hibernian, collected her things, and left the key at the desk. She had already paid her bill. He returned with orange juice, coffee, and rolls to find her bathed and dressed. Together they had come to the hospital, the pretty American had processed her admissions papers, and here she was. He had said he would be back, and she both longed for his presence and was horrified by the thought of it.

Think of something else. The floor had seemed very busy when she and Miss Talbot walked by the nurses' station. White-coated figures flew about at a furious speed; patients in bathrobes shuffled about; a cheery Mexican nurse went by, whistling. Here in her room it was very still. Miss Talbot would be back with a doctor to take her medical history, which had to be done in Italian for accuracy.

Where had she learned to speak Italian so well? Rafaella was in awe of her. She was one of the *Giant* breed, all right—tall, blonde, beautiful. She didn't seem the sort to be a volunteer, any more than Stephen did. Perhaps she was part of his film crew? *No good. Think of something else. Nothing involving what is about to happen to me, nothing involving him.* It occurred to her that she, too, could join the bathrobed figures in the corridors. Nothing prevented her. She went to the door and looked out. The halls were now mysteriously empty.

She had an inspiration. She would usefully occupy the time until the doctor came. She had a commission from a Milanese woman to design a setting for an emerald. Her client wanted something unusual. She had said it didn't matter if the design proved to be best for a brooch or a pendant, so long as it was unique.

The problem was the emerald itself. It was large, and—

like all emeralds—flawed. She would have to work the setting with cunning so that it grasped the emerald firmly in tiny prongs. No solder could be used, or the gem would shatter. She thought she would try to sketch some ideas. After all, a woman who was about to die wouldn't concern herself with a commission in far-off Milan, would she?

She had gone to get a pen from her handbag, when it occurred to her that she had no paper. She went back to her chair by the window and waited.

The man Jackie ushered in was tall and rangy. He had owlishly tufted eyebrows and an open face. Dr. Blanchard, the cardiologist.

He parked himself on the corner of Rafaella's bed, smiling reassuringly. Everything he said was in a twangy, Texas English which Jackie translated.

"Hello, Mrs. Leone. You'll be glad to know there's no need for any further heart catheterization. The X-rays you've brought from Italy are excellent. They tell me everything I need to know."

It had never occurred to her she might have to undergo *that* ordeal again. She remembered lying in the lab in Genoa, the catheter in the tender crook of her arm, watching the white, sluglike trail as it inched its way toward her heart. She could see it all on the screen, which made her feel doubly invaded. Pictures were being taken of her heart; somehow technology had conspired to make this indignity possible. There had been a little pain, but mainly a hot, rushing sensation, a feeling that she might explode.

"Do you understand your condition? Has your doctor in Genoa explained what we're going to do?"

She nodded. They were going to take a vein from her leg and create new valves. They would bypass the occluded vessels on the surface of her heart and make that organ an efficient commodity once more. While Dr. Blanchard talked about her mitral and aortic valves, complimented her on her good color, explaining that it meant her blood supply was not as bad as it might be, she concentrated on the paper she

116

needed. She must remember to ask Miss Talbot for some paper.

Dr. Blanchard, however, was far from finished with her. He needed a long and complicated medical history, made still more lengthy by the necessity of translation from English to Italian and then back again. Previous surgery? None. Childbirth? Two normal deliveries. A rather long labor the first time. Stefania, the second, a bit early. Allergies? None. Cause of death of parents? Mother of cancer, at age 55. Father, of heart attack, at age 64. Rafaella had been born to them late in life. Her mother had died when she was fifteen. Siblings? A sister, born ten years before Rafaella, who had died in infancy. She had assumed the congenital defect had been bequeathed her by her mother, but Dr. Blanchard didn't seem so sure. Childhood diseases? Whooping cough, croup, measles. Rheumatic fever? No, certainly not. Had her joints ever ached as a child? Yes, when she had a cold once, but she couldn't remember when. It was all so long ago. She told him, without being asked, that her children had been examined by her cardiologist in Genoa. Their hearts were sound.

When he examined her, his hands were gentle and sure. They seemed almost loving, and she blushed at that thought, because before last night it would never have occurred to her.

"How is it possible," she asked, when he questioned her about the symptoms which had caused her to seek medical advice, "how is it I could live to this age and never, never, feel the symptoms until so recently?" The pain, the shortness of breath, the terrifying sensation of being crushed beneath a slab of stone—all these had manifested themselves only in the last few months.

Jackie translated the question. Dr. Blanchard quirked one of his owl-like eyebrows and considered. Finally he murmured a reply that Rafaella couldn't quite make out.

Jackie translated.

"The heart is a mystery," she said. "I could write a book about the mysteries of the human heart. One day I will."

"I would like to read that book."

"For sure," said Dr. Blanchard, winking.

"*Certamente*," said Jackie.

Stephen caught Blanchard just as he was about to go back into the cath lab.

"You've seen Rafaella Leone?" he asked.

"Yes, sure. Just now. How do you know about her, Morrissy? She's Italian, not Spanish."

"What do you think?"

Blanchard rolled his eyes. "She's awful pretty," he said.

Stephen controlled himself. He needed to know Blanchard's opinion. If he revealed any personal interest in the patient in question, Fred would retreat into professionalism. He would become like Lassiter, bland and reassuring; uneasy. "How does it look?" he asked.

"Well, it looks like a hundred other times-two's. It's the mitral and aortic. She's young—should be a snap."

"What's the risk? What are the odds?"

"Why are you so interested?" Blanchard removed his glasses and favored Stephen with a deep look. Receiving no answer, he sighed and replaced his spectacles. "Look," he said patiently, "you've been around here long enough to know we don't give odds. There's always a risk with surgery of this sort. Far as I can tell, she's in a low-risk category, considering. She's a nice girl, and she's scared stiff."

"Thanks," said Stephen. He took the elevator up to the surgical floors. At this hour Lassiter would still be in one of the OR's. He entered the anteroom of Lassiter's private office and waited for the surgeon's special assistant to get off the phone. She seemed to be carrying on two conversations simultaneously; her forefinger danced over the hold button like someone operating an adding machine.

"What can I do for you?" She had concluded with one caller and relegated the other to temporary limbo.

"I have to see Dr. Lassiter. Can he make some time for me this afternoon?"

She frowned. "It's not a very good day, Mr. Morrissy. He goes straight from his last surgery to a lunch appointment."

"It's very important. How about before he does rounds?

Just for a few moments, of course. I can make myself available any time."

"Tomorrow would be better, after surgery, about noon."

"Tomorrow is too late," he said. "It's about one of the patients slated for surgery tomorrow."

She looked briefly surprised, then nodded. "I'll see what I can do," she said. "Check back with me in early afternoon." As he was heading out the door she called him back. "May I tell Dr. Lassiter what it is you wish to discuss?"

"No, I'm afraid not."

What, really, could he say? He hadn't meant to be rude, but the plain truth was that he had no idea what he could say to Lassiter. He walked back down the corridor and stopped near a window. He placed his hands on the panes and stared out at nothing. What did you say? *Be extra careful with this one, Lassiter. I know the lady.* For the first time he understood completely why Lassiter flew down the corridors, eluding the imploring eyes and clutching hands of the relatives. What could he, who had been inside more hearts than any man living, have to say to people who were concerned with only one particular heart? Beyond his easy words of reassurance, there was nothing to say. Blanchard could study his X-rays and produce an opinion, but Lassiter could only *do*.

Stephen had to talk to him, if only to act in lieu of a relative. She had no one, they thought, but they were wrong. He would act on her behalf, protect her. Not until he was halfway down the hall again did he realize that he was thinking of *them* as the enemy.

She was sitting in a chair near the window when he entered her room, and she seemed to be drawing. She was wearing a pale kimono, the color of sea shells.

"Hello." She looked up, startled. He watched her eyes register a quartet of emotions in rapid succession—alarm, recognition, relief, embarrassment?

"Where did you get a sketchbook?"

"Jackie, Miss Talbot, brought it for me. I asked for some paper and she returned with this."

"You've seen Blanchard." It was a statement, not a question. Words seemed to be jerked from him without consideration. There seemed no precedent for this conversation. No book of etiquette contained advice on the proper thing to say to the woman you've made love to the night before, on the day before she undergoes open-heart surgery. "What did he say?"

Rafaella shut her sketchbook and looked out the window. "He said I am perfectly fine and can go home tomorrow. It was all a mistake."

Sighing, Stephen perched on the hospital bed. A duplication of their positions last night at the motel. "Rafaella," he said, "please, don't. Be kind to me."

"He is going to write a book about the mysteries of the human heart."

"Who?"

"Dr. Blanchard."

"He told you that?"

"Yes, why not?" She turned again and looked at him. Her eyes were softer now. "Come sit with me on the bed," he said. "There's no room for me in that chair." Obediently, she came and sat near him. Her feet, encased in pale, washable scuffs, did not quite touch the floor. He took her hand, and together they looked out the window. A helicopter appeared in the distance; it looked as if it would smash into the Hibernian's green roof.

"I have a present for you," he said, remembering. "I bought it yesterday. A good-bye gift." The word "good-bye" hovered horridly in the room. "When I thought you were going back to Italy," he said.

"Where is it?"

"In your shopping bag with Carlo's candle." He got up, foraged in the bag, and returned with the long, flat package that had rested on the dashboard of his car. He put it in her hands and watched while she opened it and peered inside, blinking at the sight of so much color.

Certainly it was bright, which he had intended, but he wondered if he'd misjudged. A scarf was the most mundane of presents, and this one had cost a small fortune. Chinese silk, hand-embroidered, a riot of exploding green and crimson and peacock blue. She lifted it out of the box and held it up, scrutinizing. For a moment he thought he could imagine her as a thrifty, shrewd Italian housewife, appraising vegetables in a market.

"So lovely," she said. "Thank you, but it is far too costly."

"I wanted to see you wearing something bright," he said. "I know you like, ah, *blando* colors, but—"

She put the scarf around her throat, knotted it loosely so that one trailing end passed over her shoulder. In her nightgown and kimono, this arrangement had a pathetic effect. She went to the mirror, took the silver comb from her hair, and disappeared into the bathroom. When she returned, she had brushed her hair all to one side, so that it fell over her right shoulder. The scarf was tied in a huge, floppy bow; it looked like a tropical flower against the dark hair and transformed the wearer into a gypsyish peasant girl. He was enchanted.

She climbed back onto the bed, and again they looked out of the window, holding hands. "Thank you," she said.

"It had your name written on it, signora."

"Excuse me?"

"Never mind."

Lassiter sent word that he could see Stephen for five minutes outside the recovery ICU's at three-fifty. This was ten minutes before his customary raid on the waiting relatives. There were six today, and the news was good for all of them.

Promptly at three-forty-five, Stephen staked himself outside the ICU. He enjoyed a unique place in Lassiter's favor (unique among volunteers, whom the surgeon never addressed) because Lassiter was anxious that the film about St. Matthew's be accurate. Certainly he didn't think of it as a means of enhancing his reputation or bringing him more patients. He was far beyond that. What he did want was to dispel, once and for all, the notion that his hospital cut people needlessly. In the continuing war between surgeons and medical men he inevitably—and unfairly, Stephen thought—emerged as a doctor who would rather cut first and consider later.

The longest interview Stephen had ever had with Lassiter

was his first when Lassiter had given permission for the film to be made. The surgeon had lounged back in a swivel chair, long Gucci-clad feet crossed at the ankle, and said:

"Make no mistake about it. The people who come to me are beyond the point where medication alone can help. I don't operate because they want me to, or to relieve them of angina pain, or because—hell, it can't hurt them. I operate because without the surgery their lives would be dramatically shortened. Many would die within months. I place the same value on every patient who's wheeled into my OR. I do the same for a prince as I do for a Brazilian busboy. They're all the same to me."

The doors of the ICU swung open and Lassiter emerged, exactly on time. His surgical suit, pale green and immaculate, told Stephen that he'd done an unscheduled op that afternoon. In his hand he carried a stack of cards. These were imprinted with the names of the patients he had operated on that morning; he carried them so that he would be able to match the name to the heart when he met with the relatives. He walked toward Stephen briskly, then took his stance next to him, athletic body lounging against the wall.

"What can I do for you?"

"You're scheduled to do a bypass on Mrs. Leone tomorrow. A young woman from Italy."

Lassiter's pale eyes regarded him mildly. *Yes*, they seemed to be saying, *what of it? I need more information.*

"She came here alone from Genoa. I met her several days ago and I've become rather fond of her. I didn't know she was your patient until last night."

"Was she scheduled for Gold or Sadaghi?" Dr. Gold and Dr. Sadaghi were cardiovascular surgeons whose light was eclipsed by the sun of Lassiter's greatness.

"No, she was always scheduled for you. What I meant was that I didn't know she was coming in for surgery. At all."

He had succeeded in surprising Lassiter a little; the surgeon blinked once. "I won't know the story on her until I confer with Fred at five," he said. "I'll be seeing her between five-thirty and six."

"Fred says she's a regular times-two," said Stephen. Ordinarily, it would have embarrassed him to use the phrase in the company of this man, but he desperately needed to force some reassuring, human spark from him.

"Well," said Lassiter, consulting his watch, "if that's what Fred says, that's what the lady probably is." He was angling his body away from the wall, preparing to decamp.

"Look. Consider me her family, will you? Pretend I'm her—brother, or something—and I've been hanging around the hospital long enough to know the score. What would you say to me?"

Lassiter smiled. It was an elongation of his lips, merely, and without mirth. "Someone along the line must have warned you not to get involved with patients," he said. "It doesn't pay. If what Fred says is true, she'll probably be fine."

"She's only thirty-four," said Stephen. He recognized the pleading quality in his voice. He had heard it a hundred times. "My husband has never smoked a day in his life. . . . My mother lived to be eighty-six. . . . Herb watches his diet very carefully, no cholesterol . . ." Even the frailest, most high-risk cases had their bargaining points; they offered them up desperately, as bribes intended to win the surgeon's reassurance. "That should be in her favor, shouldn't it?"

"Should be," said Lassiter, "but I won't know till I've opened her up." He punched Stephen's arm lightly. He was trying to be friendly. "I'll leave a note for you after I've seen her," he said. "I must go, sorry."

Half way up the hall he stopped, turned back. He'd had a sudden thought.

"Do you want to watch?" he called. "From the observation dome?"

God, no. Christ, man! "No thanks," said Stephen. The thought of those well-manicured fingers entering Rafaella's heart as casually as if she'd been just anyone made him, literally, ill. Of course she *was* just anyone to Lassiter. And Lassiter, in offering to let Stephen watch, had been under the impression that he was acting sympathetically.

"Just remember," he called after the retreating back. "I'm her family! It's me you'll report to tomorrow."

"Check," said Lassiter. "Don't worry. No problem."

Chapter 2

Since she was the only Italian scheduled for surgery the next day, Rafaella's preoperative conference was held in her room. They were just three women in a small white room; to look at them, Viola and Jackie and Rafaella might be three friends chatting. Rafaella sat on her bed with Jackie perched next to her, where Stephen had been, and Viola sat in the chair.

Viola told her exactly what was going to happen to her and Jackie translated, but since Rafaella understood much of the English she had to hear it twice.

"—there will also be one or two drainage tubes in your side to drain fluid off your lungs," Viola was saying. She had begun the long catalogue of tubes and wires. Since she was briefing a single patient rather than an entire room of them, she was forced to look directly at Rafaella while she spoke.

Rafaella looked down at her hands, out the window, at Jackie Talbot's well-shod feet—only occasionally could she bring herself to look at the nurse. It seemed the aftermath of the surgery would be the worst ordeal. *Senza dignità.* She hoped she would be awash in a sea of drugs; she almost, but not quite, hoped she would die while still under the anesthesia and be spared the period of living death Viola described.

When she had finished her instructions, Viola shook Rafaella's hand and wished her well. Her smile seemed to promise that it would be so. Jackie remained behind.

"Since you've come alone, I'll act as your family member," she said. "I'll be available whenever you need me all during your convalescence." She looked at Rafaella's profile, which indicated a stunned passivity. "Is there anything you'd like to ask me?"

Away from those tubes, from the helplessness, the indignity. "Where did you learn to speak such excellent Italian?"

"I was married to an Italian, a Roman. Eduardo and I quarreled so much, in two languages, I picked it up fast."

"Italian men like to quarrel—sometimes they don't mean it. Was that so for you and your husband?"

"I'm afraid not. We're divorced."

"I'm sorry. Do you have any children?"

"No. But you do, don't you? Have you got any photographs?"

Rafaella took the silver-framed pictures of Carlo and Stefania out of her traveling case and showed them to Jackie.

"They're beautiful children. I know that's what you're supposed to say, but I mean it. The boy looks just like you, doesn't he?"

And so they talked on, a stilted chat at first, designed to make the shadow which was tomorrow recede a little. Rafaella was grateful to Jackie for understanding; the very banality of the conversation soothed her.

"I have to go over to the children's wing now, but I'll be back." Jackie stood up, smiled, and for one moment Rafaella felt an envy for her so intense she wondered how she could contain it. This tall, radiant girl was free to leave. She could walk out of the room on her long, tanned legs; this *Giant* girl with her golden hair and whole, undamaged heart could afford to be kind, because she was so lucky. The bile of envy was peculiar to Rafaella, and as soon as Jackie had gone, leaving her alone with the pictures of her children, it disappeared, leaving her shamed.

Carlo and Stefania seemed real presences in the room; their eyes looked reproachfully at her. Somewhere in Naples at this very moment, her mother-in-law would be crying over them as if they were already orphans instead of merely fatherless.

Regularly, on the anniversary of Aldo's death in the month of May, Gemma called Rafaella from Naples. This yearly conversation had a beautiful symmetry to it. At other times, Gemma Leone questioned, bullied, complained, was affectionate, but in these anniversary calls she managed to begin as a concerned adult and end as a bewildered child.

It was Rafaella who assured the older woman that fate had been unusually cruel in plucking Aldo away at such an early age; that it seemed unfair when so many evil, brutal people were left to walk the earth; that Aldo had been the most loving of fathers who should have been allowed to see his children grow up. By the end of the conversation Rafaella would be exhausted and drained, while Mrs. Leone, mysteriously refreshed by her outburst, would have gained enough strength to carry her through until the following anniversary.

Rafaella forgave her. She understood that fear took many forms—some people thought it possible to shout fear down. Gemma Leone could not rid herself of the feeling that it was profoundly unnatural for her son to die before her, so she reopened old wounds, shouting over the line from Naples, hoping to be enlightened.

It wasn't in Rafaella's nature to shout fear down. She carried it inside, privately, like something precious. Only Stephen had seen it, because she had offered it to him. She touched the Chinese scarf in her hair; she could feel its warmth.

One thing was clear: she must make him promise that he wouldn't ever, ever, come near her or see her in the state Viola had described. In her fear of pain and indignity she had forgotten to be afraid of death.

She knew Lassiter was somewhere on her floor without being told. She could feel his presence. All afternoon people had gone by. Fragments of conversations drifted through her open door; clattering carts trundled past. Now the atmosphere in the corridor was purposeful and tense. Even Jackie, when she came into the room a few minutes later, looked subtly different.

"Dr. Lassiter is up the hall," she said. "He'll be here soon."

"I know. I can feel him."

"I should warn you that he's a man of few words. You won't need me to translate. I only came to be with you."

"Is it so terrifying, then, to be alone with him?"

"No. Not terrifying. But sometimes it bewilders people. He seems so *casual*." Jackie hugged her purple volunteer's jacket in an anguished gesture. "Look," she said, "I'm not supposed to say things like this, but I like you so much and I'm sure you'll understand. Martin Lassiter is a great, great, surgeon, but he sometimes impresses people as being cold. He's not like Fred Blanchard—he doesn't chat and hum and pat you absentmindedly on the head. He tells you he'll fix you up, taps the foot of your bed, and wham—he's gone. He's like that with everyone, it doesn't mean a thing. He's seen your X-rays and conferred with Blanchard; he's all ready for you tomorrow. Meeting you is just a formality."

Rafaella nodded, pleased. Secretly, she wanted just such a decorous formality to exist between herself and her surgeon. It was all very well for Dr. Rinaldi and Dr. Blanchard to be friendly and encouraging, but she wanted the man who entered her heart to remain outwardly aloof. Let him save his ardor and use it where it counted. She began to explain this to Jackie, but she realized it would puzzle her. On her last day, she didn't wish to reveal so much of herself to a stranger.

When Dr. Lassiter entered the room it seemed to expand rather than shrink. He took possession of her little room as confidently as an experienced skipper might assume command of a ship. She studied him in those first moments as she would appraise a work of art.

Here is my Savior. Tall, well-made, with intelligent, pale, cool eyes. He looks a little tired. Fine lines mark his forehead. A humorous mouth used to repressing humor. Something tentative and wary in his posture. Is he afraid I will lunge from the bed and kneel at his feet, behave excessively, emotionally?

"Hello, Dr. Lassiter," she said. She held out a hand to him and he took it, murmuring her name as he did so.

"We're going to fix you tomorrow," he said, just as Jackie had predicted. "Things look fine." He stepped back a few paces, scrutinized her. "Do you trust me?" he asked.

"I think so."

"Trust me," he said, tapping the foot of her bed. "I'm the best there is. You're in the best hands in the world, the best for what you need. Do you believe me?"

"I must," said Rafaella. "Otherwise my children will be orphans."

"Can't have that. I like children, you know. Yours look like fine ones. You'll be seeing them again soon." He tapped the end of her bed again and then, as a final gesture, reached down to clasp her toes beneath the sheet. He did it lightly, with a jaunty air. "I'll see you tomorrow in Recovery." He winked, sandy lashes covering one pale eye for an infinitesimal moment, and then he was gone.

The emergency operation performed that afternoon had been on a seventy-year-old man from Oklahoma, who had arrived at St. Matthew's in grave heart failure. The fluids in his chest and lungs caused him to bubble like a coffee percolator. Lassiter had had to shock his heart back to life ten times before he could be removed from the pump and put into Recovery. He lay in one of the recovery ICU's, together with six Dutch farmers. It was a full house. In another recovery room Julio Ramirez, whose potassium level had been stabilized, still bided his time. Señora Perez and the others had long since been removed. Ramirez was beginning to be disoriented from his long stay and sometimes shouted incoherently, but the three other patients, all Dr. Gold's, were still unconscious.

In the children's hospital Lucia Camaratta's mother sang Lassiter's praises to anyone who would listen. Lucia was recovering beautifully. Another mother, a young woman from Pennsylvania, could not stop marveling over the color of her son's fingernails. For the first time in his life, they were rosy. Before they had been blue.

Night fell. Patients were fed. Televisions were turned on. On the convalescent floors, determined patients surged along, IV's trailing after them, doing their "mile" in the corridors. The floor of the patients who were scheduled for surgery the following day was quiet. The atmosphere there was one of apprehension. It was a melancholy place to be.

Jackie Talbot nearly collided with Stephen Morrissy at the elevator on the main floor. She thought he looked, for the first time since she'd known him, exhausted and unglamorous. It was the first she'd seen of him since he'd brought Mrs. Leone in that morning.

"Dr. Lassiter was exceptionally nice to Mrs. Leone," she said. "He actually spoke several sentences and commented on how handsome her children looked." Stephen nodded abstractedly. "He even patted her foot. I've only seen him do that with children."

"Are you going to her now?"

"Yes. I'm prepared to stay with her all night, if she likes."

"That won't be necessary. Look—I've got to go see Mrs. Ramirez on ten. Will you tell her—Mrs. Leone—I'll be by to see her as soon as I can?"

"Sure. They won't sedate her until about ten-thirty. Stephen? How long have you known her?"

He looked perplexed, as if she had asked an absurd question. "For a while," he said vaguely. Then the elevator stopped at Jackie's floor and she got out. Her last view of him, before the doors slid shut, disturbed her. Besides looking tired and wretched, her friend Morrissy seemed frightened. The expression in his dulled green eyes might almost have been one of guilt.

Familiar indignities, not so bad. Rather like the preparations for giving birth. Except here, of course, they shaved her leg. Since it was already hairless there wasn't much for them to do but administer the enema. When she had emptied herself, she showered in the gleaming steel bathroom. Her hands moved over the surface of her body, sadly plying the bar of hospital soap; it was the last time she would stand in a shower, her body unscarred and seemingly whole. She remembered her image of the flayed man and the night she had forced herself to contemplate her body in the mirror.

The true good-bye had been last night, but already it seemed so long ago it might have happened in a different life.

She put the white nightgown on again and brushed her hair. The Chinese scarf lay neatly folded on the bedside table. Jackie would remove all her possessions in the morning, since she would never see this room again. Viola had explained all that. Soon someone would bring her a sleeping pill. Jackie had said Stephen would come, too. It didn't matter who came first. She had reached the end of her journey and suddenly wanted only to get the business done.

When Stephen came, a little after nine, she was sitting quietly in bed, reclining a little, in the dark. Light from the corridor made it possible to see adequately. She didn't want the lights on. "Hello," she said. "I am awake."

He dragged the chair over and sat beside her bed. "I've come to stay with you," he said. "I couldn't get away until now."

"There's no need," she said.

"Lassiter says you'll be fine. He left a note for me."

"Why would he do that?"

"I asked him to. I told him to consider me your family."

"You are not. I don't want you to feel responsible for me. It isn't fair to you. And I want you to make a promise to me. You must promise you won't see me in the intensive care."

"I can't promise that."

"You must. Please."

"All right." She could tell he was saying it to placate her. Worse, by assuming she would make it to intensive care, he had slighted death.

"Do you believe in God?" she asked him.

"Once in a while. Here, God is Martin Lassiter. I believe in him. In his skill."

"I was a Catholic. When I was a little girl, I wanted to be a nun for about six weeks. That was because a friend, Graziella, convinced me. When I grew up there were only two things for girls that had *prestigio*. You could be a nun, or a movie star."

"I think you would do better as a movie star."

"But they seemed the same. I pictured myself, my life as a

nun, as if all the time cameras recorded my behavior. I was nine. By the time I was ten, I wanted to be an artist."

His fingers were stroking her cheek. It was as if he wanted to draw words from her without speaking himself.

"After my husband died, I never went to church any more. It wasn't that I stopped believing in God, either."

"You were angry at Him."

"No. I just didn't think He would notice, or care. Before, Miss Talbot asked me if I wanted a priest. I said no. It would be cowardly to go back to God just because I am dying."

"You are not dying. You will not die."

"I cheat," she said, sighing. "I pray from habit."

"Rafaella. You do not cheat, you are not a coward, you will not die."

She imprisoned his hand and held it between her own. "Another reason I could not see a priest is because of last night. How could I admit to *purezza* for three years and then—last night? He would not believe me. He would be shocked." His hand tensed in hers; he was utterly still, as if she had struck him. He had buried his head in his free hand. "Stephen," she whispered. "Stephen? I didn't mean it, I was trying to make a joke. You seem so sad. I wanted to make you laugh. I like it when you laugh."

"Some joke," he said hollowly. He moved to the side of the bed and put his arms around her. "Ha! Ha!" he whispered against her hair. "You nearly made me cry, signora. I wouldn't have thought you capable of such a joke."

"Neither would I. I think I'm going crazy." She held him tightly, concentrating on that physical act to prevent herself from speaking again. She was afraid of what she might say; it seemed some invisible dam of discretion had broken and terrible words might pour out of her, as if a demon had taken possession of her soul.

"If I could do this for you, I would," he said. "I honestly believe I would."

A West Indian nurse came in. She brought a sleeping pill and an admonition, delivered in her musical voice. Rafaella was not to eat or drink after midnight. When she left, she closed the door, and it was truly dark.

"What time is it?" she asked. By the light of his GALVTEX he examined his watch. "Ten-thirty," he said.

"I don't want to take the pill. Soon I will, but not yet."

Gradually, the room revealed pockets of light. The floodlit roof of the Hibernian pierced the gloom. "Shall I draw the curtains?" he asked.

"No. Talk to me. Tell me about your films."

She lay still, letting his soft voice lull her. He told her about pyramids and jungles, Arctic birds and great gray whales. He did not mention people or calamities. He spoke only of beautiful things, describing them precisely so she could smell the night-blooming flowers of the Amazon, flowers as large as dinner plates and colored in the mysterious, bright hues of fish that dwelt away from human eyes at the bottom of the sea. He allowed her to see the translucent green at the very epicenter of the huge waves that curled on the beaches of Australia, and she remembered something.

"When I first saw you," she said, "I thought you were once a surfer." She told him about *Sci Acquatico*, and he laughed for her.

At eleven o'clock she took her sleeping pill. As she swallowed the last of the water she knew a sudden, minor grief. No more water now. She wished she had relished the last sip more.

She became sleepy very quickly. She remembered that neither she nor Stephen had slept the night before. "How tired you must be," she said. He was holding her hand again, telling her about a cliff somewhere in Scotland where the voices of the seabirds rose, night and day, like a Siren song.

It was right for her to sleep now; she wouldn't fight it any longer. Silently, she said good night to Carlo and Stefania. Silently, she said good night to Aldo, as she always did. There was something important she had to say to Stephen, but she couldn't remember her English.

"Stephen."

"Yes."

But the effort of speaking had become too great. She could only repeat his name, again and again, in helpless gratitude.

Chapter 3

He walked beside her as they wheeled her down the corridor toward the elevators that would take her to the surgical floors. She looked very small beneath the white sheet. In her fancy, high-heeled shoes, the ones she had worn to the restaurant on the turning basin, she reached to his jawbone. The medication had made her sleepy, but her eyes were open still. He remembered how surprised he'd been when she'd first taken off her sunglasses. He had expected her eyes to be dark.

In the elevator her head turned toward him. She parted her lips, as if for a kiss. She was thirsty; the medication did that. They had moistened her lips with a wet cloth in the room. He touched her hand, but there was no answering pressure. She was beyond him now. The elevator stopped and she was trundled out toward the OR. Useless, powerless, he walked along until they had achieved their destination and she disappeared behind the doors.

Lassiter would be scrubbing now, whistling with anticipation, lost in the private world of the athlete who psyches himself up for each new combat. He wouldn't be needed for a while. He only came into the operating rooms when all the preparatory work was finished. Someone else would open her up. Probably Seales, a nice young surgeon with a freckled face and knobby wrists. Seales had once joined Stephen and Fred Blanchard for dinner. Over a carafe of potent red wine Seales confessed that he was, at St. Matthew's, mainly a mechanic. "I open 'em up, and then, when Lassiter is finished, I close 'em." Seales had ambition and planned one day to excel as a cardiovascular surgeon, but for now he was content, he said, to perform in close proximity to the King of Hearts.

On the elevator going down and in the lobby, people looked at Stephen strangely. He didn't understand until he'd gained the privacy of his motel room. Emerging from the shower, he confronted his image in the mirror, razor in hand. White stubble covered his chin; his eyes were bloodshot. He looked like a bum, or a drunk just after a weekend bender. He hadn't slept in forty-eight hours. If need be, he could go without sleep for a week, but the hand wielding the razor trembled. Just about now, he reckoned, the electric saw would be whining as it chuffed through her breastbone.

He wasn't on duty at the hospital today, but he knew he would return as soon as he had shaved and dressed. There was nothing he could do, of course. Hours stretched between the present and the moment when he would know the outcome. Nothing to do but wait, just wait.

Jacqueline Talbot, waiting for a patient in Admissions, crossed her fingers deep inside the pockets of her purple smock and wished Rafaella luck. Never had she had a patient who showed less emotion; seldom had she seen a woman more terrified and determined to behave courageously. The faces of Rafaella's children haunted her, partly because they had already known one loss and might have to suffer another. The other reason was one she didn't like to dwell on. The moment she had seen them, their grave faces staring out from the silver frame, she had thought of the children she and Eduardo would now never have.

The patient due in now was one Jackie dreaded seeing. He was, from the information she had, suffering from the deadliest of congenital heart defects, the AV—atrioventricular—commune. She knew enough to understand that most surgeons wouldn't touch such a case. The patient, Giovanni Catrine, had been born with only one chamber of his heart working. The atrium and ventricle were joined together. Inside the deformed pump, the blood fought a losing battle to gain entrance into the heart's chamber. Giovanni was traveling with his mother from an obscure village in Calabria. That was all she knew, that and the time of their arrival. By chance, the data involving his age and other pertinent facts was missing.

She wondered how long her luck could hold out. The—so far—triumphant recovery of Lucia had made her falsely optimistic. What would she do if something should happen to Rafaella Leone, for example? She thought she might very well resign, leave St. Matthew's forever, acknowledging defeat. The only loss she had ever known had been the death of her marriage. Terrible as it had seemed at the time, it counted for very little. It was a commonplace event. Most of her friends had already been married twice; two were embroiled in third marriages before the age of thirty. They were able to shuck off their former lives as blithely as a snake regenerates its skin. Only Jackie brooded over loss.

Why am I such a throwback? she thought. *You wouldn't know it to look at me.* For the first time, she wondered what she was doing at St. Matthew's. She didn't belong there; she wasn't tough enough. Any woman who found herself on the verge of tears because of a photograph of two children was not cut out to occupy a serious place in life—still less to be of any help to those who really needed it.

There were eight people in the operating room at first, not counting the patient. Two doctors, two nurses, three technicians, who were familiarly known as the pump team, and an anesthesiologist were all assembled when the groggy patient was wheeled in. She was already nearly asleep when the anesthesiologist put her under.

Dr. Seales began the preliminaries. Four electrodes were fixed on the sides of her head by the technicians who would monitor her brain waves during surgery. A strip of adhesive tape was placed over her eyes. Probes were placed in her body: one for measuring arterial pressure, one for venous, another for intravenous fluids. A catheter was inserted to remove and measure urine. All of this took approximately half an hour.

Another man entered the OR and was greeted by Dr.

Seales. He was a visiting surgeon from England who was observing the operation. He lifted a latex-gloved hand in greeting and went to stand where he would be out of the way of the scurrying nurses.

"The patient," said Dr. Seales to the English visitor, "is thirty-four years old. She is suffering from occlusion of the mitral and aortic valves. It should be a straightforward, classic double bypass procedure."

The Muzak leaped into action and filled the room with jazz. The English surgeon was startled. "What is that?" he asked.

"Miles Davis," said Seales's colleague, Dr. Irwin. "Dr. Lassiter likes him."

"Does he always operate to this sort of music?"

"No, depends on his mood. Sometimes he likes classical or pop."

The anesthesiologist indicated that the patient was well under. It was now 9:30 A.M. The small form on the table looked inhuman with its collection of probes and tubes, like a luckless voodoo doll.

"What is the patient's name?" the English doctor asked.

"Rafaella Leone," said Seales, mispronouncing her name. "Everybody ready? Right. Let's begin."

Seales cut into the inner thigh, probing for a vein. When he located one that pleased him, he pulled it out. It wriggled from the patient's leg, wormlike. Irwin received it in a bowl and cleaned it in saline solution, then examined it for any tiny holes or imperfections. "This is a good, sturdy one," Irwin said. No one in the OR thought "sturdy" a peculiar word for an object so tiny; only the visiting surgeon (a urologist), was stunned by the thought of placing twenty stitches in a vein no larger than a blade of grass.

Seales took up a scalpel and sliced into the patient's chest. A thin red line sprang up behind his sure hand from her neck to a point above her navel. The blood vessels that fed the skin had to be cauterized; for a few moments the OR smelled like a charnel house. Then Seales was ready for the saw.

He placed it over the incision, waited for the power to be turned on. The table vibrated beneath the patient as the saw bit its way through her breastbone. The retractors were brought forward and inserted. The rib cage gaping open, the heart was now obscured only by the membranous sac surrounding it. A few deft snipping movements and it was revealed to all of them—the human, beating heart of the all-but-anonymous patient. She would never see it, but nine strangers were free to examine it closely.

The heart was stippled with colors that seemed to shift and move as it rhythmically contracted. The patient was draped now. Except for the small portion of her face that could be seen between the electrodes, she was now reduced to a beating heart framed by metal retractors—a three-dimensional photograph.

Seales studied the heart for a moment. He had seen enlarged hearts, hearts flabby and gross, hearts so choked by cholesterol whole portions were the bright shiny yellow of chicken fat, hearts gray and ischemic in the area which had infarcted. This patient's heart did not alarm him.

"This is probably a congenital condition," he said for the English surgeon's benefit. "The loss of color here, and here, is due to the occlusion of the two valves. The heart is working too hard to pump blood. If we manufacture a new system for her, she should be fine. She's lucky. She might have lived twenty more years without having strong enough symptoms to send her to a cardiologist, and by then it might have been too late. The deterioration now is correctable."

He began to insert the tubes which would hook the patient up to the heart-lung machine, the "pump" which made open-heart surgery possible. Before 1955, such an operation would have been unthinkable. Coronary bypass surgery was born with the invention. Dr. Seales explained these facts to the guest, who already knew but was happy to allow the young surgeon his place in the sun. Soon enough, when Lassiter came, Dr. Seales would be only a member of the back-up team.

"The surgeon needs a bloodless, motionless field in cardiovascular procedures. If the heart continued to beat, the lungs to breathe, it would be impossible. The pump diverts blood from the heart and lungs, performs the function of the lungs, and returns the blood to the body past the motionless heart."

The machine began its work, closely monitored by the pump technicians. The patient's blood drained out through the tubing and into the machine, where it was oxygenated, then passed back through the tubing into the body. A machine now performed for the patient the functions her own heart and lungs had seen to for thirty-four years. Her heart now lay still and motionless; to the untutored eye it would appear to be dead. It was 10:15.

Martin Lassiter entered the operating room, followed by Viola Phinney. Seales stepped aside; Irwin took the bowl in which the cleansed vein lay from a sterile compartment and prepared to hand it over. Things moved rapidly once Lassiter was on the scene.

He nodded to the visiting doctor and approached the table. The wire-rimmed glasses he always wore in the OR magnified his eyes. For perhaps five seconds those cool, pale eyes surveyed the stilled heart on the table, and then he spoke into the silence.

"Okay," said Dr. Lassiter.

Plucking the tiny vein from its sterile bowl he snipped a section off. Working with deft, unfaltering fingers, he began the impossible. One end of the vein was to be sewed into the aorta, the other into the buried coronary artery. The vein was approximately one twenty-fifth of an inch across. The infinitesimal stitches, twelve, now thirteen, might be as many as twenty before he was through.

"Fantastic," breathed the English surgeon.

"Some would call it tedious," said Lassiter, who had overheard. "They're the ones who can't do it. I'm giving this patient a brand new heart, and it'll be a damn sight better than the one she was born with."

He completed the first bypass in twenty-five minutes. His record was eighteen. He began the second, in the left coronary artery, without a pause. "Yes," he murmured, pleased, "this is going to be just . . . *fine*." He slipped one hand under the motionless heart and held it up for a moment, as if to congratulate it, and then returned to the miraculous sewing. At the end of another half-hour he had completed the task. "Outstanding," he said. "Who's next, Vi?"

"The VSD, doctor."

"Okay, take her off the pump," said Dr. Lassiter.

The patient was removed from the heart-lung machine. Viola Phinney stood by with the paddles in case the returning heart fibrillated and needed to be shocked back into a regular rhythm. There was a strained moment when the heart still seemed to be motionless, but then it began to beat strongly and normally. There were no erratic rhythms. The operation was a success.

Lassiter watched the new heart he had created for a few moments, nodded briskly to himself, and left for his next operation.

"Incredible," said the English urologist.

"Yes," sighed Dr. Seales. Then he and Dr. Irwin prepared to sew the patient up. The urologist declined to remain for such a routine sight, having seen what he'd come for.

The retractors were removed, leaving a gaping, elliptical wound. There had been very little blood loss. By the time they had sewed the patient up it was twelve o'clock. Unconscious, she was taken to the Recovery Intensive Care Unit where the many life-sustaining devices she had dreaded were installed in her body. Despite the massive trauma her body had sustained, its vital signs were strong.

As Lassiter himself might have said, if he were given to any trace of humble doubt: So far, so good.

He didn't know which of the recovery ICU's she'd be taken to. Although he had a fairly free run of the hospital, certain areas were forbidden to him. He was not supposed to enter any of the intensive care units unless he was escorting a patient's kin. He couldn't pop into the OR's at will, obviously, and there was no way to track Lassiter down without doing so. Lassiter's entire morning was spent going from one OR to another.

Aimlessly, he shuttled about the hospital all morning. He rode the elevators to the surgical floor in the hopes of catching Phinney or Seales going to rescrub. The important thing was to keep moving, not to sit down like the mournful relatives in the surgical waiting rooms.

He went up to twelve to visit Señora Perez, who was in a

convalescent room now. The floor nurse, a hardy girl who rarely seemed to worry about anything, approached him with an anxious frown. "I wish you'd talk to Mrs. Perez, Mr. Morrissy. I got Juanita to warn her, you know, in Spanish, but she won't listen."

"What's wrong?"

"She won't *cough*. You know how important it is, and she just won't do it. She's real stubborn, poor old lady. Juanita told her she'd be in trouble if she didn't start coughing."

Mrs. Perez was lying in her bed looking at images on the TV screen. The sound had been turned off. Her breathing was audible, bubbly. If she didn't cough voluntarily, the fluid in her lungs would have to be suctioned out. He understood her reluctance. The pain of coughing when her chest had so recently been cracked open would be considerable, but he didn't think it was fear of the pain that inhibited her. It was fear of something else.

One of his first patients had explained this special fear to Stephen. He was afraid, he said, that the stitches would open and he would fall apart. No matter how often he was told he was sewed as tightly as the proverbial drum, he never lost the feeling that his poor, assaulted body might crack open. When he coughed, he cupped his chest, as if to catch the heart as it tumbled out.

Mrs. Perez turned her head on the pillow and watched him with impassive eyes.

"Señora," he said gently, "it is very important for you to cough." A flicker of distrust, contempt, appeared in the depths of those black eyes. She had heard it all from Juanita; she wasn't interested.

"You have had eight children in your life," said Stephen, obeying a sudden inspiration. "You must remember there were times when you had to push, even if it felt that you'd explode? Of course, I don't know. I can only imagine. But it had to be done. The coughing is like that. You won't explode, or open your stitches. It may hurt, but it won't harm you—it will help you to recover more quickly. *It has to be done, like the pushing.*"

He had captured her interest. She made a noise that seemed to be speech, harsh and low. Her voice was that of an aged grackle. He bent lower to hear her. "What does a man know?" she said. Her eyes glittered now; he had succeeded only in infusing her with anger. He thought of Rafaella being forced to cough a week from now. If she lived.

But Mrs. Perez was full of surprises. To his gratified amazement, she sat up, grasped the dinner tray next to her bed, and made a mewing sound. It grew in volume, escalating to a series of hiccuping noises; then her frail body heaved and a tortured, racking cough emerged. She repeated the process until she had brought up some fluid and lay back on her pillows, exhausted.

In his emotional state, he felt close to tears at this unexpected success. He patted her clawlike hand and made her promise to keep it up. He told her he would send her a dozen roses. The glimmer in her eyes became one of amusement.

Nearly eleven-thirty. He rode down to the surgical floor again. No one was in the corridors. The operating room which had swallowed Rafaella up was still in use. As he stared at the doors they opened and someone emerged, a man he had never seen before. The stranger removed his sterile mask and cap and proceeded down the hall toward Stephen.

He felt his heart lurch violently. The stranger's expression revealed nothing. He seemed to be lost in his own thoughts. Stephen blocked the man's path, feeling sick and nearly brutish.

"*What?*" he said. His voice was hoarse, aggressive. "What's happening in there?"

The stranger halted and looked up in polite surprise. "It's amazing," he said in a cultured English accent. "I've never seen that procedure before; the man is simply amazing."

"The patient? How is the patient?"

"Dr. Lassiter seemed most satisfied. It's all over, except for the suturing. It went splendidly."

"Thank you," said Stephen. "Thank you very much." He leaned against the wall, dizzy with relief. The stranger gave him a look of mild bewilderment and then continued on his way.

Chapter 4

The call to Genoa went through without a hitch. Jackie was used to waiting for long periods of time while the indolent Italian phone system attempted, by trial and error, to connect her, but this time the *prego* at the other end was immediate.

"I would like to speak to Signorina Anna-Laura Leone," she said. "This is Jacqueline Talbot at St. Matthew's Hospital in Houston."

"Yes, speaking," the voice cried urgently. In the background Jackie heard the voice of a child.

"Your sister-in-law's surgery went very well," she said. "She is still unconscious, of course, but the doctor says she'll be fine."

There was a silence. Not even the voice of the child could be heard. For a moment Jackie thought the connection had been broken, but then she heard the unmistakable sounds of soft weeping.

"I thought I'd better call now, because of the time difference," she said gently. "It's four in the afternoon here. She'll be awake in three hours, and I'll see her then. She won't be alone."

"Thank you," said the voice, trying to regain control. "Thank you. Thank God."

Before she hung up, Jackie heard the voices of two children break into a cheer. She knew those children. Their faces were indelibly engraved in her mind.

Another face she couldn't forget was that of Giovanni

Catrine, the AV commune patient she had admitted that morning. She had been prepared for him to be young, since he was traveling with his mother. She had also been prepared for him to look terrible. When the woman entered Admissions carrying what appeared to be an infant, Jackie hadn't made the connection. Not until she heard the Italian voice at the desk, the name repeated over and over, did she understand.

Giovanni was two years old, and he was the sickest human creature she had ever seen. Emaciated, his arms and legs like those she had seen in pictures from famine-stricken India or Africa, the child seemed incapable of sustaining life for another hour. He had nearly died on the plane. His mother was clearly hoping for a miracle.

The Catrines had been assigned a cardiologist named Parker, a man Jackie had never worked with before. Dr. Parker was older than Fred Blanchard by twenty years. He had a seamed, weary face that called to mind a basset hound. With infinite gentleness he had examined the skeletal child after the medical history was taken. He had advised Jackie to tell Mrs. Catrine that Giovanni could never withstand surgery in his present state. It was his opinion that Giovanni should be kept under observation for several days. He wanted, he said, to try a new medication. The mother nodded, passive. She would do anything, she said, to make her son well. An odd expression crossed Dr. Parker's face, and Jackie intuitively knew what it meant. It was the expression of a man confronting a hopeless case.

In the corridor she had looked at him questioningly. Dr. Parker merely lowered his eyes and shook his head.

She knew that Lassiter had operated on other AV communes successfully. Perhaps it could happen again. But for the first time she had witnessed a doctor reluctantly delivering the death sentence.

She had a brief but intense vision of the Leone children in Genoa, cheering because their mama had come through successfully, while here in Houston a Calabrian woman had traveled all these miles to have her baby die in a strange country. The vision vanished and she shook herself. It was too early to condemn Giovanni to death, just as it was too early to assume that all would be well with Rafaella Leone.

"Promise me you won't see me in the intensive care."

She had meant it too. He remembered the urgency in her voice. He had promised, but it was a promise made to be broken. She was still mercifully asleep and would be for three more hours. Jackie would go to her then, at seven, but Lassiter had given permission for Stephen to see her now.

He stood looking down at what had once been Rafaella. It was impossible to think of her as alive or human now. He knew that would change, but the shock of it was intolerable. He had been in the recovery room dozens of times, but always his concern, which was genuine enough, had been tempered by the impersonality of it. He understood now why Mrs. Reyes had promptly fainted, why some of the relatives shouted, retched, or burst into incredulous tears. At the door to the OR they took leave of people they loved, seeing them as groggy, sick, frightened human beings. They were still recognizable. Their next glimpse showed them a seeming cadaver whose every inch of human topography had been altered and violated.

No part of Rafaella remained that had not been invaded by tubes and wires and catheters. Her face was distorted by the breathing tube. Her flesh, where it wasn't painted orange, was the dull, grayish color of soiled hotel sheets. Her hands were tied down; elastic stockings to prevent blood clots from forming encased her legs. Only the regular bleeps from the equipment monitoring her vital signs assured him that she was still alive.

He forced himself to take in every aspect of her pathetic, altered form. He needed to do this for several reasons. He wanted to see with his own eyes that she had survived—at first he hadn't believed the woman was Rafaella. The other reason was less rational. He thought that if she had to suffer all this, the least he could do was force himself to look at her.

He tried to imagine the pain she would soon be feeling. Purposely, he recalled the most harrowing descriptions some of his patients had given him, but—just as no amount of time spent in ICU's could prepare him for this time—no secondhand description of pain could make him feel it.

"Please help her," he said. "Please make it not so bad." He didn't know to whom he addressed this plea, only that it was necessary.

He stayed, hands clenched in his pockets, knees locked to keep his legs from shaking, until they evicted him from the room.

The house where he had been born no longer existed. Where the Morrissys had lived until Stephen was ten was now a bleak field choked with weeds and refuse. It had been a quiet neighborhood, mostly respectable blue-collar families and the occasional company man, like Stephen's father, who had never risen very high in the ranks.

Near the primary school he had attended were the beginnings of a slum; the school itself appeared to have become derelict. The windows were boarded up or haphazardly broken. Someone had spray-painted an enormous arrow on the brick. The writing beneath was too small for him to see. He followed the direction of the arrow, driving aimlessly.

The deterioration of his childhood neighborhood did not depress him. He had no roots here. If his roots were anywhere (which he doubted), they would have to be in the Midwest, where the Morrissy family had gone when Stephen's father was fired. Why the Midwest? At ten, he had found himself suddenly living in a small Wisconsin town where the entire population was scarcely bigger than the fifth and sixth grades in Stephen's Houston school. It had been years before he had understood the reasons for the move. His mother's brother, a moderately prosperous retail lumber dealer, had offered Mr. Morrissy a job. Stephen's father went to work selling pine paneling and custom millwork, and the family was saved from bankruptcy.

None of it had bothered Stephen. At ten, he was uninterested in adult problems, which were of a very dull variety. He was waiting to grow up and manufacture a life for himself in which the problems would be major and thrilling. He never doubted his ability to achieve that goal, although he wasn't sure of how to go about it. When his sister Anne, two years younger, asked him what he wanted to be when he grew up, he replied that he thought he'd like to be an explorer. She was a placid girl who expected little from life. "Oh, I don't think you can do that, Stephen," she'd said, as if he had proposed a life of crime. It was exactly what their mother would have said.

He found himself passing a stretch of run-down houses that looked familiar, but when he scrutinized them carefully he found they were much too modern to have any connection to him. Ghosts. He headed away from his old neighborhood, since the misleading arrow had taken him nowhere, and toward River Oaks. It was his plan to drive the afternoon away, drive until seven o'clock when Rafaella would be awake.

Ghosts. The town in Wisconsin was a ghost town now, but not in the old, conventional way. It had become part of a small megalopolis—four towns overspreading their borders until they melted together to form a featureless community, a land of shopping malls and fast-food restaurants. The last time he'd been back, it was still possible to discern the skeleton of the old town beneath the new, but even the skeleton would be gone now, buried beneath Holiday Inns and K-Marts. The Morrissy family was scattered now, some blown away to other parts of America, one literally blown away, one conventionally dead.

His meek father had politely died ten years ago, bothering no one, of an infection of the kidneys. Anne lived in Chicago with her husband and children. Mrs. Morrissy passed her retirement years in a condominium Stephen had purchased for her near Pompano Beach, Florida. Leo, his baby brother, had been killed in Vietnam. He had survived eighteen uneventful years in Wisconsin, years in which he had tried to liven things up by driving too fast under the influence of applejack, only to die at twenty in a village whose name his parents were never able to pronounce.

Leo had had no luck. Luck was something Stephen had never thought much about. As he passed Eugenia Fowler's house, mechanically noting the presence of three Chicano gardeners on her sculptured lawn, he felt an uncharacteristic jolt of spiteful resentment. Why was foolish, self-centered Eugenia safe and Rafaella in such danger? Why Rafaella? Fate had seen fit to kill her husband off in a grotesque accident and to wish on her a defective heart. Unlike Leo, she hadn't even gone looking for trouble. It had sought her out.

He drove down the same street where, two days earlier, he had provided the names of the trees for her in English. What had he felt, then, his elusive Italian Widow safely imprisoned in his car? Pleasure, bewilderment, the beginnings of a sense of conquest . . . all these, and a peculiar elation at having captured her at last. He had not kissed her or made any overtures to her the night at the restaurant, although he'd wanted to. He had sensed, in her reserve, a warning. She might be the last woman in the world who would think it improper.

Driving the car through River Oaks, he had felt the barriers were down. He attributed her agitation, her sudden swings in mood, to a single source—himself. With unshakeable male vanity, he assumed the lady had decided to abandon virtue and come to bed with him, which was what they both wanted. And yet, even at that late date, he wondered why he was bothering. She was going back to Italy; probably they would never meet again. He was years past the stage of wanting to conquer a woman to prove to himself he could do it; it was too easy. He told himself he wanted to know her and wondered what that meant. In the end, he had left it to chance.

It shamed him to remember the casual egotism of his musings on Rafaella. While he had been pondering his chances, she had looked out at the Spanish moss and magnolia trees and wondered if she'd live through the next week. If he had known, if he had known.

She was still a mystery to him. At each stage of their brief relationship he had been blocked by his ignorance. After their lovemaking, just as he was beginning to put a name to his feelings, she had unloosed her thunderbolt and driven him to his knees in terror. For a moment he had seen her as the embodiment of evil—a sort of angel of death who had tried to make him her murderer. That had quickly given way to an agonized pity, a tenderness such as he had never felt before.

Where, in all this, could he recover the feeling he had been allowed to enjoy so briefly? It was buried forever now in what had come after; he wondered if he had imagined it after all.

Two more hours until she'd be awake. He passed Lassiter's house and saw three cars drawn up on the long drive. Lassiter's wife was probably playing bridge. Enough of River Oaks; he'd head for downtown Houston. He was only sure of one thing. He was not the same man he had been twenty-four hours ago. What sort of man he was remained to be seen.

Chapter 5

There was some mistake. A ghastly mistake. The anesthetic hadn't worked—she was on the table, her chest cracked open, awake. She tried to tell them, but she couldn't speak. Someone had planted a tree inside her and it was growing out through her mouth. The tree was strangling her, and she couldn't pull it out because they'd taken her arms away.

"Try to relax. Breathe through the tube. Relax."

A very loud voice somewhere close was telling her to breathe, as if she could. A woman's head hovered near, directly over her, but she did not connect the head to the voice. Now the lips were moving. They were telling her that she must not fight the breathing tube. The tree. Yes, she could breathe through the tree if she concentrated very hard. Better. She seemed to be in a train station where many people rushed about frantically. She heard the voice on the public address system announcing which trains were leaving, but she couldn't understand it. It didn't matter. She'd had some sort of accident, she was waiting to be put in an ambulance. She didn't need to catch any of the trains. She would go back to sleep.

Anesthetic hadn't worked! What did those words mean, the ones she had wakened to? They had some important meaning, but every time she was about to grasp it, the announcements for the trains blared out and it was gone. The head was near again, and another head. They were pulling at her somewhere, doing—what? Why didn't they leave her alone? Surely she was entitled to some privacy until the ambulance came.

Choking again. Remember to breathe through the tube, the tree. The lights were bright, too bright. She closed her eyes, but light seemed to penetrate anyway. She knew that pain was somewhere quite close. It was there even now, waiting to make itself felt.

A new head bobbed over her. She knew the head, the eyebrows. It was Mr. Benedetti, who taught chemistry in school. Owly eyebrows. They quirked when he smiled or frowned, either one. She and Gina had laughed often about Mr. Benedetti's eyebrows.

"Mrs. Leone." His voice was soft, not the voice announcing trains. "Mrs. Leone. You're fine, you're going to be fine. Just breathe regularly, relax. We'll have the tube out as soon as you're fully awake." What did this mean? He was consulting something above her head. She was tired, so tired. Why didn't they let you sleep in these train stations . . . ?

How long slept? Choking. Breathe. Relax. He was there again. Not Mr. Benedetti. Dr. Blanchard. Her bladder was full, she was afraid she would wet the bed. She wanted to ask him to let her go to the bathroom before they took her to surgery, but she couldn't speak. What a disgrace to empty her bladder on the operating table!

"Mrs. Leone, you're going to be fine. It's all over, dear. Just breathe, relax."

Another voice, a woman's voice, repeated what he had said in Italian. It was an angel with long, golden hair who leaned over her. A Roman accent. "Rafaella," the angel said. "Dr. Blanchard will ask you some questions. If you want to say yes, press his hand, just a little."

Jacqueline! Her name was Jacqueline. In her sudden rush of memory she tried to speak. No, no they scolded. Just press. A warm hand slid into hers, into her own hand, which she couldn't see. First English, then Italian. Was she in much discomfort? No—but how to say she felt it nearby? Did she understand about breathing through the tube? Press. Did her bladder feel full? Press, press again. Jacqueline told her it was an illusion; a catheter was draining her even as they spoke, she must not worry. The operation was all over said Jacqueline. Rafaella was fine. It was now nearly seven in the evening. Did she understand? Press.

They went away. It could have been a few minutes later when they came back, or it might have been an hour. There was no way to tell.

"Rafaella. I called your family earlier and told them. I thought you'd want to know. I heard your children cheering for joy."

Had she really said that?

And later: "Rafaella. Stephen Morrissy is in the waiting room. Do you want to see him? Two minutes is all that's allowed." She felt Jacqueline's hand slide into hers and wait for the answering pressure. *No. No.*

Finally Jacqueline went away, but Dr. Blanchard remained. He swam in and out of her sight like a great cruising fish in the watery, fluorescent light. She began to recognize other faces, too. One of the nurses who came to poke at her had wide gray eyes, another was black and had eyes several shades lighter than her skin. It was easy to get to know them because they appeared every other minute, never leaving her in peace. All around her she could feel them rushing, moving the very air in their haste. When would it be night at last?

"When was the last time you slept?"

Stephen shrugged. "It doesn't matter," he said.

"You look terrible. There's nothing you can do now, and she's going to be fine. Go get some sleep."

Jackie watched him walk off, wondering why he had been so specific in his instructions to her. "She may not want to see me," he'd said. "Make it very clear I won't come in if she doesn't want me to." She certainly hadn't wanted it. The look of alarm in her eyes was so wild Jackie had thought she was choking again, but then the hand beneath her own dropped away, as if it feared any contact would be mistaken for a yes. It was amazing how someone so incapacitated could communicate such a powerful negative reply.

All of Jackie's energy had been drained in her concern for Rafaella; she felt depleted. She would have to recharge, somehow, before she went over to the children's wing. She went down to the cafeteria and bought a container of tea.

Carrying it to the volunteers' lounge, she nearly collided with a group of berobed men who came surging around the corner, burnooses flapping, as if plotting a desert raid. Probably another sheikh was being admitted.

She had the lounge to herself and collapsed gratefully in one of the chairs. How did the doctors do it? If she, on her humble level, experienced such psychic exhaustion in ministering to sick people—how did the surgeons who cut them open and rearranged their very organs manage to carry on day after day? How could they go home and attend cocktail parties or horseshows, or make love to their wives, knowing what they did? The men who took the hospital home with them didn't last. It was necessary to keep their professional lives in separate compartments. They weren't callous; they had to survive. She knew about it firsthand because she was a doctor's daughter. Still, even the best of them had crushing doubts now and then—moments when they felt impotent and let grief intrude.

She'd been five years old when she first saw it happen. Sitting in the volunteers' lounge, sipping strong tea and dreading another encounter with Giovanni and his mother, she allowed herself to remember a day in early autumn twenty-two years ago.

Jackie was practicing a song she'd learned in kindergarten, whooping the chorus in her loudest voice. She was imagining how it would be on Parents' Day, singing to the thrilling accompaniment of the piano, standing in a ruffled dress on the wide-board stage.

Mother advanced on her, frowning. Mother told her she must be quiet when Daddy came home. Daddy had had a difficult day, and Jackie would have to have dinner in the kitchen with Willa, the cook.

Well, but *why?* She knew that Daddy was a brain surgeon. He worked at the hospital, wearing a starched white coat. His name was in the paper quite often. What could happen to make his day difficult?

"Daddy lost a patient, honey."

Where could he have lost a patient? The hospital was very large, but surely her father was clever enough to find a patient, no matter where he hid.

She woke up in the middle of the night; she didn't know why. No bad dream—just woke up. She went to stand at her window and see how the moonlight made patterns on the pin oak trees, and there was her father, right below her, swimming in the pool. He was swimming furiously, back and forth, as if something was after him. She watched, fascinated and a little afraid. She knew it was very late. Mother was probably asleep and didn't know Daddy was swimming in the pool.

After a while he climbed out and put on his blue terrycloth robe. He sat on one of the pool chairs, quite still, and looked out at the garden. He seemed to be carved out of stone; he never moved. Jackie fell asleep, right there, kneeling at her window. She woke up near dawn and looked for him, but he had disappeared. It had been a mystery. Several years later she had understood, of course, but she never did tell him she had seen him that night.

Jackie rose, crumpled her paper cup, and dropped it in the basket. In the ladies' room she ran a comb through her hair and applied fresh lipstick. Her face glowed back at her, tanned and radiant, belying her exhaustion. She had second thoughts and wiped the lipstick off as best she could. Her face would be an affront to Mrs. Catrine—a vicious reminder of just how random and indifferent life could be.

Giovanni was propped up in his bed, sleeping in a sitting position. He could not lie flat or the fluid in his lungs would drown him. Even now his breath rasped and bubbled with the edema; the sound of it filled the room. Merely to cling to life was such an effort that the child had never learned to speak.

His mother was lying on a couch which had been brought in for her. When Jackie entered she shot upright, a look of terror in her eyes. Each time someone came into Giovanni's room, Mrs. Catrine was prepared for the worst. Jackie sat beside her on the couch and asked what she could do.

"Will you post these letters for me?" Her voice was a whisper. She handed Jackie two pale blue airgrams, her hands trembling. She had a broad, peasant face and hair as black as a crow's wing. Her teeth were strong and very white. Jackie realized with a pang that Giovanni's mother, beneath the haggard, prematurely aged look her son's illness had given her, was a pretty woman. She was twenty-eight years old. Jackie imagined her, before the birth of her pathetic son, as an archetypal earth mother, broad and buxom, womb fertile enough to populate a whole village in Calabria.

"Can't I do something else? Would you like anything special to eat?"

Mrs. Catrine ignored the question. "Do you have children?" she asked intently.

"No."

"The doctor, Parker, does he have children?"

"I imagine so."

Mrs. Catrine grasped Jackie's hand in her own, squeezing painfully, as if to force truth from her. "You ask him," she whispered. "You ask him what he would do if it was *his* baby. I want to know. You ask him."

Jackie agreed, and they sat together in the dark, waiting for Parker, listening to the tortured breathing that filled the room. Even upright, Giovanni seemed to be slowly drowning.

Now that the tube was gone there was a new problem. Awful as it had been, the effort of remembering to breathe through it had occupied much time. Now she had an oxygen mask; her hands were free. With great effort she could turn her head and see the others. Only a few feet away lay a man whose chest was painted orange. He groaned fitfully now and then. Once, for no reason she could see, he shouted *"God damn it!"* This had brought the nurses running, but by the time they got to him, in seconds, he seemed to be asleep again.

He was infinitely more acceptable than the person on her other side, who had been dead for some time. When would they take him away? She didn't want to lie next to a corpse; if they left him much longer he might become a skeleton.

On the opposite wall, above her head, was a clock. It stood at just past ten, but what did this mean? Surely it must be morning now, but in this place where it was always bright there was no way to tell.

Blanchard had gone away and there was another doctor

peering at her every few minutes. He seemed to be an Indian. The next time he came over she would ask him politely to take the corpse away. She closed her eyes. She was lying on a beach. She could hear the sea, a long way off, receding over the shingle, surging back, murmuring. The cries of children playing in the waves came to her distinctly over the sea sounds. Carlo and Stefania were safe—Anna-Laura was watching them. The sun was hot, she mustn't lie here too long or she would burn. What was that? A wet cloth touched her lips and she sucked thirstily. The sun had dried her lips terribly already. She should turn over now, call the children, and prepare to go home, but she was too sleepy.

Danger! The sun was too fierce now; she was definitely burning. It touched her chest like a branding iron. Oh, she had stayed too long. Her chest was burned through, irradiated. *Help!* She was burning alive. There was a pricking sensation in her arm. She opened her eyes. The nurse with chocolate skin. A needle. Her burn was too severe to ask the nurse to help her; she was afraid to speak.

Better. Here came the doctor. She called to him and he bent down to her. She must remember to be discreet. It would be terrible if the others overheard what she had to say; perhaps they hadn't noticed yet. She told him, whispering, but he seemed confused.

"Does this patient speak English? The card says she speaks English."

She reordered her thoughts, assembled her English words like so many toy soldiers, but they came reluctantly. Again he bent down to hear her.

"That man, he is dead for a long time," she whispered. "Nobody notices. Please take him away now, he is dead."

The Indian doctor touched her hair, briefly, with kind fingers. He shook his head no. "You are confused," he said. "That man is alive. He is only sleeping."

Then he turned away and gave an order to one of the nurses. Rafaella tried to hear what it was, but she was suddenly very sleepy too. She hoped he hadn't lied to her.

Chapter 6

In Fred Blanchard's cubbyhole of an office there was a small, hand-lettered sign which read:

Surgeons go home with the setting sun,
But guess whose work is never done?

At eight-thirty in the morning he was back at the hospital, although he hadn't left until past ten the night before. Stephen thought Blanchard looked more tired than usual. Despite the fresh lab coat and fragrant aroma of aftershave, he seemed faintly seedy.

"Good morning, Morrissy," he said brightly. "Your friend is bearing up beautifully. I've just seen her. That *is* what you wanted to know, isn't it?"

"Partly."

"She alarmed Dr. Kumar for a moment last night. Seems she told him the man next to her was dead and ought to be taken away." Blanchard chuckled. "He said she seemed concerned because no one had noticed."

"Was she hallucinating?"

"No, let me explain," said Blanchard, voice patient. "A small proportion of postops will hallucinate in intensive care after they've been there for a long time. It's the unreal atmosphere of the place. Psychologically, it's not good for a patient to remain there more than three days. In Mrs. Leone's case, the disorientation was perfectly normal. She was stuffed full of drugs, groggy, still in a sort of physical state of shock from the trauma of surgery. Perfectly normal. I expect to have her out of Recovery and in one of the other ICU's today."

"What caused her heart condition?"

"It's difficult to determine absolutely. Her parents are both dead, so there's no help from that quarter. Her mother might have been taking some crazy drug during her pregnancy that damaged the fetal heart. That's one possibility. She had a sibling who died in infancy though, so unless the mama took the drug both times, we could assume a hereditary disposition. She could have acquired heart disease by an infection, streptococcus most commonly."

"What about rheumatic fever?"

"Ah, that's my theory. According to the medical history, Mrs. Leone never had rheumatic fever, but I believe she did, and it went undiagnosed."

"But wouldn't some doctor have noticed a heart murmur long before she grew up?"

"Not necessarily. Rheumatic fever's a sneaky disease. Difficult to diagnose. Fever, sort throat, joint pains, chorea, heart murmur—those are the usual symptoms. In any given case some of those symptoms can be missing or go undetected. Let's say Mrs. Leone, at eight, has sore legs and a little fever. Her mother takes her to the old family GP who assures mama it's a cold or growing pains. Her heart sounded perfectly normal through the scope even two days ago. No way to tell, no murmur. If she hadn't had a heart catheterization in Genoa, who'd be the wiser? She only went to the doctor because of unusual chest pain and shortness of breath. She was absolutely unaware of any damage to her pumping system."

"What would have happened if she hadn't had the warning pain?"

"Sooner or later, she would have. I'm just glad the pain was severe enough to send her to a cardiologist. In some cases like this, the patient ignores the pain until it becomes so severe it's too late. Occasionally an individual with the condition we're supposing will live to a good age, but generally they pop off in the prime of life. That is, if they don't die in childhood."

"Then the surgery was absolutely necessary."

Blanchard stared at him for a full half-minute before he replied. "Do you believe unnecessary surgery is performed in this hospital? Do you think I'd recommend surgery if I thought the condition could be controlled with medication alone?"

"Of course not. But I have read papers by cardiologists who think too much cutting is going on."

Blanchard put his feet up on his desk and lowered his tufted eyebrows. "The age-old war between the cardiologist and the cardiovascular surgeon still rages," he intoned. "The cardiologist believes all the surgeon's brains reside below his wrists. And the surgeon? He's sure the cardiologist is jealous, that's all. Not enough glory. The truth is that the cardiologist does all the sleuthing. We're the surgeons' watchdogs. Only if we feel there is *no other alternative*"—he tapped his pen smartly against the desk to emphasize the words—"do we advise the patient to go get cut."

"I hope you don't phrase it so bluntly," said Stephen, smiling. He hadn't smiled for so long it was a novel sensation. He did it again. "Don't come down hard on me, Fred," he said. "I wasn't implying what you think. I just had to make sure the surgery was needed, literally, to save her life."

"Steve, boy, she might have lived to be ninety without it. Might have. But if someone came around taking odds I'd lay ten to one against. And if they had a lottery to see who could come closest to her probable date of death, I'd estimate it at thirty-eight. Does that answer your question?"

"All too graphically."

"Of course you know doctors never talk like that. I didn't say it."

"Of course not."

"And now, if you don't mind, I have two caths scheduled."

"Guess whose work is never done," said Stephen. "Thanks, Fred."

The pain was still muffled behind drugs, but she could feel it coming closer again, like an unwanted guest who is about to tap at your door. Every time she coughed, as they urged her to do, it moved a step closer. Sometimes it advanced by leaps and bounds, scalding her, and then someone came to send it back down the path again.

It seemed the final, most horrible indignity that she should have to cough. What insanity ruled that someone whose chest had been cut open be forced to cough and stir that monster sleeping in her breast?

"God damn it!" The man next to her was yelling again. He seemed capable of only three words. On her other side an emaciated man coughed dutifully. Across from her she could see only feet. By the look of them, they were male. The clock said ten again, only this time it was morning. She knew because Dr. Blanchard had smiled and said "Good morning."

More than anything, she wanted someone to come and put her to sleep again. If only she could sleep until she was well enough to go to a real hospital room, she thought she could bear it.

She closed her eyes and saw, for no good reason, an old pensioner who shopped along the street where her studio was in Genoa. His legs had been crippled in an industrial accident, and he was forced to drag himself along, laboriously, using two sticks.

She followed him along the Via Vieri now, as slow as he. He went into the little *tabaccheria* on the corner, where he purchased a packet of cheap, strong-smelling cigarettes. Then on to Brandini's where he always bought the same pastry each day. Always precisely one *focaccia*, to be eaten later in his room. Next stop, the newspaper vendor. These humble errands took a long time, because of his snaillike progress on the two sticks. She always thought it was a good thing because the pensioner's days must hang heavy with nothing to do.

Once, returning from her studio, she saw Carlo dragging himself up the hallway of their flat toward his bedroom. For a moment—panic. She thought he had been hurt. Then she saw he was using two cue-sticks (they had come with a miniature billiard game) to propel himself tortuously along.

"What are you doing?" He explained, as if it were the most natural thing in the world, that he wanted to see how the old pensioner felt when he dragged himself up the Via Vieri each day. "And do you know now?" "No," said Carlo. "It doesn't work, Mama. I can't make my legs go dead. It's cheating if they aren't dead."

"Mrs. Leone."

It was a nurse with horn-rimmed glasses of the sort Maurizio wore. "Try to cough now, honey."

They meant to be kind, but they had to be so many places at once they were often abrupt. They reminded her of humming birds. Even now the bespectacled nurse was poised for flight, because she had no time to spare. Rafaella felt the liquid in her lungs seethe and bubble like boiling oil. She coughed.

"Good girl."

How much the children liked Maurizio! They brightened at the mere mention of his name. Partly this was because he brought them gifts and indulged their whims, never seeming to lose patience when Stefania told him one of her complicated stories for the third time. But there was another reason too. They liked him because he was a man, heir to all the power and privileges of the male race. When he entered the flat, a sense of security came with him. Nothing too bad could happen as long as Signor Guidi was their friend.

"Mama?" Stefania, looking sly. "Do you think Signor Guidi is handsome?"

"He is a fine-looking man, darling."

"Is he the richest man in Genoa?"

"Far from it. He is comfortable, because he has worked very hard."

"Poor Signor Guidi must be so lonely. How sad that his wife is dead. I'm sure he would like to be married again."

Carlo took a different attitude. He was equally fond of Maurizio, but in all his relations with him he seemed to suggest that he, Carlo, was his mother's chaperone. The premier man in mama's life. So long as Carlo approved of Signor Guidi's attentions to the Leones, all would be well.

But here Maurizio was, standing by her side, holding a

bouquet of carnations. "Aldo will be here soon," he said. "He is coming straight from the airport in Milan. These flowers are from him."

"Mrs. Leone."

"Please let me sleep. *Basta.* Let me sleep."

"You can have a visitor now for five minutes. Your volunteer is here."

"Stephen Morrissy is in the waiting room," said Jackie. "Would you like to see him?"

"No."

The sheikh who had come in during the night was installed in a corner suite with his entourage. Unlike his predecessor, this sheikh required more than a pacemaker adjustment. He had gone into acute cardiac failure while playing roulette at a London gambling club. From the coronary care unit in London he had made all the arrangements to fly to Houston, as soon as he was well enough, in his own jet. He had brought with him a brother, a son, his financial advisor, and a Kuwaiti cardiologist.

"Thank God," sighed Leila Coury, the Arabic-speaking volunteer.

Although she'd still have to take the sheikh's medical history and be present when he was briefed, the presence of the Kuwaiti cardiologist meant she would not be needed in the ICU.

Leila's adventures were famous in the volunteers' lounge. It fell to her lot to administer to some of the richest men in the world, and they showed their gratitude in ways that embarrassed her deeply. A Saudi prince had once ordered an Alfa-Romeo to be delivered to the hospital for her on his departure day; the last sheikh had sent her a diamond bracelet. Leila's husband did not approve of these gifts, which were duly returned.

"Couldn't you have kept the Alfa-Romeo?" Hans Wolder asked. "It isn't as personal as jewelry."

"You might have accepted the gifts and then turned the money over to the hospital auxiliary," Ernestine McGrath pointed out.

"I would have kept the bracelet and sold the car," said a young volunteer who worked in the gift shop.

"I think it's noble of Leila to be so principled," said Jackie Talbot. "Who wants to be obligated to a sheikh?"

"Be fair," said Leila. "Some of them are quite nice. The last one was a gentleman, even if he did wear those mirrored sunglasses all the time."

"And this one?"

"This one," said Leila, "has a *reputation*. He's the Casanova of Kuwait." She consulted her watch. "I'm off to the corner suite," she said. "It looks like a men's club up there."

The corner suites were the ultimate in luxury. Jackie had visited Eugenia Fowler's grandfather in one of them, and one of her patients, a Milanese industrialist, had occupied another. They were thickly carpeted, papered in striped silk, and gracefully furnished in French provincial. Each contained a glassed-in balcony and had a large adjoining room to accommodate relatives. Traditionally the cards on the doors of the suites were empty, since the hospital didn't wish to alert everyone to the presence of a celebrity, but when Jackie passed the sheikh's door later in the day she saw his name triumphantly affixed: Sheikh Ali Mahmoud el Badri. In the space where the patient's surgeon was listed was, of course, the name of Martin Lassiter.

Further up the corridor she could see a youngish man, probably the sheikh's son, pestering the prettiest of the floor nurses. As Jackie walked by, he switched his attentions to her, following her progress with hot, liquid eyes.

She loitered in front of the door where the station nurse had told her Dr. Parker might be found. She heard his deep voice rumbling inside. The name of the patient was F. G. Monroe. Whoever he was, he was laughing. One of the lucky ones, about to go home. When Dr. Parker came out, Jackie pounced on him.

"I'm sorry, doctor, but if I could talk to you—just for a few minutes?"

Parker nodded but didn't stop. Trotting beside him, Jackie explained her difficulties with Mrs. Catrine. The woman wouldn't eat the food brought for her; she had scarcely slept. She seemed to be under the impression that Giovanni was to undergo surgery at any moment, and when the hours passed and nothing happened she became frantic.

"I've tried to explain that Giovanni is under observation for the time being, but she doesn't understand. It seems to her that you're all just observing him die."

"Yes," said Parker softly. "Poor woman." He apologized for hurrying along and obliging Jackie to follow him almost at a run. "I've got to go to the cath lab immediately," he said. Jackie got in the elevator with him, determined to make him see her point. "She knows I'm not a doctor. What can I tell her? She asked me what you would do if it were your baby."

Parker turned his sad, basset-hound eyes on her and said, "That's what they all want to know. I'll see Mrs. Catrine at three-thirty. Will that be convenient?"

"Yes," said Jackie. "Thank you."

He seemed about to say something else, but the doors opened at his floor and he bobbed out. He had covered twenty yards by the time the doors slid shut again.

The conference was held in the hall, just outside Giovanni's room. What Parker had to say was bleak, and even if the child couldn't understand the words, he would be able to interpret his mother's reaction. It was impossible to know how much Giovanni understood about the world around him, but he and his mother had been a world unto themselves for so long they reacted as one.

Jackie translated the sad words of Dr. Parker, feeling them fall on Mrs. Catrine like a series of blows.

"Giovanni is very sick. His is the most serious of all heart defects, as you know. It is my opinion that he could not survive surgery at the present time. I am trying medications, but I will not lie to you. No medication I can give him will correct his condition or make him better. If, in the next thirty-six hours, he is stronger, then Dr. Lassiter will present you with a choice. He will try to operate on Giovanni, if you agree. The choice is entirely yours. I know it isn't easy, and I sympathize with you. More than I can say."

"Is the operation dangerous? If he is well enough, and he has the surgery, what are his chances?"

"It is very high-risk surgery, Mrs. Catrine. You could lose him. I'm sorry."

"And if he doesn't have the surgery?"

"I am afraid you will lose him anyway."

Mrs. Catrine bit her lip hard enough to draw blood. She was struggling to keep the tears in her eyes from flowing freely down her cheeks. "Then," she said in a harsh voice, "I will wait until he is stronger and take him home. I would rather Giovanni die at home."

"It's up to you. If that's what you choose, no one will try to stop you." Parker patted the woman's shoulder awkwardly. "Miss Talbot tells me you asked what I would do if Giovanni were my baby."

She looked at him with narrowed eyes. Jackie thought they were the eyes of someone who realizes, for the first time, how futile such a question is.

"If he were mine," said Parker gently, "I would choose the surgery. It is his only chance. I have seen Dr. Lassiter mend an AV commune more than once."

"And you have seen him fail?"

Parker nodded.

Mrs. Catrine sobbed quietly, unable to control herself, but it was a very short period of release. She thanked Dr. Parker, scrubbed at her eyes with a tissue, and returned to the room where Giovanni suffered, ready to resume her painful vigil.

"I had a son who drowned," Parker blurted out. The words seemed to come from nowhere, startling Jackie. "I'm sorry," she said.

"It's a terrible thing," he said, "the worst thing that can happen, to have your child die. I don't think a person ever fully recovers from it."

Jackie nodded, stricken by this sudden intimacy from a man she barely knew.

"How much worse to know about it in advance," he said.

"How awful that must be." His voice, though mild, contained anger.

Early in the evening, Rafaella was removed from Recovery to a regular intensive care unit. With frantic disappointment, she saw that the ICU she would now call home was an even greater beehive of activity than the one she'd left.

Some of the patients were well on the way to convalescence. One man fed himself what appeared to be gelatin. Another carried on a loud conversation with his visiting wife. What had she expected? A less frantic atmosphere, more privacy, perhaps some blessed darkness.

With only a five-minute reprieve, she was back in the land of the midnight sun.

Chapter 7

She had been here so long that they had forgotten her. She would stay here forever because the charts had become confused. When they gave her shots, she was convinced it was to make her forget.

"What day is it?"

"Wednesday," said the nurse.

"How long have I been here?"

"Eighteen hours, dear."

She felt tears welling up. "Impossible!" she heard her voice emerge in a shout of outrage. "It has been much longer," she said. "Much, much, longer."

She was behaving badly, the one thing she had resolved not to do. All around her people were behaving badly. One man had kicked over his IV stand. Another had tried to rip the tubes from his side. At first she thought it was her old neighbor, the God-damn-it man, but it seemed everyone in intensive care behaved badly at some time.

"Try to be patient, Mrs. Leone. It's necessary for you to remain in this unit—" The nurse left in midsentence, being urgently needed at another bed.

They had said she would stay in one of the ICU's for forty-eight hours, hadn't they? What was eighteen from forty-eight? Thirty. Thirty more hours. *Calm yourself, signora. Follow the pensioner down the Via Vieri.* She heard someone remarking on the state of her blood pressure. It was up. She heard the word "upset." Someone came to give her a shot. "What is this?" she asked.

"Demerol."

Better. Soon she apologized to the nurse she'd shouted at, only to discover that it was a different nurse. She was glad the visiting periods were so short. One time a man had looked from the supine body he was visiting and studied her, thinking she didn't notice. He studied her objectively, calmly, she thought, and then turned back, satisfied. And there was nothing she could do.

"You must not stare at people, Rafaella. It is very rude. How would you like it if someone looked at you like *this*?" Her mother had mimicked Rafaella's fascinated, wide-eyed look and Rafaella, aged seven at the time, had seen her point. The man she had been staring at was a dwarf. He was buying grapes at the open-air market where she and mama shopped every other weekday. He wasn't much bigger than she was; both Rafaella and the dwarf had to stand on their toes to look over the fruit stalls—but while the proprietor never failed to give Rafaella an apple or pear, he treated the dwarf just like a grown-up. She hadn't meant to stare, but her eyes couldn't seem to look away. She wondered where the dwarf had come from, if he had moved into their street, how old he was. She wondered, also, if it hurt to have to walk as he did, lumping along as if he were the captain of a deep-sea boat. Like her son Carlo, who would not be born for seventeen more years, she had wondered what it would *feel* like to be so unfortunate.

When she and mama walked off, swinging the string bag full of zucchini, peppers, and melons between them, she asked what made a person be a dwarf. Could it happen to anyone? But Mama said what she often said when Rafaella asked difficult questions: "It is God's will."

Maria Francini, Rafaella's mother. She was older than other girls' mothers, but when she was happy she sang and clapped her hands and made silly jokes. Those were the two conflicting parts of her nature—the side that liked to be frivolous, and the side that resolved all troublesome anomalies with four words: "It is God's will." She had a long list of must-nots for her daughter. Rafaella must not speak rudely to anyone who was her elder; make noise when papa was reading his papers; play with the rascally boy down the street, who would surely grow up to be a criminal; walk back from school via the interesting alleyway where tinkers sometimes gathered; forget to say her prayers, do her homework, wash her ears, brush her hair one-hundred strokes.

Rafaella's father was a schoolteacher. He taught noisy, idle boys of ten—who weren't interested—the mysteries of mathematics. He was kind and loving, often taking her in his lap and feeding her sugared cashew nuts, but when he corrected the papers of his students he pulled at his hair and swore softly. "*Santa Maria!*" he would groan. Sometimes he said worse things, and then Rafaella's mother would look amused beneath her stern, compressed-lip look and say, "Marcello! The child."

Mama had died when Rafaella was fifteen. She hadn't been ill very long, and it was a surprise. It was so surprising that Rafaella hadn't cried at first, only felt numb. She pictured her mother saying "It is God's will," speaking to her from beyond the grave, and this comforted her. When she did cry, it was alone at night in her bed—a soft, aimless weeping that had as much to do with fright as it did with grief.

Later, at her father's funeral, she had Aldo to comfort her. Lying in his arms the night after her father was buried, she told her husband about the soft curses uttered over the mathematics papers. She imitated first her father and then her mother's response. It made her laugh and cry at the same time, and Aldo wrapped his arms around her and held her very gently. They could not make love, because Carlo had been born only three weeks earlier.

Surely the pain should be gone by now? It seemed more immediate, more searing, than on the night after she had given birth. It had spread upwards, was lodged far from her womb, in her breast.

"I think I'm losing the baby!" she called to a nurse who was close by. "Something is wrong."

Stephen remembered his promise to old Mrs. Reyes and sent her a dozen roses. It had been a long time since he had sent roses to anyone, and he was outraged at the price.

Even Julio Ramirez was recovering now, and Joe Gonzalez was caring for the new arrivals. He had nothing to distract his attention, nothing to keep his thoughts from what might be going on in Rafaella's head in intensive care. He took his bulletins from Jackie, accepting her assurances of Rafaella's progress dubiously. That Rafaella wouldn't see him was not surprising, but it doubled his feeling of help-lessness.

Distraction arrived on the third day of Rafaella's incar-ceration in the form of Ivan Bell. Stephen walked into the lobby of St. Matthew's and saw a familiar, bearded figure lounging there. Ivan was talking into a small portable tape recorder. When he saw Stephen he got to his feet and gave him a reproachful look.

"I've been waiting an hour," he said. "My plane got in at ten."

Stephen had forgotten all about Ivan's arrival. He, who never forgot anything, had forgotten that Ivan existed. They had made the arrangement ten days ago; he recalled it now. Ivan was flying back to New York from the Coast and thought he'd stop in Houston for what he called preliminary impressions. Eventually, he was to write the narration for Stephen's film.

The film, too, was something Stephen had forgotten.

Ivan shifted from one booted foot to another. He was wearing jeans and a workshirt, clean but faded. Stephen had worked with him on two films and had never seen Ivan dressed any other way. His reddish beard gleamed with health, his eyes were bright with purpose. He reminded Stephen of a good retrieving dog straining to go fetch the bird. He was a fine writer; Stephen liked him and worked easily with him, but his presence just now was an intrusion.

"I'm sorry I'm late," he said. "Do you want a tour of the hospital?"

"The thing is—I'm going back first thing in the morning. The next time I come I'll be staying for a week, but this is a quickie."

"It hardly seems worth your while, Ivan."

"Not true. I've been thinking about the project a lot and something's been bothering me. I don't even understand ex-actly what these guys do. I've read all about it, I've got the general idea, I even know the medical terms—but I can't visualize it. I thought, with any luck, you could get me in to watch one of the operations today."

"I'd need to get permission from Administrative. It's a little late in the morning now; they're usually through with surgery by noon."

Who's fault is the late hour? Ivan's eyes seemed to say. *What were you doing last night? Why so sluggish—losing your touch?* What he actually said was "Can we give it a try?"

Twenty minutes later Stephen was ascending the narrow staircase to the observation dome above OR 2, Ivan alertly at his heels.

Except for a party of three visiting medical students, they had the place to themselves. Sometimes the observation dome was strictly standing room only. Color TV monitors gave a clear picture of what was going on in case the personnel around the table grew so thick it obscured a view of the action below. Today the sound system was turned off. It was impossible to hear the Muzak or the conversation; no clanking of instruments or doctors' comments reached them here. The drama, which Stephen hadn't looked at yet, was performed in silence.

"Sebastian H. God," breathed Ivan, "what a sight!"

Stephen looked. The patient had been opened and the retractors put in place. They were hooking him up to the heart-lung machine. The heart itself was still beating, contracting bravely under the circumstances, for it was a gross heart, old and worn out and enlarged. Coronary artery disease had been at work in this heart for a long time. From what he could see of the patient's face, he might be in his seventies.

Ivan was withdrawing a notebook and jotting things down in the gloom. "Who would have thought it would have all those colors?" he whispered.

"The gray parts are ischemic. Dead muscle, where there's been an infarction. That part of the heart has died." He shifted his attention to the monitor. "See that thin, bulging bit? That's an aneurysm. Lassiter will have to patch it before he starts in on the revascularization. This man's in pretty bad shape."

Suddenly the heart stopped, became motionless, as the machine began its work. It seemed pitiful in all its ravaged unloveliness and far too damaged to ever serve its owner well again.

"That's Lassiter who just came in," said Stephen. "he's just posed for a Dewars Scotch ad."

"Cool-looking devil," said Ivan respectfully. "Looks like Lassiter walked to the table, considered the heart beneath him, nodded once, and plunged in. Stephen felt Ivan flinch —they all did, the first time they watched—when Lassiter's hands entered the cavity. Gradually, as Lassiter patched and sewed and rearranged, the atmosphere in the dome became one of reverence.

"God," said one of the medical students. "He's loose as a goose."

Dutifully, Stephen provided a running commentary for Ivan Bell. When the procedure had been completed and the patient removed from the machine, Ivan was rewarded with a moment of high drama. The heart fibrillated wildly, contracting in a crazed and dangerous rhythm. Lassiter applied the paddles, jolting the heart with electricity once, twice, again. Obediently, the heart returned to normal, continued to beat regularly, and the drama was over.

The anonymous man was removed from the machine, the retractors were withdrawn, and the process of suturing the gaping wound began.

"That was fantastic," said Ivan. "I think I've got it now. How about some lunch?"

She knew what the rattling sound meant. Had she heard it more than once? It seemed to her she'd known it all her life, although that was impossible. It came, like an angel of death, when one of her neighbors was in deep trouble. Angel of life, rather. They raced with it, urged it along. When someone was about to die they trundled the rattling cart along and shocked him back to life. Electricity, the god. The body

171

arched, relaxed. The heart came back from wherever it had gone. Who had invented electricity? She couldn't remember.

It was used to shock the brains of mental patients back to a state of tranquillity; it was used to torture political prisoners, too. Who could have dreamed it could be used to coax a heart back? Perhaps they were cleverly pretending to harness the electricity for humane purposes? Perhaps this was really a torture chamber?

She was sure one of her neighbors was dead. She had looked quite recently, discreetly to be sure, and discovered a new man to her right. Where had the other one gone? He was dead, dead. They had fed a million volts into his heart and killed him. They had shocked him to oblivion.

"I have pain," she said to the nurse. "I am having pain."

"Mrs. Leone," said the nurse, "try to be patient. You have a fever. We're working on it now."

How did you work on a fever? Did the nurse mean they were on the fever's side and against her?

"Where is that man?" she whispered. "Did he die?"

"Which man?"

"There." She nodded to her right. "He is gone."

"Why yes," said the nurse, smiling, "he's gone to his room."

"When will I go to my room?"

"Soon," said the nurse. "Soon."

What diabolical liars they were! The man who had lain next to her for so many months was dead, and she would lie here forever.

"I'll have the chicken-fried steak," said Ivan. "What the hell—when in Rome, right?"

"Sure," said Stephen. He had taken Ivan to lunch at a restaurant he liked on Sunset; tonight, for variety, they were dining at the staid old Confederate Inn.

"I don't know though. Must be a lot of cholesterol in chicken-fried steak." Ivan grimaced at the cigarette smoldering in his hand. "Seeing an operation like that makes you wonder. What if my heart's a mess and I don't know it?"

Stephen assured him everyone coming to St. Matthew's for the first time had similar thoughts.

"It's funny, I've never worried about my heart," said Ivan. "When I was writing my novel—the one that never got published—I used to sit all alone, late at night, and imagine I had every fatal disease in the book. I thought I had cancer, leukemia, liver trouble, bleeding ulcers—you name it, I had it. The one thing I never invented for myself was a heart attack. I guess I thought I was too young. If I'd known about all the stuff that can go wrong with your heart I'd have had a field day."

"I've given you something new to worry about. Glad to be of service."

"I was thirty-four when I wrote that novel, and a hell of a lot healthier than I am now. It was the solitude of writing; it made me morbid. Just me and my typewriter. The times when it wasn't going well I had all the leisure in the world to imagine I was dying."

A distinguished-looking black waiter appeared to take their order. He politely averted his eyes from Ivan, who had borrowed a jacket and tie from Stephen and wore them with his jeans and workshirt. The jacket was far too large.

Ivan ordered filet of sole and a green salad. Stephen ordered another martini and lit a third cigarette. "I notice you haven't become particularly health conscious, Morrissy. What's wrong with you? You're not yourself. Don't think I haven't been wondering."

"Nothing much is wrong with me," said Stephen. "I'm worried about a patient. You caught me at a bad time, Ivan."

"What patient? Tell old Ivan. It'll take my mind off the coronary artery disease I can feel growing in my body at this very moment."

"Are all writers hypochondriacs?"

"You see? You're doing it again. Macho filmmaker allows neurotic writer to bare his soul and gives nothing in return. You guys are the jocks of the arts. Strong, silent, inscrutable. My ex-wife—you remember Roberta, I trust?—used to say you were the kind of man who wasn't allowed to cry as a kid. 'They probably beat him with a strap if he cried' was what she said."

"Not true," said Stephen, laughing. "Nobody would have noticed. My old dad wouldn't have had the energy to beat anyone. But it was nice of Roberta to care."

"I didn't think it was nice. She showed more interest in your childhood than in mine. She wanted to name our golden retriever Morrissy. 'It looks like Stephen,' she said."

"Where is Roberta these days?"

"In LA. But don't look her up just because I clued you in to the tenderness you inspired in that womanly heart. I'm still very fond of Roberta. Sometimes I think of marrying her again. Do you ever think of Natalie?"

"Seldom."

"Natalie was . . . *difficult*," said Ivan judiciously. "But she sure was good-looking." The haughty waiter brought their dinner and they ate for a time in silence. "Would you mind telling me what this is, Morrissy?" Ivan indicated an object to the right of his sole.

"That is a peach half filled with a scoop of peanut butter. Texans like it."

"Sure they do. The emergency room is only a short drive away. Let's get back to the hearts. Can I assume the old guy we saw repumped today just bought another decade?"

"You can't assume anything. He could die in the next hour or the next two days. The normal stay after surgery is ten days. If he makes it through until then there's a good chance he'll get another ten years. Without the surgery he'd live for an indeterminate period, often in severe pain. That aneurysm could have blown at any time."

"But he's got new plumbing now. What could kill him?"

"Are you sure you want to discuss this over dinner?"

"Absolutely. I may be a hypochondriac, but I'm not squeamish." Ivan produced his tape recorder and placed it between them on the table.

"Some postops infarct in intensive care," said Stephen. "The heart just dies for its own mysterious reasons. Massive trauma, failure to adapt to the new blood circulations. There are six danger signals in the recovery period. Lung malfunction—again, failure to adapt. Heart block, if the surgeon has hit a bunch of nerves called the Bundle of His. Kidney malfunction; low urine output is the clue. Arhythmic beating of the heart, sometimes remedied by electric shock. Bleeding around the graft. Fatal drop in blood pressure caused by bleeding around the heart. It's called tamponade. When that occurs, they call Lassiter at home for emergency surgery. Otherwise he isn't disturbed unless somebody dies."

"That's thoughtful."

Stephen lit another cigarette and watched Ivan demolish what remained of the sole. The sources of Rafaella's fever had not been determined. Blanchard wasn't alarmed, but he wanted her to remain in the ICU until he could isolate the cause. He had been so offhand about the fever that Stephen had wanted to hurt him. Briefly, he had wanted terribly to drive his fist into Fred Blanchard's gut just to see the look of outrage and perplexity on that calm, owlish face. As quickly as the savage impulse had come upon him, it vanished. He had been unfair.

Blanchard was the best; he truly cared. It wasn't Blanchard's fault that the first death Stephen had heard of at St. Matthew's had begun with a fever in the ICU. It wasn't even Fred's case, nor was the man known to Stephen.

He was an oldish man from San Antonio, and he occupied the bed next to one of Stephen's first charges in the ICU. Stephen could hear him begging the nurse not to do it again. "Not again," he moaned. "Try something else." Unlike the others, he was wrapped in thermal blankets. The nurse explained, when Stephen asked, that the man had spiked a fever of close to 105. Medication hadn't succeeded in taming his earlier, less dangerous fever, and now he lay on a mattress through which cold water was pumped. He shivered and twitched and moaned, lying on his icy bed of torment, because the alternative was more dreadful still. The man's heart was severely diseased; fifty percent of it had been destroyed by earlier infarcts. The fever made his heart beat faster, and a heart in arrest could not afford such effort.

"He has low cardiac reserve," the kind, distraught nurse had instructed him. "The fever is putting too much demand on him."

"Morrissy," said Ivan, switching off his tape recorder. "Do you know what I think?"

"You think your heart is fibrillating."

"Sure, of course. But something else. You've become grim. You used to be an exuberant man. Maybe you ought to get married again."

"Some of the grimmest men I know are married."

"Seriously. You don't look too good, either. Why don't you take a few days off and fly up to Dallas? Or go to Galveston—anywhere. Get away from all those pathetic hearts for a while."

Pathetic hearts. The man from San Antonio lived through his icy nightmare in the ICU, only to die of pulmonary edema three days later. His had been an unusual case. Stephen knew it well; he had memorized the particulars of that poor heart's history as a beginning student might memorize the dates of battles and treaties from a textbook. There was no similarity to Rafaella's case, no real cause for alarm, but logic had small power to comfort him. Her fever frightened him.

Stephen tried to smile in the old, mechanical way to reassure Ivan, who seemed genuinely concerned for him. "Don't worry about me," he said. "It's just grist for the old mill."

Before they parted that night, Stephen gave the writer two cassette tapes of notes for the film. They punched each other lightly, awkwardly, on the arm. Ivan pantomimed having a coronary from the contact. After he'd left, Stephen went directly to the hospital. As he entered the lobby he felt the familiar atmosphere settle on him. Fear and anxiety replaced the semi-normal feelings inspired by dinner with an old friend, and he was back where he belonged.

Blanchard told him Rafaella's fever was down. He was about to go home, leaving her in the care of Kumar. "With any luck," he said, "we'll have her out tomorrow."

Luck chose to be unkind to the patient Stephen and Ivan had seen from the dome that morning. He infarcted twice in the recovery ICU and died just before dawn.

Chapter 8

Three white walls, one blue. Windows, sky beyond them. Daylight, true light. Silence. Bliss.

"Thank you," she whispered.

Jackie had even taken the photographs of her children out and placed them on the metal ledge, where she could see them. There were flowers there, too. Jackie brushed her hair, gently working the bristles through the matted mane, working on one strand at a time. Rafaella lay still, submitting to this kindness gratefully.

In her breast there raged a clawing beast or a dreadful fire—whatever could cause pain was there—but she thought she could bear it. She felt humble and exalted both, like Saint Bartolomeo, and she knew she could tolerate the pain because at last she would be free to combat it on her own terms. They had broken her, split her open, cut into her heart, tested her to the limits of her endurance, and she was still here. She had survived.

"How many died?" she asked. She was a general, concerned for her men. In her mind, not the clash of sabers but the clattering of the cart.

The hand wielding the brush paused. "Nobody died," said Jackie.

"Someone did. I know someone did." She tried to raise her hand, but she felt too weak. She saw the ugly bruises, black on the tender flesh of her inner arm. Her hand hurt. The comforting rhythm of the brushing resumed.

"Nobody died in the ICU where you were," said Jackie firmly. "You imagined it."

"But somewhere else?"

Jackie sighed. "Yes, early this morning. A man in his seventies."

"What was his name?" It seemed important that she know as much about the man as possible. "Where did he come from?"

"I don't know. Don't think about him, Rafaella. He was old and very sick. Concentrate on yourself. By tomorrow you'll be able to get up and walk a bit."

Jackie bathed her face and held the pillow to her chest while she coughed. The coughing was agony. It seemed she might split apart. She had a vision of the unseen sutures gaping open, ready to pop like a defective zipper. No matter how many nurses and doctors told her this could not happen, she never quite believed them.

She lay back, exhausted, making her battle plans. She would live from incident to incident. In a little while Jackie would help her to the bathroom, an adventure so arduous she couldn't imagine it. In an hour, when the children returned from school, she would hear their voices. In the meantime, there was coughing and pain and the attentions of the nurses who still came in and fussed at her. There were the small discomforts and the large ones. She tried to hold on to the victorious feeling which had claimed her at first, the elation at having survived, but it was going to be difficult.

"Such lovely flowers," she gasped. "*Peonia.* What are they called in English?"

"The same, peonies. I thought you'd like them." Jackie was considering her oddly, head cocked to one side. "Don't you want to see yourself in the mirror?" she asked. "Most people do."

"I am afraid."

"If you only knew how much better you look! Let me show you, Rafaella." Jackie foraged in her shoulder bag and extracted a gold compact. She came close, cupping the mirrored lid in her hand, and showed Rafaella to herself.

A white ghost looked back. Beneath the frightened eyes were shadows that matched the mauve peonies. There was a bruise of deeper mauve near her left nostril. Her lips were colorless and cracked a little. She was recognizably human, but that was all that could be said of her. And Jackie had said how much better she looked!

"You see," said Jackie triumphantly, "you're still there, honey. In a few days you'll be beautiful again."

"I was never beautiful," said Rafaella. "It doesn't matter what I look like, so long as I get better, does it?"

But Jackie grinned, as if to say she knew better, and picked up the brush again.

Jackie knew the pattern now. Occasionally a patient defied the pattern, but generally she could almost predict what would happen when they came out of intensive care and were put into private rooms.

Relief at having been released from the ICU made them euphoric for a time, but all too soon they became depressed. They were in constant pain which the drugs could not completely mask, and they were expected to begin the process of healing themselves. Machines and tubes had performed their functions for them; now they had to reenter life, at a time when they were weak and ravaged, all on their own. It was a painful process, and frightening.

Many of them believed they would never again be able to draw a free breath or walk normally—they couldn't see beyond the pain and anxiety of the postoperative period because they were so diminished. Gradually, as the days went by and they improved, they were drawn slowly back into the routines and preoccupations of everyday life.

Rafaella was in the depressed period, although she did not complain. Jackie saw it in the vacancy of her eyes, the listlessness of her movements. She did not—as a patient of Ernestine's once revealed—believe that a part of her soul had departed when her heart was opened, but she did think she had been changed unalterably.

"I will never be the same," she said once, as Jackie helped her back to the bed. She said it softly, speaking to herself, in Italian. When Jackie assured her she was wrong, Rafaella seemed astonished. She hadn't realized she'd spoken aloud.

When she talked to her children she was cheerful and sounded full of hope and vitality. Afterward, she often cried.

She had called them three times in the two days she'd been in the private room, as if to reassure herself that they remembered her.

More flowers stood on the metal shelf now. Added to Jackie's peonies were a large spray of mixed flowers from her family, an extravagant bouquet of roses from someone called Maurizio, and a pot of white violets from Stephen Morrissy.

Rafaella seemed to dread the thought of seeing Morrissy. She begged Jackie to send her excuses to him. She wasn't well enough, she said. In the middle of an examination she alarmed Blanchard by suddenly gasping. "Are you having pain?" he asked. But Rafaella merely shook her head. "I just remembered something," she said.

When Blanchard had gone, she drew Jackie close and whispered, in conspiratorial tones, "Something dreadful. When Mr. Morrissy brought me here, he checked me out of the hotel. I had paid in advance, but I forgot about the telephone calls." Her eyes were wide with fright; she might have been confessing a mortal sin. "Don't you see?" she whispered. "He must have paid for them, he never told me and I forgot, and they were calls to Italy, expensive calls—" Tears were in her eyes. Her color was the highest Jackie had ever seen it.

"It can't matter, Rafaella. Please, be calm. It's not important."

"Yes, yes, it's very important. Where is my purse? I must have my money now."

"Your valuables are all locked away, *cara*. You can pay him back later, can't you?"

Rafaella sank back against the pillows in despair. "How will I know how much is owed to him? He has the bill, you must find out. And then, please Jackie, unlock my money so I can pay him."

Jackie saw how agitated she was. She was breathing hard; it wasn't good for her. "Of course," she soothed. "I'll do that right away, Rafaella. Just be calm. As soon as I see him, I'll find out."

As she went in search of Stephen she realized that the reason for Rafaella's heightened color was simple to explain.

She was blushing. She had admitted that Stephen had settled her hotel bill, a fact that had immense significance to her.

The curiosity Jackie had felt at the beginning had mounted steadily, and no one was willing to satisfy it. Morrissy hung around like a banished lover and Rafaella—who had other things to worry about—blushed when discussing telephone bills.

"Miss Talbot." She turned to confront Dr. Parker who was pursuing her down the hall. "Can you be present in Mrs. Catrine's room at eight o'clock tonight?"

"Yes. Has something happened?"

Parker nodded. "Dr. Lassiter wants to come to a decision about Giovanni," he said.

What he meant was: Lassiter wants to operate and needs Mrs. Catrine's permission. Jackie felt a wave of stubbornness take hold of her. She wanted to tell him that she would not be present to play the voyeur at the scene of Mrs. Catrine's agonizing decision. She wanted to explain that she had hoped Giovanni would blessedly die in his sleep or miraculously recover enough to go home to Calabria and live the rest of his brief life there.

"I'll be there," she said.

Stephen was just leaving. She ran after him and caught him at the door.

"What is it?" His voice was harsh with alarm, his eyes narrowed against bad news. Poor Stephen, she'd frightened him.

"She's fine," she said hurriedly, repeating the litany he must be so tired of hearing. "There's a minor problem, Stephen, nothing medical."

Now he looked wary. She saw something else in his green eyes, too. A tentative pleasure. He thought she was going to say Rafaella wanted to see him. "It's about her telephone bill," said Jackie softly. "She's very upset because she owes you money."

"*Her telephone bill?*"

Jackie explained, emphasizing how important it was to Rafaella's well-being to settle her debt. Stephen ran a hand through his hair, shook his head disbelievingly, and gave a mirthless laugh.

"Christ, I don't have the bloody bill. I don't remember how much it was."

"Well, make up a figure then. I'm supposed to go get her money and pay you immediately."

"Is she going crazy up there, Jackie?"

"They all do, a little. Don't worry. In a few days she'll be much different."

"Tell the signora she owes me eighteen dollars."

"Do you have change for a twenty?" Jackie handed him a bill.

"What's that for?"

"Stephen—I've got to be able to say I put the money in your hand. She'll ask me, better believe it. She'll know if I'm lying."

"Can't I just hand it back to you in that case?"

"You can buy me lunch some day and tell me just what's going on."

Stephen shook his head again, passed Jackie two singles, and said, "You're all crazy."

Jackie understood that the "all" referred to women in general.

"Be patient, honey," she said.

He gave her a smile of dazzling irony and left the hospital without a backward look.

"You owed him eighteen dollars," said Jackie. "I paid him."

"You swear?"

"Yes, Rafaella. Cross my heart. I think you hurt his feelings."

"Don't say that. It isn't true."

"Come on, Rafaella, it's time to walk a little."

Slowly, shuffling like an old woman and clinging to Jackie's arm, she allowed herself to be guided out into the unknown world of the corridor. She blinked, as if she'd stepped outside on a particularly bright day, and looked away when another patient came creeping toward them. She seemed very small to Jackie, who towered above her in her high-heeled sandals. She glanced up once, a child seeking her mother's approval. Then she stared straight ahead again. Her face was white, locked in lines of such determination that she looked, in profile, like a woman setting off to commit murder.

Her hair was coiled up in the old style. Jackie had done it for her, fastening the knot with Rafaella's silver comb.

One good thing about being rich was that you always had a swimming pool. Jackie kicked off, feet against the dove-gray tile, and backstroked the length of the pool. At the opposite end she turned quickly and executed a rapid butterfly stroke back again. She alternated the two for a quarter of an hour, then floated quietly on her back, looking up at the stars.

Her parents were out. Except for Willa, the cook, the house was empty. Safe and sound in River Oaks, floating on her back in the turquoise, underlit water, her perfect, un-scarred body covered, barely, by a hundred-dollar bikini—what could be wrong in the world?

She got out, toweled herself, and poured a glass of wine. She wasn't going to think of them tonight, she was going to drink half a bottle of wine, relax, maybe play the piano for a while. Then a long, hot bath, a novel for escape until she was blissfully sleepy, and bed.

Except it didn't work that way. Mrs. Catrine's face came sharply into focus, as if she were tapping for admission to Jackie's garden. Rafaella also lurked in the wings of her consciousness. Mrs. Catrine was the more urgent.

She had accepted everything Lassiter said without a hint of emotion, unblinking, unmoving. Even when he told her he could offer her no assurances, only hope, she did not respond. Jackie thought she'd gone beyond grief now into an area of numb resignation. She had participated in the meeting only once; when Lassiter told her the decision was hers she lifted a hand wearily and nodded. It was as if she'd dismissed an orderly who'd been summoned to fetch a bed-pan. Lassiter had fulfilled his purpose and was no longer needed. It was the first time Jackie had ever seen the surgeon look uncertain.

Rafaella was another matter. She seemed deeply frightened now; when a spoon fell from her tray, clattering to the floor, she flinched and cried softly. She had taken to worrying about the man who'd died again.

"What was his name?" she had asked Blanchard. "Where did he come from? How old was he?"

Blanchard had turned a look of disapproval on Jackie. Volunteers were not supposed to discuss deaths with patients. "Why are you so concerned about him, Mrs. Leone?"

"I want to know. Is there a rule against it?"

"His name was Joseph Surtees. He was seventy-six years old, and he came from Chicago."

"Joseph Surtees."

"Do you feel better for knowing his name?"

"*Grazie.*"

When they were out of Rafaella's earshot, Jackie had asked Blanchard for an explanation. "Do you think she feels it was a trade-off? Mr. Surtees's life for hers?"

"I wouldn't go that far," said Blanchard. "Probably she imagined something in the ICU. Flying on drugs, hallucinating—we can't ever know what fragments are lodged in their minds after a long period there."

Jackie took her wineglass and padded over the tiles to the French doors of the music room. She switched on a light, bathing the room in the amber glow her father favored after long hours in the glare of his hospital, and walked to the piano. Her mother was the musician in the family, but Jackie loved to play when no one else was home. She was far from an accomplished musician; her style was to ramble along, playing fragments of songs and half-remembered snatches of classical pieces which segued into show tunes. She tinkered with some Debussy, crashed out "March Slav," played as much as she could remember of an Italian folk tune Eduardo had liked.

Rafaella, she thought, was feeling guilty for having survived. This seemed so odd to her that she wondered if the woman could be, after all, slightly unbalanced. On the other hand, how could Jackie—who had never undergone any surgical procedure more serious than a tonsillectomy—possibly understand what it was like for Rafaella?

Volunteers were supposed to be encouraging, helpful, and friendly, but they were forbidden to concern themselves with strictly medical problems. Rafaella's state of mind lay in neutral territory, but there were overlaps. If Jackie tried to interest Rafaella in the problems of other patients, it would take her out of herself, but it could also be harmful.

The plan that kept springing to mind was a dangerous one. What Jackie wanted was to bring Rafaella into contact with Mrs. Catrine. She thought the benefit to both women would be considerable. Rafaella could talk to Mrs. Catrine in her own dialect, probably, and she was a mother, too. She could give her the sort of sympathy and comfort the male doctors were incapable of providing and Jackie herself was too alien to provide.

And Rafaella? She would be thrust back into a world of other human beings and freed from the tyranny of living in her own confused mind. Jackie firmly believed in the therapeutic effects of helping others, but she couldn't judge whether Rafaella was strong enough to do so. And there was the great danger that Giovanni would die. If that happened, there was no telling what damage his death might do to Rafaella. In her fragile state, it might even harm her physically. Jackie thought she'd ask Blanchard's opinion.

She took a deep swallow of wine and told herself not to meddle. Then she began to play "The Yellow Rose of Texas" and banished the hospital and all its inhabitants from intruding on her peace in River Oaks.

Chapter 9

Nighttime was the worst. They gave her sleeping pills and some medication for the pain, but more often than not she lay awake for hours.

Frequently, Aldo seemed to be with her. His spirit entered the room. She could always tell when he was close to her because then she would become unaccountably sleepy and struggle to stay awake.

Was it possible she'd come so close to death their spirits had nearly touched? She knew he would be proud of her for surviving, for their children's sake, but the memory of her weakness the night before she entered the hospital made her sick with shame.

What had seemed natural, even loving, at the time, now seemed so bizarre she could not believe she had allowed it. Was it possible she was a different woman than she had thought herself all these years? Had vanity played a part in her behavior, or only fear? If she had died in the arms of a stranger in a Houston motel room, who could ever explain to her children?

She pondered these questions endlessly and found no answers. It seemed obscene to even consider her body as anything but a ravaged battle zone; the fact that it had participated in the act of love less than a week ago now appeared as a disgusting, cruel joke.

The fact that her coconspirator had sent her flowers was the cruelest joke of all. At least there had been no message. Only his name.

The ride in the wheelchair seemed almost festive. Jackie pushed her down the hall where she was used to taking her snail's-pace constitutionals, and the IV trundled merrily along beside them, guarded by a nurse. They passed several of the patients Rafaella now nodded to on her walks.

"Going home already?" called a man in a plum-colored bathrobe. He was Dutch and spoke good English, but he pronounced the word "home" so that it had two syllables. Jackie answered for her.

At the nurses' station a hawk-eyed young man in a burnoose observed her with interest. He made a little bow as they passed by. "Who was that?"

"The sheikh's son," said Jackie. The nurse made a little sound of disapproval, clicking her tongue between her teeth and grunting slightly. She was a young black woman whom Rafaella particularly liked because she had an infallible technique for helping with coughing. She was able to hit Rafaella's back, without causing pain, and miraculously the smart tap of her broad black hand never failed to dislodge the liquid.

Jackie and the nurse told her about the sheikh while they waited at the elevators to the children's wing. He had undergone successful surgery—a double bypass like Rafaella's own—and the volunteer who helped with him reported the son's words: "My father has the heart of a lion."

How much had been going on while she lay recuperating in her white retreat, oblivious to all needs but her own! Now that she could walk her "mile" and bathe herself, standing at the washbasin, there was no excuse to be so unaware. They were taking her to the children's wing now because they needed her help.

The poor Catrine woman, she thought, what choice on earth could be so terrible as hers? Now that she had decided for the surgery, the waiting must be unendurable. Jackie had warned her that the child was ghastly to behold, the mother almost savage in her self-imposed solitude. Of course—she was a Calabrese, wasn't she? They were brave and stubborn. Americans wouldn't understand Mrs. Catrine's attitude, but Rafaella did. There was a chance that Mrs. Catrine would resent her for being a northern Italian—almost as alien as an American—but Rafaella had been married to a Neapolitan, and she had children of her own. They had a bond.

In the children's wing they passed room after room papered with bright clown faces and capering, fanciful animals. In one she saw a baby, no more than six months old, lying in a barred crib with mobiles dancing overhead. "Thank God it was I who was sick, and not one of the children," she thought.

A little girl with long dark braids approached them on a red tricycle. Jackie called to her in Italian, and she cycled up to them, speaking shyly.

"This is Lucia Camaratta," said Jackie formally. "Signora Leone. Lucia had surgery ten days ago—see how lively she is now?"

Rafaella felt the unpredictable, emotional tears hovering close behind her eyelids. The child reminded her of Stefania at the age of three, and she ached to touch her. *"Buon giorno, signora,"* said Lucia, taking Rafaella's hand. She asked why Rafaella was riding in a wheelchair. "Because I have had an operation like you. It would be much nicer to have a tricycle." Lucia smiled, but seemed bewildered.

"I thought only children had this operation," she said.

The atmosphere outside the Catrine room was palpably different. No babble of television, no glimpses of sunlight through the door. The curtains had been drawn against the day. The nurse withdrew, and Jackie tapped once, then wheeled her into the room.

There was a smell in the room. It was compounded of several things, all unpleasant. The indefinable odor of sickness mixed with the even more indefinable odor of defeat was joined by the smell of Mrs. Catrine's unwashed and uncared for body.

Beyond, on the bed, an emaciated figure, gnarled and mummylike, lay propped on the pillows, gurgling. Rafaella felt her wounded heart throb in pity; it was an actual sensation, pinpointed deep in her tightly laced breast. Jackie introduced the women formally and then left the room. They had agreed Rafaella would stay for a quarter of an hour. She spoke now, in the dialect Aldo had used.

"Signora," she said, "I am sorry your only son is so ill. I have two children. I can understand."

Maria Catrine thanked her for her concern. Beyond them the gurgling, quieter now. "Will you push me close to Giovanni's bed?" Rafaella thought she understood something of great importance. Because Giovanni was so gravely ill, the doctors didn't treat him as they did the other children. They observed him clinically. They were prepared to go to extraordinary lengths to save his life, but she imagined they displayed no tenderness toward him. This was not from indifference, but because they thought he was too sick to notice or understand. Perhaps they were right, but his mother would notice. She would care.

Up close his drawn, skeletal face resembled that of a spider monkey's. His lips were tinged with blue. "Hello, Giovanni," she whispered. "Hello, darling." With infinite care she touched the sparse, dry clumps of black hair adhering to his skull. Above his bed the tumbling clowns on the orange wallpaper seemed grotesque. She continued to caress him, murmuring little nonsense words of greeting, as she would to any sick two-year-old. There was a light of sorts in those eyes. It was dim, nearly extinguished, but it showed awareness. At the beginning he had looked at her with distrust. Now he seemed more tranquil. She placed her forefinger in the tiny dry cup of his hand and drew his own fingers around it.

When Mrs. Catrine wheeled her away from his bedside, he seemed to be sleeping. "You understand, signora," she said gruffly. "The others"—she made an eloquent gesture with her hand—"to them he is just one of God's mistakes."

They sat in silence for a while, and then Maria Catrine told Rafaella the name of her husband—Giovanni, also—and his profession. He was a vintner's salesman. Rafaella replied with the names of her children and the name of her dead husband. Mrs. Catrine inquired politely after Rafaella's health, and then she cried a little, soundlessly, while Rafaella held her hand.

When she had finished crying she said, abruptly: "I am sorry I cannot offer you coffee." Her sorrow was real; she was humiliated by her inability to provide refreshment for a guest. "To tell you the truth," she said, lowering her voice and looking around as if spies might be present, "the coffee in this hospital is a disgrace."

When Jackie reappeared, the two women said good-bye, calling each other signora courteously. Rafaella promised to come again. *God bless,* they said.

"There is something you can do for that woman," said Rafaella as they were trundling down the corridor. "It would be a great comfort to her."

"What, *cara?* I'd do anything to help, but she never asks."

"Get an espresso pot and some strong Italian coffee. If she could have coffee in her room—" Rafaella shrugged. There were things an American couldn't understand, even if she had been married to an Italian man for a time. She pictured Jackie's ex-husband and thought he would not be the type to take his coffee at home; it would be impossible to explain the importance of the espresso to her.

"Of course I can do that. It never occurred to me."

"I know the kind of coffee she would prefer. I'm not sure you can buy it here though."

"Don't underestimate Houston," said Jackie. She reached down and touched her charge's shoulder lightly. "You amaze me sometimes, Rafaella. Honestly you do."

At 9:00 P.M. the visitors left. She could hear them in the hallways, calling good nights, promising to return at noon. The voices came in a variety of languages. As they straggled toward the elevators they spoke to each other politely, often in broken English, sometimes in broad Texas twangs. They were close in the peculiar way of strangers who have watched their respective loved ones struggle and endure.

Rafaella sat in the chair near the window, hearing their voices fade. This was the loneliest time, when night approached and all the visitors went away. It seemed unbearably sad to hear the voices diminishing; she knew her feeling

190

was unreasonable but nothing could assuage her sadness at this hour.

She also knew Jackie spent an unusual amount of time with her because she was alone, but Jackie had other patients, a life of her own. Dr. Blanchard looked in often, too; besides his daily examination he popped in whenever he was on the floor to say a quick hello. They were kind, and she appreciated it, but she didn't want them to pity her.

Her television was on, the volume very low. A man was talking about droughts. It was a word she didn't know, and he said it over and over. She remembered her lonely hours with the television at the Hibernian, the silly movie with the irritating heroine. It seemed impossible that those images had flickered on that screen only a week ago.

Basta. Stop feeling sorry for yourself. It was uncomfortable in the chair, but she was tired of lying in the bed. She couldn't find any position in which to sketch without pain, and even reading was difficult. She was beginning to be able to brush her hair; that was something anyway.

How dare you, how dare you feel sorry for yourself!

What if she were Maria Catrine, waiting for the morning, knowing it might well be the last night she'd spend with her son? She had seen her once more, shortly after dinner. Mrs. Catrine was bathed and wearing a fresh dress. Her hair was plaited neatly around her round head. "All your doing," Jackie told Rafaella later. But really it had been the coffee. Mrs. Catrine was able to offer her a cup of strong espresso, and that age-old gesture of hospitality and friendship had buoyed her.

Strange to think such a simple thing could please a woman in Maria's tragic situation, but Rafaella understood. Deprived of everything familiar, caught in a world whose every movement was alien to her, she had had no human dignity. *Let Giovanni live,* Rafaella thought. It wasn't impossible; Lassiter had worked miracles before.

A rapid-fire burst of Arabic echoed through the halls, followed by the night nurse's reproving voice. She had an overwhelming desire to go to the door and see what was happening.

Consuelo, the Cuban nurse, was holding her head in her hands and asking God to give her strength. Outside the corner suite the sheikh's live-in relatives were trying to maneuver an enormous floral offering, shaped like a lion's head, through the door. It was entirely fashioned of red and white roses; Rafaella could smell them half a corridor away.

They turned it this way and that, but it was three-dimensional and every angle failed. Roses dislodged themselves from the wire frame and fell at their feet. One of the men looked up and caught her watching. He made a hopeless hand gesture, palms turned up to heaven. It seemed a very Italian gesture, and she laughed.

Later, when the nurse called Addie came to help her to bed, she asked how the problem had been resolved. "It's still out in the hall," said Addie. "In the morning the florist is sending someone to redo it smaller. Honestly, I'm surprised they didn't hire a helicopter to bring it in through the balcony."

Another nurse came in, her hands full of mutilated roses.

"These are for you, Mrs. Leone. The sheikh's brother told me to present them to the young lady down the hall." The roses had no stems to speak of. "What are you going to do with them?" Addie asked. "Where can we put them?" She, who could maintain a cool head in the face of cardiac arrest, seemed utterly unstrung at the prospect of finding a suitable vase for the roses.

"Never mind," said Rafaella, "I'll think of something."

And so she lay in the half-gloom, lightly sedated, with the roses strewn over the blanket. Her fingers touched them now and then, releasing their powerful scent into the air, and it pleased her. She thought of Italy, of gardens long ago, and then it came to her: from the moment the strong espresso had passed her lips in Maria Catrine's room, she had been missing Italy. Her children and Anna-Laura she missed continuously, but this was different. The roses, the espresso, Maria Catrine, the hand gesture of the struggling Arab, had made her long for home.

"I want to go home," she whispered.

She thought she might dream of home that night, but

instead she dreamed that Stephen Morrissy had come into the room and was looking down at her as she slept. "You shouldn't be here," she told him. "But stay. Please stay."

In the morning the roses, deprived of water, were shriveled and brown at the edges. She had known this would happen, and she scooped them up and dropped them into the wastepaper basket by her bed. There was nothing else to do with them; they had served their purpose, under the circumstances, as best they could.

When Jackie came, she asked her to write letters to her children. There was something she had to tell them.

"Of course I will," said Jackie. "But you'll be home before the letters get there."

"All they have had is my voice on the telephone. It is important for them to have a letter. One for each."

Jackie seemed to understand. She sat, legs crossed, in the chair near the window. While Rafaella dictated, she wrote the words out in her neat, American, boarding-school hand.

Rafaella addressed her daughter first. She told Stefania she was very well and getting better every day. She described meeting Lucia Camaratta in the Children's Hospital, and how like Stefania Lucia had seemed. She said she missed her terribly and loved her—how? She had been about to say "with all of my heart."

"I love you very much," she amended. "I will be back soon, and we will be a happy family once again."

Carlo's letter was much the same, except that in honor of his superior age and his maleness she took a more mature tone. "There is a sheikh from Araby here, who had precisely the same operation as mine," she dictated. "His son goes about saying: 'My father has the heart of a lion.' "

"*Dal cuor di leone*," repeated Jackie. "Lion-hearted." She smiled. "Is your son proud to have the surname Leone?"

"Oh, yes. Very." Rafaella thought of the curious formality with which Carlo signed his school papers: *Giancarlo Sebastiano Leone*.

When she had finished, signing "Your Mama, who loves you," Jackie assured her she would mail the letters out immediately. There was a frightened, vulnerable quality to

Jackie's eyes this morning. For all her professional cheerfulness, and the genuine friendship which lay beyond it, she was preoccupied and anxious.

"I am thinking of him, too," said Rafaella. "And of his mother."

Neither of them spoke Giovanni's name.

The observation dome over the operating room reserved for Giovanni was packed full. An opportunity to watch surgery on an AV commune was rare, and the atmosphere was one of solemn expectancy. None of the gallows humor so prevalent among residents and medical students prevailed today. The mortality rate for this procedure was estimated at eighty percent; there were only a handful of surgeons who would even attempt it. Lassiter had done the trick before, but he had also failed.

The saw sliced easily through Giovanni's breastbone. There was no cracking sound, no pop. He seemed impossibly tiny to survive such an assault, but they had all seen surgery performed on younger children. It was rumored that Lassiter had first practiced inside a matchbox to perfect the precise movements required to maneuver in such a small space.

Giovanni's heart was huge, grotesque. The blood shunted, fighting, to get in and out of the malformed pump and make its way to the single chamber of the pitiful heart.

"That's the sickest heart I've ever seen," said one of the observers.

And yet it had performed heroically. It had labored harder to keep its host alive for two years than a normal heart would have done in three score and ten.

Lassiter peeled back a flap of heart muscle and stitched it to the thoracic cavity in order to have a clearer field. Giovanni's heart, motionless now, seemed less dreadful. Deformed it might be, but without the awesome spectacle of the blood's frantic effort to gain entry, it could almost be regarded as a candidate for cosmetic surgery. Lassiter could not supply the child with the missing chamber, but with great luck he might be able to resuspend or replace the valves. There had been a celebrated case in which a child consigned to death by local cardiologists had appeared, at death's door, at St. Matthew's. Lassiter had discovered that she didn't have a second hole in her heart after all. *Ostium primum*, bravo! A stroke of luck! Some tricky stitching of a Dacron patch and she was leading a normal life within six months. Pictures of her riding her pony arrived at the hospital, fondly inscribed by the grateful mother.

Giovanni had no such luck. The heart was every bit as sickly, as cruelly deformed, as it appeared to be. Lassiter sewed, stitched, and reconstructed for two hours, but when Giovanni was taken off the pump, the heart failed to activate.

He was shocked over and over, taken off the pump and put back on. Dr. Parker, the cardiologist, walked to the door and came back, like a man performing an exercise. Lassiter worked for over an hour. The paddles descended again and again. Lassiter reached deep within the cavity and did something mysterious there, but it wasn't to be. Sixty-seven minutes after he was taken off the pump, the men in the OR acknowledged that Giovanni Catrine was dead.

Martin Lassiter shook his head. No. For one moment his gloved hand hovered over the table, as if he were about to slam it down in a gesture of defeat, and then he turned and left the room swiftly. Viola Phinney followed him, her shoulders slumped.

"Aw, shit," said one of the observers in the dome.

Dr. Gold moved forward to begin the process of sewing Giovanni up. In death, he seemed no larger than a kitten.

Chapter 10

Maria came to say good-bye. She was dressed in a dark traveling suit, and she brought Rafaella a basket of grapes.

"What can I say?" said Rafaella. "How can I ever tell you how sorry I am?"

"Don't cry," said Maria. "We did our best. Nothing more could be done. We're going home now. Soon you will be home, too. I will always remember you. *Grazie*."

"*Addio*," said Rafaella. "I will always remember you too."

They exchanged addresses, knowing that they would never write, but knowing, also, that they would never forget each other.

Rafaella put on her kimono and set off on her mandatory walk down the corridor. The Dutchman passed her, going the other way, and they saluted each other like two passengers on a cruise ship. The sheikh had been brought up from intensive care; presumably the unwieldy floral tribute had been scaled down in time to welcome him. She passed a door whose patient card bore the name Santiago and wondered if Stephen Morrissy came into this room as a volunteer, but there were several Spanish-speaking volunteers, and there was no reason to assume that Morrissy had business on her floor.

She half hoped to see him now. She told herself her motives were selfless; after all, he would be relieved to see how well she was doing. Common decency obliged her to reassure him, she thought, and then she blushed at the word "decency." What she had meant, of course, was common courtesy.

She had reached the end of the hallway. She still hurt, sometimes quite badly, but the pain had settled into something she recognized, like an old enemy. Her leg no longer hurt where they had taken the vein, but she secretly believed there would be a lake of fire in her breast forever. It would diminish, but never disappear entirely.

"Lookin' good!" called a voice from one of the rooms. Inside she saw the round little man who always wore a monogrammed robe and a button with a smiling face. He was sitting on his bed, legs dangling over. She waved to him and continued on her way past the nurses' station. Jackie had told her that the man with the Smile button was reputed to be a retired gangster, but to Rafaella he looked like a benevolent parish priest.

The door marked Santiago opened and she felt her body tense with anticipation. She halted, standing completely still, aware of a quickening of her breath, but the man who came out was no one she had ever seen. To her astonishment, she heard her voice addressing him, asking if he was a volunteer.

"Yes. I'm Joe Gonzalez. Is there something I can do for you?"

"Do you know Mr. Morrissy?"

"I certainly do. Do you want me to send for him? He's not in the hospital just now, but I'm sure I could locate him for you."

"Oh no, no—not necessary." She was babbling, blushing, speaking in broken English. "Would you tell him, when you see him, I am recovering very well? Tell him I am fine and send my best wishes."

"There's only one problem," Gonzalez said gently. "I don't know who you are. Who shall I say is recovering very well?"

"Mrs. Leone. Thank you." She turned away, seeing herself as Gonzalez would—a madwoman in a kimono creeping up the hall toward her lair.

In her room she examined her image in the cold fluorescent light of the bathroom mirror. She did not look mad, only ill. The tears she had shed in Maria's presence were still visible as tracks on her cheeks. She hadn't even wiped her eyes with a tissue. One forgot such things. She wasn't nearly as strong and well as she had felt herself to be when the Smile man called his encouragement. She was a pale, sickly creature, creased and worn. Lucky to be alive. Maria's child was dead; Maria would become pregnant again and dread that the child under her heart might be born like Giovanni— either that or she would never let the vintner's salesman near her again and the marriage would go on, year after year, infused with bitterness and defeat.

She thought of her own children, strong and untainted. She, Rafaella, could still become pregnant. What if she was pregnant even now? Grotesque thought, appalling. Calm yourself, she thought. It would not be possible to go through what I have done without losing a child, would it? What if, what if? She couldn't ask. The idea of asking Dr. Blanchard was so dreadful she could only imagine it as a sort of ghastly joke.

"By the way, Dr. Blanchard, is it possible to conceive a child on the evening before one enters the hospital for open-heart surgery and have it survive? I just thought I would ask."

"But surely, Mrs. Leone, there's no chance—"

"Of course not! You insult me, doctor. I told you—my interest is purely academic . . ."

A nurse entered the room carrying a pot of azaleas. She helped Rafaella back to bed and handed her the card which had come with the flowers. It said, "We pray to see you soon, dear Rafaella. All our best wishes and hopes for your recovery." It was signed Michele and Gemma Leone.

Aldo's parents.

Dr. Lassiter came to see her at six-thirty. She watched his pale, Anglo eyes as they scanned her chart. She looked for a hint of grief, a message which would tell her he felt the loss of Giovanni, but she saw nothing.

"You'll be leaving us soon, Mrs. Leone," he said. "You're a very satisfactory patient." He gave her one of his dry little smiles: a joke.

He was as immaculate and glamorous as ever, but she

suddenly detected something shifty in his glance. This was so unlike him she studied him carefully when he was looking away. It was as if he'd been in the sun too much and damaged his vision temporarily. He couldn't look at any one object for too long. Rafaella wondered if anyone had expressed sympathy to *him* after Giovanni's death.

It was possible that everyone shunned him after a tragedy because they didn't know what to say; he was far too great a figure to approach with ease. It wasn't right. Apart from Maria, Lassiter was the person closest to the child who had died. He knew him most intimately, having worked with his own hands to save him, and surely that was a sort of closeness. Lassiter had gambled, and failed. He had, in the best faith, killed Giovanni. The child would have died anyway, but it was Lassiter who'd been the instrument of his death. Surely he deserved sympathy.

"Doctor," she said, "I am sorry about the little boy who died."

She thought she had angered him. He gave her a look of such flatness it was as if he'd told her she was speaking out of turn. He continued to look at her, furtive gaze now gone calculating, and at last he nodded. "We were all sorry," he said in his light, uninflected voice.

"Yes, I knew you were, but I wanted to tell you *I* was sorry. For your sake."

He smiled, but it was not a smile which offered encouragement. "For my sake," he said.

"Yes. When a child dies there is such a great sadness. Everyone offers sympathy to the parents and feels grief for them. I remember you said you liked children, and I thought you might be sad, and maybe nobody thought to say they were sorry to you."

"I cannot afford to be sad," said Lassiter. "I have no time to be sad." He looked away, out the window, then at the flowers, and finally back to her. "No—that's not true," he said. "I allow myself to be sad, but only for a moment. Then I convert it to anger. Anger is more useful. Are you understanding me? Good. Sadness is not useful. You can't build anything on it. But anger? Anger is a fine adversary. I am angry that I could not save Giovanni. I won't live long enough to see the day when his condition could be as easily remedied as a deviated septum, and *that* angers me."

"Are you ill?"

"No. I mean that I would have to live to be a hundred and fifty. Maybe only a hundred. It's a great shame I can't live forever, Mrs. Leone, because I am a genius. *Genioso?*"

"If you are a genius, doctor, then you will find a way to live for a hundred more years."

"Not my field," said Lassiter. "Thank you for your sympathy."

"It is nothing," she said politely.

"No," he said, reaching down and tweaking her toe as he had done on the night before her surgery. "It is something. Definitely something."

"What is a drought?" she asked.

"A drought," said Stephen, "is a period of dryness. It is when the land receives no water, and the crops die and the reservoirs dry up. No rain. Why do you ask?"

"I heard a man talking about it on the television. What is a deviated septum?"

"Rafaella. Certainly it wasn't discussed on the same program?"

"Dr. Lassiter told me the phrase." She explained, and Stephen told her what a deviated septum was.

"When I first saw you," he said, "I thought you might be a journalist. Something about your alertness that day in Admissions, your air of observing. Maybe you should be a journalist. You have a remarkable ability to make people talk."

She laughed, a bit anxiously he thought, and fiddled with the bed covers. They were not at ease with each other. All the wordless emotion which had passed between them in this room on the eve of her surgery had fled. It was replaced by a peculiar aura of false gaiety. Her laughter, her amusing questions about droughts and deviated septums, were barriers against emotion, as she intended them to be.

When Joe Gonzalez had relayed her message to him, he had felt two separate things—joy, because she was asking, in her typically roundabout fashion, to see him, and irritation that it had taken her so long. All the irritation vanished when he entered her room and saw her lying in her bed, propped on her pillows, looking like a Renaissance artwork that had strayed into a modern hospital.

She seemed so fragile, yet there was color in her face which had not been there before. Beneath the pale skin a faint wash of apricot was visible. It was proof of her improved circulation. One of her hands was bandaged lightly. He supposed it was a minor infection from one of the blood pressure tubes. Her dark hair, pulled up and fastened with the silver comb, had a glossy sheen that reminded him of the blue light reflecting from a purple plum. She was drawn, a bit, from her recent sufferings, but he thought she looked very lovely. She had a secret beauty, not immediately visible to everyone, which he had seen from the first. His awareness of that beauty, the day he had glimpsed her sitting in the admissions office, made him feel he had *discovered* her. It was emerging now and would continue to emerge until the promise became a glorious reality. He was as pleased and excited by her transformation as if he had created her.

He could tell her none of what he was feeling. He could only wait and take his tone from her. *Your move, signora.*

Of course she had launched into one of her exasperating little apologies. She hadn't intended for him to actually visit her, had only wanted to send him a message. She was sure he was busy and had other patients to attend to, but she wanted to thank him for—yes—his kindness. The word "kindness" hovered in the air, embarrassing them both. Then had come the gaiety, the request to be enlightened about droughts. He watched her trying on various roles, groping for the proper attitude. There was nothing he could do to help until she had exhausted her small supply of trivia. Her determined courtesy, her attempts to put him at his ease—annoying though they were—had to be admired. They were a part of her courage.

"Ah," said Stephen at last, feeling like a character in a

bad play, "these are your children. I never saw these photographs." He stretched a hand toward the silver frame. "May I?"

She nodded graciously.

The little boy resembled her to a degree quite amazing. He could have seen his image anywhere in the world and known he was Rafaella's son. When his fascination with the uncanny similarity had worn off, he felt a brief pang because he had no children to show her in return. The daughter, he presumed, favored her father. Her dark eyes stared at Stephen accusingly.

"Stefania looks very like my husband." She spoke of him as if he were still alive.

"Aldo," said Stephen. Her eyes widened, as if he had insulted her, but she nodded. He got it now. He wasn't allowed to utter the name of the adored departed one. He was surprised she didn't travel with a photograph of Aldo, a portable shrine.

"I am relieved that you're doing so well," he said. "I wish you had allowed me to see you earlier, but whenever I asked, Jackie told me you didn't want to see me."

"It wasn't necessary," she said meekly. Now she would tell him she was sorry that he had worried.

"I'm sorry—" she began, but suddenly he was laughing, unable to control himself. Her polite little comments, her dodges and withdrawals, might be maddening, but the fact that he could predict them now made him very happy. A moment ago he had been jealous of a dead man, and now he was laughing because he thought he knew her better than anyone in the world.

"What is so amusing, please?"

"You, signora, you. You've just come through an ordeal so gigantic I can't begin to imagine it, and right now all you can think of is how to make me disappear. You want to pretend it—we'll call it *it* to spare your delicate sensibilities —never happened. 'If I am very polite and superficial to Morrissy he will vanish, and I can go home and resume my life as the chaste Madonna of Genoa. Now that I am healthy I can look forward to many years of selflessness and celibacy.' But it won't work, Rafaella. I won't vanish, and you are not a saint."

Her hands were held before her as if in surrender; her face was flooded with color. "Please," she said, "don't say any more." He was appalled. Dr. Morrissy's shock tactics were right for her, but not now. She was still in a delicate condition. He walked to the bed, took her hands, and lowered them gently to her sides.

"At least be my friend, Rafaella. We are friends, aren't we?"

"But I'm going away."

"I know that. But will you grant me the pleasure of your company until you go? After that—we'll see. Will you stop shutting me out, hitting me over the head with politeness? I don't want to be thanked for my kindness. My attention to you is completely selfish. I want to be with you."

She nodded. He bent and kissed her forehead. "*Bene*," he said. "Now, I imagine you're getting tired of hospital food. I've located a restaurant that specializes in Genovese cuisine. I can return with the dish of your choice in an hour. *Pesto?* Or is that too common? I've been told it's the ultimate Genovese treat."

"I would adore to have *pesto*," she said. There were tears in her eyes, but Stephen pretended he didn't notice. "And wine," she said. "Dr. Blanchard lets me have a little wine."

"What kind?"

"Do they have Santa Maddelena in Houston?"

"I'll find it."

When he returned an hour later, she was waiting expectantly. Her eyes were shining, and she was wearing the Oriental scarf he had given her.

Ceremoniously, he uncorked the Santa Maddelena and poured a glass for each of them.

"You even remembered the thing for opening the wine," she said, as if he had performed a feat of heroic measures. She lifted her glass. "To your health," she said, and there was no irony in it, no recognition that it was not his health which was important.

He opened the little containers of *troffie*, and the rich

smell of the *pesto* filled the room. She watched while he arranged the plates and silver on her tray, letting him take care of everything. He felt very happy, performing these small services for her.

He wasn't sure, but he thought she was happy too.

She wanted to design something very special for Jackie as a token of her everlasting gratitude. She had envisioned a bracelet, for Jackie liked bracelets. She could see it on Jackie's slender tanned wrist—a delicate affair of links which would be clasped by a heart.

On the morning after her supper with Stephen, she sat trying to sketch the little heart which would be the bracelet's focal point. It was to be free form, a fanciful heart meant to remind the wearer of Rafaella always. She had imagined telling Jackie to watch for a package from Italy—a small thank-you, she would call it, for patients were not supposed to gift volunteers.

The little hearts she sketched were ugly, deformed in her eyes. Her fingers couldn't seem to fashion the simplest heart —even the conventional kind a five-year-old child could draw were beyond her. These hearts were shattered, fragmented, and violated like her own.

Tall, beautiful Jackie had a glorious life before her. She had no need of a foolish bauble which would only remind her of people less fortunate than herself. Jackie would soon meet a man who would make her forget about the philandering husband who had hurt her so deeply.

Rafaella tore the page of hideous little hearts in half, then in quarters. She went on tearing until the thickness of the bunched paper resisted her fingers. She would think of some other way to thank Jackie.

Her hand crept under the kimono, under the nightgown, and she touched the hard seam at her throat. It felt shiny and enormous. She couldn't bring herself to look. She shut her eyes and was presented with a vision of Jacqueline Talbot and a man who loved her. He was one of the *Giant* people, of course—he would have to be. Jackie's radiant health and vigorous beauty required it. Like called to like.

He would be tall, probably fair haired, and he would be very athletic and adventurous.

Rather like Stephen.

On their last night together, Stephen read to her in Italian. He had discovered a book of short stories in the hospital library. Neither of them had ever heard of the author. She lay very still, listening to his endearingly atrocious Italian as he read her a selection about a lonely peasant boy's adventures in Rome.

The book was small; his hands seemed to dwarf it. She thought of all the strange and wonderful places in the world he had been to and of all the others still waiting for him. He was not cut out to sit by sickbeds reading, even less to enter the world that was hers in Italy. It was a world of work and small children and neighbors and family. There was no adventure in it. It pained her to think of how soon he would grow tired of being her friend.

They had agreed that she would go to sleep early on this last night. The flight tomorrow would be long and tiring. Stephen wanted to fly as far as New York with her, but she had refused. He was to take her to the airport, that was all.

When he came to kiss her good night—a gentle kiss for a convalescent, mouth brushing cheek or forehead—she drew his face to hers and kissed him on the lips.

Chapter 11

Jackie came at eight in the morning with Rafaella's possessions and discharge papers. Rafaella was already dressed and waiting for her.

Dr. Blanchard came to say good-bye, and Consuelo and Addie. So many good-byes and thank-yous. Good-bye to the Dutch farmer and the brother of the Lion of Kuwait. Good-bye to the sheikh himself, who was now walking his mile in flowing robes. Good-bye to the man with the Smile button. Tears flooded her eyes at the realization that she would never see these people again; although they had so recently been strangers, she felt closer to them than to anyone in the world at the moment of parting. Dr. Lassiter was already in surgery; she had said her good-bye to him when they spoke of his genius, but she begged Blanchard to say it again, thank him again.

"Aren't you going to say good-bye to Stephen?" Jackie asked. "Isn't he coming to the hospital?"

"We said good-bye last night." His name on Jackie's lips, so casually and unexpectedly uttered, caused a sensation of pain surprising in its intensity. "Can we go to the airport now?" She avoided Jackie's eyes. "I would like to get there early."

And so it was Jackie who drove her away from the hospital; Jackie who sat beside her as they glided down the long, curving drive which had brought her here ten days ago. Good-bye to the hospital.

Good-bye to the Hibernian and the green lawns where the makeshift tents and stalls had been. She remembered sitting on the bale of hay, discovering that his eyes were the color of hazelnuts. "My husband is dead," she had told him.

"Are you comfortable, Rafaella? Is the air conditioning too high?" Jackie was solicitous, cheerful.

"I am fine." She wanted to tell Jackie how kind and good she was, to thank her and wish her all the luck and happiness in the world, but the words would make her too emotional. She could not afford to break down now at the end of her long trial.

Once they had passed the Hibernian and swung out onto the highway, nothing seemed familiar. Rafaella tried to find one object she remembered, but everything seemed alien. She had been so terrified during that other ride that all its particulars were blocked from her memory. It was all going by too quickly now; they were approaching the airport with a bewildering speed. It wasn't really a very long journey. Rafaella felt as a woman does on returning to her childhood home only to find it much smaller than she had remembered. *Is this all?*

In the airport waiting lounge, she told Jackie of her abortive plan to design a bracelet for her. She tried to make her failure seem amusing, but Jackie embraced her, holding her tightly so that the perilous emotion threatened to return.

"I'll miss you," whispered Jackie. "I'll write to you."

"But wait," said Rafaella. "I want you to have something to remember me. You must take it." She produced the Oriental scarf, neatly folded, from her purse.

"But it's yours! It's so beautiful, Rafaella—I can't imagine anyone wearing it but you."

"It was only to wear in the hospital. To lift my spirits. I won't wear it in Genoa. Please. It is all I have to give you."

In the end, of course, she took it. She knotted it around her neck loosely, smiling her gratitude. Rafaella thought she looked like a bird of paradise. *Good-bye, Jackie.*

The flight boarded early and she was relieved to be among the first passengers to get on the plane. She heard her name being called on the public address system as she was walking toward the point of no return. The urgent voice wanted Mrs. Rafaella Leone to come to the courtesy phone. The request was repeated several times, but Rafaella ignored it. She tried not to picture the caller, the way he held the receiver in his hand. At last the sound of her name, echoing through the vast building, died away and was no more.

She boarded the plane without looking back. She sat quietly in her seat, waiting to go home where she belonged.

ITALY

BOOK THREE

Chapter 1

At Cristoforo Colombo Airport in Genoa, a woman standing behind the arrivals barrier drew many glances. She wore a trouser suit of a gaudy lime shade. Beneath it frothed a blouse of tropical colors, caught too tightly at her plump throat in a floppily tied bow. On her head was perched a rakish hat, decorated with erect pheasant feathers. The woman was approaching forty, and her costume was more suited to someone twenty years younger, but it wasn't the oddness of her dress which made people look at her.

In the shade of the festive hat the handsome dark eyes never ceased their searching, scanning movement. Her whole body inclined toward the ramp where debarking passengers streamed down. She was tense, anxious, in spite of her dashing clothes. At seventeen minutes past midnight—the connecting flight from Milan was late—she waited in the milling crowds like someone plucked from a frivolous party to be present at an historic event.

Anna-Laura. Rafaella saw her first. She had a quick view of her before Anna-Laura was obscured by the flow of travelers. She recognized her immediately—but how odd she looked! This small, round person, dressed so peculiarly, was the woman she had composed so many mental letters to during her exile. She was the one to whom she had entrusted her children. Rafaella moved toward her, continuing anonymously, caught in the instinctive flow of the homecoming or holidaying people who had flown with her from Milano.

Beside her, a strong young woman moved easily forward, shifting the heavier of her two bags from the right hand to the left. Her husband ran along, accompanying her, outside the barrier. He was calling out to her, shouting details of domestic life; during her absence there had been a leak in the roof and some damage in the kitchen. The woman moved on, imperturbable.

All around Rafaella was the sound of her own language. The worried husband spoke in the Genovese dialect, and for a moment she was surprised to hear it. It had not yet registered that she was home. Everything was too hurried, too loud. She had lost sight of Anna-Laura now, and not a single face in the jostling, noisy crowd was familiar.

She wanted, suddenly, to be back in her room at St. Matthew's where everything was orderly, predictable. She had a vivid image of the corridors where she had progressed, first with her IV and then triumphantly alone, on what the nurses called the Road to Recovery. The corridors, the nurses' station, the neat cards on the doors—all appeared in her memory with supernatural clarity, and she felt a longing for them. After all, she knew every inch of her hospital room, knew it more intimately than any other place she had ever inhabited, and it seemed cruel to her that she would never see it again. On the Road to Recovery she had had a goal; here she was only one of many who concerned themselves with things like leaking roofs.

A group of nuns fluttered together and then parted, revealing Anna-Laura once again, and an astonishing thing happened. Anna-Laura caught sight of her and waved frantically, her face transfigured by a smile of joy, and the entire picture changed. Rafaella saw, not the clownish little woman almost absurd beneath her feathered hat whom she had glimpsed beyond the barrier, but her sister-in-law. Someone she loved.

Drawn by the lure of that potent smile, she hurried toward it. Anna-Laura battled her way toward her, nimbly dodging the embracing couple of the leaky roof, almost colliding with two of the nuns in her haste. Like a blazing emissary from another world, her hat knocked askew, she hurtled toward Rafaella, sure and elemental as a comet.

Rafaella felt her traveling case fall to the floor as her sister-in-law seized her hands and drew her into her arms.

She smelled the familiar odor of Anna-Laura's perfume mingled with her unique scent, which had always reminded her of basil and honey; her body registered the warmth and pressure of Anna-Laura's large breasts pressed—because she was shorter by a head—against her stomach. Ordinarily, she would stoop to embrace Aldo's sister, but now she let Anna-Laura take her in her arms as a child would, bemused and oblivious.

"Oh—Rafaella! I am so happy to see you! But I mustn't forget—is it all right to hug you tight? Do I hurt you?" She drew back anxiously, then kissed her on both cheeks. "Let me look at you! But, *cara*, you look marvelous! A little tired, perhaps, but such a long flight—oh, Rafaella!" Tears trembled on her heavily mascaraed lashes; her wonderful flashing smile came and went, as if it didn't know how welcome it might be but was powerless to stifle itself. Her hands trembled, setting the bangles on both wrists into a jangling symphony of love and agitation.

"I put the children to sleep at ten," she said, speaking into Rafaella's neck, "but they'll be up again to welcome you home. Signora Lenti is with them now—oh, Carlo resented that, let me tell you, but I thought it was only right—"

Rafaella nodded, her head bowed down and crushed against the pheasant feathers. She wanted to tell her sister-in-law that she was stunned with gratitude and speechless with emotion, but that would be a contradiction. Words ballooned in her consciousness and had no meaning. She clung to Anna-Laura. They formed a small island in the moving flow of human beings, immobile and impregnable. All around them people jostled and moved onwards, curious but kind, unheeding.

"Come," said Anna-Laura. "We'll collect your suitcases. Do you need a wheelchair?"

Rafaella shook her head.

Shortly afterward, enclosed in the close, warm atmosphere of Anna-Laura's orange Fiat and speeding west toward the city, Rafaella felt herself growing faint. She asked her sister-in-law to open the window. Anna-Laura cranked the window down and Rafaella breathed in the scent of octane and brine which heralded the approach to her city. Better, she thought. Slowly, she counted off the familiar sights contained in the small world of the Fiat.

The sagging door of the glove compartment, which could never close because Anna-Laura crammed it so full of miscellaneous objects. The flip-flop sandals demurely resting on the dashboard, in case their owner's feet wearied of high heels. Beneath them a stack of pamphlets and unopened mail. In the rearview mirror she could see the ever present stack of students' papers cluttering the back seat. They were piled neatly enough, two apples and a russet pear weighed them down, for Anna-Laura—who was constantly dieting— often ate lunch on the run. Next to them was something familiar which made Rafaella catch her breath.

"Stefania's goldfish bowl?" she asked.

Anna-Laura sent her a quick look, then understood. Squinting in the rearview mirror, she smiled and shook her head. "No," she said, "but it's identical. Sundance died while she was in school, so I went to make a match. Butch Cassidy was fine, so I left him in the bowl and took Sundance in a glass to the shop. I wanted to make sure, *cara*, that Stefania couldn't tell it was a replacement—that one has eyes like an eagle."

"But two bowls?"

Anna-Laura sighed. "Somehow I broke the glass, and the shopgirl—oh, she was a true Genovese—made me buy another bowl. Would she put the new Sundance in a plastic bag? She would not. Therefore: two bowls. I must hide this one so Stefania doesn't see it."

"She is a big girl now," said Rafaella. "You spoil her." She said it affectionately, but her sister-in-law's hands tightened on the wheel.

"I thought—" Anna-Laura did not finish the sentence. It was too clear, what she had thought, and she was right. They both knew it.

The motorway curved precariously to the left. Rafaella could sense the huge cranes and cargo containers of Savona looming in the darkness, some miles away but visible. They would avoid Savona and drive toward the other, mightier port, toward home. The wind rushed in through the windows now. Rafaella heard a rustling sound and, too late, the thud of the fruit as it slid from the papers and fell to the floor of the car.

Majestically, the papers flew up and enclosed the interior of the Fiat in flapping commotion, as if half a dozen doves had been released from their cages. Rafaella forgot herself and grabbed for a flying paper as it swooped toward the window; the sudden movement caused a deep ache in her breast and frightened her. Anna-Laura was trying to crank the window up, cursing softly and maintaining a steady course with great effort.

"Oh, *shit!*" cried Anna-Laura as one of the sheets of paper flew through the window and sailed off on the wind. Behind them, a driver honked angrily. The window closed on an escaping sheet, and Anna-Laura swiped at it angrily, trying to release it. The paper tore in her hand and the car careened, causing more honking from the rear.

Rafaella's alarm receded. This, after all, was what she was used to. Anna-Laura had navigated a thousand perilous journeys without coming to grief, and she would navigate a thousand more. While her sister-in-law apologized for the disturbance, telling her in a dignified manner that she had wished, for Rafaella, a peaceful and calm journey home, Rafaella sank back against the seat and laughed softly. Her laughter came in little, measured gasps, and Anna-Laura glanced at her with alarm.

"I'm *laughing*," she soothed. "Sometimes I cry and laugh both at the same time, but you mustn't pay attention. I'm so tired; perhaps I'll sleep." She heard herself, heard the words, and hoped Anna-Laura would understand. She reached out a hand, forgetting that Anna-Laura's plump fingers would be clenched on the wheel, and felt the cloth of the lime-green trouser suit beneath her palm. She patted the sturdy thigh, wishing she had the strength to tell all she felt, but she had been in the air for many hours and felt her energy draining as if giant fingers were pushing it through a sieve.

"I trust you," she murmured. It seemed the greatest compliment she could offer. She hoped Anna-Laura would appreciate the immensity of it. Before she slept, hunched in her corner of the Fiat, she had a vivid image of the couple at the airport. She saw the young husband skipping along on the other side of the barrier, keeping pace with his wife. The woman wore a sleeveless dress of a soft blue material. Her bare arms were brown and strong as she juggled the cases and smiled, listening.

Where had she been, that woman? Where had the nuns been? *How small the world is, after all,* she thought.

And how dangerous.

"The stairs?" Anna-Laura was looking anxious again. "You can walk up the stairs, *cara*?"

The short sleep in the car had both disoriented and refreshed her. The sudden exhaustion which had overcome her was gone, but in its place came a sense of unreality. The Fiat was parked in front of a large white house, once handsome, on the Via Vieri. The house was flanked by others, much like it, but each building had some small distinguishing characteristic to mark it from its neighbors. The tiled roofs were of a uniform terra-cotta shade, but the doors were painted different colors. The house they were parked in front of boasted a door of turquoise-blue; flowers, closed for the night, spilled from the ground-floor window boxes in lavish profusion. They were carefully tended by the owner, Signora Lenti, who lived on the first floor.

The second floor was divided into two flats, and Rafaella and her children inhabited the third floor. She could see lights in the windows of her flat. The shutters were open to the warm night air. Behind those windows her children slept. They were there, and yet Rafaella could not really believe it.

Anna-Laura's voice seemed unnaturally loud as she stood, suitcases at her feet, inquiring about the stairs. Next door at the window, faces appeared. First Signor Rossi peered out, then, at his shoulder, his wife. *Buona sera, signora!* they called politely, as if it were early evening rather than past one in the morning. "Welcome home," added Signora Rossi. "It is good to see you again."

Rafaella smiled and nodded. The Rossis were kind people; they meant no harm, but they were unable to restrain their curiosity. They would not ask about her health. The fact that she was standing next to her sister-in-law on the Via

Vieri rather than returning on a stretcher was good enough for them. She thought she heard a sound at the second-story windows of her own house and moved forward. In another moment the entire neighborhood might rouse itself and appear, leaning out of windows, to welcome her back.

Anna-Laura moved ahead of her, carrying the large case and the smaller one. The Neiman-Marcus shopping bag was left behind. "Leave it," hissed Anna-Laura. "I'll come back for it."

"Do you need help with the luggage, signorina?" Mr. Rossi asked solicitously.

Rafaella lifted the bag and followed her sister-in-law, declining with thanks. The stairs were shallow and easy to navigate. All was quiet on the second floor, but she could hear Signora Lenti moving excitedly to the door above. Long before she had reached the top she could see her landlady's face peering over the landing, wreathed in smiles.

Signora Lenti darted down and wrested the shopping bag from Rafaella's hand. She kissed Rafaella on both cheeks and called upon the Holy Mother to witness such a triumphant return. She discussed Rafaella's absence as if she had passed a week or two on the Riviera lying in the sun. "Oh, it's done you a world of good," she cried. "Anyone can see—isn't it true, signorina?" Anna-Laura admitted that it was so and tactfully maneuvered Mrs. Lenti back into the flat. Rafaella followed.

In the small, square room that served as an entryway she could see stacks of unopened mail neatly reposing on a low table. Beyond, the sitting room was waiting, and somewhere, still deep in sleep, her children.

"I thought you might be hungry after your journey," Mrs. Lenti said. She led the way into the sitting room and gestured, like a conjurer, at a table laid with refreshments. There was a pot of espresso, a saucer with thin lemon peels, a decanter of red wine, and a plate piled high with pastries.

Rafaella felt her exhaustion return. Rituals must be observed, even now, and Signora Lenti—old and alone with no family of her own left living—would be distressed and hurt if Rafaella did not sit down with her and celebrate her return.

The room, so alien at first, began to assume its double familiarity within seconds. Double, because the furniture crammed into it had had two lives. In the more spacious quarters she had inhabited with Aldo, it had seemed perfectly chosen, the furniture of a woman of taste who had studied art and had an eye for harmony. Here on the Via Vieri, the cherished pieces were more like old friends who had been reduced to living communally. Was the spot on the wine-colored love seat new, or had the velour been rubbed to a shiny thinness without her noticing? Had the bookcase near the door always protruded so that entering or exiting was a cramped activity?

"The children," she said softly. "I want to see the children."

Anna-Laura was removing her feathered hat. Briskly, she ran her fingers through her hair and started toward the rear of the flat. She nearly collided with Carlo, who came hurtling past the bookcases and into the room. The light almost blinded him, and he stood, clad in his pajamas, tense with emotion and still half asleep.

"Mama," he said. "I heard you." He walked toward her shyly, his bare feet so soundless on the carpet that he might have been gliding over water. "I wasn't asleep," he said defiantly. "I was waiting."

He seemed so large to her, as if he had grown half a head in her absence, yet when he allowed her to pull him close he was the proper size. She bent and kissed him, feeling her arms close around the small, sturdy body in an involuntary movement as natural as that of the lungs drawing air. Gone were Anna-Laura and Signora Lenti; the room contained one person only. She and Carlo were an entity, a mother and her son, and they were one creature, indivisible.

Beneath the jacket of his pajamas she felt the deep trough, from neck to the base of the spine, and the ribs radiating outward. It seemed a miracle that she had created this miniature man, and for a moment she experienced again the wonderful sense of power and immortality she had known on the night he was born. Then he stepped away from her embrace, a worried furrow between his brows. He was afraid of hurting her. Already he was assuming the protective, manly attitude he had preserved ever since his father had died. "You should sit down," he said sternly.

She took his hand in hers and led him toward the door.

"Let's go and wake your sister," she said. "Stefania must join us."

At the door to the children's room he tugged on her hand. "She's in your bed, Mama," he said. "Anna-Laura said she could sleep there." They passed the room intended to be the marital chamber but now curtained off to accommodate Carlo and Stefania and halted outside the door to the small bedroom where Rafaella had slept ever since the death of her husband.

A small light had been burning and cast its glow over the large, ornately carved bed which occupied most of the space in Rafaella's bedroom. Stefania slept in the precise center of the bed, one hand gripping the coverlet and the other flung over the edge of the mattress. Her dark hair spilled over her face; she lay, belly down, her body making such a small hump beneath the bed clothes Rafaella felt suddenly afraid.

She went to her daughter's side and gently drew the covers down and smoothed her hair aside. Stefania was wearing a new nightgown of a pleated, salmon-colored material. Rafaella recognized it as something from the open-air market two roads away—it was inappropriate and somehow whorish. Doubtless Anna-Laura had succumbed to Stefania's pleas and bought it for her. Her daughter's face was serene and beautiful in sleep; from the neck up she seemed to be a *quattrocento* angel.

Carlo reached out and seized his sister's arm. "Gently, Carlo," Rafaella whispered, but Carlo tugged and prodded expertly. Stefania groaned and rolled away, like a hedgehog compressing itself into a protective ball, but when she heard her mother's voice she struggled up from sleep. Stefania battled her unconscious state, striking out with her hands. Her eyes opened and registered the image of her mother, and instantly she was scrambling up, tossing her hair back, smoothing her nightdress down over her thighs, and smiling.

"Mama!" she shouted. "You came home!"

Rafaella felt, in her daughter's embrace, some of the reviving strength Carlo had brought to her. Stefania slid easily down from the bed, already eager to describe the injustices perpetrated by her teacher during Rafaella's absence, and the three of them joined hands and walked to the sitting room.

Rafaella sat on the large couch, a child on either side, and accepted a glass of Bardolino and a cup of espresso from Signora Lenti. Anna-Laura bit into a pastry, her strong teeth smiling around the flaky crust.

"So," she said, gesturing to the children, "doesn't your mama look magnificent?"

"May I have some wine?" asked Stefania, seizing the moment.

"Yes, *carina*," said Rafaella. Signora Lenti brought two small glasses from the kitchen, and Carlo and Stefania were given wine.

There was a moment of confusion when everyone tried to think of the proper toast. To drink to Rafaella's health seemed somehow wrong. It was such a casual toast, a sop to the fates, and not solemn enough for such a momentous occasion.

"To your safe return home," said Signora Lenti, and they all drank obediently.

"To Mama," said Stefania.

Anna-Laura put down a second pastry, glaring at it as she would at an enemy, and lifted her glass. Her eyes, as she drank to Rafaella, were suspiciously moist.

It was nearly two in the morning when Signora Lenti went shuffling somewhat tipsily down the stairs to her own flat. Rafaella felt her eyelids as a great weight which, if allowed to fall, would remove her from the place where she wanted to be. All that she loved was in the room, and to leave it seemed unthinkable. She remembered the Neiman-Marcus shopping bag, still standing in the hall, and roused herself.

"Shut your eyes," she commanded the children. "Don't open them until I say." She asked Anna-Laura to turn the lamps off, and then, in the darkened room, she lit the giant boot-candle. By the flickering light she placed the cowboy hat on Stefania's head.

"It's a cowboy hat!" shrieked Stefania. "I can tell!"

"Open your eyes."

Stefania plucked the hat from her head and examined it with delight. Carlo, more circumspect, leaned forward to appraise the wax boot. He got up and walked around it, nodding as a master craftsman might at a novel and awe-inspiring object.

"*Stupefacente*, Mama," he said.

They sat, for a time, in the light of the Neiman-Marcus candle, feeling happy and blessed. Rafaella was unaware of her body; she believed, just then, that her greatest triumph had been to safely shepherd gifts from America to her home. It occurred to her that Anna-Laura, too, had a gift, but when she tried to mention it her sister-in-law laughed and placed a finger over her lips.

It was Anna-Laura who helped her to bed. She knelt and removed Rafaella's shoes, sat beside her and unbuttoned her blouse. Rafaella submitted gratefully while the capable hands undid the silver comb and let her hair fall free. She sat on the edge of the bed, docile as a child, clad in one of the old-fashioned slips Anna-Laura found so amusing. It was cut high, and there was no way to detect what had happened to the body beneath. "I'll sleep like this," she said.

Anna-Laura drew the covers over her and left. Rafaella could hear her clearing away the cups and glasses, preparing to sleep on the couch in the sitting room. Faintly, in the gloom of the bedroom, she could make out the shape of the carved pineapples on the headboard. It was really true, then. She had come home.

She closed her eyes and saw one of the visions that sometimes appears to those who are overtired but do not long for sleep: she was disembodied, hovering over the earth and looking down; she could see the Ligurian coast from her great height, see where it curved inward in a great sweep to form the Bay of Genoa. Eastward, toward Nervi, the coast grew wild, unruly, but the port town of her birth seemed safely cupped by the shoulders of the land. Somewhere, far beneath, she lay in her own bed. Many miles to the west, across Europe and the Atlantic, she could just make out the vast land mass which was America.

She turned away from the westward continent and continued to hover, peacefully, over Italy.

Chapter 2

She discovered, to her surprise, that she didn't want to get out of bed. On her first day back, Anna-Laura brought her breakfast on a tray. It was midafternoon, and she had slept for twelve hours.

Anna-Laura strode about the room, opening the shutters and beginning the chore of unpacking. She wore last night's lime-green trouser suit; in the light from the window she looked tired and a trifle pale.

"Was it awful, sleeping on the couch?" asked Rafaella. She knew from experience that the couch pitched slightly downward, making one feel off balance. She herself slept there whenever her in-laws descended for a visit.

"No, I slept very well." Anna-Laura walked to the bureau and deposited a pile of underclothing. She shook out Rafaella's dresses briskly and placed them on hangers. Her vigor was apparent even in such small tasks, but she was hampered by the fact that the large bed took up most of the available space in the room.

"There's a package on the bottom. It's for you."

Rafaella watched while her sister-in-law ripped the tissue paper and withdrew the blouse she had selected at Neiman-Marcus a lifetime ago. It was precisely the sort of item she herself would never wear—a blouse designed to call as much attention as possible to whoever put it on. Anna-Laura loved it.

"Oh, beautiful," she sighed, holding the blouse to her cheeks and caressing it sensuously. The sight of the fuschia and lime colors so close together made Rafaella wince. "Perhaps not with those trousers," she said, laughing.

"That's the trouble with you, *cara*. You don't take chances." Anna-Laura heard what she had said and turned awkwardly. "I mean with clothes." She shucked quickly out of her jacket and blouse, standing in the center of the room in her lacy brassiere. She was quite unselfconscious, as always. Her recent bout of dieting had taken an inch from around her waist, but she was still chunky and ample; she would be so to the end of her days. Her round arms were firm, her shoulders plump and padded. Rafaella could see the line where her bathing suit ended; Anna-Laura's breasts, round and smooth, were paler beneath the line. She was naturally dark skinned, as her brother had been, and in the sun she turned the shade of caramel.

Rafaella slid farther beneath the covers, feeling herself pale and wasted, hollow. She didn't want to look at that stocky, healthy body. She knew a momentary dislike for its owner and then felt deeply ashamed. This was Anna-Laura, whom she loved. Anna-Laura, who had to suffer the indignity of her mother's pity because she had never married. Gemma Leone was forever clipping magazine articles which offered hints on how to make the most of your best features; Anna-Laura's best features, according to her mother, were her eyes and her bosom. Gemma seemed to imply that if Anna-Laura only tried hard enough, Signor Right would drive over the horizon in a white Alfa-Romeo and spirit her off to a life of marital respectability.

Rafaella forced herself to watch while her sister-in-law thrust her arms into the new blouse and buttoned it with a flourish. Anna-Laura tucked the blouse into the waistband of the green trousers, grimacing at her broad hips, and surveyed herself in the mirror.

"Gorgeous, no?" she asked. "When Signor Nelson sees me in this, he will forgive me." She blew Rafaella a kiss of thanks.

"Who is Signor Nelson?"

"The student whose papers flew out the window last night. He is with Citibank, a very ambitious young man. It was his grammar test."

"From the *politecnico?*"

"No. One of the private students."

Anna-Laura taught Italian to Americans, English to Italians. In addition to her duties at the school, she tutored students at her flat farther up the Via Vieri. She was a scrupulous and excellent teacher, her private pupils a democratic mix. She lavished as much attention on the son of a career diplomat as she did on a Genovese taxi driver who was planning to emigrate. In her flat was a large corkboard upon which dozens of cards and messages from all over the world thanked her—in Italian and English—for what she had done.

"Do you have classes tonight?"

Anna-Laura shook her head, flinging her hands out as if students were of little importance. "I am here for you," she said. "I have a leave of absence, *cara*. Don't worry. I can stay for as long as you need me."

Rafaella knew it was absurd. Her sister-in-law lived five minutes away. There was no earthly reason why she should have to stay at Rafaella's flat; Signora Lenti could be counted upon to help, and Rafaella was strong enough to look after herself and the children. All these thoughts sprang to her lips and were suppressed. She needed Anna-Laura's presence for a time. She would be selfish.

"The children will be home from school in an hour, Rafaella. Do you want to get up? Shall I help you?"

It was then that Rafaella realized she had no desire to leave her bed. What business had she in the world where women with smooth, dark flesh could bare their bodies in the sunlight without anxiety?

"No," she said. "I'll stay here for a while."

"But wouldn't it be good for you to move about?"

"I'm still sleepy." Rafaella inched lower in the bed, pretended to yawn. The sunlight, so different from the probing, harsh light of Texas, the very sunlight she had looked forward to seeing again, seemed an affront. "Would you close the shutters?" she asked meekly.

Anna-Laura gave her a searching look, her eyes beautiful in sympathy in a way Gemma Leone would have applauded.

Then she shrugged slightly. "If you like," she said. She went to the window and restored the room to darkness.

"*Grazie*," said Rafaella.

Long after her sister-in-law had left the room, she lay motionless in bed. In her chest was a soreness which was not, precisely, pain. Now and then she felt the need to cough. Obediently, as she had learned to do in Houston, she summoned up the ugly little sound. She coughed from reflex and wondered if she would ever really want to leave the bed again.

Maurizio Guidi stood at the entrance to the sitting room. He held flowers, twisted in a paper cone, in one hand and a bag of pastries from Brandini's in the other. Despite the warmth of the summer evening he was dressed in suit and vest as always. From the top of his expensively barbered head to the glowing tips of his shoes, he radiated a prosperous respectability. He handed the pastries to Stefania, who had come rushing to his side. His hand rested on her head for a moment in an affectionate gesture, but his eyes were on Rafaella.

He spoke her name. In a room accustomed to the voices of women and children only, his voice had a particularly deep and commanding sound.

"Rafaella. This is a happy day."

She rose to meet him. In the end, of course, she had gotten up and bathed and joined her family. She hadn't wanted to alarm the children. She wore an old dressing gown which she'd found at the back of her closet. It was long and loose and covered her from neck to ankle.

Maurizio took her hand in his, then bent to kiss her cheek. All his movements were exaggeratedly gentle, as if he did not wish to alarm her.

"You were very kind to visit the children so often while I was away," said Rafaella, "and the flowers you sent me were lovely. Thank you, Maurizio."

He inclined his head eloquently. Without words he let her know she had no need to thank him. His reproachful smile suggested that her thanks wounded him. Thanks were for mere friends or kindly acquaintances like Signora Lenti; Maurizio felt himself to be one of the family.

Rafaella allowed herself to be pressed gently back into her chair. Holding the flowers on her lap, dressed as an invalid or a high priestess, she was the central figure of a drama, one who did not understand her cues or know her lines. What, for example, was she expected to say to Maurizio? In all the time she had known him, she had never seen him show great emotion. Except for his explosions in heavy traffic, Maurizio Guidi was calm and rational—a model of strength and responsibility.

Tonight he seemed a stranger, capable of revealing weaknesses she didn't wish to see. His eyes, normally clear and vivid as if he could see for great distances, had assumed a vaguely furtive look. He glanced at her, then away. With the children he took on a proprietary air. It was as if during her absence he had become an important factor in their lives.

Anna-Laura took the flowers and went in search of a vase. When she returned, she brought with her a bottle of Maurizio's favorite cognac and a glass for him. Where had the cognac come from? Rafaella had never kept it in the flat; it was far too expensive.

"*Brindisi!*" he said, lifting his glass and drinking Rafaella's health. He turned to Anna-Laura. "She is blooming," he said, as if Rafaella were not in the room.

"Signor Guidi took us to Pegli last Saturday," said Carlo. "We went to an open-air concert."

"He's going to take us again," said Stefania. "Whenever we like."

"Whenever your mama likes," corrected Maurizio.

Stefania rushed from the room so suddenly they all started. Her feet went thudding up the hall. "Remember Signorina Freda," said Anna-Laura automatically. Signorina Freda was a retired schoolteacher who lived in the flat beneath. She often slipped neatly penned notes under the doorway of Rafaella's flat asking for consideration. She was retired, she wrote, and had hoped to live out her days in peace and tranquillity in the Via Vieri. It disturbed her to hear the pounding of childish feet above her, and if Signora Leone would only caution the children about their movements, life would be infinitely more pleasant.

Rafaella sympathized with Signorina Freda; at the same time she could not force her children to walk at all times like patients in a convalescent ward. She tried to compromise by asking Carlo and Stefania to remove their shoes in the flat. Her children, like Japanese, were accustomed to slipping out of their shoes at the door, in order to appease the downstairs neighbor. Tonight Stefania was wearing stylish sandals with clattering wooden heels. Her stay at Anna-Laura's had made her forget.

"Remove your shoes," Carlo called like a drill sergeant.

Stefania returned, barefoot and wearing her cowboy hat. She stood in front of Maurizio, glancing up coquettishly from beneath the brim. "See?" she said. "See what Mama brought me from America?" She spun around, pivoting gracefully so he could admire it from all angles.

Rafaella watched her daughter with mixed emotions. A part of her basked in simple pride at the child's prettiness. She loved the prancing little feet, delicate and twinkling, and the sly, curved smile. She also loved the moving spill of Stefania's glossy black hair, and the wit and liveliness in the dark eyes—her father's eyes—as she struck new poses for the delight of Maurizio.

What chilled her was the knowing, seductive quality of Stefania's movements. How could a child of eight imitate, so unerringly, the wiles of a grown-up woman? Maurizio was enchanted. He laughed indulgently, reaching out and pulling the brim of the hat low on Stefania's forehead, pretending to draw a six-shooter and challenge her to a duel.

"And what," he said when they had exhausted this game, "did your mama bring for you, Carlo?"

Carlo, as if aware of his sister's excesses, sat expressionless in his chair like a diplomat. He smiled a conspiratorial smile at his mother and waved one hand. "Something wonderful," he said casually. But he, too, was only a child, and soon he went to his room and returned with the Neiman-Marcus candle.

Ceremoniously, Maurizio lit the candle with his expensive cigarette lighter. "Only for a few minutes," said Carlo. "I don't want it to burn away."

Stefania was sitting on the arm of Maurizio's chair. At first she perched decorously, but by degrees she permitted her body to curve toward his until she was all but slumping against him. Her skirt had rucked up, and one leg was nearly exposed. Maurizio patted the leg absentmindedly, pulled her down so that she was sitting on his lap, her head against his chest. He shielded her face with one large, capable hand. In the other he held his brandy glass. His eyes continued to dart furtively in Rafaella's direction; if their glances met he smiled before looking away.

"Time for bed," Anna-Laura told the children.

"Signor Guidi will carry me," said Stefania languidly. "I am much too tired to walk." She looked up at Maurizio, lifting her arms in a movement both pleading and sensual. Rafaella saw her daughter's hand splayed against the adult man's chest, mutely coaxing, and spoke abruptly.

"Stefania! Stop pestering Signor Guidi and go to bed. Now!"

She heard her voice, shrill and shrewish, pierce the room. It was the voice of authority, and it astounded her that she could still produce it. Instantly she was appalled. She had been home for less than twenty-four hours and already, witchlike, she had shrieked at her daughter. Stefania's eyes grew large with hurt and betrayal. Didn't her mother realize, the eyes seemed to say, that it was for *her* sake?

Anna-Laura was marshaling the children, taking charge. In another moment they would be gone, marched up the hall, and Rafaella would be alone with Maurizio. She called out to Anna-Laura that she would put the children to bed.

"I am still very tired," she said to Maurizio. "Forgive me."

He got to his feet in one smooth movement, as if he had been prepared for this moment all evening. In his eyes she saw some of the urgency she had perceived earlier and wondered again what it was she was required to say.

At Carlo's bedside she knelt and took him in her arms. "Tomorrow," she said, "I am going to go for a walk. Will you come with me, after school? Perhaps we'll see the pensioner who walks on two canes." He nodded happily and kissed her.

Stefania was a different matter. She lay hunched on her side, perplexed and withdrawn. "Stefania," said Rafaella. "I'm sorry I raised my voice. Signor Guidi works so hard—he only came to welcome me back—and I didn't want him to—"

To what? Stefania rolled over, always ready to forgive immediately. "He is old, Mama," she said, "but Signor Guidi has a lot of energy. He's fun. He makes me laugh."

Rafaella bent her head, inhaling the vital scent of her little girl. If Anna-Laura was destined to call to mind basil and honey, and Carlo almonds, then Stefania was a blend of peaches and some elemental, chemical odor she couldn't identify. She stroked her daughter's hair and wondered how much Stefania could recall of Aldo. She did not wish, no matter how kind and competent he was, for Maurizio to assume the role of father to her children.

"You had a fine father," she whispered close to Stefania's ear. "Do you ever remember Papa?"

But Stefania was—oh, blessedly, Rafaella was to think later—asleep.

Nina was the next to visit. She came to the flat the following afternoon. Rafaella saw her from her window, swinging up the Via Vieri, dressed in tight blue jeans and an American T-shirt. The words emblazoned on the shirt jiggled and swayed over Nina's small, unfettered breasts. Sunlight streamed down on her straw-colored hair and she was momentarily so radiant it seemed she might burst into flame.

Directly beneath the window she smoothed her hair and assumed a more serious expression. It was a look meant to be appropriate for visiting an invalid who also happened to be her boss.

Rafaella met her at the door to the flat, still wearing the long, loose dressing gown. She saw that Nina's T-shirt said Ohio State University.

Nina did not embrace her, but she smiled and touched her

shoulder gently. "You look fine," she said. "Better than fine. You look as if you've been in the sun."

This, Rafaella knew, was true. Everyone who remarked on her color, her "blooming" as Maurizio would say, struggled to keep the surprise from their voices. They had expected her to be pale and gaunt, and instead she appeared healthier than she had in years. Only frank Nina was capable of appraising her so casually.

"The operation improved my circulation," she said.

Nina nodded. She rummaged in her large shoulderbag and came up with a small package wrapped in tissue and the notebook in which she kept accounts. She put the notebook on a table and handed the parcel to Rafaella. "Small present," she said. "In fact, very small."

Rafaella unwrapped the tissue and discovered a single cake of expensive, carnation-scented soap. It was a soap she particularly liked; she had mentioned it once to Nina and was touched that the girl had remembered.

"Thank you, Nina," she said. She offered coffee, but Nina asked for Coca-Cola. Nina subsisted on a diet of carbonated beverages and unfiltered cigarettes, which she smoked constantly. She had confided to Rafaella that she was a "night person" and could not bear to go to bed before dawn, even if she had to get up early the next morning. By rights, she should have been a dissipated, trembling creature with nicotine stained fingers and a rasping cough, but she was, at twenty-two, as healthy and glowing as a prize colt.

"Shall we do business?" she inquired, lighting a cigarette and glancing at her notebook.

"Has there been any?" Rafaella could not imagine that much had gone on in the Bagatelle studio in her absence.

"Yes, yes." Nina ran her fingers through her long hair and began to recite, day by day, the transactions she had supervised. On the very day Rafaella had left, the department store on the Via Marconi had requested a consignment of buckles for their new line of ornate belts. "They're to be worn with designer jeans, of course," said Nina, unconsciously smoothing her own sleek hips. The sister store in Milan was also interested in the buckles. The proprietor of a small, elegant boutique in Rome had sold all of Rafaella's earrings and was considering a new gimmick.

"Single earrings for men," said Nina. "Unique, one of a kind."

"What sort of man wears earrings?"

"Lots of younger men do, signora. Just one, you understand. They have one pierced ear. It looks quite dashing."

Rafaella began to feel weary as Nina triumphantly outlined the volume of her business. She should be glad she was achieving such a following, but all she could think of was oceans of belt buckles, acres of earrings, burying her in a glittering pile of trivia. What did she care for men with pierced ears or vain women intent on dressing like latter-day buccaneers?

The lady from Milan had written to ask when she might expect the design for her emerald to be submitted for her approval. She would be in Genoa in mid-July, and hoped that Signora Leone would have something to show her at that time. Finally, Nina herself had sold three pieces at the studio. Two had gone to Austrian tourists, and the third was purchased by the wife of one of Maurizio's associates.

Nina looked up from her notebook and smiled with pride. Surely, she seemed to say, Rafaella would be happy to hear of such a productive time. Rafaella tried to show some enthusiasm, but it all seemed unreal, beside the point. What *was* the point? Somehow she had forgotten in the past weeks that she was a businesswoman. She had obligations. She had to support her children and herself. It was no longer enough to lie and listen to the signals her wounded body telegraphed to her. This activity, her only activity recently, was not enough. More was required of her.

"I tried to work on a design for the emerald," she said. "Nothing came right."

Nina paused and seemed to come to a decision. She flipped through her book until she'd located the page she wanted. She handed it over to Rafaella with a tentative gesture. "I was just scribbling," she said. "You know, just for fun? I thought maybe something like this?"

On the page, sketched in Nina's light, rapid hand, were

several crude ideas for the emerald's setting. The one she had liked best, and refined, was a small, breaking wave. Tiny filigree tendrils represented the tossing froth; the emerald itself, caught and held in the wave's arc, would suggest the green underbelly of the sea. It reminded Rafaella of something, but she couldn't remember what. Nina had sketched the piece, finally, in three dimensions. It was complete.

Rafaella handed the book back. "It's lovely, Nina. I can't imagine doing anything better."

"Consider it your coming-home present. With the soap."

"No. The design is yours. You must have the credit, Nina."

"I can't sculpt it, though, or cast it."

In the end, Nina agreed to bring the small tools Rafaella would need for the preliminary cast to the flat. She was flushed and proud. Although the setting would come from the Bagatelle studio, Rafaella insisted it be called a Nina Rossilli original.

"Who knows?" said Rafaella. "Perhaps we'll end up as partners."

"You're not angry?"

Rafaella stared at her in amazement. Why should she be angry? Below, in the streets, they heard the cries of children returning from school. The voices floated up and through the open windows like a choir of starlings. The summer term would soon be over and the children, anticipating their freedom, were noisier than usual.

It occurred to Rafaella that Nina was afraid she was jealous or annoyed by such ambition in her assistant. Nina still lived in a world where such things seemed important. It was a world which no longer had significance or meaning.

"I'm proud of you," she said gently.

They heard footsteps pounding up the stairs, and then Carlo came into the room. He was always the first to arrive home. He deposited his bookbag and greeted Nina politely. He hovered near the door, glancing at his mother with puzzled eyes.

"You're not dressed," he said at last. "I've come to take you for your walk."

Rafaella remembered her view of Nina, swinging easily up the street, and pulled her gown more tightly around her. "Perhaps tomorrow, darling," she said. "I'm a little tired now."

Nina left then, and Carlo remained near the door. He was too old to consider a walk with his mother a treat, and so he did not say, as Stefania might have, *You promised.* Instead he wrestled with the conflicting emotions warring inside of him. Rafaella could read his mind; her son wanted to be tender and considerate—he did not wish to tax her beyond her endurance—but he also felt himself responsible for her welfare. At the age of eleven, Carlo tried to be both son and surrogate husband.

"It would be good for you, Mama," he said. "You said yourself you were supposed to walk a little every day."

She looked at the defiant face, the blue eyes wavering between authority and the desire to be commanded, and felt she might cry. "Ah, Carlo," she said. "Don't look like that. You'll break my heart."

They both heard the words at the same time. Rafaella rose and pointed to the clock on the table, laughing shakily. "Five minutes," she said. "I will be ready in five minutes."

As she was searching for a pair of low-heeled shoes to wear on her walk with Carlo, she came upon the shoes she had worn the night Stephen had taken her to the restaurant on the turning basin. Their heels, slender and high and frivolous, poked accusingly from the neat little storage bag. She stretched out a finger and touched them wonderingly, these artifacts from another life. She could recall the precise feel of the sultry air on her bare arms; the soft lapping motion of the bayou, the white ship passing out to sea, the taste of the wine she had drunk—all filled her memory and became more real than her own bedroom.

She had succeeded in banishing his face. Whenever it threatened to invade her consciousness she summoned the myriad demands and details of her domestic life until, overmastered by reality, the image faded and assumed its proper place in her life, which was nowhere.

Like a clever ghost who demands admittance, he now

entered her bedroom in a way she could not have anticipated. Touching the high heels of the shoes she had worn
made her remember the steep and pebbly path to the restaurant. She could feel the perilous path beneath the soles of
her feet, and then, in logical sequence, she felt the touch of
his hand, his arm beneath the cloth of his jacket, as he
guided her safely up the hill.

Carlo was calling to her from the living room. He wanted
to know if she was getting ready. In his voice she heard
impatience and concern. She shut the closet door and was
returned to reality.

Chapter 3

She dreamed that Fred Blanchard, the owly-browed cardiologist from St. Matthew's, was her husband. He told her all the nurses at the hospital were going to buy earrings from Bagatelle to wear in the operating room. Then he stepped into an airplane and flew back to work in America. "I'll see you next week," cried Rafaella, waving into the sky. "Don't forget to cough," he called back.

"Are you experiencing any pain?" asked Dr. Rinaldi in real life. She was lying on his examination table, feeling his fingers lightly traversing her scar. She shook her head. "Only a little soreness," she replied. "Not real pain."

He was well pleased with her, it seemed. She was in fine shape, Dr. Rinaldi told her. Better than new. He was especially impressed by the neatness of the scar which ran from neck to navel. He commented several times on the scar, approvingly, as if it were a thing of beauty, and she did not reply.

She had not confronted it yet. Her ploys for avoiding the sight of her own body were numerous. It was important to conceal this fact from Dr. Rinaldi, she knew. She felt she was well acquainted with the scar in any case. Her fingers knew the feel of it; her body was aware. Beneath her flowing dressing gown she felt secure, but in street clothing she felt an odd alarm.

On that first walk with Carlo, she had worn a high-necked dress of a light, summery material. The sun had been strong, and against all reason she had feared that it could penetrate the thin material and reveal her to passersby. She had glanced uneasily into the plate-glass window of the tobacco shop. There she had seen only a slender woman walking with a small boy. Nothing marked the woman as peculiar, except the worried frown between the brows.

Dr. Rinaldi told her to dress and join him in his office when she was ready. Blindly, as she had done ever since the operation, she clothed the upper part of her body. When it was covered, she slipped into her skirt and shoes quickly. The scar on her inner thigh, where they had taken the vein, was healing nicely. It did not disturb her, even though it ran a zigzag course and showed red against the tender flesh. Disfiguring as it was, she thought it the kind of scar anyone might have. It had a casual, devil-may-care attitude. Once, in the bath, she had imagined it had come to her as she climbed over a stile in a country meadow. A nail, embedded in the wood, had ripped at her there. It had required many stitches.

"Do you have any questions?" Dr. Rinaldi asked when she sat across from his desk. "Is there anything troubling you?"

"No," she said.

"Your children? How are they?"

"Fine. They're fine."

"Do you ever feel depressed?"

"Never."

"You are a lucky woman, signora. Extremely lucky."

"Oh, yes," said Rafaella. "I know."

As she was about to leave, Dr. Rinaldi asked her about Martin Lassiter. What was the great doctor like? Was he conversational, friendly? Rinaldi asked these questions with a convivial air, as if Rafaella had recently attended a concert so legendary that people slept in the streets for days in order to be first in line to secure a ticket.

She searched for some small tidbit which might please her cardiologist. Since she had been asleep for the main event, she could only appease him with trivia.

"He wears Gucci shoes," she said at last.

"Ah," said Dr. Rinaldi. "A man of fashion."

When she stepped back out into the sunlight, a little puff of wind blowing off the sea tugged at the floppy ties of her blouse. She pressed them flat with both hands and imagined the breeze plucking her clothing away, revealing the long, straight, shiny path that divided her torso to hundreds of curious eyes. Since Dr. Rinaldi's office was part of a clinic, nearly everyone in the vicinity would flock to view her with professional curiosity.

But, how lucky you are, signora, they would murmur. *You have been mutilated by masters!*

Carlo and Stefania were still in school. Anna-Laura, seamless and plump as a fresh melon, was shepherding her students through the intricacies of grammar at the *politecnico*. Nina would be speeding toward the studio on the pillion seat of her boyfriend's motorcycle, Maurizio returning to his office after a comradely solicitor's luncheon of cold seafood and wine.

And Dr. Blanchard, whom her subconscious had inappropriately joined her to in holy matrimony? He would, she calculated, be waking up in River Oaks, or wherever he lived, his mind full of angiograms and the living bodies to which they were connected. Lassiter would also be waking up, but here her imagination failed her. She could not picture Dr. Lassiter asleep or rubbing his eyes in the first moment of wakefulness or eating a boiled egg.

Whenever she thought of him she saw him standing at the foot of her bed, poised for flight and yet uniquely *there* for her. It was as if he was pulled in so many conflicting directions that it took a supreme act of will to anchor him to the floor of her hospital room. Each time she pictured him she felt a secret wave of happiness and gratitude lulling her into a calm state of mind, leading her away from common events and into the world of high adventure they had shared together.

It was an intensely personal feeling and could never be described. She was sorry to have been so flippant with Dr. Rinaldi, but if she had tried to explain what Lassiter was like she would seem irrational. She couldn't say that she loved him. It was a love that asked nothing. She never expected to see him again, nor did she care to; but in some way he would always be a part of her now. She had never felt that way about the doctor who delivered Carlo and Stefania, nor was she a woman who automatically revered doctors. She knew her feeling was one that could only be understood by those who had had the same operation. *Dr. Lassiter had been in her heart.*

She boarded a bus at the Piazza Della Valli and took a seat. She had been told to expect wild shifts in her emotions following surgery, but so far, at home, she had remained much the same. After the first great joy of seeing the children again, she had settled into a sort of weary numbness. She thought she was sad, and mourning for something, but she didn't know what it might be.

An old woman, dressed in dark cotton, stared at her with what seemed disapproval. Next to her, a man read his newspaper, folding each page back with an annoying fastidiousness, as if to make sure no word escaped him. Rafaella saw that he had just finished reading an article about an OPEC conference.

She wondered if the sheikh had gone home yet and tried to imagine what had happened to the enormous wreath of roses.

Just before the bus veered over toward the Via Vieri, a woman boarded with her little boy. The child let go of his mother's hand and ran ahead, down the aisle, jostling knees and causing the man with the newspaper to frown.

"*Stefano!*" cried the mother, rebuking him so sharply he froze where he was standing. "*Stefano.*"

Rafaella felt a shudder pass over her at the name. It was as if the woman was shouting at her. She wanted to repeat the name, softly, to herself, and then the feeling passed. All she knew, when she got off the bus, was that the sensation of mourning had come closer.

Sometimes, Rafaella wondered how a couple like Michele and Gemma Leone had produced two such offspring as Aldo and Anna-Laura. Although it was possible to trace some of Anna-Laura's emotional excesses to those of her mother, where had the wit, the grace under pressure, the genuine kindness, come from? Gemma tried to be kind, but she lacked fine instincts and was too absorbed in her own small interior world—a world in which people were always insulting her, or failing to understand how sensitive she was—to ever help anyone.

Aldo had been even more a mystery. He seemed to have been a changeling, sneaked into the nursery when no one was looking and marked with the name Leone. Rafaella used to imagine that the real Leone baby—peevish, colicky, and demanding—had been the bane of its unsuspecting foster parents' life while Aldo, son of some gentle prince, had brought delight and beauty into the chaotic home of the undeserving Leones in Naples.

She had mentioned this fantasy once, and he had laughed and pulled her close. "I am just like my father," he'd said, "but with an important difference. He is an unhappy man, and I'm a happy one."

Rafaella found this an unsatisfactory explanation. Michele Leone was withdrawn and silent. He was unfailingly courteous to Rafaella and occasionally he showed signs of affection toward his son and daughter, but something was missing in him. She had seen him sit for over an hour without speaking unless someone addressed a direct comment to him. Rafaella thought it was his way of escaping from his wife, who talked enough for both of them.

Michele Leone was an engineer, close to retirement age now, who shared no common interest with his spouse. Rafaella knew, because Aldo had told her, that Michele was interested in European history; he had an extensive library and had once dreamed that he would write a book on the *Risorgimento*. This information had stunned her because the small, neat man with the dark moustache and melancholy eyes seemed incapable of dreaming anything.

If Michele was an unhappy man, Gemma didn't seem to notice. Her endless lists of grievances, the terrible burdens she had been made to bear, were things she discussed cheerfully and exhaustively, confident they were as interesting to others as they were to her.

"My mother's misfortunes make her very happy," Anna-Laura often said. It was true. So true that when a real misfortune came to her—the untimely death of her son—she did not know how to express her sorrow. She had been feigning unhappiness for so long that she could not cope with genuine despair. It had been Michele who had wept when Aldo died.

Rafaella was thinking of her in-laws because she expected a phone call from Naples at any time. Anna-Laura had fended her mother off, saying that Rafaella was sleeping, but soon enough that excuse would not avail. The phone in the hallway would ring, and at the other end the effusive voice of Gemma Leone would rush into the flat, poking and prodding, trying to elicit guilt and sympathy, trying to connect itself to a life which had eluded her.

She had just settled down with Nina's sketch and a lump of wax and her tools when the phone rang. Anna-Laura had taken the children out to dinner; she was alone.

"Stefania, darling, it's your *nonna*. Will you let me speak to mama, my pet? I have waited and waited to hear her voice, Stefania, but she is always sleeping. She can't be sleeping now, because it's time for your dinner. Have you eaten yet, *carina*? Are you having proper meals?"

Gemma's voice roared down the wire like combers crashing on a beach. Rafaella thought of the design for the emerald, and changed the image. Gemma's voice was more like the charge of a rogue elephant. She waited for her mother-in-law's diatribe to wind down. When Gemma paused for breath, she said, "This is Rafaella."

"But I thought you were Stefania! You sounded like her, you know." An accusatory inflection. Rafaella, she seemed to say, had been craftily posing as her daughter.

"I'm sorry, *Nonna*."

"Are you very weak, then, *cara?* Has something happened to your voice? Anna-Laura has told me you look very well, Rafaella. Are you hiding something from me? It can't be healthy for you to sleep so much."

"It was only for the first few days. I'm fine. Please don't worry about me." She told her mother-in-law she had seen the doctor and described herself as convalescing splendidly. She asked after Gemma's health.

"Who can care about the aches and pains of an old lady?" Gemma asked rhetorically. "When you are young, the whole world takes notice. Nobody cares for the miseries of old women." She laughed, to show it had been a joke. "But seriously, Rafaella—you must tell me exactly how you feel. I imagine it will be weeks before you are yourself again."

"Dr. Rinaldi says at the rate I'm going I will be back to normal in two more weeks," said Rafaella. This was not precisely true. Rinaldi had been less definite, but Gemma needed absolutes. Two weeks was a measure of time she could conjure with. She would mark them off on her calendar. In exactly two weeks she would call and say: "Well, are you yourself again?"

"Let me give you the benefit of my greater years, *cara*. When I was in bed after the female business, I found a teaspoon of mineral oil in warm water most beneficial. You must have it every morning, before your breakfast. It will keep you regular."

Rafaella agreed to the mineral oil. She then listened to a catalogue of the mortally ill and dying in the Leones' neighborhood. Signora Arioli, Rafaella would remember her, was being eaten away by a voracious cancer and would not last the year. The younger daughter of the Gioffre family appeared to be inflicted by a debilitating disease of the central nervous system. A man in Michele's engineering firm, a junior partner from the Posillipo area, had been involved in an automobile accident and might still lose his right arm.

"Sometimes it seems it would be better not to be born, eh?" Gemma sighed. "So much horror in the world, *cara*— so much sorrow. What's the use?"

"I don't know, *Nonna*," said Rafaella. She was used to the litany of death and disease; she sometimes suspected Gemma of inventing calamities when none existed.

"But why am I being so morbid, Rafaella? Just when you need to be encouraged? It is a miracle, darling, a miracle— what they have done for you. I didn't trust the American doctor, you know. Signora Arioli told me he used to put monkeys' hearts in human bodies until they stopped him, but that was a long time ago. If he has helped you, he has my blessing forever."

The call rambled on for a time. Gemma informed her daughter-in-law of numerous small details in her life: a shop-girl had been rude to her, a pane of glass in the parlor window had mysteriously cracked, necessitating the services of a glazier, who had charged twice what the job was worth. At last she wound down. "Shall I have a word with my darlings?" she asked.

"Anna-Laura has taken them out for supper," said Rafaella.

There was a shocked silence. "*Cara*—surely not. They must want to be with their mama after such a long absence. It is most important for families to dine together, Rafaella. Especially"—her voice took on a misty quality—"when there is no papa. When I was a young girl, my parents never left me. We were always together. I never ate a meal away from them."

Rafaella heard a male voice, muffled in the distance. Then Michele Leone was on the other end. "Rafaella," he said calmly. "Welcome back. Get all the rest you need. Call us if there is anything we can do."

"I will," she said gratefully. Explosive sounds issued from the background, but Gemma was not to be allowed back on the line. Perhaps, she thought, her father-in-law was a greater ally than she had known. She put the receiver down and went back to the room where her tools were in readiness.

She took up Nina's sketch and studied it, kneading the wax in her other hand. She wished Aldo were alive so she could ask him if he ever had eaten a meal, in his childhood, away from his mother.

On her fifth day back home, Rafaella woke to euphoria. She could not recall a time when the prospect of getting out of bed had seemed so pleasing. She threw the shutters back and let in the pearly light of early morning. How calm and peaceful her street was at this early hour! How beautiful the stately white houses, snug beneath their tiled roofs. Directly below, the furled petals of Signora Lenti's geraniums glimmered with dew and waited for the sun to tease them open.

Why was her bedroom so bare? She had put away the photographs and personal mementos before she went away to America. It was time to restore them. From a drawer she took her wedding picture and a photograph of Aldo, taken shortly before he died, and placed them on the bureau next to the framed shots of Carlo and Stefania. There they were —her family. Better.

She put on the flowing dressing gown, washed her face and cleaned her teeth, and brushed her hair until her scalp ached. In the kitchen she restrained herself from humming as she brewed the coffee because Anna-Laura was still asleep on the couch. She cut melon for all of them and boiled some eggs, English style. When the espresso was ready she took a cup to Anna-Laura. Kneeling beside the couch she surveyed her sister-in-law's face with compassion. Fine lines radiated from her eyes, and in her sleep she frowned slightly. Anna-Laura was tired from assuming Rafaella's responsibilities as well as her own.

"This is your last night on the terrible couch," she said when Anna-Laura's eyes opened. "Tonight you will sleep in your own bed."

"What's this? Did I keep you up with my snoring?"

"You don't snore, love. You're perfection itself."

Anna-Laura humped herself up beneath the covers and extended a hand for the coffee. "You're cheerful this morning," she said.

"I feel wonderful. It is time to stop dragging about. I am going to go to the studio after the children are in school. I feel *stupendous!*"

Anna-Laura smiled. "Good," she said. "But you won't overdo, will you?" She touched Rafaella's cheek. "You'll be sensible?"

"I find a teaspoon of mineral oil taken in warm water every morning extremely beneficial," said Rafaella, imitating Gemma's confidential tones.

"But what good is it to advise you?" finished Anna-Laura. "Who listens to the advice of an old woman?"

They collapsed in laughter, leaning against each other, giddy with mirth at Gemma Leone's expense.

When the children awakened, Rafaella was leaning out the window carrying on a lively conversation with Signora Lenti, who was pinching dead leaves from her potted flowers. They exchanged looks of surprise—even under normal conditions their mama was not in the habit of shouting from the windows.

While she dressed Stefania's hair, making two small braids at each side and letting the rest hang free, she instructed Carlo to run through the words of his spelling test for her. Even when he faltered over *sdrucciolevole* twice, she merely laughed and made a face at him. Again the children exchanged looks. Rafaella was generally stern if you missed the same word twice. And something else—what about Stefania's hair? How many times had Stefania pleaded with her mother to be allowed to experiment with her hair? First she had wanted to have it cut off very short and permed into a frizz of ringlets like her friend Maria. Mama had pointed out that Maria's hair was naturally curly; Stefania's, like her own, was straight. She did not think it becoming for little girls to alter the hair God had given them. Of course, she didn't mention God, as *nonna* would do, but the implication was clear. Stefania might do anything she liked when she was grown, but while she was still a child she would abide by her mother's decisions.

And now, here she was, happily creating chic little braidlets—exactly the sort a famous model affected—and bringing the mirror so Stefania could admire herself. Such was the power of her reflection in the mirror that Stefania forgot to wonder at this aberrant behavior, but Carlo was still wary.

Rafaella stood at the head of the stairs, blowing kisses as the children trudged off to school. She and Anna-Laura had another cup of coffee together, and then Anna-Laura, too, went off. Rafaella bathed, using the carnation soap Nina had given her. She did not look at her body but allowed her hands, slippery with soap, to linger over the scar. Soon she would force herself to look at it. She would wait, sensibly, until it had healed to a thin, white line. She dressed in white trousers and a pale blue tunic with a Mandarin collar. Her fingers trembled with impatience; she was eager to be outside. She hummed along with the music that came from her portable radio. It was tuned to a station that offered frequent news flashes, and the tunes were old, nostalgic. She felt they were almost unbearably beautiful.

244

On the street everything seemed to be twice as brilliant and colorful as it ought to be. She had never taken drugs, but she remembered descriptions she had read of the effects of LSD. If this was what it was like, she thought, then everyone ought to be fed massive doses of lysurgic acid. She thought of the wonderful changes it might bring about in Gemma Leone, for example. Gemma might look at her cracked windowpane and see, not a potential expense, but a waterfall of diamonds.

The euphoria persisted throughout the day. On the Via Acquatania, where Bagatelle was located, she felt she had strayed onto a stage set. The red and white canopy awning over Brandini's sparkled like a Christmas candy, just as she had remembered it. Promptly on cue, the pensioner who walked with two canes came dragging up the street. She called good morning to him, so full of good will she ignored the unspoken custom and delayed him in conversation.

He was polite, bewildered. "You've been away, signora," he said. "Were you having a holiday?"

"Yes, yes," she cried, hearing her laugh ring out with the precision of fine crystal rapped by a tiny hammer. "Yes, signore, on holiday!"

In the studio the display cases seemed to welcome her back. No wonder shops in Milan and Rome vied for her designs—they were works of art! She had been far too modest to style herself a bauble merchant. She avoided the back room, sensing that the austerity and whiteness might prove too clinical for her present mood. She would work later. For now, she wanted customers. She wanted to stand in her little shop and carry on brilliant conversations with whoever wandered in. Let them be strangers, by all means! She extracted a brooch from its little nest of velvet and pinned it to the collar of her tunic.

Toward noon, a customer came in. She was a German, a woman of about Rafaella's age, but stout and matronly. She carried a map of Genoa folded in one hand and spoke English.

"These are nice pieces," she said. "Very original."

"Thank you," said Rafaella.

The German woman leaned on the cases, surveying the

treasures within. At last she pointed to the brooch on Rafaella's collar. "You have any more like that?" she asked.

Rafaella brought her hands up, lightly touching the silver trapezoid at her neck. She unclasped it easily and handed it to the German woman.

"No, no," the woman said. "Do you have any you will sell?"

She seemed such a nice woman. Despite her Germanic attitude, she had an endearing smile and a soft voice. Rafaella noticed a small ladder in her flesh-toned tights. Even as she watched, it snaked up the woman's leg. Her customer, so confidently attired, was unaware of this imperfection.

"I will sell this one," she said. "You may have this one."

The woman's blond brows shot up in a gesture of incomprehension. She thought, no doubt, that Bagatelle's owner was so hard up she would sell her own ornaments. Rafaella laughed. "Take it!" she said. "It is a present. You understand? It's yours." She tried to thrust the brooch on the German; their two hands danced over the counter in a strange *pavanne* of misunderstanding. "Have it, as a gift," Rafaella said, but the woman shook her head and retreated. The last view she had of her was a sad one. The woman walked out of the shop and briskly up the Via Acquatania, the sun showing, with merciless clarity, the white path arrowing up her leg.

When the children came home, they found their mama absorbed in cooking. The flat was full of the spicy, olivey smell of the seasoning for *cima*. Rafaella danced a little two-step in the kitchen as she chopped and sautéed. Anna-Laura was coming for dinner, she told them. Even though their aunt would sleep at home from now on, the table would be incomplete without her.

"Can Signor Guidi come too?" Stefania asked.

"He can," said Rafaella, laughing, "but I have not invited him." Two bottles of wine stood uncorked on the kitchen table.

"Will we drink all that?" said Carlo. "All by ourselves?"

His mother laughed again. The knife flashed in her hand

as she attacked some mushrooms. "We may, darling," she said. "Who can tell?"

"Stefania hasn't removed her shoes," said Carlo. There was nothing bullying or tattletalish in the remark. He was simply reporting, as a junior officer might to the general, an infringement of the rules.

His mother turned. "Carlo," she said, "just for this one time let the child wear her shoes." She embraced him, her hands still holding the knife. "Stefania!" she shouted. "Dance on the signorina's head! Make as much noise as you like!"

Carlo coaxed his mother out to watch the news on television. They gathered, a family, in the center of the sitting room. Rafaella settled back on the couch, a glass of wine in her hand. The announcer talked about boring things, like the fluctuating state of the lire and a scandal within the *regione*. His mother nodded wisely, as if she and the man on the television were old friends. She seemed less happy when pictures of a minor earthquake in Greece flashed on the screen. Carlo noticed that she shut her eyes when the camera panned over scenes of devastation. "It's all right now, Mama," he said, when the camera had returned to the large, calm face of the announcer. "The earthquake is over."

But it was not all right. The announcer assumed a solemn look and told them that the body of a kidnapped industrialist had been recovered after six weeks. He had been found in a deserted warehouse a few kilometers from Milano, shot through the heart and mutilated in ways the announcer apparently found too horrible to disclose.

They were subjected to a close-up of the remains. The industrialist, in death, reminded Carlo of nothing so much as a monkey he had once seen in a copy of *National Geographic*. The lips were drawn back in a horrible parody of a smile. Anyone could see that the smile was the product of pain, not happiness.

"No," his mama said in a low voice. "Oh, no. I don't want to *see!*" She bent forward deeply, and the red wine in her glass spilled over the front of her blue tunic. It was as if blood had seeped from her mouth. Carlo watched with a horrified fascination as the red stain spread over her front.

She hunched forward, hiding her eyes. She seemed to be weeping. He touched her shoulder timidly and told Stefania to turn the television off.

In the sudden silence, Rafaella's small sobs sounded like the inarticulate peeps of a wounded bird.

Chapter 4

"You forget, Rafaella, I have raised children of my own." Maurizio's voice was calm, affectionate. "I understand what Carlo is feeling at the moment."

"Ah, but then you understand everything, don't you?" She knew she sounded spiteful, but the fact that her own son had telephoned Maurizio for advice was painful to her.

Maurizio sighed the sigh of a patient man. He raised a hand as if to touch her arm and then withdrew it. "Who would you have him turn to, Rafaella?"

She made no reply. The answer was obvious; but it was quite impossible for Carlo to turn to her when it was her welfare that concerned him. She was not angry at Maurizio or at Carlo, but at herself.

She and Maurizio stood in the first-floor *galleria* of the Palazzo Rosso on the Via Garibaldi. When he had asked if she would lunch with him to discuss an important topic she had suggested meeting here. It was a place that had always pleased her, and it was so public he would see she was not encouraging intimacy. She stared straight forward, at a painting she had seen a hundred times before. It was a sixteenth-century portrait of a woman attributed to Micheli Parrasio. She had always loved it because the young woman seemed so incredibly modern. Why had she never noticed how much the Parrasio resembled Nina?

"I wonder," she said to Maurizio, "if I hired Nina because she looked like this girl?"

"Carlo loves you very much. He is concerned for you. He called me because I am the only adult man to whom he can speak." Maurizio took her arm and led her along to stand in front of a painting which showed the resurrected Jesus displaying his wounds.

"Do I behave like a madwoman, then?" Rafaella looked away from the mutilated palms of the Christ and surveyed a group of women nearby. One of them had been looking at Maurizio with interest. She lowered her lids when Rafaella's eyes met hers. What had she seen in Maurizio Guidi to inspire such a frankly approving stare?

He was wearing tinted glasses; he looked, today, rather like a prosperous film producer. The gray in his brown hair gave him a distinguished, commanding appearance. Rafaella realized that Maurizio, when she'd first met him, had not been much older than she was now. He was telling her that she did not behave like a madwoman, no, far from it, but that she was showing a streak of erratic behavior so unlike her it alarmed Carlo.

They climbed the stairs of the palazzo to the second floor. Here was Christ again, depicted by Rubens, carrying the Cross on his shoulders. Rafaella began to wonder why she had chosen this place for her conversation with Maurizio. This beautiful palace, with its soaring marble staircases and magnificent proportions, seemed dedicated to the glorification of suffering. As an art student, she had viewed the paintings displayed along the Via Garibaldi with an eye for line and space, texture and color. Now all she could see was a celebration of cruelty.

She turned to the Vandykes and wondered why so many small things seemed significant. What had she dreamed of, and forgotten, in those hours of the Intensive Care? The lush green background in a Dürer painting reminded her of something with an immediacy which was almost painful. But what? She thought if she could only submerge herself in that aching green she would find the answer to a cosmic question. She had been cheated, robbed, of whole parts of her life, and Maurizio would never understand. If she tried to tell him, he would say that her behavior was erratic.

"I want to help," he said. "That is all I have ever wanted —to be of some use to you."

"I know," she said. "I know, Maurizio."

They stepped out onto the little terrace which overlooked the roofs of the Old City. Here, looking down on the six-teenth- and seventeenth-century palaces lining the Via Gari-baldi, it was possible to believe the world an orderly and exquisite place.

"It is impossible for me to understand what you've been through," said Maurizio, "but I do know one thing. You must allow yourself to lean on someone. You can't do every-thing alone, my dear."

"Thousands of women are alone, Maurizio. They man-age."

"Is that all you ask of life—simply to manage?"

"You make me sound very dull. Perhaps I am. I'm not adventurous and brave like Anna-Laura. Just to manage seems an heroic feat to me. I am an extremely ordinary woman, Maurizio."

Even as she spoke the words, she knew they were not true and felt a sense of loss. She would never be an ordinary woman again. She would recover and stop behaving in strange ways and raise her children; she would be courteous to strangers and kind to animals. But she would never, never, feel whole.

"*Bene*," she said, startling Maurizio. She had made a deci-sion. If she was going to be a sort of ghost, at least she would be a ghost who did not frighten others.

On a warm day in early July, Rafaella rang her sister-in-law's bell, prompted by impulse. It was close to noon, and she had no idea whether Anna-Laura would be at home at this hour. The children were in school, Nina at the shop. She thought it would be pleasant to spend an hour at Anna-Laura's flat, talking and sipping coffee. She had bought fresh vegetables at the open-air market; perhaps she would make a salad.

Anna-Laura's flat was on the ground floor. The door opened tentatively and Anna-Laura peered around the edge, looking startled. When she saw Rafaella she became dis-tinctly flustered.

"*Cara*," she cried. "I wasn't expecting you." She wore a

rose-colored robe, belted at the waist, and her feet were bare. Rafaella began to apologize, but her sister-in-law opened the door wide and insisted she come in.

A small man was seated at the kitchen table, his hands clasped around a glass of what looked like Cinzano. One of Anna-Laura's private pupils, no doubt, come for his lesson. He had removed his jacket and hung it neatly over the back of the chair. His shirt sleeves were pushed up, revealing pale arms lightly laced with dark hairs. He seemed alarmed but rose politely when Rafaella entered the kitchen. Introductions were made. Anna-Laura said the man was *il dottore* Castelli, a doctor of dentistry, and called him Paolo. She put her arms around Rafaella and introduced her, effusively, as her dearest sister.

"It is a great honor to meet you, signora," the little dentist said. He clasped her hand and then remained standing, as if awaiting orders. Anna-Laura was darting about the kitchen, peering into the bag of vegetables, bringing glasses from the cupboard, and drawing up another chair for Rafaella.

"But I mustn't disturb the lesson," Rafaella said. "I'll come another time."

"No, please—I was just leaving, signora."

"The lesson," said Anna-Laura, "is over for today."

Dr. Castelli winced. Rafaella felt sorry for him. He was so diminutive and vulnerable. Despite his profession, he looked shabby. She wondered why he felt the need to study English.

"Do you have an international clientele, *dottore?*" she asked.

"Oh, by no means," he said. He emphasized the words, as if to put to rest forever any suspicion that he might be successful. "I practice here in Genoa, signora."

Rafaella smiled. That much she had guessed. He spoke the local dialect—all but incomprehensible to other Italians. It was a dialect she could speak as easily as she could academic Italian or the Neapolitan dialect of the Leones. Dr. Castelli was nervously donning his suit jacket now, glancing at his watch and gathering his cigarettes and lighter from the table. Anna-Laura watched him, arms folded.

"*Ciao*, Anna," he said. He repeated that it had been a

great honor to meet Rafaella and then all but fled from the room. Anna-Laura went with him and returned moments later. She sat at the table and poured herself a large glass of Cinzano. "That man is always in a hurry," she said. She looked at Rafaella over the lip of the glass, her eyes ironic.

"Why does Dr. Castelli need to learn English?" Rafaella asked.

"He doesn't. Paolo has no English, *cara*."

"But the lesson? You said it was finished."

Anna-Laura continued to regard her over the glass. She shook her head, rose, and went to the sink. She began to wash the tomatoes Rafaella had bought, turning the water tap on so high that the room was full of the sound of rushing water. "You are priceless!" she shouted over the noise. "Beyond rubies, Rafaella. Absolutely priceless." She turned the water off and returned to the table.

"Paolo is my lover," she said.

Rafaella tried to connect the word "lover" to the furtive little man who had just left. It seemed impossible that Anna-Laura could refer to him in those terms.

"Did you think I taught my students dressed like *this*?" Anna-Laura pointed to the robe, her bare feet. It was obvious she was naked beneath the rose-colored material. Now that Rafaella really looked, she saw that Anna-Laura had recently been engaged in the act of love. There was a soft, loose quality to her lips which was never apparent at ordinary times. She looked tousled and sleepy. A horrifying thought occurred to her.

"Did I *interrupt* you?" she asked. She could not meet her sister-in-law's eyes. She felt that Anna-Laura was mocking her for her naïveté; her face had grown hot with humiliation as if it were she who had been caught in a compromising situation.

"No. I told you—that man is always in a hurry."

Rafaella tried again to picture the lovers at their noon tryst and failed. Her imagination faltered each time she recalled the pale, defeated arms beneath the dentist's rolled-back shirt sleeves, the weak, apologetic mouth. Anna-Laura, so vital and strong—how could she have conceived a passion for such a colorless little man? Dr. Castelli did not seem equipped to move a woman so powerful and shrewd as her sister-in-law.

"Do you love him?" she asked.

Anna-Laura laughed. "Look, *cara*," she said. "Let me explain something to you. Love is not so very easy to find. It's not a measured commodity—so much for you, so much for me. It isn't democratic. Some people get more than their share, some get almost none.

"Paolo is a lonely man; I am a lonely woman. If we can make one another happy now and then, why not? Who suffers? I would rather have love, you understand, but in place of it I will gladly take what I can get. I am not going to turn my back on pleasure, Rafaella."

"Do you want to marry him?"

"*Madonna mia*, you are a child. Younger than Stefania! Paolo is already married, *cara*. Why else do you think he comes to see me between eleven and noon? *Il dottore* has five children and a wife who grinds her teeth when she performs the marital duty. He will never divorce her, and I wouldn't marry him even if he did. Do you understand now?"

"Yes," said Rafaella.

While Anna-Laura went to dress, she prepared the salad. She saw herself as a relic from another age, shocked because her sister-in-law had a lover. The shock was real. From the moment she'd realized, she had felt it shake her with amazement. There was no moral judgment in her shock. She did not dispute Anna-Laura's right to seize some happiness wherever she might find it.

Neither, on close reflection, was her objection on aesthetic grounds. Dr. Castelli seemed unprepossessing to her, but who was she to judge? If it had been within her power to confer a handsome, vigorous lover on Anna-Laura she would have done so, but lacking the power she accepted Paolo.

No. What made her hands tremble with revelation as she sliced the tomatoes was something else. She had been thinking of Anna-Laura only as Aldo's sister and her own dearest friend—a cherished prop in her life who did not exist when she was out of sight. Was she so selfish, or withdrawn, that she thought of people only in relation to herself?

She wished she could apologize to Anna-Laura. In her years with Aldo, she had experienced what Anna-Laura coveted. She was obscurely lucky, it seemed, just as Dr. Rinaldi had said. Misfortune had cloaked her luck in its dark folds, but somewhere, deep inside, it might be flourishing still.

Carlo watched his mother carefully now, alert for the small signs that told him how she was feeling. He thought she was getting better, but he remained vigilant. She had never again pranced about with the terrifying gaiety she'd shown the night the television news made her weep, and Carlo was immensely relieved. Better, he thought, for her to be sad than to pretend to a happiness she did not feel.

Signor Guidi had explained some things to him the time he'd telephoned him at his office. For one thing, he said, the sort of operation his mother had undergone did strange things to people. These things were temporary, but while they lasted they could be most distressing. The effects differed from person to person and Rafaella—shy and independent both—was likely to feel them more than someone of, say, Anna-Laura's temperament.

"What kind of things?" Carlo had wanted to know.

"Some people feel they have lost a part of themselves during the surgery," Signor Guidi said. "For a time they are depressed because such an amazing thing has been done to them and they cannot remember it."

Carlo remembered a teacher at his school who had been absent for many weeks following an operation on his gall bladder. He mentioned the teacher and asked if he, too, would be depressed.

"A gall bladder is not a heart, Carlo. We are very superstitious about our hearts."

His mother was not superstitious. Of that he was sure. Anna-Laura rapped on wood and crossed the street to avoid black cats, but Mama had never done such things. Still, he understood what Signor Guidi meant. The day she had told him he would break her heart, for example. That day had meaning. He could not imagine his teacher, driven to distraction in the classroom, saying "*Basta!* You will break my gall bladder."

Carlo understood many things. Some of them would have surprised his mother, if she had known. He understood that she was wary of Signor Guidi, and why. She knew he would like to take care of her, marry her, and provide them with every comfort. It disturbed her because she knew everybody thought she ought to accept him. It was the sensible thing to do. It would be good for all of them. Some people might even think she was selfish to pass up this chance; knowing this, his mother felt guilty.

Although Carlo liked Maurizio personally, a part of him felt a keen hostility whenever Signor Guidi entered the flat. His mother seemed cornered then, like a gentle forest creature taken captive and unwillingly displayed. Carlo always remained near her, so she could feel his support.

Another thing he understood was her shyness about the scar. She wasn't vain, like Stefania or his friend Marcello's mother, who never appeared in public without lipstick and mascara and was always sneaking looks at herself in mirrors. No. His mother liked things to be neat and orderly, simple but well arranged. He knew because he was that way himself. The curtain that divided his part of the bedroom from Stefania's might as well have been a barrier against chaos.

On Carlo's side, everything knew its place and stayed there. His sketching pads, his books and records, the model cars and airplanes he had constructed—all were ranged neatly on shelves or hung from the ceiling on wires. Every night before he went to bed, he checked to make sure that each object was where it ought to be. The Neiman-Marcus candle stood below the window now to the right of his poster of the American model, Cheryl Tiegs.

Stefania's half of the room was a demilitarized zone. Her underthings and school shirts lay in a jumble on the floor, where they stayed until mama crossly told her to pick them up. Dolls she hadn't played with in years lay everywhere, their arms askew and hair pulled out in clumps. Presiding over the whole mess, Sundance and Butch Cassidy, whom she always forgot to feed, swam about in murky water. Stefania was definitely a slob.

His mother covered herself so thoroughly, he thought, because the neatness of her body had been violated. She didn't want to reveal her scar any more than she would bring a stranger in to view Stefania's unmade bed.

Coming home from school, pondering these thoughts, Carlo decided he would stop in at his mother's studio on the Via Acquatania. He could see Nina through the window. She was behind the display cases, reading a fashion magazine.

"Good afternoon, *bello mio*," she said, looking up with a big grin. She always smiled broadly at him, as if she found him vaguely amusing. It made him blush when she called him handsome, because Nina was sexy. Today she wore a thin purple tank-top as a concession to the heat, and he could make out the shape of her *poppe* beneath. "Your mother is in back," she said.

Rafaella was seated at the work table, head bent. She was examining a small wax mold through a magnifying glass. Before she turned to him she selected a tiny tool, no larger than a toothpick, and made some minor adjustment. Then she gave him all her attention.

"What do you think of this, Carlo? Give me the benefit of your excellent artistic eye."

She put her arm around him and squeezed lightly while he scrutinized the minute sculpture. It looked for all the world like a fleecy head of cauliflower. He told her so.

"*Bene.* That is exactly what it is supposed to be."

"It's very pretty," said Carlo, "but why would anybody want to wear a cauliflower on her dress?"

"To know the answer to that question," his mama said, "one would have to ask Signora Fabiola Grippa. She commissioned it."

Carlo thought his mother looked exceptionally pretty today. She wore a coverall over her blue shirt, here in the studio, and her hair was braided into a loop and secured with her silver comb. On her feet were sandals with little blue ties that looked festive and summery.

Carlo found himself thinking about the scar. Was it so awful? On warm days in the past, his mother used to wear sundresses with thin straps over the shoulders. He remembered a locket that had lain against her slender throat. Was it there now? Last summer, when they had gone with Anna-Laura to the beaches, she had worn a blue-and-white-patterned bathing suit, modest by modern standards, but somehow prettier than the bathing suits of other mothers. Would she never go to the beach again?

As if reading his mind, she turned to him with a sorrowful expression. "You know, darling, that we can't have a real holiday this summer? There isn't enough money. I'm sorry. I'll try to make it up to you."

"It doesn't matter. Who wants to have a holiday?" In his desire to make her feel better, he went too far. He maintained that holidays were boring and stupid. Personally, he thought it would be much nicer to stay close to home. There were a million things he wanted to do in any case.

She nodded solemnly, but he could see she didn't believe him. When he left, Nina winked at him over her magazine. "*Ciao, pescino mio,*" she said.

Little fish! He narrowed his eyes to show her she was out of line. He was too old to be called little fish; it was vulgar and insulting. He walked home, cutting dangerously across the Via Acquatania and narrowly avoiding a speeding car. He made a rude gesture at the driver.

He thought of the holiday he would be missing this summer. He knew it was true about the money, but something was troubling him. Holidays meant the mountains or the sea. His father had died in the mountains, and his mother would not be wanting to go to the sea. It was quite possible they would never have a holiday again.

Old Signora Lenti was sitting in front of his house. She had brought her plastic lawn-chair out so she could snoop on the comings and goings of everyone in the street. Later, his aunt would no doubt come over bearing fruit or pastries. Stefania was probably home from school already, singing along to some silly tune on the radio, practicing to be a rock star when she grew up.

Too many women! thought Carlo, trudging up the stairs.

He thought of the beach at Nervi with longing. He could almost feel that exhilarating shock that came when a sloping wave broke over him—the first wave of the day. He could feel the sun piercing the boiling surface of the sea, smell the mingled aroma of brine and tanning oil and orange rind.

On the landing midway up the stairs, he paused and shut his eyes. He was breast-deep in the water, bobbing gently with the current. Before him he could see the great humps of rock where the sea had cut deeply into the coastline. Cars, tiny from this distance, swarmed along the bluffs. He scanned the shore until he found what he was looking for. A figure, recognizable by her blue and white bathing suit, was propped up on her elbows watching the ocean with vigilant eyes. She raised her arm and waved.

Carlo continued up the stairs. He removed his shoes just inside the door to the flat and scanned the letters lying on the floor. He had written away to a post office box which promised to send him sea monkeys, but there was no reply yet.

He noticed with some interest a letter addressed to his mother. It came from America and was enclosed, not in the pale airmail envelopes used for transatlantic correspondence, but in a heavy, cream-colored envelope. There was extra postage fixed on. Whoever had sent the letter, he thought, must be very rich.

Rafaella read the letter from Jacqueline Talbot over and over again. It was a short letter, friendly and breezy as Jackie herself, but she read it as if it were the most valuable of documents. Jackie wanted to know how she was coming along; she said she would like to hear from Rafaella some time. Things at the hospital were much the same said Jackie. There were no sheikhs at the moment, but an English television personality was installed in the corner suite, and he insisted on singing old-time music hall numbers to the nurses.

"Do you remember poor little Giovanni? A child from Ceylon, born with the same defect, was admitted this week.

Dr. Lassiter operated two days ago, and so far the surgery is a success."

She concluded with best wishes and love. "Love, Jackie," she penned in her easy, American way.

Rafaella lay in her ornate bed, the letter in her hands. Mention of Giovanni made her cry a little, but the tears slipped down unheeded. Chiefly, she saw the hospital with a poignant clarity, much as her son, earlier, had seen the beach at Nervi. The corner suite, the nurses' station—all appeared to her as places she had known in a period of great happiness.

Signora, she told herself, *this is crazy.*

She dreamed of a large theater in which Dr. Lassiter and Jacqueline Talbot performed variety numbers. At one point, Jackie, dressed in a sequined showgirl's costume, lay down in a box and allowed Lassiter to saw her in half. When she bounded up, radiant and flexible on her long legs, the audience cheered maniacally.

Next to Rafaella, beating his palms together and cheering along with the best of them, sat Maurizio.

Chapter 5

In the dull dog-days of mid-July, a letter was delivered to Stephen Morrissy's motel room in Houston. It came from Italy. The post mark was Milano, the writing masculine, but all the same he felt his entire physical being quicken at sight of it.

It was written on the sort of airmail paper which had always baffled him. If you opened it in haste, half the message was lost. The trick was to use an old-fashioned letter opener or the flat edge of a butter knife, but since neither of these tools was in his immediate possession, he carried it about for half a day before an opportunity presented itself.

In the volunteers' lounge he borrowed Hans Wolder's pipe knife and slit open the pale blue envelope. Then he replaced the letter in the pocket of his jacket and carried it about with him all day on his rounds like a time bomb.

He was preparing to leave Houston. He had been hanging around the hospital long enough to absorb what he had come to find, and the atmosphere of the place was beginning to work a strange effect on him. He both wanted to leave and felt, in advance, the sense of bereavement that leaving St. Matthew's would bring to him. He was in limbo, and the letter in his pocket seemed the only possible tie to a place where something important had happened to him.

Although he couldn't put a name to what it was that had happened, he felt that the course of his life had been altered. It was as if the Italian Widow (he tried not to think of her by name) had been dropped into his life to teach him something. Then, just when he was beginning to learn, she had vanished, leaving him unformed, the lesson half learned.

He recognized the egotism of such a thought—that she should have been made to suffer merely so that an obscure mortal named Stephen Morrissy might learn some home truths about himself—was a ridiculous, repugnant theory. He detested mushy mysticism and resented her for making him entertain such thoughts.

By doing her vanishing act so expertly and leaving him without so much as a good-bye, she had succeeded in severing their connection forever. It was too clearly an act of utter rejection. It allowed him no room. He imagined writing a letter to her in Genoa and having it returned unopened, an Italian version of Return to Sender penned in her neat hand on the envelope. *A class act, signora. Performed with surgical precision.*

Before he went out to dinner that night, he pulled the letter from Italy from his pocket and opened it angrily. Just as he had known, it was not from her. An Austrian filmmaker he knew, who was currently living in Milan, wrote to remind him of a film festival coming up in August. It was to be held in Geneva. Friedl included some gossip about a woman with whom Stephen had once had an affair.

He tried to remember what the woman had looked like and could picture only her flamboyantly dyed hair. He crumpled the letter up and sailed it into the wastepaper basket. His anger was not at the harmless Friedl, who only wanted to keep in touch, but at himself. The fact that he had carried a letter from Italy around all day, and put off reading it because of the disappointment it would bring was humiliating.

He went to a large and noisy restaurant for dinner and ate without pleasure. He contemplated calling Eugenia Fowler and going to the house in River Oaks. He would make brutish, impersonal love to her—she no doubt preferred it that way—and forget about the Escape Artist.

On reflection, the thought of Eugenia was as devoid of pleasure as the food he had just eaten, and he got back in his car and drove to the hospital. He was not on duty, but St.

Matthew's was the temporary focal point of his existence. He had once thought of it as his set, but now it seemed nearly a refuge. A home away from home, if he had had a home? Stephen shrugged off his self-pity with extreme irritation. Everything was as he liked it. He was free, obliged to no one, and lucky in his career. The last thing he needed, after all, was to become involved with a repressed widow. and her chaotic family.

He imagined her children as whining and spoiled. As he walked up the steps to the hospital entrance he pictured the Leone family gobbling pasta in a shabby kitchen in Genoa. The little boy was yelling at his mother, who stood at the stove like a slave, guarding simmering cauldrons. Whap! She turned around and smacked the children—one-two—bawling at them like a harpy from a farcical Italian film. Tears and shrieks all round.

His spiteful scenario pleased him. He nearly walked into Dr. Blanchard, who was leaving for the night, and apologized absently. Blanchard brought the real world back; the moment Stephen saw the familiar, tired face the grotesque phantom Leones faded. The babble in the kitchen was gone, and he heard the PA system paging a Dr. Berger with flat, noncommittal tones.

"Come to me for a check-up, Morrissy," said Dr. Blanchard kindly. "You look like hell."

Rafaella had always loved the Old Town, the Centro Storico, best. In the mornings, when the children were in school, she often took a bus to the Via Gramsci and wandered through the twisting alleyways and covered mazes of old Genoa until it was time to go home at noon.

By night a person might find trouble here. Thieves and pickpockets lurked; vendors selling cheap contraband cigarettes and wristwatches waited to prey on the credulous and greedy. Every Genovese schoolchild knew better than to visit the docks after dark, but in the clear light of a July morning the Old Town delighted her.

At noon she returned to prepare lunch. Then she did the

marketing and went to her studio where she worked until time for the children to come back from school. There was a pattern to her days now, and she was somehow soothed by the regular passage of time as the summer progressed.

Evenings were the hardest. All the bright promise of the day seemed sucked away. Lately she had begun to make elaborate dishes for the evening meal. The preparation and washing-up bit a large chunk from the empty hours.

She was rigorous about the children's homework, especially now that term was almost over. Carlo and Stefania complained, but she turned a deaf ear. Her severity, she told them, meant she loved them more, not less. Italian children were notoriously spoiled. In the warm summer evenings they accompanied their parents to cafés and sat up, cosseted, long past their bedtimes. She was torn between the desire to pamper them and the sure conviction that a woman alone had to be twice as strict.

Sometimes Anna-Laura came to keep her company in the evenings. She had taken to working on a piece of long crochet which she bullied about as they talked. Rafaella wondered if it was destined to become a scarf for Dr. Castelli but couldn't bring herself to ask. Maurizio, too, came to the Via Vieri flat, but his visits were brief and formal. He always proposed jaunts to the Riviera di Levante, easy weekend trips designed to delight the children without tiring her. "Perhaps when school is over," she always said, and then felt guilty.

She retired early, lying propped in bed with the old art history books she had read as a student. She attempted, several times, to write to Jacqueline Talbot, but each attempt ended in failure. Her words seemed stilted, ungracious.

She was happiest on her morning walks. No one knew her on these anonymous wanderings; no one sought her opinion or scrutinized her with anxiety. If she tired of the Centro Storico she could warm herself, as she would by a grate fire, in front of the tapestries and frescoes in the *palazzi* lining the Via Garibaldi or Balbi. Nobody urged her to turn her attention to a Crucifixion or the passion of a holy martyr. She could stroll into the Treasury, where the green chalice used by Christ at the Last Supper was claimed to repose, and who would stop her? Who was the wiser if she entered the baroque portals of the Nunziata like any other tourist?

None of it was new. This was her city. She had walked every step of it at one point in her life. Aldo had asked her to be his wife in front of the cathedral of San Lorenzo. As a child, as a student, as a bride, she had at some time visited all the places she was rediscovering, but she felt she was seeing them now for the first time.

One small dissatisfaction marred her peace on these walks. She wished, vaguely, that she could serve as someone's guide. Someone who had never seen her city. So many foreigners passed up Genoa, seeing only the thriving port, the jumping-off place for Corsica and Sardinia, and remained forever ignorant of the beauty that lay within.

She remembered Stephen Morrissy's words, spoken apologetically. "I've been to Rome, and Milan and Venice, but I never got to Genoa."

Whenever she thought of him, she chastised herself like some member of a medieval order. Rafaella felt that to think of him was a disgrace; therefore, she made sure that any memory of him was accompanied by a painful, humiliating, countermemory.

The poor man, she would think, while standing in front of a Luca Cambiaso fresco. He imagined he would have a pleasant, diverting time with a volcanic Italian widow—nothing serious, just a day or two of Mediterranean *passione*, ardent and perhaps a bit comical to an American—and then *Ciao, signora. Grazie mille!*

Whenever a small, reasonable voice would insist that he had been decent and honorable far beyond what the situation required, she silenced it by replying that his attentions had been prompted by pity. Pity and guilt. He had no reason to feel guilt—the deception had been hers—but Anna-Laura had assured her all American men were bowed down by guilt, imagined and otherwise.

He had hoped, like Paolo Castelli in his noon raids on Anna-Laura's body, to lose himself for an hour. Instead, poor Stefano had found himself dragged back to the very world he had been seeking to avoid. She pictured the time when he would tell someone of his misadventures with the crazy signora from Genoa and forgave him. They were even.

Even-Stephen, she thought, recollecting some long-forgotten American slang, and pushed him from her mind

Nevertheless, on her walks in the city, it was he who walked beside her. She saw Genoa through his eyes, and it became strange and wonderful to her.

"These mussels come from Barcelona," said Maurizio.

"How do you know?" asked Carlo. "How can you tell?"

"One knows," said Maurizio. He gestured toward the half-moon bay below them. "Once they were plentiful here. No more."

He seemed curiously sad; it was in his voice. This was so unlike him that Rafaella darted a quick look in his direction, but he was now busying himself with the mussels.

"Are they less good for being Spanish then?" she asked softly.

He smiled and took a sip of wine. "No, no." Far below the terrace where they were sitting, they could make out the figures of fishermen tying nets and pots for lobster. "You see those fishermen?" Maurizio asked the children. "A little over a hundred years ago, this village boasted a fleet of a thousand ships. There is a nautical school here, once famous. Those fishermen are the descendants of celebrated sailors."

"What happened to the thousand ships?" asked Stefania.

"Steamboats came, of course," Carlo said with impatience.

"Yes, that's right," said Maurizio. "Steam and power boats. With their advent, Camogli turned back into a little fishing port."

Stefania, who had seen Camogli only as a place featuring delights like the aquarium and marine museum they had toured, was silent for a moment. "It's still pretty," she said at last. Then she returned to her plate of *torta pasqualina*, forgetting the past glories of a town which offered current pleasures.

They were lunching high above the westerly bay of the

Mount Portofino peninsula. "Pretty" was not the word Rafaella would have chosen, although the faded pastel shades of the houses were exactly that; the region was rugged and wild, studded with the ruins of Romanesque churches and watchtowers erected for the sighting of pirates. The sea beat against the coves and inlets of the promontory. Here, just twenty kilometers from Genoa, was a coastline which could be viewed two ways, like a puzzle in a child's book. Look at it in one light and it was a picturesque fishing cove; examine it again and it became a haunted place of savage beauty.

"Well," said Carlo philosophically, "that's progress, Signor Guidi."

"*Senza dubbio*, Carlo. But here progress reversed itself. Progress always means that one group will shoot ahead, another fall behind. It is intriguing, don't you think?"

Carlo paused, his fork halfway to his lips. "In England," he said, remembering a recent history lesson, "they smashed up machines when they were invented. The men were afraid they would lose their jobs, so they broke the machines."

"Laborsaving devices. For every laborsaving device that is invented, thousands of laborers are out of work."

Stefania was fidgeting about in her chair. She asked permission to go and explore the cypress grove on the terraced slope beneath them. Rafaella was about to tell Carlo to run along and look after her, but one look at his absorbed expression stopped her. She told Stefania to be careful and granted permission. Stefania ran off, holding her hands to her cowboy hat to keep it from blowing off in the sea breeze.

"What is the answer?" demanded Carlo with the fierceness of the very young. He expected, demanded, a solution from the adult male who sat across from him.

"That is up to you," said Maurizio. "Your generation will inherit that problem, Carlo. It is a very old one, but never more pressing than now."

"Maybe we'll ban progress," said Carlo seriously. "We'll pass laws saying *basta*—enough, now. Life is easy enough." He looked at his mother and flushed. "Except, of course, we wouldn't ban medical discoveries."

Both Maurizio and Carlo glanced at her uneasily. They

were thinking, she knew, that without a machine invented only twenty-five years ago, she would be approaching the end of her life.

"Well, Carlo," she said, smiling at his earnestness, "it's an all or nothing proposition. In your government of the future, it would be cheating to make allowances."

"Anyway," said Carlo, "I am going to be an artist. Artists don't concern themselves with such things."

When he, too, had excused himself and disappeared into the cypress grove, Rafaella turned to Maurizio. "You seem melancholy today," she said.

Maurizio removed his tinted glasses and looked out to sea. His gray eyes took in some of the light reflected in the blue bay and became a shade paler. He looked vulnerable. He took her hand and held it in his own, lightly, without pressure. "I am never melancholy," he said. "Only discouraged, sometimes."

Rafaella sat motionless, almost afraid to breathe. She wanted to show some sign of her gratitude and friendship to him, but she was afraid it would be misinterpreted. Once more she felt imprisoned by his goodness and resented it.

Maurizio inclined his head upward. "At the Santuario del Boschetto up there," he said, "the sailors and their families still make votive offerings to the sea. Each year they commemorate the worst storms of the Mediterranean." He put his glasses back on and signaled for the check. "The world thinks of we Genovese as merchants and traders," he said. "They forget we were sailors and adventurers, too."

They drove back above the sea on the Via Aurelia. When they headed inland toward the heart of the city, Rafaella felt relieved. The wild Ligurian coast, which she had always loved, now seemed a place of menace. Only in Genoa in her crowded flat was she completely safe.

The purple silk flower in Anna-Laura's hair had begun to slide down. It was flopping against her cheek when she entered the kitchen.

"You cannot hide here like a servant," she whispered to Rafaella. "You are here to enjoy yourself, *bella*." She fussed with the flower, reanchoring it, and took Rafaella firmly by the arm. "I will introduce you to some very interesting people," she muttered.

Rafaella sighed. She had been happy at her post in the kitchen, loitering near the table piled with bottles of wine and whiskey. Occasionally she helped a guest to ice from Anna-Laura's bucket, a task which required little effort and conversation. She followed her sister-in-law reluctantly into the party's vortex, where the music had become deafening and smoke hung in the air as dense as sea fog.

The occasion was Anna-Laura's annual party for students, given on the night the *politecnico* closed for the summer. Each year she opened her flat to them, laying on a mammoth spread of food and drink, and watched proudly while they danced until dawn and shouted to each other in their new languages. The Italian speakers practiced English; the English and Americans spoke in outlandish Italian. Rafaella had always found these parties exhausting, but she would not dream of failing to show up. It was Anna-Laura's night of triumph. She seemed to love her pupils with the sort of ardor usually encountered in primary-school teachers. She beamed with pride at their humblest accomplishments and often petted them. They were her children.

Rafaella watched them converging on a long table, diving and pecking at the mountains of food like hungry gulls. There were platters of *antipasto*, huge bowls of seafood salad, salamis and cheeses and pastries and an entire ham. "You are too extravagant," she murmured. "Next year, let them give a party for you."

"Oh, no, *carina*. They are my livelihood! They keep me going, and besides, I love them."

The flat was in a cul-de-sac at the very end of the Via Vieri. Outside, cars and motorcycles and mopeds kept arriving, discharging more guests until it seemed Anna-Laura's flat would burst at the seams. The music escalated in volume. It was the sort of music Anna-Laura loved best—an international nightclub wail, owing much to American disco —which Aldo had always called Via Veneto music. Some of the *politecnico* students had begun to dance.

"Oh, here comes Signor Nelson," cried Anna-Laura. She

lowered her voice. "He is the one whose paper blew out the window the night you came home."

Rafaella was introduced to Signor Nelson, who spoke to her in a slow, formal Italian. His wife was full of praise for Anna-Laura. "I don't *parla* myself," she said, "but the *professoressa* has Ken speaking like a native, don't you think?"

Rafaella smiled, agreeing politely. It was just as well, she thought, that he did not speak like a native. The Genovese dialect would be incomprehensible to Berlitzed executives.

Anna-Laura guided her from group to group, introducing her to Americans in business suits, fierce young Italians wearing T-shirts with the arms ripped out. She met Mrs. Lutz, a schoolteacher from New York on sabbatical who spoke a graceful, flowery Italian which might have gone down well in the court of the Medicis. Here were the Dell Bondis, a Piedmontese couple recently arrived in Genoa, who learned a new language every year. They spoke English as if their very lives depended on it. Here was Gino, a glamorous and skilled hairdresser planning to set up shop in Rome. English would be useful, no? He flirted with Rafaella, grinning and flexing his muscles. He wore, she saw, one earring.

Gino's hot black eyes appraised her frankly. His body began to weave to the music. Wouldn't she like to dance? Sure of his erotic power, he had reverted to his native Italian. Rafaella blushed and told him she had a bad ankle. It was Anna-Laura who went pistoning out onto the makeshift dance-floor with Gino, and Rafaella slipped back to the relative calm of the kitchen.

A large American in early middle-age, his long hair bound back in a red bandanna, was scrabbling about in the ice bucket. "Hi," he called over his shoulder. "I'm Bob Babcock. *Mi chiamo* Roberto Babcock." He plunked ice into his glass and waited for her to introduce herself. When she did, his eyes narrowed in surprise. "No shit!" he said. "I would never have figured you for the *professoressa*'s sister. You seem so different. I thought you were English."

"We are certainly very different," she said. *Don't dare say anything bad about her*, she thought.

But nothing, it seemed, could have been further from Bob Babcock's mind. He seemed determined to tell her his life's history. Wedged as she was between the drinks table and the refrigerator, she was a captive audience. Bob Babcock told her he had been born in Denver to stiflingly middle-class parents. Blinded by their ambitions for him, he had done the whole trip. "*The whole trip*," he repeated meaningfully. Medical school, an internship, all of it. Yet all the while, he said, he had sensed a big trap opening beneath him. If he stayed in America and became a specialist, his fate would be sealed. He had dropped out years ago and bummed around Europe. He had a small trust fund—he confided this sheepishly—sufficient to support him, frugally, wherever he went.

"I've been on Sardinia for a year," he said. "I came to Genoa last April, and headed straight for the polytech. Wherever I go, I sign up for a course at the local polytech, and do you know why?"

Rafaella shook her head.

"That's where you find the real people. The salt of the earth! Not in the universities. Not with the arty crowd. In the polytechs." He drained his glass and gave himself more. "What do you do?" he asked.

Rafaella considered. She had never yet mentioned her recent ordeal to a stranger. Here was Bob Babcock, a bit of a fool, who traveled the world in hopes of extracting the salt of the earth. Why not make him the first? She would never see him again; it couldn't matter. He had once been a medical student—it might even interest him on some long-forgotten, academic level.

"I have just had bypass surgery," she said brightly.

Signor Babcock's face sharpened. He leaned closer. "When?" he whispered. "Where?" Anyone watching them would think they were arranging an assignation.

"About six weeks ago now. In Houston."

"Dr. *Lassiter*?"

"Yes."

"Son of a *bitch!* Dr. Lassiter? St. Matthew's?"

"Yes."

"Oh, wow," said Bob Babcock. "Are you okay?"

"As you see."

"It's funny," he said. "That's what my parents wanted me to be. A heart surgeon."

It struck her that this earnest man, only a few years younger than Stephen Morrissy, had been arrested forever in the period of his youth when he had "dropped out." Perhaps Anna-Laura's opinion—that all American men were children—was formed on the likes of Bob Babcock. He became even more conspiratorial, making vague movements with his elbows as if to seal them off from the rest of the crowd.

"Listen," he said, "tell me. What was he like?"

Rafaella considered. "He was shy and very businesslike," she said. "He saved my life. He wore Gucci shoes."

Chapter 6

Her solitary morning walks were a thing of the past. Now that the children were out of school, Rafaella devised new ways to keep them occupied.

On weekends, they drove with Anna-Laura to the suburb of Pegli for the open-air concerts and plays. Maurizio took Carlo and Stefania to the outdoor swimming pool at Arenzano and once as far as Albisola, where the children swam and Rafaella admired the celebrated ceramics at the museum.

There was, about these outings, a curiously joyless flavor, as if the children knew they were being entertained and felt it their duty to have fun.

Weekdays dragged by for Rafaella. Her earlier routine, which had made her feel so secure, had been broken.

"Mama," Stefania would say, coming from her friend Maria Panero's house, "Maria is going to Switzerland for three whole weeks!" Or, "Maria has her very own stereo record-player."

Once, as Rafaella sat quietly in the kitchen, mentally balancing her accounts, Stefania burst in with further news about the fortunate Maria Panero. "Maria has a *pocket calculator*," she shouted.

"Maria has a father!" Rafaella shouted back. Instantly she felt deeply ashamed. So great was her mortification she buried her face in her hands. *Shame, signora,* she counseled; *control yourself*. When she looked up to confront Stefania, the room was empty. She went to her daughter's room and found Stefania, with a sheepish look, tapping fishfood into Butch and Sundance's bowl.

"I would rather be me than Maria," the child said, speaking to the room at large. "Maria's mother always has headaches, and she has nasty, long fingernails like a witch. She is always polishing them, and she misses in places."

"Now Stefania, that's no reason to speak rudely of Signora Panero." The reproof was mild, and she could scarcely keep from laughing. A current of understanding ran between her and her daughter. If Stefania was quick to irritate, she was even quicker to forgive. Her way was oblique. By attending to the goldfish without being asked, she admitted that she, too, had faults.

Carlo was another matter. He was very good at amusing himself. He disappeared for long stretches of time, and when he returned he was vague about what he had done. She could not coop him up in the flat during the long, sunny days of summer, but neither could she allow him complete freedom. He was only eleven.

"Where have you been, Carlo?"

She stood at the head of the stairs, arms folded. He was half an hour late, and her mind had conjured up dreadful images—Carlo running with a pack of insolent boys, throwing sticks at passing cars, lighting illicit and dangerous fireworks which managed, each summer, to be smuggled in from the port. Worse, Carlo, not heeding the traffic, struck down at some perilous intersection, bleeding in the road.

"I was with Marcello," he said defiantly. "He showed me how to use his skateboard." He gestured at a scrape on his knee, as if offering evidence. "Marcello has a skateboard," he said. "From America."

"*Stupendo*. And where did you and Marcello use this marvelous device? In the street?"

"Of course not," he said. His tone was withering. "I am not a fool, you know. We went to the *campo di giuoco*." Except for the word "playground" he might have been a grown man trying to maintain his dignity in the face of an hysterical woman's accusations.

July dragged toward its end, and the flat became airless

274

and oppressive. Even the temperate climate of Genoa, shielded by the mountains to the north from the sultry air of midsummer, seemed insupportable to Rafaella. She thought, now and then, of the small but airy house she had inhabited with Aldo. Fragrant breezes blew through opened windows there; the children had separate rooms. There was no fretful spinster dwelling beneath them, and from her windows she could look down on the small, manicured park beneath. When she looked down from her windows on the Via Vieri, she saw the sparse gray locks of Signora Lenti, seated in her plastic lawn-chair like the benevolent warden of a women's prison.

Anna-Laura went off for a ten-day vacation to the Seychelle Islands. She planned these annual holidays with great care and frugality, poring over travel books and eliciting the opinions of friends before she would make her decision. A former student who now worked in a travel agency had helped her to book cheaply; according to Anna-Laura, ten days on the Indian Ocean would cost her less than ten days in Genoa.

Stefania was impressed. "*Zanzibar*," she sang, on the way to the airport. "Romantic Zanzibar."

"Let's hope so, *anima mia*," said Anna-Laura. She wore a dashing safari suit and extremely high-heeled shoes. Her toenails were painted in an iridescent orchid hue. Rafaella, who had watched her pack, knew there was a matching orchid bikini in her sister-in-law's luggage. *Let her find romance*, Rafaella prayed fervently and then wondered what she had meant. She had a vivid image of Paolo Castelli and wondered how he would spend the hours between eleven and noon for the next ten days.

They waved her off gaily, watching the plane ascend in a trail of silver until it became indistinguishable from the heavens. Back to business. "Now," said Rafaella, "you will be very silent and very kind to me. Mama is going to drive."

She slid behind the wheel of the orange Fiat. It was now hers to do with as she pleased until Anna-Laura returned. It was an awesome prospect. She and Aldo had owned a Fiat also, but a larger one, a 132 GLS. In the days of her marriage she had driven it often, with speed and precision. It was an old friend; she had never expected to encounter danger in the Fiat and never did.

When Aldo had died, the Fiat, along with the house, had been sold. Her only experience behind the wheel of a car these days came when Anna-Laura went on holiday. She could see the faces of the children, pale and tense, reflected in the rearview mirror. They had taken her admonition seriously.

She turned and regarded the two sets of eyes, one dark and one pale, and saw the history of her life, past and present, reflected there. She was looking at herself, and all that had made her what she was, and at Aldo, and what they had made together. Anna-Laura might wing off to the Seychelles, orchid toenails gleaming with anticipation but— much as she loved her—she had no responsibility in that quarter.

Carlo and Stefania were different. They were flesh of her flesh, hers to protect and love and keep safe, however she might accomplish such an awesome feat, and at this moment they were, dear God, afraid. It must not be allowed. It reversed the natural order of things. They were afraid for her, and that fright robbed them of their childhood. *The child must not become the parent until the time is right*, she thought. *The child who becomes the protector is damned, doomed, lost.*

She smiled at them. "Don't worry," she said. "Don't you remember? Mama is one hell of a driver."

On the *sopraelevata* she knew a moment of panic. Surely the cars which streamed along, honking, bleeting, intent on passing her, were instruments of death. The large van grunting behind her was malevolent; its driver would easily ram her into the barricade and speed on, shrugging. Her hands gripped the wheel so hard she felt a half-remembered ache shoot up her arms. What if she had a heart attack? But that would not happen, would it? She was, as Lassiter would say, repumped. Brand new. The driver of the bellicose van was more likely to have a heart attack than she.

Her hands relaxed on the surface of the wheel, which had become slick with her sweat. She felt her body uncoil, fall into the loose and natural rhythm of driving. It was easy, once you abandoned the thought of evil, random harm. It was only driving! The children's faces in the mirror became less strained.

No sudden calamity here—only Mama, transporting them back home.

She took vows and became a nun. Her order was a strictly cloistered one. They lived in a fortress, surrounded by groves of lemon trees, high above the sea. The colors in the dream were exceptionally vivid—the green of the foliage and the blue of the sea were as bright as something from a child's picture book.

Guests climbed the steep hill to visit with her. She talked to them from behind a grate in the wall. One day the mother superior told her to go out in the garden and sit on a bench beneath an olive tree. She did as she was told, sitting with her hands clasped looking out to sea. The mother superior told her a film crew was coming to make a *documentario* about the order; if she looked hard enough she would see the sails of their boat approaching.

Suddenly the mother superior frowned. "This will not do," she said. She was looking down at Rafaella's feet. Rafaella followed her gaze and saw to her consternation that her feet beneath her long robes were clad in high-heeled sandals. Her toenails had been painted in a glimmering lilac hue. She began to protest, to tell the mother superior that these were the feet of her sister-in-law, when she was wakened by the shrilling of a bell.

The bell alarmed her. In the first disoriented moments of wakening she was sure it was the telephone, and telephones did not ring in the middle of the night unless there was something wrong. She lay very still, heart pounding, waiting for it to ring again, but the flat was silent. It was three in the morning.

A fresh breeze rushed in through the louvered slats of her shutters. It smelled like crushed flower petals and seawater. She slid from the bed and went to the window, unlatching the shutters and looking out onto the darkened street. It had begun to rain lightly—large, warm drops fell erratically into her outstretched palms.

The breeze stirred again, and she heard the bell, clearly this time. It was the clashing of Japanese wind-chimes—a melodious tune that sounded unbearably lonely in the still hours of the early morning. Signorina Freda must have bought them at the open air market and hung them in her window, beneath. Rafaella pulled the shutters closed and stood before the mirror on her bureau, lighting a lamp.

The face looking back at her was not that of a cloistered nun, but something of the dream still clung to her and she felt half inside it still. Now was the time.

She unbuttoned the many small buttons on the front of her old-fashioned nightgown, until it was open to the waist. She turned, presenting her profile to the mirror, and slid the gown down, holding it around her middle with hands grown cold. In the mirror a slender woman, arms perhaps a bit too thin, hair tumbled and messy with sleep, peered cautiously around to meet her image.

Slowly, the woman turned and presented herself to the glass, full front. Her gaze moved down to confirm what she had seen only fleetingly or from her peripheral vision, as children think they see goblins scurrying under their beds from the tail of the eye. Here was a woman who had bathed by candlelight, dressed with head averted. What the woman did not see could not exist. Her body, from belly to throat, was an unoccupied territory, like the Empty Quarter in the Arabian Desert.

Now she surveyed this quarter carefully, an explorer. It was less horrid than the explorer had feared. The red line, fading she supposed, but still angry, was neat and straight. There were no livid clumps of scar tissue, no puckered patches where a stray bullet, say, might have ripped into her. Nothing disturbed the consistency of her skin. Just the red line. A breast stood on either side, like a sentry guarding a checkpoint.

Yes, less dreadful in terms of disfigurement, but more because it was so unnatural. She thought of a doll Stefania had wanted when she was very young. It had glossy, lifelike hair and a piquant face. Small bumps marked the breasts of the doll; she even had a saucy, swelling pubic mound. Rafaella remembered the soft, comforting rag dolls of her own youth. Reluctantly, she had purchased the doll for her daughter. Stefania changed the doll's costumes many times each day, and Rafaella could never look at it without revulsion. It had been cheaply manufactured, and where the child saw only its sophisticated, fashionable *élan*, the mother saw the seams where it had been hastily joined.

"Why did this happen to me?" she asked the woman in the mirror. There was nothing of self-pity in the question, only an honest desire to know. Not *why me?* or even *why did something so out of the ordinary, so unpleasant, happen to me?*

Why did *this* happen to me? This particular thing?

She returned to the bed and lay for some time, willing the dream to come back. She wanted to sit looking for the sails at sea, her worldly feet concealed by the folds of her long habit. She heard the wind chimes from time to time and imagined they were bells on buoys at the foot of her cliff.

Flying from Houston to New York, Stephen looked into the dutiful face of the flight attendant and realized she reminded him of his sister Anne. They shared the same good looks, marred by a kind of spiritless acceptance of whatever came their way. *We don't ask for much* might be their motto.

Many miles to the north, Anne was living her life in Chicago. She was, presumably, happy enough. It had been months since he had called her, months since she had dropped him a line. If he were to meet her on a street in some city—New York, for example—things would be awkward between them. Gradually, events from their childhood, the common glue which bound them, would appear in their conversation, and they would end by acknowledging a reluctant affection. It seemed wrong somehow.

The Morrissys had never been a close family. Stephen's father was kind, ineffectual. A life of defeat had made him taciturn. His mother showed little emotion, perhaps because she couldn't afford to. Leo, clearly an afterthought, had come along when Stephen was eleven years old. When Leo was seven, Stephen had left to go to the university. Since he had never really returned, except for brief, filial visits, Leo had forever remained a little boy to him, a pesky little brother.

Leo filled his thoughts now for no reason he could discern. Staring out at cloud banks over Atlanta, Stephen remembered teaching Leo to swim, building him a platform for his Lionel trains, and allowing him to ride (if he was in a very good mood) on the handlebars of his Schwinn bike.

Once Leo had stowed away in the back of the Morrissy car on an evening when Stephen was taking his girlfriend—Debbie? No, Diane—to a drive-in movie. Leo hadn't been discovered until they were passing a corn field halfway to the movie. Stephen had been furious, but Diane was charmed and flattered because she thought little Leo had a crush on her.

He saw now that he'd always liked his brother best. Secretly, he applauded all the things he'd pretended to find annoying about Leo because he knew they were alike. Neither of them was willing to settle for dull tranquillity. Each wanted to make his mark on life—Stephen at seventeen and Leo at six—because to merely accept what came your way, as their parents and Anne did, was an admission of defeat. In their separate ways, they wanted adventure.

I had all the luck, Stephen thought. *Poor Leo had none.*

"How do you *do* it, man?" That was Leo at seventeen, visiting his brother in New York. They had seen a rough cut of a film Stephen had made in Mexico, and Leo was all admiration. Already he saw Stephen as a celebrity. "How did you learn to do all that?"

But when he'd tried to explain to Leo, his brother grew restless and agitated. "I don't know," he said. "I'd like to be a racing driver. Or maybe a foreign correspondent. It's impossible back there, Steve. Dad wants me to be an accountant or sell millwork. Ma just wants me to go to college —she'd settle for anything. They don't understand what you're doing." He had flushed with discomfort, sitting on a cushion in the Perry Street apartment. There was something he wanted to say, but his native decency prevented him. At last outrage prevailed.

"They think you're some kind of *failure*," he said.

Stephen knew this was true. When his mother telephoned, she never neglected to ask why he chose such depressing topics. Famines, wars, and social unrest were things Mrs. Morrisssy wished not to think about. "Why couldn't you make a cheerful movie, dear? Something that would lift people's spirits?"

The flossy nest of clouds gave way to a pure and blazing blue. He turned from the window and encountered the passive gaze of the woman who looked like Anne. She seemed to accuse him. Back to the window.

Not long after Leo's visit to New York, he turned eighteen and joined the marines, seeking the adventure which had always eluded him. Perhaps he had expected Vietnam to be an extension of those hot summer nights when he drove the country roads, drunk on applejack, desperately hoping for something—anything!—to transform him.

Two years later with his then wife Natalie, Stephen had returned to Wisconsin to see his brother buried. What was left of Leo came by air in a bag and was implanted in the cemetery west of the town. No doubt a Ramada Inn now presided over the spot.

He would never forget a fragment of conversation he had overheard back at his parents' house after the funeral. His wife and his sister were huddled together in the kitchen, arranging cold cuts on a platter for the wake.

"Well," said Anne, "I guess this will give Stephen ideas for a new film."

"Grist for the old mill," replied bitter Natalie.

The worst of it was that he had thought of such a film, standing at his brother's graveside. It would be a film that suggested the essential loneliness contained within the American heartland—a bleak, cosmic loneliness, a suspicion of ultimate defeat, that prompted boys like Leo to search for real life elsewhere. He had imagined it as a tribute to his little brother's misplaced energy and spirit. It was all he could do for Leo now, but the voices in the kitchen were judging him and finding him wanting. Lacking in feeling.

What did they know? They were wrong, his sister and his ex-wife. Because they lacked whatever it was that inspired emotion in him, they presumed he had none. He could never have told Natalie that he had loved his brother because she would have stored the knowledge in her private arsenal of weapons, trotting it out in some reprocessed form to defeat him in an argument.

The flight attendant was trying to foist a tray on him. It contained a sandwich, which looked as if it had been sculpted in wax, a sticky bun, and a square of some kind of jelled fruit. He shook his head no, feeling an impulse toward rudeness, and shifted his cramped legs. Beneath his seat lay an attaché case containing all his notes on the hospital and Dr. Lassiter. Papers and tapes, suggestions for Ivan Bell and technical notations—all had been crammed into the case in his last hours in Houston.

He would be returning in October, but his good-byes at St. Matthew's had seemed final to him. He had dined with Blanchard and with Lassiter—who proved to be as decisive over a menu as he was hovering over a heart—with the same sense of ceremonious farewell he had experienced with headmen and bureau chiefs on other locations all over the world.

It was Jackie Talbot who unwittingly provided a symbolic conclusion to his weeks in Texas.

"Where did you get that?"

Jackie had touched the Oriental scarf at her throat with hesitant fingers. "She gave it to me," Jackie said. "She wanted me to have something to remember her by."

"Who?"

"You know. Rafaella."

Rafaella. She did exist after all. Jackie Talbot had mentioned her name.

"I bought it for her. It was a present."

Jackie had looked down at her Bloody Mary, which was called a Cardiac Arrest in the popular restaurant where they were dining, and then unknotted the scarf with uncertain fingers.

"I'll buy you a new one at Marcus," said Stephen. He felt it was ungentlemanly and gauche of him to take the scarf back, but Jackie understood. "I'll get one like it," he amended. "No two are alike."

Jackie passed the scarf over to him, smiling sadly. "So long as you remember," she said. "No two are alike, Stephen."

Beneath his seat, folded neatly among the tapes and papers, lay the scarf. In the next week, he would fly to California and then, when he had settled himself, on to Europe. He had legitimate business in Geneva, didn't he, and Geneva wasn't so very far from Genoa.

They even sounded alike.

Gemma's voice was weak, faltering. "The heat," she gasped. "It is unimaginable, *carina*. We are having an exceptionally hot summer. I don't think I slept a wink last night."

"I'm sorry," said Rafaella.

"Michele can sleep in any discomfort, any condition. Naples in August, Alaska in January, it is all the same to him. Isn't it just like a man?"

This question was fraught with unseen land mines. Gemma revered the male race, yet thought it permissible, occasionally, to suggest that they could be insensitive. To agree was to invite a lecture; to demur would bring a wounded, superior silence. No one could suffer as nobly as Gemma.

"I have had a postcard from Anna-Laura," said her mother-in-law with a sigh. "I am sure you have had one, too. Tell me, Rafaella, why does she go to such dangerous places? Why must she fly halfway around the world where there are revolutions and mercenaries and volcanoes? She will return with dysentery. Or a sea urchin could bite her! The bite of a sea urchin is extremely dangerous and very painful. The spines become imbedded in the flesh."

"Anna-Laura is very capable. What makes you think she will be bitten by a sea urchin?"

"I did not imply that she *would* be bitten, *bella*, only that it is a possibility. Why are you so emotional? Is something wrong?"

Rafaella shifted the phone from one hand to another. Whenever Gemma called, the receiver seemed twice as heavy. "She'll be back in a few days," she said soothingly. "She works hard, *Nonna*—she deserves her holiday."

"Has something happened to one of the children?"

"Why do you ask?"

"I know you, darling. You are so cool, so reserved. I can tell something is troubling you. You must confide in me."

"Nothing is troubling me. Nothing is wrong with the children, and Anna-Laura will be home soon. Everything is perfection."

"You're in a hurry? Young people are always rushing somewhere."

"I was on my way to the studio."

"Such close work," said Gemma. "Such tiny figures. Pick, pick. Picking away with your miniature tools, my love, like a little bird. I could weep when I picture you at your workbench! Aren't you afraid it will ruin your eyes?"

Rafaella stifled unfilial laughter against her sleeve. She had already heard Gemma's rendition of the Neapolitan bonnet-factory girl. Angela, a pious but poor friend of Gemma's youth, had been orphaned at an early age and taken work in a factory where she sewed sequins on hats. The blooming girl had begun to squint before she was twenty. At twenty-five, she was sent to a colony for the blind. *Una cieca.*

"My eyes, at least, are excellent."

"I wish," said Gemma, "I could say the same for my legs. The arthritis is much worse, *carina*. Sometimes I hobble from my bed. That is why I have decided we should stay at Anna-Laura's. The stairs at your flat—*Madonna mia!* Of course, it is for your sake, too. In your condition you should not sleep on that crazy couch."

Rafaella heard her mother-in-law's words without comprehending at first. It came to her in a flash that Gemma was discussing the impending visit. Every year, to escape the oppressive heat of Naples and visit her adored grandchildren, Gemma descended on the relative cool of the Via Vieri flat. Here she set up camp and dictated for two weeks. Michele sometimes came too; generally he traveled down by train for the weekends only.

Gemma was giving her the date, a week in advance, and the precise arrival time of their train. "Of course, even though we'll stay at Anna-Laura's, we will be at your flat all the time," she said. "The other is only a sleeping arrangement, Rafaella. I will help you in every way, *cara!* Arthritis or not, you can depend on me."

"We will be so glad to see you," said Rafaella. She leaned against the wall now, imagining the flat as it would be soon. How could she have forgotten?

As soon as Gemma had bidden her farewell, she fled down the stairs. Signora Lenti was planted in her chair, reading a newspaper. "Nearly time for the children's grandparents to come, isn't it?" she asked. Her eyes were full of innocence. She wasn't prying, nor had she listened in the hall. Signora Lenti merely marked the passing of the seasons by certain events which transpired beneath her roof. The visit of the senior Leones was one of them.

"Yes, nearly time," said Rafaella. Dear God, it must be August!

Chapter 7

Gemma Leone sat in the precise center of Rafaella's couch, leaving room for no one else. Although it was not particularly warm in the room, she fanned herself with a magazine.

"This flat seems to get smaller every year," she said.

"That's because there are so many people in it when you come," said Stefania. Rafaella glanced at her daughter but saw no malice there. Stefania was simply pointing out the truth. Seven of them were packed into the room, and it looked like the terminus of a busy train station.

Anna-Laura perched on one arm of the couch; Stefania, on the other, wriggled imperceptibly away from her grandmother's clutching embrace. Rafaella sat across from them, with Carlo cross-legged at her feet. Michele occupied the armchair, and a kitchen chair had been fetched to accommodate Signora Lenti, who had toiled upstairs to pay her respects. She sat humbly, half hidden by the television set. Whenever there was a lull in the conversation, she leaned forward with the inevitable, polite question.

"And how was your journey from Naples, signora?"

"Better not to ask," said Gemma. "Why do they call a train a *rapido* if it creeps along at a snail's pace?"

Signora Lenti frowned in sympathy. She was formulating another question. As always, she played directly into Gemma's hands, inquiring about the signora's health, comfort, peace of mind—topics upon which Gemma could discourse for hours. Anna-Laura leaped in to prevent her.

"Your new coiffure is most becoming, Mama. So intricate! What gave you the idea to have your hair frosted?"

Gemma fanned herself more vigorously. She seemed flustered, offended. The pages of the magazine flapped open and she gave a little cry of irritation. Everyone looked at her warily, with the exception of her husband, who was staring out the window.

"*Nonna*," said Stefania, "I will bring you a proper fan." She ran lightly from the room, sending a significant look in her mother's direction, and returned with a pleated paper fan, a memento of a trip to a Chinese restaurant. She took the magazine from her grandmother's hands and replaced it with her treasure. "*Grazie*, darling," said Gemma. Her voice trembled with emotion.

Stefania, peacemaker, stepped back and all of them watched while Gemma, like an intricate machine momentarily thrown out of kilter, resumed her fanning. She wore a fashionable trouser suit of turquoise-blue, and her eyelids were colored to match. Her nails were carefully shaped and painted with lacquer. A number of bangles jingled on her wrists. As Rafaella studied her, it became suddenly apparent that the becoming new hairstyle, springing up in intricate whorls from Gemma's head, was in fact a wig. Oh, dear. Poor Anna-Laura. With the best intentions in the world, she had committed the first offense. Now she would have to suffer.

"And you, signore," said the voice from in back of the television set. "How have you been this past year?"

There was a silence. "Michele," said Gemma sharply. "Signora Lenti is asking you a question."

Michele Leone's head swiveled about in polite confusion. As always, he seemed to have been awakened from a dream. When Signora Lenti repeated her question, he assured her that he was in excellent health and had been so for twelve months. He thanked her for asking and then resumed his surveillance of the window. Before he did, though, he glanced briefly at Carlo and smiled. It sometimes seemed that Michele and Carlo could communicate without words, but what comfort it brought either of them Rafaella could not imagine. She rose and went to the kitchen.

While she placed the espresso cups on the tray she could hear her mother-in-law starting in on Anna-Laura. Didn't

Signora Lenti agree that it was scandalous for an unmarried woman of nearly forty to run off to a place like the Seychelle Islands? Wasn't it asking for trouble? Did Signora Lenti know that to tan too deeply was to court skin cancer? Anna-Laura looked, said Gemma, like a *Siciliana*.

"I think she looks nice, *Nonna*," said Carlo daringly. *Bravo, Carlo!* Rafaella lingered over the simple task, trying to block out the sound of the gathering storm. Soon Signora Lenti, terrified by her position of catalyst, would excuse herself and shuffle downstairs. She debated taking away a cup and leaving only six, but the timing was tricky.

When Gemma had first seen her she had folded her in her arms, softly exclaiming at Rafaella's fragility, her paleness. Michele had pointed out that Rafaella was not, in fact, pale, but his wife did not listen. There had been that brief moment of complicity with her father-in-law—a moment in which he had smiled at her in a way achingly reminiscent of Aldo—and then, after the decorous kiss on each cheek, he had retreated into his private world.

She added a plate of thin lemon slices to the tray, and spoons and sugar. Carefully, she arranged the *amaretti* biscuits and wondered what else she could do to postpone the moment of return. She heard a movement in the living room, and then Signora Lenti was at the kitchen door, thanking her and explaining that she had to feed her parakeet. Anna-Laura hovered behind.

"Where are we now?" Rafaella asked when Signora Lenti had made her departure.

"We are at the stage where Mama feels she is losing her audience."

"Could we create a diversion?"

Anna-Laura shrugged. "Too late."

Like soldiers at the ministry of war, they huddled in the kitchen, planning strategies. At last it was decided that Anna-Laura would ask Carlo to show his grandmother his latest drawings.

"*Coraggio*," said Anna-Laura. "It can't go on forever, *bella*."

Rafaella watched her sister-in-law leave the kitchen. She heard her voice, unnaturally distinct, bid Carlo to bring his sketches. The rigid pattern of the next ten days stretched before her, as inflexible as the schedule of a convicted prisoner.

Gemma and Michele would be with her constantly. Brief outings would occur, as stretches of relief, but these would be fraught with difficulty and stress. Gemma thought that the children, on a drive along the coast, should remain in the car at all times. Family dinners almost staggered her when she tried to imagine them. Gemma would inhabit the kitchen like a mythological high priestess pronouncing the knives too dull to cut, the oil not virgin enough. Everyone would eat too much and emerge with indigestion, except for Carlo and Stefania, who had stomachs of cast iron. On the evening when Maurizio—as was his custom—took them out for a meal, Gemma would be so polite that a great silence would settle over the table. Her father-in-law, who disappeared for long walks as these visits wore on, would spend more and more time in the bathroom when forced into close proximity.

Even as she was thinking about him, the pipes sounded resoundingly from inside the walls, and she knew he had sought refuge. She bent her head, laughing softly against the barrier of her arms, and thought it would be comical if she did not have to be present.

Carlo must have presented his sketches, for she could hear Gemma's voice raised in pride and disapproval. "These are very good, Carlo! Truly, I have never seen such talent in a little boy, but, *ragazzo mio*, why such a spirit of violence? This dragon, here, with the fire streaming out of his nostrils? Why so fierce? Why couldn't he be a kind dragon? Why the fire?"

Carlo's voice was flat, dispassionate. "Fire is what dragons breathe, *Nonna*."

Anna-Laura's voice, reckless, "What would you have them breathe, Mama—olive oil?"

Stefania's voice, cajoling, "Carlo is the best artist in his class. The teacher admires his drawings."

"She can admire them," said Gemma. "She is not related to him by blood. I am only suggesting improvements, eh, Carlo?"

The pipes sounded again beyond the wall, as if Michele had contributed to the discussion in some definitive way.

Rafaella picked the tray up and prepared to enter the room and defend her son. She was reminded of an old American television program which had been popular in Italy ten years ago.

Signora, she told herself—*This is Your Life!*

"A letter for you," said Carlo, sorting through the mail, "from America." He handed her an oblong white envelope and went off to the kitchen in search of something to drink.

Rafaella held the envelope carefully in both hands, staring at the postmark. It was from New York. It was addressed to her in a sprawling but legible hand, and contained no return address. She was afraid to open it and so she sat, motionless, feeling the texture of the paper with her fingertips.

"Is it from that lady at the hospital?" Carlo called.

"No."

She took a long time in opening it, as long as possible. She extracted the single sheet of paper and unfolded it. The writer of the letter addressed her as "Dear Signora." Her eyes flew to the signature.

Yes.

Stephen Morrissy told her, rather formally, that he was going to Geneva on business. After that, he expected to be in Italy briefly. He said he would call her while he passed through Genoa and named a date. He hoped she was in good health. "I would very much like to see you again," he concluded. That was all. He signed the letter with both his names, first and last.

She read it several times, then folded it and replaced it in the envelope. Carlo had come quietly into the room. She wasn't aware of him until he spoke.

"Mama? May I have the stamp?"

She found she couldn't bring herself to rip the envelope. "Later, Carlo. I will give it to you later."

She sat for some time, holding the letter and questioning her feelings. The very suggestion that he would be here in

Genoa instead of half a world away filled her with a sensation so peculiar she felt nearly ill. Impossible that he should be here, intruding on her real life. Yet she wasn't really astonished; in the well-guarded interior of her most secret self was something which insisted on a lack of astonishment. *Of course*, it said. *Of course.*

Sifting through the fear and joy and anticipation assailing her in alternating waves, she came upon a thought: So this was how it happened. Not white sails on the horizon, herself in robes at the summit of a cliff, but a plain white envelope, delivered through normal channels and handed to her by her son.

All six of the Leones sat in Maurizio's drawing room, off the Piazza Madellena. They were dressed quite formally in honor of the occasion. It was the first time Signor Guidi had invited them all to his home.

"What a handsome residence," Gemma said, looking around at the oil paintings, the Etruscan sculpture, the silver candlesticks. The elegance of Maurizio's rooms seemed to intimidate her; she was more subdued than usual.

Epifania, the old woman who cooked and kept house for Maurizio, entered the room with a tray of drinks. She wore a crisp white apron over her black dress, and a little white cap; her walnut face was split wide in a welcoming smile. Gemma stirred uneasily.

"Yes," she repeated, "a handsome residence. But don't you find it too large, signore, all on your own?"

"It suits me," said Maurizio simply.

He had bought the house thirty years ago for his bride, who died in the first year of Rafaella's marriage. Rafaella looked for the portrait of Giulia which had always hung in the drawing room and discovered it was gone. In its place hung two seventeenth-century maritime maps, framed ornately.

When they had all been served, Maurizio lifted his glass and proposed a toast. "To our dear Rafaella," he said, "who has returned to us."

The words were so unexpected she felt warmth spread

over her cheeks. She lifted her glass and bowed her head as they all drank. The children lifted their glasses of watered-down wine with a cheer. Anna-Laura cheered also. The others drank quietly, and in Gemma's eyes Rafaella saw something awaken.

Our dear Rafaella? So that's how it goes, eh?

The long double doors at the end of the room stood open, giving out on a small garden. Carlo and Stefania asked permission to go outside and visit the goldfish pond. They walked off, Carlo in his long-trousered suit and his sister in a white linen dress; they might have been going to make their first communion. Rafaella saw them sitting in the twilight, side by side on a pink marble bench, and was flooded with emotion. How beautiful they were, her children! They seemed too far away, as if she were looking at them through the wrong end of a telescope, and she wanted to call them back. Carlo looked up and waved. All was well.

I would very much like to see you again.

The room was sweet with the fragrance of the white flowers standing everywhere in silver bowls; beneath it she could smell an expensive cleaning polish mixed with attar of cloves. Everything here was lovely and harmonious. Nothing was cramped or mean or incongruous. Even the sounds of traffic from the Piazza Madellena were muted. There was no doubt that the mistress of such a house would dwell in peace and comfort, surrounded by beautiful things.

Even Gemma bloomed in such a setting; she was softer, less abrasive. The speculative look in her eyes remained, and Rafaella wondered what she was thinking. So far the look was not resentful.

When Epifania announced that dinner was ready, Maurizio came to Rafaella and took her arm, leading her to the dining room. Place cards in silver holders had been provided at each setting. Maurizio, of course, sat at the head of the table. Rafaella sat across from him. Here, long ago, Giulia Guidi had presided at dinner parties. On less formal occasions, the Guidi children, now grown, must also have dined here.

Anna-Laura was exclaiming over the beauty of the place

settings, the gleam of the Florentine silver. "Oh, Maurizio," she sighed, "you do have an eye for lovely things."

Gemma smiled and nodded, catching Rafaella's eye. "Oh yes," she said. "He does." This time her expression was unmistakable. She did not disapprove at all, quite the opposite. If Aldo's widow married Maurizio Guidi it would not be a betrayal. Aldo had been young and ardent, the husband of Rafaella's heart. Now that she was older and marred by illness, now that she found herself struggling to support her children—who could blame her if she married an affluent older man for security? Even Aldo could not object. Rafaella was lucky, indeed, to have such a suitor as Maurizio.

The look in Gemma's eyes was definitely one of congratulations. A shrewd, woman-to-woman look. Rafaella looked away.

I would very much like to see you again.

Epifania entered with the first course, a cold salad of fish and vegetables in parsley sauce. Michele Leone gave a soft sigh of happiness, which startled everyone. *Cappone magro* was one of his favorite dishes.

Rafaella clasped her fingers around the stem of her wineglass. She waited until the slight trembling had ceased. Then she spoke, keeping her voice light and conversational.

"I had a letter from America today."

Five pairs of eyes looked up politely. Only Carlo's gaze quickened.

"One of the volunteers at the hospital will be passing through Genoa," she said.

"The girl who called me?" Anna-Laura asked. "The one with the Roman accent?"

Rafaella explained that the volunteer was a man. She said he had been very kind to her. The volunteers were amazing she said, giving so much of their time to people they would probably never see again. She talked on at some length about their kindness and devotion, until it seemed she might be describing a group of saints.

"Well," said Maurizio, his tone almost paternal, "that will be nice for you, to see someone who made your stay more comfortable."

"No doubt you feel grateful," said Gemma.

"Yes. Grateful."

She realized they all pictured the impending visitor as a mild, gentle soul, perhaps rather effeminate in nature. Why else would a man volunteer to work at a hospital? It was something none of them could imagine an Italian male doing.

Epifania brought the veal and pasta. More wine was poured. The subject of the volunteer was dropped. No one had shown much interest in him, anyway.

Carlo lay on his bed, arms folded behind his head. He stared at the poster of Cheryl Tiegs without seeing her. The house was quiet for once. Stefania had gone out shopping with *Nonna*, and his mother was at the studio, working. His grandfather was in the flat watching television with the volume on low, and Carlo was able to think things over in peace.

He knew that his father had proposed marriage to his mother while standing in front of the great lion at the San Lorenzo cathedral. It was a story he had heard often enough. Papa had known her for a month only, but he was sure he wanted her for his wife. Although his name, Leone, meant lion, he lacked courage. What if she refused? He took her to San Lorenzo to draw the necessary courage from his name-sake, and she said yes.

Signor Guidi had all but proposed to his mother the night before, and he had done it without words. Soon he would find the words. He felt that Michele and Gemma were his allies in the matter, and he would act quickly.

The letter was something he still couldn't understand. When he had seen her, sitting so still, her eyes far away and unreadable, she'd seemed stricken. He was afraid she'd had bad news. Guiltily, Carlo had considered reading the letter on the sly, but she kept it in her bag and he had no chance. Now that she'd announced the letter's contents, he was be-wildered. What was there in the visit of an American man who seemed to be a sort of nurse to make her look the way she had?

Carlo slid from the bed and made his way into the living

room. His *nonno* was reading the newspaper, paying no attention to the images on the television screen. He looked up and smiled.

"Do you want to go for a walk?" Carlo asked.

Michele turned the set off and fetched his hat. They went down the stairs together in companionable silence. When they'd crossed over into the Via Acquatania, Carlo asked his grandfather why he'd kept the TV on when he wasn't watching.

Michele turned the question over, knitting his brows. "I suppose," he said at last, "I have grown so accustomed to the sound of another voice, forever talking, I can no longer read without it."

Carlo nodded. They strolled along, feeling the late afternoon sun on their shoulders, not speaking. Carlo liked walking with his grandfather. When he was smaller, they had held hands on their walks. Now that he was so big they walked apart, but occasionally Michele's hand reached out and lightly cupped his head.

When they reached the *tabaccheria* on the corner, Michele went inside. Carlo could see him buying the cigarettes, filling his thin case with them, doing everything with the slow, deliberate movements which were his nature. When he came out of the shop, he handed Carlo a little sack of licorice candies, and they walked on.

Outside his mother's shop, Carlo paused. There was a customer inside talking to Nina. Nina wouldn't tease him or call him little fish in front of a customer. Now was the time.

"*Nonno*," he said, "I have to give Mama a message. Will you wait?"

He went straight through to the studio without announcing himself. Rafaella was studying a belt buckle, which had already been cast in silver. When she looked up her eyes were bright, as if she might have a fever. "Hello, my love," she said. "What brings you here?" Her eyes clouded. "Is something wrong?"

"No. I'm just walking with *Nonno*. I thought I would stop in to tell you something."

She leaned forward expectantly. Between the white vees of

her collar he saw the thin pink line. Carlo stepped closer, so that he could not be overheard.

"I just wanted to tell you—" How to say it? Best to be frank, he thought. "You don't have to marry Signor Guidi if you don't want to."

To his embarrassment, she seemed to be struggling to contain laughter. Her eyes grew brighter still. She took his hand and held it to her cheek.

"Thank you, Carlo," she said. "Signor Guidi is a wonderful man. I like him very much. He hasn't asked me to be his wife, but if he ever did, I would have to refuse."

"Because you don't love him."

"Correct." She kissed his hand, returned it to him. "Are you disappointed, Giancarlo?"

"No."

It was the truth. Despite the splendid things he could have if his mother married Maurizio, it would not be worth it. Not if she didn't love him. He would feel guilty and wretched; something would be taken away from him forever.

He went back through the shop, smiled casually at Nina, and rejoined his grandfather. Michele handed him the licorice candies again, and they resumed their walk.

Chapter 8

"The man from the hospital. When will he come to see us?" Stefania was brushing her hair a hundred strokes. With her head bent low the dark strands nearly touched the floor.

"I'm not sure that he will, darling. Perhaps he'll just telephone to say hello."

Stefania straightened, eyes wounded. "Oh, *no*," she wailed. "I was counting on *seeing* him."

"But he may be in a hurry, passing through. I thought the best thing would be for me to meet him in town. That way *Nonna* wouldn't have to be bothered."

"But *Nonna* is baking sweet cakes for him. I heard her tell Anna-Laura."

Sweet cakes, thought Rafaella. Of course. Gemma would assume that her daughter-in-law would be incapable of receiving a man anywhere but at her home. "We'll see," she said.

"Oh, please, Mama. *Please*."

"Why is it so important to you, *bella?*"

"I've never really seen an American."

"That's nonsense, Stefania. You've seen dozens of them."

"Not close up or to talk to. Not in our flat."

Rafaella sighed. "We'll see, darling," she repeated.

This was the day he had said he would arrive in Genoa. Rafaella was determined to treat it like any other day—a Wednesday in August, her in-laws nearing the end of their stay with her—but of course it would not be possible. Each time the phone rang her throat constricted with anxiety, and each time she answered and found Nina on the other end or one of Stefania's friends, she felt equal parts of relief and disappointment.

She couldn't go to the studio, her refuge, for fear that he would call and find no one there. Worse still, Gemma might answer if he called in the afternoon.

"Is he an older man?" Gemma asked, on arriving. "Will he have trouble with the stairs?" She plumped down in the armchair, massaging her legs. "What's so funny?" she demanded. "Wait until *you* have arthritis, *cara mia*, and you won't laugh at those stairs."

"I'm sorry," said Rafaella. "It's just that he won't find them difficult."

"Americans are so soft! They have elevators everywhere. I merely thought the stairs in this establishment might be difficult for an American. Especially if he is elderly."

Rafaella was about to explain that the American was not elderly—who had said he was?—when Michele made one of his rare pronouncements. "There are only two flights," he said. "We are not discussing the Spanish Steps, Gemma."

Gemma rose stiffly and took the plate of *ravioli dolci* to the kitchen. Rafaella followed her and saw her mother-in-law standing pensively at the kitchen sink. Her legs in their reinforced stockings were planted wide; from the waist down she seemed combative, but her shoulders slumped and she looked, on closer inspection, defeated. What obscure sorrows moved her now? Rafaella pitied her.

She crossed the room and put an arm around Gemma's shoulders. "I wasn't laughing at you," she said gently. "I'm sorry if your legs are hurting."

"You are a good girl, Rafaella. I mean well, you know." For a moment, the older woman leaned against the younger. Then she straightened briskly and touched the curls of her wig. "We have the sweet," she said. "Now—what for dinner? What would the gentleman like for dinner?"

"I don't know that he'll be with us then," said Rafaella patiently. "We must not plan for him; it might make him uncomfortable."

"Well, he will definitely wish to take coffee and the sweet with us. This man was kind to you, and I feel it my personal duty to show our gratitude. It is important for foreigners to see how closely knit our good Italian family life is, don't you think?"

A new idea assailed her. "He is a family man himself, isn't he? Why does he travel without his wife?"

"He isn't married, *Nonna*."

Gemma's brows shot up. "That settles it," she said. "A lonely man like this one, all by himself in a country strange to him—he will definitely want to be with a family."

The sound of the phone shrilled through the flat. Stefania sprinted to the hallway and bellowed into the instrument, her voice loud with excitement. It was only Anna-Laura, calling to say she would bring some flowers by later.

"Flowers do so much to brighten the atmosphere," said Gemma. "Signor Guidi's flower arrangements were most attractive, don't you think?" Her eyes bored into Rafaella's meaningfully. "Of course, Signor Guidi's house is elegance itself. He can afford the finest flowers, eh *carina?*"

Rafaella excused herself and went to her bedroom. She sat on the edge of the bed, clasping her hands together tightly. Like it or not, it seemed Stephen would be drawn into the chaos on the Via Vieri. Her whole family had willed it. She believed she was capable of defying their collective will, even the children's, but something prevented her.

At first she had imagined herself meeting him in neutral territory. She would breeze into the little restaurant near the Centro Storico, say, and show him the restored Rafaella. She was on her own turf here; she would be the guide this time. She had seen herself quite clearly in these fantasies—she was witty, casual, sophisticated. The frightened, half-crazed Rafaella he had known in Texas had disappeared utterly.

Gradually, these rosy pictures had been eroded by her certain knowledge of their fraudulence. She was infinitely better, stronger, than she had been, but she was neither sophisticated nor casual. *Above all, signora*, she told herself, *you are not casual. You never have been; you never will be. It is not your nature.*

It was just as well that he should see her as she was—a woman enmeshed in a chaotic family life which was sometimes wonderful and sometimes the stuff of low comedy. To present herself as anything else would be a deception, and she had already deceived him once.

She thought of the worst that might happen. Alone in her bedroom, she invented scenes—principally involving Gemma—which made her blush with anticipated humiliation. In Gemma's mouth she placed inconceivably embarrassing comments; she allowed Signora Lenti to shuffle into the proceedings, Signorina Freda to bang on the ceiling with a mop handle and scream for quiet. She imagined how cramped the sitting room would be—it would grow hotter and hotter, and the knees of everyone present would nearly scrape against the knees of everyone else. Stephen would feel constrained to eat more of the *ravioli dolci* than he wanted. Stefania would do her cowgirl act with even greater lubricity than she had manufactured for Maurizio. *Maurizio!* Bring on Maurizio, too, by all means! He might call, unannounced, with a sheaf of flowers. Another kitchen chair would have to be fetched.

When all the ghastly possibilities had been exhausted, she felt very calm. In American films, characters sometimes said *Take it or leave it.*

"Take it or leave it," Rafaella said, alone in her bedroom. "This is what I am. No mystery here."

It was nearly five when he called. He asked to speak to Signora Leone. He was speaking in Italian, and rather more fluently than she remembered. Didn't he recognize her voice?

"This is she. Welcome to Genoa, signore."

At the other end a windy, roaring sound. She heard a car horn, passing voices. He was in a telephone booth. *I would very much like to see you again.* That was what she wished he would say. Instead, he inquired politely after her health and the health of her children. He told her he was staying at the Colombia-Excelsior, near the main railway station.

"A fine hotel," she said judiciously. It was the most expensive, at any rate. She thought it might cost him eighty thousand lire a night there.

"It seems a beautiful city," he said. "I've been walking around. I'm at a place called Piazza Colombo now."

"Oh, but that is nothing! You must go to the Garibaldi, and you should take the funicular to Monte Righi."

"I thought," he said, "I would like to see the Via Vieri."

"There is nothing of note here." She smiled against the cup of the receiver.

"I think otherwise."

"My entire family is here," she said, lowering her voice. "It is the time for my in-laws' annual visit. They are very eager to make your acquaintance, signore. They wish to express their gratitude."

"And you, signora?"

She clasped the receiver firmly. "I would very much like to see you again."

"What time?"

She told him to come after dinner, if that would be convenient. She named the time and cautioned him not to take a sweet after his meal. "You will be required to eat," she said. When the conversation was about to be terminated, she had a sudden thought. "Do you know how to get here?" she asked.

He laughed. "Don't worry," he said in English, "I'm very good at finding my way."

She had forgotten how tall he was. He stood at the door of her flat like an emissary from the New World, looking as out of place on the Via Vieri as an oak among cedars.

"Hello, signora."

Hazelnut eyes. She wanted to go on looking at him, undisturbed, just looking, in this first moment of their reunion. Fortunately (for it would have embarrassed her, in retrospect), Stefania rushed into the entryway.

"Bring him in, Mama," she hissed. Then she stopped dead in her tracks and looked up at him. The look was one of amazement; she had expected someone quite different. She twirled a strand of hair in her fingers nervously.

"*Buona sera, signore,*" she said in a small voice.

"*Buona sera, signorina,*" said Stephen, smiling.

When they entered the living room the looks of surprise were more carefully masked. Michele rose to shake hands. He was sitting next to his wife tonight; it had been agreed that the guest should have the armchair. Gemma, who had been prepared to welcome the stranger effusively, was so alarmed at the difference between her vision of him and the reality that she could only nod primly when they were introduced.

"This is my son, Carlo"—a manly handshake, Carlo's eyes unwavering and somehow fierce—"and my sister-in-law, Signorina Leone."

"My name is Anna-Laura, signore. There are so many Leones in this room you will be confused." She smiled brilliantly—the provocative, irresistible smile of a worldly woman. She was trying to show him that one of the Leones, at any rate, was living in the twentieth century.

He sat in the offered chair, and there was an interval of terrible silence. Stefania discreetly surveyed his shoes, loafers, while the room grew smaller. He seemed to take up a lot of space. Although his hair was by no means long, it was longer than what they were used to seeing. The shaded lamp behind him cast a nimbus around the fair hair.

"So," said Anna-Laura, clearing her throat. "You've come from Geneva?"

He replied that he had. The weather had been overcast and dull, which was surprising. Rafaella listened, not to the prosaic words but to the fluency of his Italian. She thought he had been practicing. Occasionally he stumbled a little.

"I teach English," said Anna-Laura, switching to that language. "If you tire of Italian, just say so, signore."

Gemma straightened, alert. "I have no English," she said.

"I have some," said Carlo.

"Me too," said Stefania.

Rafaella watched him turning in all directions, trying to pacify everyone. Gemma leaned forward and asked what sort of business had taken him to Geneva. Stephen could not understand her Neapolitan accent and looked helplessly to Anna-Laura. When the question had been translated, he replied that he had attended a film festival. A lamb to the slaughter.

"But, Signor Morrissy,"—Gemma pronounced it Morizzi —"films are for leisure. What a lucky man to be able to fly so many miles to go to the cinema."

Rafaella thought it would be a good moment to escape. She excused herself and went to bring the coffee and *dolci* in from the kitchen. Stefania followed her.

"Is he a film star, Mama?" she whispered.

"No, a filmmaker, *carina.*"

This same information was being imparted in the living room. She could almost hear Gemma's gasp, followed by a long spurt of Italian.

"My mother says she has given up going to the movies," said Anna-Laura. "She says they are nothing but an excuse to show unclothed people behaving disgracefully." Anna-Laura's voice was just ironic enough to apologize to Stephen without offending Gemma.

"Really, your aunt has become quite a diplomat," said Rafaella. She sent Stefania in with the plate of sweets.

"*Nonna* has made these especially for you, signore," said Stefania. "They are her specialty."

"Please tell your mother that I am a *documentary* film-maker," Rafaella heard Stephen murmur. Then he thanked Stefania.

"Mama went to a *documentario* not long ago," said Stefania.

"Did she?"

"It was about starving children with legs like matchsticks."

Rafaella watched, unseen, from the kitchen. At Gemma's urging he picked up one of the *ravioli dolci.* She observed the curve of his strong fingers. The collar of his shirt was open and she could see his smooth, brown throat. He was tanner than he had been in Texas. Where had he been in the sun? "*Squisito,*" he said, complimenting Gemma on her pastry.

"You shall have many more," she said, as if speaking to Carlo.

Rafaella entered the room and set the tray on the low table. She began to pour coffee into the thin cups. She felt his eyes on her and willed her hands to stay steady.

Stephen jumped to his feet, alarming everyone. "I forgot," he said. "I brought wine and left it in the car."

"The gray Mercedes," said Carlo, who had been admiring it from the window. "It's a stupendous car."

"Is it nicer than Signor Guidi's?" asked Stefania.

"No comparison."

"It doesn't belong to me. I borrowed it from a friend in Milan." He turned to Carlo. "If your mother doesn't mind, you can come down and have a look at it while I get the wine." He had lapsed into English.

"What is he saying?" Gemma whispered loudly.

"May I go look at Signor Morrissy's car?"

Rafaella nodded. Carlo went off with Stephen, hands in pockets, walking casually.

"He has a friend in Milan," said Gemma when they had left. "Why would he have a friend in Milan?"

"It's allowed, Mama," said Anna-Laura.

"He isn't elderly, not at all. Rafaella, you implied that Signor Morizzi was elderly. He can't be over forty."

"He is forty-four, *Nonna*."

"His Italian is most peculiar. Sometimes he sounds like that Spaniard who used to live over the coffee shop in Naples."

Stefania had come back into the room wearing her cowboy hat.

"I thought he had come from Geneva," said Gemma, "and now he says Milan."

"One thing is certain," said Michele. "He won't have any trouble with the stairs."

"Not this one," said Gemma darkly. "He is not the man Rafaella described, not at all—"

"Shhh, *Nonna*, they're coming back!"

Stephen placed two bottles of wine on the table. It was the Santa Maddelena she liked; he had remembered. "*Grazie,*" she said. It emerged almost in a whisper, and then the confusion resumed.

While Anna-Laura went to fetch glasses for the wine, Stephen admired the cowboy hat. Stefania did not twirl about or perform for him as she had for Maurizio, and when he complimented her she smiled and looked down, her lashes casting shadows on her cheeks. It was a very pretty sight, but she was unaware of it this time. Rafaella saw that Stephen made her genuinely shy.

Michele roused himself long enough to drink Stephen's health. "We are grateful to you," he said.

Gemma went on at some length about their gratitude, all of which had to be translated. It was a formal speech, very gracious and dignified. At the end of it, she said, "And now I suppose you will be going home? To America?"

Stephen looked at Rafaella directly. "Please tell your mother-in-law I have two days to spend in Genoa. Two more days before I must go back."

It was another hour before she found herself alone with him. There was an interminable time during which he was forced to shake hands with everyone, thank Gemma for her delicious *dolci*, and tell the children he hoped to see them again. When he went to the door Rafaella went, too. Carlo sidled along beside her, but Anna-Laura called to him and he dropped back.

Stephen stood leaning against the open door. In his eyes was a tentative smile. Behind them, they could hear Gemma's voice rising and falling like a calliope. Rafaella refused to apologize for them, but she put her hands to her head and laughed softly to acknowledge the chaos.

Stephen's lips turned upward. He bent his head and laughed too. "I am honored to have met your family," he said, speaking in a voice so low she could scarcely hear him, "but I wonder if it would be possible to see you alone?"

She wanted very much to touch him but couldn't think how to do it; it seemed an impossibility.

"Without your chaperones," he continued.

"What is keeping Rafaella?" Gemma called loudly.

Hastily, she named a restaurant in the Old Town, and said she would meet him there at noon. There was nothing but silence in the living room now—the silence of listening.

"Until tomorrow then," said Stephen. He ran lightly down the stairs and disappeared, leaving her so suddenly she felt bereft.

Chapter 9

In a maze of covered lanes in the Centro Storico was the small restaurant Rafaella liked. It occurred to her that Stephen might find it difficult to locate. The streets were narrow and twisting, the buildings a bewildering jumble to a stranger. One had to climb a steep flight of stairs from which there was a tantalizing view of the sea and then turn at a sharp angle. There the restaurant, little more than a *trattoria*, was squeezed between an ancient palace and a fruit market.

She walked more swiftly, jostling people and apologizing. What if he thought she was playing some bizarre joke—naming a rendezvous which did not exist? She came to the foot of the old stone staircase. Nearly there. Her heels clicked importantly as she hastened upward toward him. At the top she felt a little breathless and paused to lean against the stone archway. The sea was green today; it soothed her.

She began to walk on, and then she saw him. He was standing not three feet away from her, looking out to sea. His back was to her; the lines of his body were alert. He was waiting.

"I was afraid you would get lost," she said.

He turned to her, smiling. "I told you," he said. "I'm very good at finding my way."

"Why did you wait here instead of at the restaurant?"

"I like it here. I knew you had to come from that direction, unless you came by sea."

They walked to the restaurant slowly. Stephen kept his hands in the pockets of his jacket. He wore a suit of faded blue denim and a checked shirt, soft and old. Rafaella was glad she had dressed casually. Walking beside him in her floppy white pants and shirt, she thought others would see them as a couple on holiday.

Still, she was different from the others. When they were seated at the small table, she saw what the difference was. Everywhere she looked, she saw the bare arms and shoulders of women. The women displayed their tanned flesh proudly; they had been offering themselves to the sun. Only the old native ladies covered themselves in stifling black. Widows or not, they wore black always. Rafaella, buttoned to the throat, was as protected as they. A white widow.

She looked at her hands, folded on the pink tablecloth, to avoid the sight of the half-naked women all around them.

"What would you be thinking about?" asked Stephen. "At this precise moment?"

She looked from her hands to his face. He had removed his sunglasses, and his eyes were serious, as if he wanted her to answer the unserious question.

"About lunch," she said. "Are you fond of squid?"

"Ah, signora—what a poker player you would make."

Between them was a pink carnation in a slim ceramic bud vase. She fixed her gaze on the carnation. "You should not ask people what they are thinking at a given moment," she said. "It is likely to be something uninteresting."

"I'll tell you what I was thinking," said Stephen. "I was thinking of the color inside a particular kind of seashell." He picked the little vase up and turned it in his hands. "A more prosaic man than myself would say you were blooming like a rose or like this carnation, but I prefer to compare your color to the seashell."

The waiter appeared. After some consultation, they ordered aperitifs. Neither of them, it seemed, was hungry. The waiter sighed politely and went away.

"Rafaella," said Stephen, "you are blushing. You may be the last woman on earth to actually blush."

The dream she had had, on those July mornings of her solitary walks, became a reality. She was his guide; she showed him Genoa. From the time they left the *trattoria* to the time in late afternoon when they stood in front of the Palazzo Balbi Durazzo, he made no more references to sea-shells or blushing. They talked of neutral things.

On the dockside—where the sun beat so brightly against the harbor it made her giddy—he told her how much he liked her children. They watched a ferry steam off in the direction of Sardinia. Gulls screamed in its wake, wheeling endlessly.

"Carlo looks just like you," he said. "Does Stefania look like her father?"

"Exactly. A copy."

Walking back through the twisting maze of alleyways, heading for the Via Garibaldi, he asked who was with the children now. Had her in-laws resented her going off to meet him?

"My mother-in-law thinks it is improper for a woman to go anywhere without her husband. If the woman doesn't have a husband, she ought to stay at home. Especially a widow. Allowances can be made for old family friends."

"Like Signor Guidi." He smiled at her astonishment. "I asked Carlo who Signor Guidi was. He said, 'a kind old man who is my mother's lawyer. We dined with him the other night.'" He imitated Carlo's solemn, manly intonations so perfectly she laughed. "Quite diplomatic, that Carlo. He protects you like a royal guard."

She led him into the Via Garibaldi without preparing him for what he would see and had the pleasure of witnessing his awe. He stood speechless on the avenue of palaces, struck dumb by the perfection of the white marble buildings—a man who had stepped from one century to another without warning. "A hidden city," he said at last. She bypassed the *palazzo* where she and Maurizio had stood before the bleeding Christ and took him instead to the Palazzo Bianco.

"I never much liked Saint Sebastian," he said, standing under the Lippi painting. "He always seems to be enjoying his martyrdom too much."

"That is the nature of saints," she told him.

"Your mother-in-law would like this painting."

"She prefers female saints," said Rafaella. "Especially

ones who pray to God to make them ugly so that they cannot tempt men."

He laughed out loud, startling the guard, who laughed along with him to be polite. He was a small man, dressed in a splendid uniform, and his duties were few.

Stephen told her he had completed his research for the film on St. Matthew's. It was the first time the hospital had been mentioned, and she felt suddenly shy. The film would start shooting in November, he said. He was living in California now. Before he had left Houston though, Lassiter had invited him to dine at his private club. They had talked, not of the film or the hospital, but about deep-sea fishing.

By the time they reached the Via Balbi, it was late in the afternoon. She would be expected back. "We will go into the Balbi Durazzo," she told him, "and then I must go home."

They stepped together into the seventeenth century once more. The pastel frescoes, the Vandykes, the tapestries which seemed to have collected the light of three hundred years within their glowing threads, enclosed them.

"When do the children usually have their evening meal?"

"About eight. But I must go back very soon."

"When you do, tell Signora Gemma that Signor *Morizzi* is taking the children out for dinner. Of course, you must come too. Otherwise I might get lost and take them to a place with topless waitresses by mistake."

"I don't think—"

"Your sister-in-law can handle them. She seems to be a resourceful woman."

They rounded a corner and found themselves in the Hall of Mirrors. Dozens of Rafaellas lifted their hands helplessly. Dozens of Stephen Morrissys took the hands and held them firmly.

"Please," he said.

"How can you even contemplate such a thing? We hardly know this man. How can we trust the children with a stranger?"

"He is not a stranger to me," said Rafaella. She had resolved to keep patient and calm, but the sight of Gemma working her way into a rage made her temples throb. "I am their mother, *Nonna*, and I will be with them too."

"And what about *that?*" Gemma whirled from the counter where she was slicing eggplant and pointed her knife at Rafaella. "It doesn't look right, you going off with that man in his big car. What will people say?"

Anna-Laura, who leaned against the door, an ironic observer, had said nothing. She smiled at the predictability of her mother's words. Her eyes telegraphed a sympathetic message, but still she kept silent. *This is your fight, carina,* she seemed to be saying.

"How do we know what kind of movies he makes? He tells you *documentario*, and you believe him." Gemma laughed softly—a significant, mirthless laugh.

"He is making a movie about the hospital in Houston. That's why he was there, *Nonna.*"

"The way he looks—I don't trust him. So big and tanned, and all that hair, *biondo*, he looks like a man who doesn't work for his living."

"He can't help the way he looks, after all."

Anna-Laura had decided to join the fray. She took a seat at the kitchen table. "Be fair, Mama," she said. "You are discriminating against Signor Morrissy because he is good-looking."

"Not true. He is not my style of man. He came to this house without a tie. He lacks manners."

"Mama—do you remember when you met my dentist in the street? Dr. Castelli?" She shot a wickedly gleeful look at Rafaella. "If this Morrissy looked like Castelli, you wouldn't have any qualms about him at all."

"That is bad logic, Anna-Laura. The *dottore* is not proposing to take Rafaella to dinner." She wheeled about, assailed by a new thought. "Why isn't this Morizzi married? If he is so successful and respectable, why doesn't he have a wife and family?"

Anna-Laura spread her hands and looked at her sister-in-law. "The ball is in your court," she said in English. Rafaella projected her mind's eye to a great altitude. Three women were standing in a kitchen, arguing. The woman to whom the kitchen belonged was being cross-examined by another woman, who had been the mother of her husband, now dead. The subject of the interrogation was fully adult. She had borne two children and lived through open heart surgery. She knew the situation was ridiculous, yet she felt powerless to deny the wrath of her mother-in-law. She felt the woman might be able to look into her eyes and read the truth: that she had allowed another man to go where only Aldo had been.

"Probably," said Anna-Laura, "he is divorced, Mama."

"I believe he is," said Rafaella.

Gemma closed her eyes and released a long, hissing sigh, as if the realization of her worst fears released her. "So," she said. "You wish to take the children and go out on the town with a divorced playboy. America has obviously changed you, Rafaella."

Michele Leone thrust his head in, turtlelike, at the door. He had been reading in the living room; as usual, they had forgotten about him. He glared at his wife, but when he spoke his tone was mild.

"*Basta*," he said. "Rafaella is thirty-four years of age. She will do as she likes."

Silence descended on the kitchen, and Michele withdrew. Gemma's bosom heaved with indignation, but she obeyed. Anna-Laura's fine, dark eyes held an expression new for them. Behind the look of amusement and sympathy Rafaella always saw there lurked a wistfulness. Beneath it lay envy.

She left the kitchen and went to get ready. Her father-in-law glanced up from the magazine on his lap. "*Grazie*," she whispered. He winked at her, a gesture so rapid and slight it might have been a facial tic.

From the children's room came a thick silence. They had been listening, of course, to every word.

The interior of the Mercedes smelled expensive, like a fine new leather glove. Carlo loved riding in it and hoped when he was a man he would have friends who would lend him such a car. It did not occur to him to want a Mercedes himself. What impressed him about his mother's American friend was Signor Morrissy's air of being at home wherever he went. Think of dropping in on Italy and having a friend in Milano who would lend you a Mercedes, just like that!

They were turning off at Ruta, where you could see all of the Portofino peninsula, as if from an airplane, and taking the road to Santa Margherita Ligure. They had passed Camogli, where Signor Guidi had taken them for lunch last month, long ago. His mother was speaking to her friend in English. Stefania, beside him, leaned forward to listen. How like her!

Last night, after dinner, Stefania had embarrassed Carlo so many times he had lost count.

"Are there many movie stars in the *documentarios?*" she would say, or, "Is it true that mini-skirts are coming back?" Always he answered these questions seriously, and with care. Carlo asked him about the places he had been and what he had seen there, and Signor Morrissy answered these questions with an equal precision, as if they were the same. He was being polite. *Nonna* was assuredly wrong in what she had said in the kitchen earlier—Signor Morrissy had very good manners.

"Is anyone hungry?" The question came from the front seat, lazy and good-natured. Morrissy had simply proposed that they drive along the Riviera di Levante with no destination in mind. When they felt hungry they would stop. This proposal was so novel—so American—that Carlo was enchanted.

"I am about to starve!" cried Stefania.

"Carlo?"

"Whenever."

"*Bene,*" said Signor Morrissy in his strange accent. "We will stop at Santa Margherita Ligure."

The Mercedes continued its downward plunge on the steep descent toward the sea. Stefania was talking, like a tour guide, about the orange trees they would see at their destination, the *margherita* bushes, like snowballs when they bloomed, when the goat appeared.

They rounded a hairpin curve, and there the goat was, an elderly goat, doddering along before them on the road, his tail matted and flea ridden. Signor Morrissy slammed the brakes, and the Mercedes halted so suddenly that they were all thrown backward, against the upholstery.

"Oh!" his mother cried in a stricken voice. "Oh, Stephen!"

The goat bleated once and scrambled off to safety. Carlo saw the brown hand on the steering wheel fly off to protect his mother from harm. When the danger was past, the hand briefly took hers and patted, reassuring. "*Va bene*," he murmured. "It's okay."

Stefania, recovered, draped herself over the front seat. Her eyes were wide with revelation. "*Stee-ven?*" she breathed. "Is that your name, your *nome di battesimo?*"

"That's it," he said. "Stefano."

"We share the same name, signore. We have the same name."

"In honor of that coincidence," said Signor Morrissy, "I will make sure we have a very good lunch."

All the way to Santa Margherita they bantered about sharing the same name, but Carlo watched Stefano's eyes in the rearview mirror. They were nearly always on the road, steep and treacherous, but whenever conditions permitted, they rested on his mother.

She sat erect and a little tense after the episode of the goat, but on her lips was the ghost of an enigmatic smile.

"If his name isn't Morizzi, what is it?"

Gemma was washing her hair at Anna-Laura's flat. She bent over the sink, the upper part of her body encased in a bath towel which was tucked into her brassiere.

Anna-Laura filled a pot with warm water and poured it over her mother's head. "It is Morrissy, Mama." She pronounced it correctly. "That's how it's said."

"Yes, an American name." Gemma's voice emerged gurglingly, muffled by the water.

Anna-Laura looked at the place where the towel creased her mother's back. The material bit deeply into the flesh, which had become friable with age. Gemma's arms trembled as she braced herself against the sink. Anna-Laura could remember when the arms were firm, the flesh smooth and resilient.

"But what was it before? Americans always come from someplace else, unless they are red Indians. What sort of name is Morrissy?"

"Probably Irish, Mama."

"*Santa Maria,*" groaned Gemma.

Chapter 10

The two days came and went, and Stephen did not go home to America. The weather turned sultry by Genovese standards, and children sat up with their parents half the night in cafés.

"I thought you had to go back to America," Rafaella said to him.

"They will have to do without me for a few more days."

At his request, she had taken him to her studio on the Via Acquatania. He sat with her in the back room, watching while she sculpted in wax. Her slender fingers were quick, assured; they had, in abundance, the confidence the rest of her lacked.

Even now they weren't alone. Her assistant was in the shop, separated from them only by a curtain, a few feet away. Stephen felt himself drawn into a situation nearly medieval in its ramifications. There sat his signora, modern in her tan trousers and blue coverall worn for work, a twentieth-century woman whose life was lived by feudal standards.

Stephen was required to juggle half a dozen conflicting elements merely to see her. The children, for example. He liked them and knew they liked him, but their grandparents had come all the way from Naples to see them—it would be improper of him to monopolize the little time they had together. The children would not mind, but toward the senior Leones he would be committing a cruelty. Carlo and Stefania filled him with admiration. At their young ages, they had learned, in their separate ways, to be diplomats. He might have been repelled if this diplomacy had been learned to pave the way for their own ends—more treats, more gifts, more attention—but it seemed to him that they had perfected these skills in innocence. They wished to protect their mother and keep the small unit of their family alive and well. Their guile was so guileless it filled him with a pity that was nearly heartbreaking.

When Carlo regarded him with his fierce, possessive eyes —the eyes of his mama—Stephen tried to reassure. When Stefania practiced her version of womanly seduction upon him, he was grave and appreciative. He understood the motives from which their behavior sprang, and was surprised at the vast reserves of patience untapped within him. They were allies, really.

But were they? The culture was so different, so foreign, he wondered if he had already overstepped some boundary invisible to him. He had passed time in far more exotic places, where men and women went naked and mutilated themselves and each other in the name of beauty and of sexual purity, where adultery was courtesy and thieving punished by death, but he had never felt such an outsider before— because he had never wanted anything from them. Feeling alien, he realized, had to do with expectations. The man who wanted nothing was forever safe. The man with expectations was suspect.

Back to square one. If the mother-in-law did not so clearly regard him as a fiend from hell, he might have had a shot at entertaining them all, but Signora Gemma would have nothing to do with him. Rafaella seemed to feel her duty toward her mother-in-law as some sort of sacred trust —she knew the woman was comical but defied her with dread.

Then there was the Signor Guidi the children mentioned so frequently. It was obvious, from Stefania's meaningful looks, that Signor Guidi had some proprietary interest in Rafaella. Perhaps, in this corner of Italy, a dead man's lawyer assumed control of the widow. Nothing would surprise him anymore.

Anna-Laura was his ally, but her powers were limited. She was generous and good, but being thoroughly modern herself, she could not quite penetrate the medieval labyrinths of Rafaella's mind.

Stephen sat on, quietly observing. The white, bare walls of the studio were as she had described them to him. It seemed as austere as the cell of a nun. His signora shuttled back and forth between this cell and the larger cell of her flat, imprisoned by responsibility and her quaint sense of honor.

"What are you thinking, at this precise moment?" she said suddenly. Her lips were curved in a playful smile; a good sign—she was teasing him.

"I was wondering—how old is Signor Guidi?"

The smile faltered, and she lowered her head over her work again. "He is fifty-two," she said presently.

"Ha! The kindly old solicitor is not so ancient as Carlo made him sound."

"Carlo is only eleven," she said. "Maurizio may seem quite elderly to him."

Maurizio. Dashing name. He wanted to ask more questions but reminded himself that he was treading perilous ground here. He had to observe protocol, behave with decorum. The Italians called it *garbo*. A man who behaved with *garbo* was a courteous gentleman.

"Why are you laughing?" To his surprise, she was caught up in a spasm of mirth. Her eyes were squeezed shut, her shoulders shook with it. She looked like a little girl— Stefania, giggling. When she could speak she told him how Gemma, before his arrival, had feared the stairs would prove too much for him. She switched into her mother-in-law's Neapolitan dialect, imitating her with great skill.

"You do her very well," he said.

"I have had years to learn," said Rafaella. She shook herself guiltily. "Poor woman," she said. "It is wicked of me to laugh at her."

Nina thrust her head between the curtains. "Signora— telephone! From Milano."

Rafaella excused herself and Nina came into the studio to flirt with Stephen. Her provocative smile, her twitching little buttocks in their tight denim, were harmless proofs of her powerful femininity. She meant nothing by it. She sat on the edge of the worktable, crossing her legs.

"So, signore—how much longer will we have the pleasure of your company?" She lit a cigarette and exhaled noisily, throwing her hair back.

Stephen said he wasn't sure, not much longer he was afraid, and smiled at her pretty tricks. She reminded him a bit of Jackie Talbot. Automatically, he fell into the easy postures of meaningless flirtation. It wasn't until she laid her bare arm next to his hand in order to compare their suntans that he thought: *I am not behaving with garbo.*

He withdrew from the small flirtation, no doubt bewildering her. The woman he wanted came back then, and he was flooded with longing. She resumed her work and Nina went back to tend the shop. He watched the nimble fingers again, the small, well-turned wrists. Beneath the blue coverall, he knew, she wore a shirt buttoned to the neck to conceal her scar. This fastidious concealment touched and saddened him. With the longing came a touch of the hurt and resentment he had felt when she'd pulled her disappearing act. She'd left him without a word, a note. If he had not followed her, come literally to her doorstep, he would never have seen her again. She was quite capable of living out her life without ever sending him a word, a sign. Her passivity angered him. *Garbo* was abandoned.

"Why did you go away like that?" he asked. "Why? Did you think it wouldn't matter to me?"

Her fingers tensed, her whole body stiffened. She raised her head to look at him but seemed unable, or unwilling, to meet his eyes.

"Would you ever have written to me? Talk, signora. Explain something to me. Does it matter to you whether I stay or go? Is it of any importance?"

She raised her hands, fingers touching, and held them together before her. Her fingertips were just beneath her chin; she looked as if she were praying.

"Please," she said. "Don't ask me such things. Not now."

"When?"

The telephone rang in the other room. They could hear Nina's voice, important in answering, assume a casual tone. The caller was someone known to her.

"Signora," she called. "Your sister-in-law!"

Sighing, obedient, Rafaella marched through the curtains to answer yet another summons from her demanding family.

"I thought he was going away," wheezed Gemma. She had been to a doctor, hastily procured by her daughter, who assured her that it was not asthma she suffered from. It was an allergy of some sort. He prescribed tablets.

"He changed his mind," said Anna-Laura.

"Do you know what I think?" Gemma hooked a finger, summoned her closer. "I think America has turned Rafaella's head. She is not herself, Anna. It is all that man's fault—he has put strange thoughts into her head."

"*Ridicolo*, Mama." Anna-Laura's voice was sharp. She was tired of playing middleman, weary of her mother's excesses, and envious of Rafaella. Her own lover, Paolo, was an inferior and spiritless man. She waged a daily battle—lately, not daily, but whenever time could be snatched—to wring some passion from him. Rafaella, who had gone off to have her heart cut open, had somehow attracted the attention of a prince, while *she* made do with a frog. It was unfair. Anna-Laura would know what use to make of Signor Morrissy, but Rafaella didn't have a clue.

"You are being ridiculous!" Anna-Laura felt shame at such thoughts about her sister-in-law, whom she honestly loved, and the shame made her anger grow.

"Who is ridiculous?" Gemma shouted. "Not me, little girl. *Not me!* You, who fly off to the Indian Ocean in search of adventure—you are ridiculous! Rafaella, who had the love of my son, the finest man to ever walk the earth—Rafaella, who lets her head be turned by a big *biondo* who will take advantage and then desert her—*she* is ridiculous!"

"How can you talk that way? Why do you hate him, *Nonno?*" Stefania stood in the doorway, eyes bright with anger. "I think he is the nicest man I ever met. Don't talk about Mama that way, and don't talk about him that way, either!"

Overcome by her outburst, fists clenched and knees trembling, Stefania waited for God to strike her dead for such impudence. When He did not, she offered a final salvo:

"He and I—we share the same *name*!" She broke into a storm of weeping and ran from the room. They heard her feet go thudding up the hallway.

The tears of Stefania were bright and hard as diamonds. Gemma's tears, when they came, seeped from between her eyelids like pond water, old and from a static source. "She is so like Aldo," Gemma whispered. "The image."

Anna-Laura felt the familiar pity springing in her breast. Her mother could always do this to her; it was the old trick, but not a trick. Her mother was grieving. It was real.

Gemma stirred on the couch; she shook her head. "Help me, love," she said. "I must go to her. *Dio mi perdoni!* Anna—forgive me! I love you, Anna."

Anna-Laura helped her mother to her feet. Together, they walked toward the sounds of weeping.

Triumphantly, Stephen spirited her away for an hour. He telephoned her at the flat, expecting to hear the usual pandemonium in the background. She answered on the first ring, her *prego* breathless; behind her voice was silence. Gemma, she explained, had been stricken since yesterday with allergies. She was lying down at Anna-Laura's; the tablets the doctor had given her made her sleepy. The children had gone with their *nonno* to the cinema. She imparted this information neutrally, her voice even and calm.

When he asked her to meet him at the cafe in the Old Town, she agreed immediately.

He sat waiting for her, an undrunk Cinzano at his elbow. For the first time in weeks, he wanted a cigarette. From his vantage point—an outdoor table, one of half a dozen strung out along the cobblestones—he would see her come toward him. She would have to appear at the head of the yellow stone stairs and descend to reach him.

He framed the scene cinematically to capture the antiquity of the shallow steps, the steep pitch of the tall, narrow buildings enclosing this part of the maze. A fat calico cat slunk from a doorway opposite and shot up the alley. All cats were sleek, here. They lived off the fishheads from the open-air markets and were indulged by the merchants.

A trio of schoolgirls appeared at the head of the stairs, behind them a portly man who fanned himself with a Panama hat. The girls stopped abruptly, pointing to something in the distance, perhaps looking out to sea, and the man was forced to wait. He spoke to them sharply and the girls giggled and ran on. Stephen ordered another Cinzano from the waiter, and set it at her place.

Now a woman in a pale gray dress materialized above him. Her dark hair hung free, past her shoulders. At her throat, a white silk scarf, on her feet, high-heeled shoes more frivolous than the rest of her costume. A man at a nearby table discreetly watched her legs as she descended.

"Stephen," she said, sitting opposite him, "I hope you have not waited long?"

"About forty-four years," he said.

"*Scusi?*"

"I used to be Mr. Detached. Also Mr. Objective. You have changed me. You have a responsibility toward me, signora."

She laughed in a puzzled way. "Have you had too much to drink, Stephen?"

He stood up, held out his hand. "Come with me," he said. "I have something to tell you."

They climbed the stairs together, her hand in his. She did not ask their destination. Only once, before they came to the Colombia-Excelsior, did she speak. "We didn't touch the Cinzano," she said. "It was wasteful."

"Yes," he agreed, "I know. You are thrifty and virtuous, and you are right, but this is more important."

She sat beside him in the taxi, looking straight ahead, her hand still in his. There was no way, he thought, she could not have known where they were going. This was her city. Near the Stazione Principal she seemed about to speak, but did not. They passed through the doors of his hotel in silence and walked to the elevators. He wondered if she was remembering the Hibernian.

The elevator was silent and efficient. He had chosen the Colombia-Excelsior because one of the filmmakers in Geneva had told him it was comfortable. He had not come to Genoa to be a tourist and didn't mind that it was a modern hotel. Now he was pleased. In a colorful *albergo*, a small *pensione*, many curious eyes would be on them. The chambermaid would call a sly greeting, embarrassing his signora. Here they were anonymous.

Outside the door to his room he glanced sideways at her. She looked as if she were going to her doom. He unlocked the door and she followed him in. The chambermaid had tidied everything and drawn the curtains against the assaulting sun. There was a marine light in the room, dappled and green. Rafaella stood near the door, pretending to look about the room with interest.

He removed his jacket, placing his key and a handful of loose change on the glass-topped bureau.

"The room is nice," she said. "Probably far too expensive."

"The view makes it all worthwhile," he said. "Come and see."

She crossed to the window and stood beside him. He drew the curtain aside, revealing a view of no particular interest. Sloping rooftops, the shapes of loading cranes at the port. He let the curtain fall and took her hand, placing it on his breast so she could feel his heart, the accelerated beating. He was so sensitive to her touch that he could feel her fingers trembling.

Slowly, like a cat prowling for the perfect resting place, she drew close to him, replacing her hand with her cheek, laying her head on his breast. She kissed his shirt. He felt her hair, still warm from the sun, beneath his hands as she turned her head against him. She seemed to be denying something, shaking her head no, but he knew it was only her feverish protest against happiness; the usual.

She came to lie with him on the bed. Half-turned toward him, she whispered a word in Italian he did not understand. He remembered her as she had been in his room in Houston. She was afraid, now, as she ought to have been then. He stroked her hair, her cheeks, and watched her sigh beneath his hand.

"This is all I need," he told her. "I want much more, but this is what I need now. Only to be close to you. Alone."

His hands went where they would, almost idly. He

touched the fine small bones of her knees beneath the soft gray of her dress, and traced the line of the legs he and the other man had watched descending the stone stairs. Her heart beat into the cup of his hand, and she was no longer afraid.

She lay in his arms quietly now, allowing their lips to meet. She held him to her and there was a surprising strength in her arms.

"I ran away because I could not bear to say good-bye to you," she said. "I thought it wouldn't matter so much to you."

"You were wrong."

She told him of the dream she'd had. "I was a nun with painted toenails," she said. "I was waiting for your sail to show, far out at sea."

Only once did her body stiffen and move from him. He touched the scarf at her throat, having a sudden need to kiss the place where her pulse was, in the hollow, and she started in alarm.

He loosened the silken material and drew it away. A few inches above the vee of her collar was the evidence of what had happened to her, and what she dreaded for him to see. He kissed the warm neck, gentled her. It was more than a month since she had left the hospital. It was not too soon for lovemaking, not by medical standards, but it was too soon for her.

Unsatisfied desire, the insistent need of his body—not likely to be given what it wanted for some time—produced a poignant pain not felt since adolescence. Nevertheless, he was perfectly happy as he lay with his signora in his arms.

"Stefano," she murmured, "I am sorry I am such a difficulty."

He smiled. He had won the first round of the battle and wanted her to be tranquil and rested before he introduced round two.

Chapter 11

"California! How can you go there?"

Anna-Laura's astonishment was so great she allowed the water to spill over the top of the flower vase and slosh to the floor. Cursing, she slapped the tap shut and reached for a towel. "How can you, Rafaella?"

"By going to the airport with Carlo and Stefania, boarding a plane for Milano, changing there—the same way I went to Houston, *carina*."

"Very funny." Anna-Laura mopped at the puddle of water distractedly, then went back to arranging the roses in the vase. They were Morrissy's gift to her—a thank-you. "It is not so simple, Rafaella, is it? Where will you find the money? A holiday in California would cost the earth. The airfare alone is prohibitive." Unconsciously, she was assuming a schoolmistress's voice. Rafaella had never heard it before.

"The roses were his good-bye gift to you," she said softly. "I, too, have a gift." She produced the tickets from her bag and held them up. She had a week to make up her mind; after that, the tickets could not be canceled.

Anna-Laura caught her lower lip in her teeth and nodded.

"*Bene*," she said in a tight voice. "I would go like a shot myself, Rafaella, but I am not you."

"You disapprove?"

"Who am I to disapprove? The children would love it."

That was what Stephen had said. "*Promessa*, they'll love it." He had described the sugary sand, the great arc where the sky and sea merged; he had painted pictures for her of

Carlo and Stefania, ecstatic on American roller skates, gliding along beneath the palm trees.

"You surprise me," said Anna-Laura. "I have always thought you were too innocent. Chaste and pure, like a nun. You go off to have surgery and return with a rich lover who follows you about—I can't make sense of it."

The words were meant to hurt, and Rafaella felt their sting. This was the one quarter where she had not expected to encounter resistance. "He is not my lover," she said.

"*Gesù Cristo*—he will be if you go to California! Did you think he would pay all that money for the pleasure of your sweet company alone?"

She saw it was useless to explain. How could she make Anna-Laura understand what she herself did not? He was so clever, her Stefano—anticipating her objections at every turn. He was not particularly rich, he told her, although he was well paid. It was just that he had no one to spend money on but himself. Everything in his life was borrowed, temporary, like the Mercedes and the beach house in a place called Malibu where they would stay. Would she deprive him—to say nothing of the children—because of stubborn pride over money?

That was where he was especially clever. He spoke of the California idyll in terms of the children's pleasure and his own, never hers. Thus she was made to feel she would be selfish if she refused him, and allowed to hold the prospect of her own pleasure secretly. He had been gone for two days now, and she longed for him. It would never again be possible for her to pretend he did not exist.

"Anna," she said tenderly. "I loved Aldo with all my heart. If he had lived I would have wanted no one else for the rest of my life. He has been dead for more than three years, Anna."

Anna-Laura bowed her head, standing over the vase of roses.

"I know," she said.

"I am not betraying anyone."

"I just don't want you to be hurt, *cara*. All men are not Aldo, Rafaella. This one may think you are more sophisticated than you are—there could be a misunderstanding."

Rafaella laughed to herself at the thought of Stephen believing her sophisticated. Of all men in the world, he had the least cause to think it. Her own fears were very different than Anna-Laura's, and they were many.

"If I don't go, then I will never know," she said.

Anna-Laura straightened, then hurtled across the room. She caught Rafaella in a bear hug, burying her face against her shoulder.

"I'm jealous," she wailed. "I'm *jealous!* That's what ails me, *bella*."

They swayed together in the kitchen, one sniffling, the other comforting, until the sound of Gemma's key was heard turning in the outer lock. They sprang apart, hastily smoothing their hair. Anna-Laura scrubbed her eyes with her knuckles and returned to the flowers.

Gemma came into the kitchen with a string bag full of groceries. She stopped at sight of the extravagant roses beneath her daughter's hands. "For you, Anna?" she asked incredulously. "One of the students?"

"From Signor Morrissy, Mama. He must have ordered them before he left."

"*Santa Maria*," said Gemma. "Why does he send *you* flowers? He is certainly fickle."

Rafaella began to unpack the groceries. This was to be Gemma and Michele's last night in Genoa, and a mammoth dinner would be cooked. Michele had taken the children down to the waterfront to buy fish for *buridda di pesci*. She wondered how she could justify ruining their last night with the news that their daughter-in-law had become, or was about to become, a fallen woman.

Anna-Laura took the vase to the living room, and her mother followed. Gemma spoke in a low voice, but it was perfectly audible to Rafaella.

"What is the matter with *her?*" she asked. "She is so quiet."

"She's fine, Mama."

"I know what it is," said Gemma dourly. "She is missing that Irishman. Thank God he went away."

Rafaella slipped a hand into her bag and felt the tickets lying there on the bottom. A week to decide.

Gemma sneezed. "Anna—take the roses somewhere else, darling. I think they are aggravating my allergy."

"I am glad *Nonna*'s gone," said Stefania. "Sometimes I don't love her at all."

"She means well," said Carlo. It was something he had often heard his mother say. "It could be her Time of Life."

"What's that?"

"Old age makes women cross. When they get old and quarrelsome it's called their Time of Life."

"What about men, Carlo?"

"Men don't have one. That's part of what makes us superior."

Stefania kicked him lightly in the shin; he pulled her hair half-heartedly. It was not a real quarrel.

Carlo was bored and dispirited. His friend Marcello had gone off on holiday to Lago Maggiore, and in a small and private way he missed his grandfather's silent affection. Stefania seemed more devastated at Signor Morrissy's departure than that of her grandparents. Carlo was both sorry to see him go and relieved. His mother's eyes were too happy when she was around the American man. Carlo liked her to be happy, but he wasn't sure it was good for her. Not like that.

Just as he was thinking of her, she entered the room. Stefania began to list her grievances. Carlo had said men were superior, had pulled her hair, but Mama ignored her. Her eyes had the very glint he distrusted. Without any warning, she said something amazing.

"How would you like to go to California for two weeks?"

"California? In *America?*" Stefania's jaw hung open.

"Signor Morrissy has invited us. He has a house there, on the beach."

Stefania let out an ear-piercing scream of happiness. Foolishly, she danced around the room, hugging herself.

"You said we could not afford a holiday this year," said Carlo. His mother blushed.

"Signor Morrissy has provided us with airplane tickets."

"Then we have to go," cried Stefania.

"By no means. They can be canceled before a certain date. Carlo? Wouldn't you like to see California? Swim in the Pacifico?"

How could she ask! It was shameless of her, playing him like that. "Do *you* want to go?" he asked. She nodded yes.

"Then so do I," said Carlo.

Her eyes were searching his face very carefully; she was disturbed by his reticence. Sometimes she didn't seem to realize how grown-up he was. He had been head of this family for three years now, ever since he was nine, and he thought he was doing pretty well. She ought to realize.

When she called Stephen in California his voice sounded clipped, metallic. "Morrissy here. Leave your name and number and I'll get back to you when I can. Thanks. Wait for the beep."

By the time she understood it was some sort of a machine, the ugly signaling tone had come. The experience so flustered her she gave all her information—the time of their arrival, the number of the flight—in rapid Italian. Then she hung up.

When he called back a few hours later, he was laughing. He apologized for the machine. He told her he would be at the airport and said she had made him very happy. Behind his voice she heard a rhythmic murmuring.

"Is that the sea I can hear?" she asked.

"Yes, darling."

The foreign word touched her with delight, as if he had put his hand on her back or caressed her hair.

"Could you understand everything I said about the flight?"

He repeated it back to her correctly.

"I was afraid I waited too long after the bleat," she said.

Dr. Rinaldi assured her she was well enough to travel and expressed good-natured envy over her trip to California. She asked him if there was anything—anything at all—she was not well enough to do. She could not bring herself to mention the term. She, a widow.

"*Va bene,* signora," said Dr. Rinaldi. "Everything is allowed." He gave her a peppermint candy as she left and patted her shoulder.

She went home and made the dreaded call to Naples. She explained her intentions to Gemma, who listened in ominous silence. No sobs or shrieks came flowing northward, only heavy, stertorous breathing. When Rafaella had finished, repeating that it was only for two weeks, assuring her mother-in-law that it would be good for the children, apologizing for the distress she was causing, there was a silence so palpable it seemed electric. When Gemma broke it, her voice was low and harsh.

"There are words for women like you," she said, "but I won't lower myself. You are stealing my grandchildren." Then she slammed the receiver down.

Hands shaking, Rafaella carried Butch and Sundance down to Signora Lenti and asked her to feed them in Stefania's absence.

The day before she left, she bought two postcards showing scenes of Genoa. On one she wrote to Jacqueline Talbot, thanking her for her letter and for everything she had done. She told Jackie she was well and happy and said she would write again at a later date.

The second postcard was harder to write. She wasn't at all sure the recipient would remember her—why should he?—but she felt the need to send her thanks. Dr. Lassiter's card showed the statue of Cristoforo Colombo.

It seemed fitting.

CALIFORNIA

Chapter 1

The boards of what he called the "deck" and she called the *loggia* were warm beneath her bare feet. She held a coffee cup in her hands, reluctant to set it on the railing because it, too, was warm, and she drew comfort from it. Even though it contained a liquid both murky and weak from the Mr. Coffee machine in the kitchen, it was something familiar and homely. A cup.

Everything else was strange. People here did not wear clothing. They lived in bathing suits, going half naked everywhere. The man from a neighboring house, who was doing some sort of exercise on the sand, she had seen in the little market on the Pacific Highway. He'd been wearing his swimming trunks and a T-shirt, his female companion a pair of shorts and her bikini top.

The man's dog, a black and white spaniel, joined him, bounding from the house, and together they walked to the edge of the sea and began to run. Ocean and sky were a clear, hard blue laced through with silver; it hurt her eyes to look at them.

From inside the beach house she heard Stephen's voice, but it was the machine. He had taken the children with him on some errand. They had left before she was awake. Curious, she went into the house to hear who the caller might be. A woman's voice, rapid and intimate, urged him not to forget to come to her party. Her name was Betsy. Before she hung up she made a kissing noise.

Rafaella walked through to the kitchen and unplugged the Mr. Coffee machine. The owner of the beach house—

another filmmaker—liked machines. There were utensils in the kitchen whose purpose she could not even imagine, and a horrifying device for chewing up leftover food which terrified her.

"Don't put your hands anywhere near it!" she'd told Carlo and Stefania. "Promise, promise!"

"Of course not, Mama." Offended looks—did she think they were lunatics?

Ever since she'd arrived she'd been assailed by fears for them. The maniac speed of the cars on the freeway, the unsafe appearance of the car in which Stephen had met them ("Stupendous, Mama—it's an old Mustang convertible!"), the crashing surf, nearly at their door—all threatened to harm them. Even their sleeping arrangements alarmed her. Carlo and Stefania shared a room on the lower level, sleeping on two lofty platforms reached by a ladder. The room belonged to the filmmaker's children, who visited him when their mother permitted, and Carlo and Stefania loved it. "What if you should roll over and fall in your sleep?" she had asked, but no one had heard.

"Where will my mother sleep?" Carlo wanted to know.

"In the main bedroom," Stephen told him. Before Carlo could ask, he said there was a couch which turned into a bed for him in the living room. Carlo nodded, satisfied.

She slept in an enormous bed in a room whose windows faced the sea. She heard the surf in her dreams, it seemed—that, and the little click of the digital clock as it measured off the minutes of the night. She had her own bathroom, with a glassed-in shower, a bewildering number of nozzles and taps, and tiles of blue and green.

She felt like a guest in a luxurious foreign hotel, where the proprietor assumed responsibility for her children. She tried not to voice her fears for the children, not wanting to seem ungrateful, anxious, strange.

Alone, midmorning sun dazzling into every corner of the house and following her everywhere, she wandered through the rooms. Stefania's Dr. Scholl's sandals lay in the hallway, where anyone could trip over them. She picked them up and returned them to the children's room. In her own bedroom she opened the closet door and looked at Stephen's clothes hanging there. She touched the shirt he had worn on his last day in Genoa, a dark suit she had never seen him wear.

"Morrissy here". . . Once more she heard his voice in the empty house, above her. This time the caller was a man named Ivan Bell. He left a number in New York.

Back in the living room, she studied once more the framed photographs hanging everywhere on the walls. The filmmaker decorated his home with scenes from his own life. He was a man of about Stephen's age, thin and dark; he looked like a scholar. In one photo he stood on the bridge of a sailing ship, in another on snowshoes surrounded by sled dogs. His life, like Stephen's, was built on activity, movement, and adventure; there were no pictures of him sitting quietly with his children or standing in a suburban garden.

She moved to examine the photo she'd already studied a dozen times. In it the filmmaker and two other men stood in a clearing somewhere in a jungle. All of them carried machetes in their belts. To the filmmaker's left stood an Indian, to his right, Stephen.

It was a much younger Stephen who looked out at her from his jungle clearing. His hands were hooked in his belt; he wore high boots and the kind of jacket made popular by Fidel Castro, and he was smiling. She thought of stifling heat, tormenting insects, poisonous snakes, malaria, the jungle—held at bay with the machetes—creeping back even as he stood there. Danger everywhere, and in its midst Stefano, smiling, happy. Loving danger.

"Don't you see what dreadful things could happen to you?" she asked the photograph. "Danger is everywhere—you don't have to go looking for it. It finds even the most cautious people sometimes, but you—you *look* for it."

As if by magic, she heard his voice on the steps to the *loggia*. They were back.

"Look!" cried Stefania, bursting into the beach house. "Aren't they beautiful?"

She held a pair of white roller skates up for Rafaella's inspection. The wheels were acid green. Behind her, Carlo flourished black boots with orange wheels. "Stefano is going to take us to Santa Monica Beach to try them out," he said. It was the first time he had called Stephen by his name.

Rafaella looked at the skates. For a moment she envisioned broken ankles and gashed knees, but the moment passed and she saw instead a woman whose fears were unnecessary. There was no need to fear the worst at every turn—she had been doing it reflexively, by habit. *Basta.* She laughed at herself, out loud, puzzling Carlo and Stefania and making Stephen smile.

"They look quite marvelous," she said.

The house was a mansion. There was no other word for it. She had never been in a house so grand, or seen a private swimming pool so large. Stephen said they were in Bel Air.

The woman called Betsy kissed Stephen with affection and referred to him as "angel." Her kiss was more noise than action; it sounded as it had done on the phone. She took Rafaella's hands and held them, surveying her in a way that would have seemed rude except for the admiration in her eyes.

"Rafaella!" she said when they had been introduced. "Your name is as lovely as you are."

Betsy's skin was tanned in such a way that she looked as if she had been dipped in liquid bronze. She had wheat-colored hair, cut short as a boy's, and wore what appeared to be a strapless jump suit. Rafaella thought her very beautiful, but when she asked Stephen if Betsy was an actress he looked surprised.

"She's a photographer," he said. He explained that the mansion belonged to her ex-husband, who was away in Portugal. They were still good friends. He led her through the house to the garden in back, where fifty people stood drinking beneath the jacaranda trees. Everyone ignored the lighted pool.

It was too complicated, she thought. Nobody stayed married here in California, where even photographers were as glamorous as movie stars. It was all impermanent. A red-haired woman in a mauve caftan slit to the thighs waved at

Stephen. She *was* an actress, he said, but Rafaella had never seen any of her pictures.

Apparently Betsy drew her friends from all quarters, for there were artists and writers from the East Coast, actresses and directors from the West, lawyers, agents, teachers, real-estate brokers, comedians, restaurant owners, orchid growers, a Rolls-Royce dealer, and some gentlemen and ladies of leisure. She wondered if they found her odd—a wild flower tossed by accident into a jungle of riotous blossoms.

A man who wore a T-shirt with tuxedo trousers had way-laid Stephen. He wanted to know about the editing of a certain film and listened raptly to Stephen's explanation. Rafaella listened too. Much of what he said was technical and lost on her, but it gave her pleasure to hear the authority in his voice.

Stephen hovered near her in the next hour, protective and somehow anxious. She had noticed that women here did not remain by their mens' sides as they would at home, but mingled freely so it was difficult to know who was attached to whom. She didn't want Stefano to feel encumbered; when he turned to speak to a woman who had hailed him, she wandered down the lawn toward a trestle table covered with pink linen. A high, three-quarter moon sailed up in the sky, gilding the people in the perfumed garden who had strayed beyond the artificial lights. She saw a couple standing in the moonlight, gesticulating angrily near a little marble bench. In that perfect lovers' setting, they were quarreling.

The woman Stephen was talking to was black and very slender. She moved with the grace of an antelope. A dancer? Her long, shapely fingers rested for a moment on his lapel as she laughed at something he had said.

At the table, people were heaping their plates with food. She moved toward them, smiling so anyone could see she was enjoying herself.

"I loved your last film," said an older woman dressed in silver pants. She ladled crabmeat on her plate and smiled at Rafaella. "This is going to be your lucky year."

"Thank you," said Rafaella.

A courteous man was preparing a plate for her. She tried to decline, but he would not understand. He handed her the plate and took her to one of the little tables by the side of the pool. A uniformed servant refilled her champagne glass, and the man sat opposite her.

"Where're you from?" he asked, saluting her with his fork.

"Italy." So far, so good.

"I knew you weren't American. Just to look at you. What are you doing here?"

"I am visiting a friend."

The man gestured expansively. The water from the pool briefly stippled his face. "All this," he said. "Must seem pretty strange to you."

"I think it is like River Oaks, maybe."

"Say," he said. "You've been in Houston?" He shook his head. "Crazy city. Texas is no damn good, honey. You stay here, you'll like it." He chewed, swallowed. "I've been here ten years now. No regrets. None." Absentmindedly, he drank from her glass. She saw that he was tolerably drunk.

"You've got a look, a quality. You're something different here. You'll do fine."

"Thank you," said Rafaella.

The teen-aged girl from the beach house next door was paid an enormous amount for watching television with Carlo and Stefania. Before she scuttled down the steps of the *loggia* she cast a strange look at Rafaella and said, "Do you have baby-sitters in Italy?"

"Yes, love. Also electricity and television and running water."

"Carlo and Stephanie were really good," said the girl. "Well—good night. See you, Steve."

Rafaella went to the children's room and climbed the ladder to Carlo's bed. He slept serenely, as if impressing the baby-sitter with his adulthood had been tiring. Stefania—Stephanie!—lay on her platform, knees drawn up to her chest in fetal position. Her cowboy hat lay at the foot of the bed, along with her new roller skates. Rafaella drew the covers over her and Stefania stirred.

338

"Have a nice day, Mama," she murmured. "When it is tomorrow, have a nice day."

"I will, my love."

"That's what they say in America. At the market, the lady told us to have a nice day." Sleep pulled at her, but she resisted it. She reverted to Italian. "Were there film stars at the party?" she asked.

"I think so," said Rafaella. "Who can tell?"

They walked along the beach close to the water's edge. The imperfect moon had slipped low, but the crests of the choppy nighttime waves were touched with its silver. Rafaella held her shoes in her hands, walking beside him, and they did not touch.

"What was the name of your wife?" she asked.

"Natalie."

Rafaella pictured Natalie. She would look very like Betsy, wouldn't she? She would have been perfect and assured, blonde and smooth and commanding. Yet "Natalie" seemed an exotic name for an American. Perhaps she was the color of dark coffee, like the black girl in Bel Air whose pink tongue had showed so prettily in her mouth when she laughed and touched his arm.

Carefully, in formal Italian, she asked him if he had loved his wife very much. Loved Natalie.

"No," he said. "I thought I did, but it wasn't so."

A great, unworthy sensation of happiness seized her, followed by disapproval. How could a man marry, thinking he loved, only to find it was an illusion? Impermanency; casual actions, meaning nothing. "I wish I could see one of your films," she said.

It seemed nothing could be more simple. Due to yet another miraculous machine, a film by Stephen Morrissy could be screened for her in the privacy of the beach house. It was in the collection of the absent filmmaker. "Whenever you like, Rafaella."

"Now," she said.

He took her shoes, carrying them easily in one hand, the

339

heel-straps hooked over his thumb. She remembered the machete. "Okay, signora," he said.

She followed him back to the house, climbing the stairs behind him, steeling herself to the danger she would see him courting on the flickering screen.

Chapter 2

Stephen announced that he was going to go rock climbing. He was packing a bag. Very calmly, she watched as he packed a pair of roller skates, a machete, and a bottle of vodka.

"What will you eat?" she asked.

"Not necessary," he replied.

She knew he would die and was resigned to it. She was feeling only a vast and empty desolation. She could hear a high wind somewhere approaching. It would blow through her soon. She tried to explain about the wind, but he was too absorbed in his packing to hear her. She picked up a little half-liter bottle of wine and threw it at him to get his attention. It struck him squarely on the temple, and he reeled. The wine was everywhere, dark and sinister. It coated the walls of the beach house and trickled down his face.

"Oh, Rafaella," he said in the saddest imaginable voice, "look what you've done." Then he fell to the floor. She was sure he was dead, but she could not rise and go to him. She had become paralyzed and sat weeping, immobile, while he died.

The light in the room was the pale, oyster-colored light of just before dawn. The first thing she saw when she opened her eyes was her own hand, clenched on the pillow and revealed to her by the clicking digital clock's orange glow. It was very silent in the beach house; even the ceaseless murmur of the sea was muted. The clock said it was four-fifty-two.

She was still full of the unspeakable sadness of the appalling dream and unwilling to admit that she could be, even in her unconscious, a creature of violence. Long ago, her mother had explained that dreams were merely the result of what had happened the previous day. Maria Francini, if she were alive, would say Rafaella threw the bottle at Stephen because she had seen a film before she went to sleep. A film in which dangerous objects were thrown with intent to harm.

Rafaella knew better. She had been angry at Stephen for placing himself at risk. Unable to speak her anger, she had taken the coward's way and slain him in her sleep.

She got out of her bed and walked through to the living room, slipping down the hall as silently as a thief.

Stephen lay on the convertible bed, breathing evenly, in deep sleep. He lay on his side, and the sheet that covered him had slipped down to his waist. He wore a white T-shirt and—from what she could see at the opposite end of the bed—pajama trousers of navy blue. With a pang, she realized that the convertible bed was not really long enough to accommodate him; the leg which was not bent dangled over the edge, its bare foot sadly uncovered.

His face was pillowed on one hand; the other hand was flung upward, as if searching for something. She knelt beside the bed and studied him. There was something unseemly and not fair about such close scrutiny when he was unconscious, but it could not be helped. She felt very daring, like a member of a secret and prohibited army taking illegal photographs. His eyelashes were straight, girlish; his mouth, in sleep, soft and vulnerable, the lips slightly parted. The arm which cradled him showed a powerful muscle against the white cloth of the shirt, but the other arm, thrust up, seemed less formidable. The pressure of his head had cut off the circulation there, she saw, and a vein stood up along the tenderer flesh of the inner arm in protest. She studied his topography avidly, wishing to draw the sheet down and see him altogether, but fearing to wake him.

She had discovered the reason for the crescent-shaped scar on his back, the one she remembered beneath her fingers from a different life. Quite casually, he had mentioned it to her the night before in the middle of the film he had shown her. Glass. It had been caused by a shard of flying glass in Belfast, and the glass was flying because a Molotov cocktail had been hurled at a shop.

"Right after we shot that sequence with the children, a store halfway up the street exploded in front of our eyes. I remember it exactly, because a little piece of glass flew fifty feet and caught me in the back like an arrow." That was all he had said, smiling as if at a happy memory, and instantly she had remembered the feel of his skin there, where part of a shop window in the North of Ireland had changed the texture of his back forever.

Watching the film, she had been both proud and dismayed. In the subtlest and most heartrending way, it showed the viewer how irredeemably lost and wrenched from their moorings the lives of the Belfast children were. Stephen's technique was not to moralize, but to show through the impartial lens of his camera the daily fiber of life in a place where boys no older than Carlo manufactured bombs and carried guns.

At the end, when the credits crawled down the screen and she saw his name, she felt a pride in his accomplishment which overcame everything else.

"Are you Irish?" she asked him, remembering Gemma's label for him.

"I suppose I am. My grandparents came from Ireland." He had turned on her, a look of amusement in his eyes. "That's not why I showed you the film, Rafaella. It's ten years old—the only one I have a copy of here. I like to think I've improved."

"It is a wonderful film, Stefano. Thank you for showing me."

And then they had parted, the lady of the house and her projectionist, and she had gone to sleep and dreamed that she had killed him with a half-liter bottle of wine. And here she stood, in the approaching dawn, watching him while he slept and wishing she could protect him from all the perils of the world without depriving him of his life's blood. It was not possible, she thought, to keep safe a man who distilled beauty and valuable emotion from calamity, violence, and danger.

He stirred, a little, in his sleep, and Rafaella half hoped he would waken and find her there. What then? She waited, her heart seemingly stopped, but instead of waking he plunged deeper into sleep, and she was abandoned.

She remained by his side, her mind fixed on images of flying glass and machetes hooked in belt-loops, until the first rays of the sun glanced over the sea and turned it from slate to the palest, tenderest, hue of green.

Already, Stefania had made a friend. She brought her to the beach house one afternoon, introducing her as casually and confidently as she might a child at home.

"Melissa lives up there," she said, waving vaguely up the beach, northward. "I am going to show her my room."

Melissa was a long-legged, pretty little girl of Stefania's age. Rafaella watched her follow Stefania downstairs, heard them giggle together at some small shared amusement. Presently they came upstairs and went to sit together on the topmost step of the deck. Their voices rose and fell in animated conversation. Rafaella listened, fascinated by her daughter's lack of shyness about her imperfect English. She did not hesitate, groping for the proper grammar, but plunged recklessly along in a sort of pidgin English. Occasionally she lapsed into Italian, and then Melissa would guess at her meaning.

"No—not *that!*" Stefania laughed. "Not to eat, to wash the hair."

It seemed they were talking about strawberry shampoo, a new passion of Stefania's since she had seen it in a market.

Beyond them, she could see Stephen and Carlo. Stephen was standing at the water's edge, while Carlo bobbed about, chest deep in the gentle swells of a calm sea. The children ran in and out of the ocean constantly, like amphibious creatures at home in either element. It pleased her to see Carlo, sleek as a seal and calling companionably to Stephen, but on days when the waves were high she felt twinges of the old alarm.

"My father and mother are divorced," Melissa's voice came to her from the deck. "My father lives in Arizona. Where's yours?"

"He was dead," said Stefania.

"He *is* dead, you mean. That's too bad, Steffi. I'm really sorry."

"Okay," said Stefania, "let us go to swim."

Rafaella went to her bedroom and put on the blue-and-white swim suit she had bought for a trip to the Adriatic coast two years before. She took down the old shirt of Stephen's she borrowed to wear while sunbathing. Carefully, she buttoned it over the suit, knotting the tails at her waist. In a large straw carryall she deposited her hairbrush, a plastic container of tanning lotion, a paperback book she was reading to improve her English, and a writing tablet containing a half-written letter to Anna-Laura.

Upstairs again, she added two oranges from the enormous refrigerator and Stefano's sunglasses, which he had left on the kitchen table. The two little girls had left the deck and were down at the water's edge, hopping about and waving at Carlo.

She stepped out into the sunlight, ready. They were all facing away from her, seaward, and nobody noticed her descent from the house to the sand. She always tried to join them at such moments, unobtrusively, a familiar presence who lay by the edge of the water, securely covered in a man's shirt. The sun had begun to tan her legs to the color of the sand which lay beneath the sugary, covering layer. She glanced down and noticed the darker color of her thighs, the new paleness of her unpainted toenails, pale by contrast.

She walked toward them across the sand. Her beach chair was empty, waiting for her. An odd sensation came over her as she measured her steps on the scalding sand—she was about to step into a tableau when she joined the others and make it complete. The children cavorting in the sea, the man who stood at the edge as if guarding them, lost in his own thoughts—none of them had meaning or cohesiveness without her. She was needed or they could not hold together.

She arranged herself in the little low chair in her customary position, one leg draped over the other to conceal the long scar on her inner thigh. Carlo had swum farther out; he had almost reached the high ridge of the ocean's floor which humped up at that distance and formed an underwater ledge. It was called a sandbar. As she watched, he doubled himself up and stood erect, ankle deep, triumphant at his achievement. He walked along the sandbar; he seemed to walk on water.

The two little girls watched this feat with delight and Carlo waved to them. It was a cocky, condescending gesture, and Rafaella saw in it the entire history of her son. She straightened in her chair and willed him to swim back, humbly, to her side. Instead he caught sight of her and waved with a new fervor. He pointed in her direction and Stephen turned, understanding him.

He came to her, sinking easily to his knees beside her.

"You were very prophetic when you mentioned *Sci Acquatico*," he said.

"*Scusi?*"

"Never mind," said Stephen. "It's a mild sort of joke, signora. You are getting brown."

As always, at any reference to her physical self, she felt the need to withdraw, like a tortoise teased by cruel boys. "A little," she said.

"Oh, yes," said Stephen mockingly, "only a little. All things in moderation, Rafaella."

"What is wrong with moderation, please?"

"It has its place," he said.

Calmly, pretending not to understand him, she began to peel an orange.

"Can you swim, Rafaella? I just realized—I have no idea whether you know how to swim."

"Of course."

"Wouldn't you like to go in the water? It's especially warm today. Very nice."

She was struck with the oddness of it—that he, who had flown her half-way around the world, who had endured her presence and her children's now for nearly a week, did not know if she could swim. This small point seemed to sum up the strangeness of their relationship more than anything else. It had taken her three days to join them on the sand, and only now was he venturing to ask her. He was offering his ocean for her pleasure.

"Perhaps another day," she said. Her voice sounded flat, ungracious. *This isn't me*, she wanted to say. *I must have a little more time*. Instead she took his hand and held it in her own. "I am not a very good guest, am I, Stephen?"

He smiled, answering her with a non sequitur. "It will be all right, Rafaella," he said. "*Va bene*."

By chance Rafaella saw a picture in the Los Angeles *Times*. She did not recognize the man in the photograph at first, but her eyes returned to him. A slight man he seemed, curiously colorless despite the easy grin he displayed for the camera. It almost seemed he had eluded the camera and was offering only a shade of himself. The man was Martin Lassiter.

"That isn't right," she said aloud. "That isn't Dr. Lassiter."

But of course it was. Lassiter was being accused in print of having a God complex, whatever that might be. She read on indignantly. A British cardiologist, addressing a medical convention in Los Angeles, charged that Lassiter was too quick to operate. The doctor claimed that many St. Matthew's patients could as easily be helped through medication. He maintained that the reverential attitude toward surgeons in America was setting a dangerous trend.

"What does *he* know?" She spoke aloud, alone in the beach house. She felt rage at the stupidity of the doctor who criticized the man who had saved her life. It wasn't *his* heart at stake or his hands that worked magic. "Bystander!" she hissed.

She had felt this peculiar, protective impulse toward Lassiter once before. Not wishing to pry, she had come across a document of Stephen's on his desk one day. It was weighed down by a stone from the beach to protect it from blowing away, and for a moment she had feared the stone had fallen from the careless hand of Carlo or Stefania.

She didn't intend to read the letter from Ivan Bell, but certain words leaped up from the page. Ivan wrote that he was having problems with Lassiter's image. "I've never much liked doctors," he wrote, "and this one seems like an arrogant son of a bitch, no?"

347

She had replaced the flat, stippled stone, feeling dislike for Ivan Bell, and said nothing.

She studied the newspaper photograph again, seeking a hint of the slyness in those pale eyes, the slightly wounded quality behind the confident smile, but they were missing. Dr. Lassiter was wearing his most public look.

Carefully, she cut the article from the paper and took it to her room. She wasn't sure why, but it seemed the proper thing to do.

That evening, she heard Stephen ask the children if they had cut something from the paper.

"No," said Carlo, bristling. "I wouldn't cut up your newspaper, signore."

"Not me, Stefano," her daughter said.

"It doesn't matter," he said.

She took the clipping to him and handed it over without comment. He read it with interest and then excused himself to make some telephone calls. Of course! She grew hot with shame when she realized it contained important information for him and for his film. It might subtly alter his approach, and here she had squirreled it away like a mad old hermit— one of those unfortunate women who collected documents and clippings and muttered to themselves, alone in their imagined archives.

She went out on the deck and watched the moon rise. It seemed to be born from the womb of the sea. At its height it would make a path on the waters; when she had been a child, she had believed it might be possible to swim along the silver path until she reached the moon.

Melissa appeared at the bottom of the stairs, looking up anxiously. "Is Steffi coming?" she asked.

"Where, my love?"

"She's going to sleep over at my house, remember?"

As if on cue, Stefania appeared on the deck carrying her Alitalia flight bag. She announced that she had forgotten nothing—neither pajamas nor toothbrush. A well-organized child. She kissed Rafaella and assured her she would be a polite and cheerful guest. *More than I am*, thought her mother.

"*Ciao*, Mama."

Carlo joined her. Together they watched the girls walk up the beach toward Melissa's house. Rafaella put her arm around her son's shoulders, drawing him close to her. There was a small resistance, a pulling away, and then he relaxed and leaned toward her.

"Are you enjoying yourself, Carlo?"

There was a silence, as if he wanted to be scrupulously fair in answering the simple question. "Yes," he said slowly, "in my own way. Not like Stefania. In my own way."

She told him what she had believed, when she was small, about the moon's path on the sea.

"Really, Mama?" He looked up at her, indulgent and incredulous. "I wouldn't have believed that. Not even as a baby."

She didn't remind him that he had, until the age of five, believed he was the only human being on the face of the earth who dreamed at night.

Chapter 3

She watched him while he worked. It wasn't so different from the times when Aldo had brought blueprints home from the office and pored over them at his desk. It was mysterious. Stephen sat at a portable typewriter, consulting a sheaf of papers sent by the man, Ivan Bell, and tapping out thoughts as they came to him. He didn't appear to be a very competent typist. Occasionally, he picked up a small tape recorder and spoke into it. It was a far cry from the man with the machete, a different side to the work.

He had promised to take her to a lab where she could see how films were edited; he had some unfinished business there, he said. He had also, almost as an afterthought and with deceptive casualness, asked her why she had cut the item about Lassiter out of the Los Angeles *Times*.

"Didn't you want me to see it?"

"It wasn't that." A pause. "I'm sorry."

"Don't be sorry," he said. "For Christ's sake, signora, it doesn't matter! I would have seen it anyway. I just want to know why you did it."

Rafaella had shrugged. "I don't know. An impulse."

Now, pretending to read and watching him do battle with the typewriter, she wanted with a force verging on desperation to explain herself to him. This need presented itself in the form of a very large stone which seemed to be lodged in her throat. He murmured into the recorder, discarded a sheet of paper, and hit the keys with large, unskilled fingers.

She spoke around the stone.

"I didn't like to see him criticized," she said.

"What?" He turned around on the swivel chair, perplexed.

"It made me angry to read what they said about him. What do they know? *I* know him better than they do. They have no right!"

He removed the horn-rimmed glasses he wore at the typewriter and passed a hand over his eyes. "Terrific," he said. "That's just great, Rafaella." He got up and went to the window, looking out with a distracted air. He spoke as if addressing the deserted beach, the waning moon.

"This is the biggest emotional outburst I have ever heard from her," he said. "Who would have guessed the signora's passions could run so high over a little bad press for Lassiter?" He touched his forehead to the glass and laughed softly. "You are incredible," he said, turning to her. He had reverted from his new, fluent Italian to the peculiar half-Spanish of their earliest encounters.

"You should have been a master criminal," he said. "You have all the qualifications, Rafaella. You are brave, you are secretive. You are brilliant at disguising yourself, and not bad at making getaways, either. Who would have thought an article about Lassiter could provoke such loyalty, such rage?"

"Why are you angry?"

"Allow me to explain something. We ordinary folk have all sorts of petty emotions which you, apparently, do not experience. Jealousy is one of them—very common among us. You will find this amusing, I'm sure. I am jealous because you have just expressed more passion on behalf of Dr. Martin Lassiter than you have ever done for me."

"But no one has criticized you," she said. A part of her knew it was an infuriating remark to make, but it was also true. Another part of her felt the unworthy, adolescent thrill that came at his admission of jealousy.

Stephen looked to the heavens for sympathy. It was a comic gesture, yet deeply meant. More than anything, she longed to go to him and step into the circle of his arms and make things right, but the same stone which had lodged in her throat now seemed tied to her ankles, like a millstone. She felt robbed of all the simple, womanly devices which had once been available to her.

351

"You are wrong about one thing," she said. "I know how to feel jealous. I feel it all the time. I was jealous of Jackie, much as I liked her. I envied her for being beautiful and whole, but I was also jealous. They are two different things. Where are you going?"

At mention of Jackie, Stephen had held up both hands. Now he indicated that he would be right back. She was to wait. She could hear him rummaging in the hall closet, searching for something. He returned with an object wrapped in plain white tissue paper.

"Speaking of Jackie," he said, "I caught her wearing this one day, signora." He ripped open the tissue and the glorious Chinese scarf spilled out. "She said you had given it to her."

"I did." For one moment she was horrified, imagining that Stefano had accused Jackie of thievery. "I truly did, Stephen."

"It didn't suit her half as well as it did you. I told her I wanted it back because I planned a trip to Italy, and she surrendered it without a murmur. I'm afraid I did not behave with *garbo*, but neither did you. It is definitely not courteous to give away gifts, Rafaella."

He held it out to her, and such a world of memory seemed contained within the glowing threads she felt imprisoned, as if by magic. She thought if she stared long enough at the Chinese scarf all the jumbled images of things lost to her might be returned. It contained the green curl of the mighty waves, as well as the night-blooming flowers of the jungle—all the wondrous things he had lulled her with on her last night before surgery.

"Please," she said. "Help me now."

"Stand up."

"What if I can't?"

"You can. You've walked the mile. Just walk to me, now. It's no good if I come to you—it's your turn, Rafaella. After you do this one thing, I'll help you forever. If you'll let me. Okay? Come on, signora. Just get up and come to me, the way you did in Genoa that last day."

There was sand on the floor. She felt it beneath the soles of her bare feet as she rose.

352

"Do you remember when you met me in the Centro Storico, came flying down those steps? The man sitting next to my table was studying your legs. With rapture. You had an audience and you didn't even know! Now there's just me. Just me, Rafaella. Come, darling."

"I am also jealous of Betsy and all the others at the party. I'm jealous of your wife." She took a few steps toward him.

"She has not been my wife for years," he said, laughing.

"I am jealous of Maurizio."

A few more steps. She remembered Maurizio's words the day they lunched at Camogli. Something about the Genovese being sailors and adventurers.

"Come, Rafaella. We will run out of people to be jealous of before you get here."

"Don't make me laugh," she begged. "This is—" she searched for the right phrase in his language to describe her feelings. "This is—a big deal for me."

"For me, too," he said.

She was close enough now to see that the hazelnut eyes were darkened with the intensity of his emotion. He was frozen still, not allowing himself to advance toward her in any way. Almost there. A journey of some fifteen feet, much longer than her flight from Genoa to the western edge of America.

"Here I am," she said.

Stephen gave her the Chinese scarf, folding her fingers around it. She held it to her cheek, thanked him as if he had only now gifted her with it. His eyes flickered; he seemed about to speak. Quickly, she prevented him.

Her arms slid around his neck with a demonic speed all their own, as if they realized the importance of snaring him before he could say anything. Physical contact was more needed than words—she had already made him talk and talk. She had made Stefano sing for his supper at his own table, when all she really wanted was to devour the feast with him.

She stopped his lips with her own. They had never kissed standing up, and she rose on her bare toes so he would not have to bend so far. She felt herself grow taller and taller, rising up in his arms like an arrow released from a magical bow.

She hoped he would continue to hold her very tightly so she would not escape.

The wind rose in the night, and the sound of the waves on the sand was furious to her ears. They crashed, one close on the heels of the other, so that the air was full of a continuous roar and boom. There was no grace period between waves—only the chaotic sound of the unrelenting, spiteful ocean.

She lay in Stephen's arms, listening fearfully. She had been awake for an hour now, ever since three o'clock when she'd opened her eyes and discovered she was too happy to go back to sleep. Carefully, so as not to waken Stephen, she had lifted her head from his chest and studied his face in the digital dawn. What pleasure she found in this activity! Unlike her guilty, secretive pilgrimage to his bedside on the morning of her nightmare, every part of him seemed now a part of her.

Her body, somehow heavy with the evidence of their lovemaking, still hummed with echoes of the pleasure which had flowed between them. She placed her hand on her breast and fell her heart beating, calmly, there. Her fingers touched the scar: a hard, straight line which would never go away. Disfiguring, yes. She wondered if she could ever make love to Stephen in the full light of day, but it was not a terrifying prospect any more. Where once she had thought of herself as mutilated, now she was merely *disfigured*. Imperfect. It did not stop Stefano from wanting her.

She lay back down, her head on his chest. The warmth of the male body in bed, beside her, half under her, seemed as necessary to her life as food and water. She had lived without the warmth for so long she had forgotten its healing nature. Safe within the fortress of her reserve, her aloofness, she had ignored what Anna-Laura had always known—life was a disorderly, chaotic business, undemocratic, punctuated by infusions of joy and sweetness, jolted and shattered, when you least expected it, by cruel surprises. If you walled yourself up against the daily assault of life, you might succeed in barring pain, but you banished joy as well.

You managed to fool yourself, if you were determined enough, until the day you noticed the worldly, painted toenails beneath the nun's plain habit.

Stephen stirred, murmured something unintelligible. His hand settled on her hair. He slept. She lay against him in perfect happiness until the wind began to rise. The tumult of the ocean grew until the sound of the surf reminded her of the beating of a monstrous drum.

Not long ago the sound would have filled her with terror. All the old fears a practiced mind could summon up would have crowded around her bed: Carlo, wrenched from sleep by the booming of the ocean would sit up violently and plunge from his platform bed; Stefania would waken in a strange house, terrified; the waves would creep up the beach and engulf them all. She, this former Rafaella, would leap from the immediate dangers to the ones in the future. She would imagine Stephen going off one day to some troubled part of the world where she could not follow him. There would be a call in the night or a cable. Stephen would be swallowed in an earthquake, drowned by a tidal wave, shot by a sniper, deprived of his life by a rare, tropical disease.

The newly formed Rafaella did not really believe any of these things would happen, but the violent sound of the sea made her draw closer to the man beside her.

"Rafaella?" His voice was sleepy, yet strangely alert.

"I am here. Go to sleep, Stefano."

"It's only the wind," he said. "It happens, sometimes."

Chapter 4

Stefania, in her scarlet bathing suit, was learning how to ride the waves. She and Melissa paddled out, then crouched tensely, glancing over their shoulders, waiting for the precise moment to fling themselves toward shore. Rafaella could hardly bear to watch.

The surf was high today, just as Stephen had told her it would be. The fury of the night wind had passed, and the day was hot and sunny. The jogger and his spaniel had already set out, as usual, calling to Rafaella to have a nice day. Everything seemed to have settled into the usual Californian perfection, but she wasn't sure she trusted the waves. They had gathered their strength far out to sea and beat upon the shore with a vengeance.

She forced herself to watch while the two little girls hurled themselves forward. They were borne along on the surface of the waves like mermaids, shrieking with glee. Stefania and her friend rode almost to the shore, then rose up on unsteady legs and paddled out again. The ocean's blue was dotted with the forms of children, all playing the same game.

Now her daughter waved to her, laughing. She and Melissa had become careless, drunk with pleasure. Rafaella saw the malevolent form of the huge wave hanging over them; it bulked above them like a stippled mountain glacier and halted its downward progress long enough to confuse them. Melissa, more practiced, dived beneath the wave and emerged some yards further on, paddling furiously, but Stefania was dragged under.

"*Stefania!*" She screamed her daughter's name and ran into the water. It beat against her legs with a throbbing, warm rhythm surprisingly lacking in ferocity. She had expected to enter a maelstrom.

Almost at her feet, Stefania emerged, coughing and laughing. The left strap of her bathing suit had been knocked down by the force of her underwater journey. Modestly, she pulled it up before rising from the sea like a miniature Venus.

Rafaella went to her, pulling her up and into her arms, but Stefania was not in the least in need of comfort. "Did you see that?" she asked. "Oh, Mama—what a ride!"

Her legs, Rafaella saw, were studded with a myriad of tiny scrapes where the shells and stones of the seabed had wounded them. They were small wounds, but each minute gout of blood made her shudder.

"*Basta*," she said. "Enough danger for today, Stefania. Come into the house and I'll put something on those cuts."

"The seawater will heal them," said Stefania. "Please, Mama. It's so much fun."

"The waves are too high."

Stefania regarded her with affectionate contempt. "They're *not*," she said. "Melissa says they are nothing! They get twice as high, and sometimes there is a thing called an undertow, but today is just perfect." Her expression was frankly pleading, and then it changed to one of sly, adult conjecture. "Here comes Carlo," she said. "Stefano is with him."

While her mother turned, Stefania willfully swam out again to ride the waves with her friend. By the time Rafaella had turned, she was far out in the water again.

"What are they doing, Mama?" Carlo asked. His eyes, her eyes reborn, swept the arc of the sea and counted the many children there. "Is it a game?"

"They are riding the waves, Carlo."

"How do you do it?"

She explained, as best she could. If you hurled yourself along the water at the precisely right moment, she said, the force of the wave would bear you safely in to shore. If you missed you were sucked under the sea and dragged along the ocean's bottom, and your legs were cut a bit by all the little shells, but you survived.

Carlo listened intently. In his face she could detect the longing to join the others, to have an adventure, but when he spoke it was with his customary air of adult judiciousness.

"I will swim out and tell Stefania to return, shall I?"

"No," said Rafaella. "She is enjoying it. She has become quite an expert."

He called to Stephen. "Is it dangerous?" he asked.

"No more than most things."

Carlo pondered and made his decision. "If you don't mind," he said to his mother with *garbo,* "I'll give it a try."

"Go," she said. "Your sister will show you how. Go and learn."

He remained, looking up at her to make sure he had heard her correctly. When he was satisfied, he waded into the sea. He breasted the swell of the first wave, disappearing from sight, and then bobbing up again, swimming steadily out toward the place where his sister—a crimson dot against the horizon—waited for the next wave.

Rafaella watched him. At her back, she felt Stephen drawing steadily nearer toward her. Soon he would be close enough for her to take his hand. The closer he came, the farther the swimming form of her son appeared, but it was not Stefano who drove the boy away; it was the natural order of things.

For a moment everything was as it should be. She had no doubt that she was at the hub of the cosmic wheel—an important chip in the mosaic of the universe.

The one who approached would stay, and the one who seemed to be leaving her would return.

She turned, smiling. Stephen called something to her, but the drumming of the surf made his words inaudible. She walked to meet him halfway. There was something urgent in his approach, yet when they came together he merely touched her cheek with his warm hand and said:

"A call for you. It's Anna-Laura. I thought you'd want to talk to her."

Rafaella ran over the sand toward the steps of the *loggia*. How casual Stephen was! Every moment of silence on the transatlantic call represented unimaginable numbers of lire.

Anna-Laura would be calling to ask if she was returning to Genoa on schedule. She would want to pick her up at Cristoforo Colombo as she had done last July.

As she ran, slipping in the hot sand, she planned what to say. Yes, she would be returning. Yes, she would appreciate it if Anna-Laura could be waiting, although it wasn't necessary. The children were thriving in California; the sun shone steadily. She had the beginnings of a tan. It had been the perfect holiday.

Midway up the steps, it occurred to her that Anna-Laura, of all people, deserved to hear the truth—but what was it? Although she would certainly appear, children in tow, back in Genoa on the appointed date, it was not the truth of the matter. The truth was that she might return to America or live in New York, or Rome or Houston or anywhere at all. Her life was no longer to be lived on the Via Vieri, or not for long, because that life was a thing of the past. The new life was as yet formless and uncharted. For a moment she imagined the negotiations and compromises which would have to be forged and felt a backward-sliding impulse toward weariness, but she shrugged it away. She refused to be daunted.

They would find a way. Between them—a *Sci Acquatico* man and a woman whose legacy was that of adventurers—a plan could be made.

She grasped the receiver in sandy fingers, only to hear her sister-in-law's voice locked in intimate conversation with that of the international operator.

"So true," said Anna-Laura. "The world has become a small place. A village. What, do you think, is the price we pay for such intimacy?"

Rafaella waited, politely, for the dialogue to run its course. While she waited, she looked out to sea. All of the children, Carlo, Stefania, and Melissa, were huddling before the crest of a mammoth wave, preparing to trust its power to propel them safely back to shore. The wave peaked, and they were lost to her sight.

"*Prego!*" she cried, interrupting Anna-Laura's transatlantic flirtation.

"Is it you?" Anna-Laura's voice. Seductive, sharp, suspicious.

Stephen stood at the lip of the shore, guarding the children as surely as if he had been born to such a task. The sight of him canceled her fear for their safety.

"Yes, it's me," she said.

While she watched, the sea lifted their slight bodies and bore them gently back. They emerged laughing and whole, intact.

"Listen," said Rafaella. "I have something to tell you."

"Yes?" In Anna-Laura's voice there was a quick, indrawn gasp of excitement, mixed with the familiar impatience and affection Rafaella knew so well. "What, *carina?* Tell me!"

She began.